ENSLAVED

ELISABETH NAUGHTON

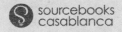

Published by Sourcebooks Casablanca, an imprint of Sourcebooks, Inc.
P.O. Box 4410, Naperville, Illinois 60567-4410
(630) 961-3900
Fax: (630) 961-2168
www.sourcebooks.com

Printed and bound in Canada.
WC 10 9 8 7 6 5 4 3 2 1

For Darcy and Helen, who read the books my brothers won't. I'm so thankful to have you as sisters!

Destiny waits alike for the free man as well as for him enslaved by another's might.

—Aeschylus

Chapter One

THE BLOODY VOICE WAS BACK.

Not that it ever completely went away, but most days he could deal with it. Today it was like a pounding drum, growing louder each and every second. The sound so intense, it left him wanting to stab his eardrums with a hot metal poker just so he didn't have to listen anymore.

Come to me. Bring me what I seek. You know you can't deny your destiny.

Gryphon twisted in the May sunlight, squinted through the trees, searched for the source of the voice that continued to torment him. But it wasn't close. Not in this vast Montana forest, not in the remote village down the hill to his right, not among his warrior kin, who'd been eyeing him as if he were bat-shit crazy for the last two months. No, this lovely voice was in his head. *Inside* his body. Calling to him every hour of every day, drawing him toward a darkness he feared might soon consume him.

Panic and a need to break free tightened every muscle in his body, pushed him to do *something*. He couldn't give in to the darkness. He wouldn't let it have him. He'd seen its wrath firsthand, knew the horror it would unleash. No matter what, he had to keep fighting that voice. He couldn't let go and…

"Gryph? Dude? You okay?"

Gryphon startled at the gruff voice—the *real*

voice—coming from Titus, his Argonaut kin, standing in the shadows of a large pine. A lock of wavy hair fell free of the leather tie at the nape of Titus's neck, brushed his weathered cheek. The guardian tipped his head, narrowed his eyes, seemed to study Gryphon more intently. A descendent of Odysseus, Titus was the keenest of all the guardians, and he had the ability to hear others' thoughts. Could he hear the voice too?

"Gryphon?" Titus asked again, this time crossing the small clearing toward him, his knowing hazel eyes honed in on Gryphon's face, his boots crunching over dried needles and broken sticks as he moved. "Maybe we should take a break."

Oh, yeah, Titus could hear it.

Shame, fury, helplessness welled inside Gryphon. Before Titus reached him, he stepped out of the guardian's way and beat feet for the hillside, where his brother Orpheus was scanning the small village with binoculars. "Stop treating me like a freakin' five-year-old. I'm fine."

Titus's boots stilled, and he heaved out a heavy sigh. Without looking, Gryphon could see the *you're not fine, you're fucked* expression on his kin's face.

He didn't need the pity from Titus. He could barely handle the way Orpheus looked at him, as if he had some terminal disease. Did they think they were helping with their constant coddling and useless baby-sitting? Gryphon scratched at the back of his neck, dragged his hand down his chest, and clawed at the skin hidden under the thick henley and leather strap that cut across his torso. Things would be a helluva lot better for everyone if they'd just leave him alone. Couldn't they see that?

Come to me, doulas. *You know you want to*. *Stop fighting me*.

He clenched his jaw, rubbed his ear against his shoulder. Flexed and released his hand so he didn't draw his blade against the only threat out here he could see: himself. Stopping next to Orpheus, he tried like hell to ignore the voice and asked, "What do you see?"

Orpheus lowered the binoculars, shot him a way-too-fucking-concerned look. "Nothing. No movement. Looks like a ghost town. You okay?"

Gryphon ground his teeth at the question—and the worry he saw on his brother's face—took the binoculars, scanned the distance. Saw the same thing Orpheus had, nothing but empty houses and swaying tree limbs. No humans, no Misos—half-breeds who often lived together in isolation—not even a damn dog roaming the empty streets.

He handed the binoculars back to Orpheus as he fought the need to strike out and kill something...*anything*. As Titus came up on his left, he caught sight of the ancient Greek text on the guardian's arms. The same text that covered all the Argonauts' arms, marking them as guardians of their race. He'd served with them for over a hundred years, but now everything felt different. It was first mission since Orpheus had rescued him from Underworld, and Gryphon knew Orpheus was re sible for his being included today. The other guar Theron, Zander, Demetrius, Cerek, Phineu had Titus—they didn't think he was ready. But Or argued that getting back into the routine of hunting Atalanta's daemons as Argonauts ha for millennia, was an important step in his

His recovery.

From the hell of the Underworld.

And Atalanta…

The last thought sent a tremor through Gryphon's entire body. A tremor that triggered a bitter hatred, turned his vision a blinding, glaring red and amped the need to annihilate exponentially.

"Gryph," Titus said jovially—way too jovially— "why don't we hang out up here while Orpheus goes down to see if Nick needs help."

Nick was the leader of the half-breed colony where Gryphon and Orpheus had been living the last two months. He was already in the village below, looking for survivors of what they suspected was a daemon attack. And he had a tendency to eye Gryphon as if he had three heads too.

Fuck them all. Gryphon was sick and tired of being treated like an invalid. It wouldn't stop until he showed them that he could hold his own, just as he had before. It wouldn't stop until he proved he was the same guardian he'd once been.

Before Orpheus could agree, Gryphon stomped down the hill toward the silent village. And felt like screaming, because even he knew he wasn't that *ándras* anymore. He twitched, he heard voices, he felt the need claw himself free of his own skin every second of ry day…nothing he did made any of it stop. Not the way the Argonauts made him go to, not the time or on e from the Underworld, not even being out here and don mission again. And after the things he'd seen ing to qu when he was in the Underworld, he was start-ion whether he'd ever be that *ándras* again.

Only I understand you, doulas. *Only I can ease you. Give in. Come to me.*

He swiped at both ears with his hands, scrubbed his fingers through his hair, and pulled hard so he wouldn't scream as he headed down the hillside. If he started hollering like a psycho, they'd surely lock him in a padded cell. And he wouldn't go back to being imprisoned. Not even by them. Never again.

A growl echoed to his left just as he reached the bottom of the hill, followed by a frigid burst of air that signaled daemons were in the area.

His adrenaline shot up. He reached back for his parazonium—the ancient Greek sword all the Argonauts carried—just as Nick stepped out of the shadows.

Screw that. This was Gryphon's kill. His blood grew hotter with the promise of a knock-down, drag-out, blood-letting fight.

The first daemon came around the side of the house, stepping between Gryphon and Nick. The beast lifted his head—a grotesque mix of cat and goat and dog—and narrowed glowing green eyes on Gryphon. Then he drew in a deep whiff and growled, "You."

"Me, you son of a bitch." Gryphon lifted his blade. "And I've a message for you to take back to your bitch of a leader."

Nick swore at the beast's back. Up the hill, Orpheus shouted, "No!" Someone cursed as boots pounded across the earth. But Gryphon didn't listen. He was already charging, already losing the voice, the pain, even himself, in the fight. As his blade met sword and flesh and bone, he was already proving he was *more* than the guardian he'd once been.

He was everything he didn't want to be.

—∾∾—

Tonight was the night. No more fooling around.

Maelea's stomach churned with a mixture of apprehension and excitement as she sat at the long rectangular table in the two-story dining hall of the half-breed colony and only vaguely listened to the conversation around her. Part of her felt a pang of sadness that she'd soon be leaving. Another part was eager to get away. Even after two months, she was never going to be one of them.

Though Orpheus claimed she was safe here, Maelea knew she wasn't. Those around her weren't safe either. Hades was hunting her. He'd find her sooner or later. He'd do whatever he could to stop her from reaching Olympus.

And Olympus…well, that was something worth running for. Something worth fighting for. Something worth even dying for.

"Maelea?"

Maelea blinked, realized she was zoning out, and refocused. Looking down the table, she eyed the female who'd called to her. Dammit…what was her name? Harriet? Holly? No, Helene, that was it. Her gaze skipped from face to face before faltering on Skyla.

Though Skyla was no longer one of Zeus's assassins, she had the senses of an elite warrior, and her eyes zeroed in on Maelea as if she were a hawk closing in on its prey.

Maelea glanced quickly away from Skyla's knowing green eyes and looked to Helene. "What? I'm sorry. I didn't hear you."

"We were wondering if you would be willing to help

out with the decorations for the festivities. Katia said you have a real eye for color."

Katia… Maelea glanced back over the table and remembered she'd helped the female decorate a nursery for one of the other colonists. But for the life of her, she couldn't remember what festivities they all were talking about. "Um…"

"Nick's favorite color is blue, so I was thinking we'd use that as our starting point," Katia said from across the table. "He's going to be so surprised. A hundred and fifty years. Hard to believe, isn't it?"

Right. The celebration to commemorate the one hundred fiftieth year of Nick's leadership. Maelea had heard a few of the other females in the castle talking about it last week. As it was a surprise for Nick, everything was hush-hush, but Maelea had a hard time imagining Nick being surprised—or excited—about anything. The Misos leader always had a stoic expression. And with that scar down the side of his face…Maelea shuddered. He was downright scary looking. The man had no use for her, had made it more than clear he wasn't happy Orpheus had brought her here. So she stayed as far from him as she could.

Just another reason it was good she was finally getting out of this place.

"Well?" Helene asked. "Can you help?"

Maelea nodded and worked up a smile. "Sure. Why not."

"Wonderful." Helene turned back to the others and dove into the party plans.

A whisper of guilt rushed through Maelea. By tomorrow she'd be gone. If things went as she hoped, in a few hours she'd be nothing but a memory. And though she knew that was the best option—for everyone—a tiny place deep inside couldn't help but wonder what it would be like to be a real part of this community. Part of a family. She'd never had that. Not in all her three thousand years. Before coming here, she'd spent most of those years alone. And the few times she hadn't, well, those times she'd learned the loss of love was a thousand times worse than not having it in the first place.

She'd gotten a small taste of family these past few months. And she liked it, more than she should. The longer she stayed, the harder it would eventually be on her when it all ended. And no matter what Orpheus claimed or how safe he and Nick thought they could keep everyone, she knew reality. She didn't want to be the reason all of this finally came to a screeching halt.

As the females talked, Maelea's gaze drifted to the wide, arched windows that looked out to the blue-green lake and the majestic mountains beyond. Dusk was just settling in, making the lake look dreamy and inviting, but to Maelea it was one more barrier to her escape. The colony was nothing more than an enormous castle built by a Russian prince on an island in the middle of a glacial lake in the wilds of Montana. That prince, whose wife was Misos, had been killed before either reached the protection of the castle, and Nick's people had come to inhabit it after their colony was destroyed somewhere in Oregon. The hows and whys didn't much matter to Maelea—but even she recognized the safety this location provided.

It would be a thousand times safer once she was gone.

Silverware clinked against the old wood table, and

as conversation continued around them, the female to Maelea's right leaned toward her friend on her other side and whispered, "Did you hear they took him out today?"

"Who?" the other female whispered back.

"The blond Guardian. The one they keep locked on the third floor."

Maelea's interest piqued. They were talking about Gryphon, Orpheus's brother. She tried not to look like she was listening, but inside something jumped to life.

"The crazy one?"

"Yeah. He went out hunting with Nick and Orpheus and one other. Have you seen him? There's something not right about him."

"I heard a rumor he was quite the playboy…before," the other said, her voice lowering. "That females in Argolea used to flock to him."

Before. Before being sent to the Underworld. Before being rescued by Orpheus and Skyla. Before coming to live at the colony.

The first lifted her plate and pushed back from the table. "Well, he's no playboy now. Any female would be stupid to get within fifty feet of him. He's unstable. I'm really hoping they don't let him out for the celebration. Can you imagine what would happen?"

Maelea watched the two walk toward the end of the room to deposit their dishes, and even as relief that dinner was finally over rippled through her, so did a wave of trepidation. If Hades caught her, the same fate that had befallen Gryphon awaited her. Only she wouldn't survive the Underworld. She was sure of it.

Her determination resolidified, Maelea scrambled for her own plate. She'd found the way out days ago, had just been waiting for the right moment to bolt. Tonight the sentries would change shift at two a.m. And Hawk…he wasn't as observant as some of the others. If she timed it right, she'd be past him before he even saw her.

She headed for the end of the dining hall. The china nearly slipped from her fingers when Skyla sidled up next to her.

"Volunteering for the decoration committee. Look at you getting all involved, Maelea. I barely recognize you anymore."

Maelea bobbled the plate in her hand, worked to keep her expression neutral. "I don't know what you mean."

They reached the end of the room. Skyla set her utensils on the high counter after Maelea. "Sure you do. You're different since you've been here. In a good way. Dare I say it? More human."

Maelea steeled her nerves as she faced the blond Siren. Most days she liked Skyla. Skyla had become more than an unexpected ally, she'd become a friend, and she made Orpheus happy, which gave Maelea at least a little bit of hope that there was happiness out there—not for her, but at least for others. But the Siren was too perceptive. And right now Maelea didn't need anyone probing into her intentions. If Orpheus got one whiff she was planning to run, he'd do everything he could to stop her. It was way past time Orpheus stopped feeling responsible for her. He had plenty of other things to worry about—most importantly, his brother.

"I'm not human, Skyla. We both know that. If I've changed, it's only because I'm working hard to fit in. That is what you and Orpheus asked me to do, isn't it?

Fit in? And stop being such a…what was it Orpheus called me? A ghoul?"

A slow smile crept across Skyla's face. "He's such a smartass."

Yeah, well, he was also right. Hades had cursed her to walk this world alone for all eternity, and that's exactly what she'd done, not only for her safety, but for the safety of those around her. And the fact that she was willingly going back to that now, after experiencing life at the colony, depressed her more than she liked.

"Look," she said, desperate to get away from Skyla before she gave anything away, "I promised some of the children I'd read them a few stories in the library before bed. Are we done here?"

Skyla's face softened, but those knowing eyes of hers didn't lessen in intensity. "There you go, being all involved again."

Involved. There was a word Maelea had never expected anyone to use to describe her. The colony was the first place she'd felt safe enough to risk getting involved. Only now she knew her safety was in jeopardy. The continual hellhound sightings in the Pacific Northwest told her that Hades had not given up searching for her. That he'd never stop hunting her.

As that depressing thought sank in, Maelea turned for the hallway. But before she reached the threshold, her chest constricted as if a heavy weight had been dropped on top of her.

"What's wrong?" Skyla asked, her hand brushing Maelea's long-sleeved shirt.

"I…I felt something weird come into the castle. Something dark. Something…evil."

Concern morphed to alarm in Skyla's eyes. Skyla knew Maelea could sense energy shifts on the planet—a gift of being caught between two worlds. Just as Skyla opened her mouth to answer, the cell in her pocket hummed.

She pulled the phone from her jeans, lifted it to her ear. "Orpheus, thank gods…Where are—? No, Maelea and I are—" Her face paled. "Oh shit. I'll be right there."

"What happened?" Maelea asked as Skyla stuffed the phone back in her pocket.

"Something bad," Skyla answered, crossing the gleaming hallway floor toward the elevator. "It's Gryphon."

Maelea stopped with Skyla at the elevator, watched as the Siren frantically pushed the call button. "Is he hurt?"

"No. Worse." Skyla looked up at the wood-paneled doors. "Where the hell is that damn car? In Zimbabwe?"

"What could be worse than being hurt? He's not dead, is he?" Why the thought of his death disturbed her, she didn't know. She didn't even know the guardian. Hadn't once talked to him in the months they'd both been here.

"No," Skyla answered, a frown cutting across her mouth. "But he might be soon, if Nick gets a hold of him." Her voice lowered so no one else could hear them. "Orpheus said he mutilated an entire horde of daemons. And then he wouldn't stop. Titus and Nick are both getting stitched up in the medical clinic as we speak."

Maelea's eyes grew wide. "What happened?"

"According to Orpheus, Gryphon attacked them."

Chapter Two

"I DON'T CARE WHAT YOU THINK HE'S *GONNA* DO, I CARE about what the hell he *did* do."

Nick's booming voice echoed off the walls as Maelea followed Skyla down the hall in the medical clinic on the second floor of the castle.

"Nick, shit." Orpheus's voice now. Frustrated. "You know he didn't intend to hurt you or Titus."

"Tell that to Titus," Nick said. "Or no, wait, you can't, because he's in frickin' surgery."

Skyla rounded the corner, but Maelea pulled up short. Shit. What was she doing here? This didn't concern her. In a matter of hours, she'd have nothing more to do with these people. The best thing for her would be to turn right around and head back upstairs.

But just as she was about to, she peeked into the room. And caught sight of Nick sitting on an exam table, chest bare to reveal chiseled abs, a healer at his side stitching up his arm. His pants were bloody and ripped, and red lines streaked his skin, but he didn't seem to care. His attention was focused solely on Orpheus across the room, and the *don't fuck with me* expression on his scarred face piqued Maelea's curiosity all over again.

Relief rushed over Orpheus's features when Skyla stepped into the room, but he didn't move to kiss her cheek as he normally did when he saw her in the castle, and Maelea had the distinct impression it was because Nick was watching them.

"Where is he?" Skyla asked.

"He's fine," Orpheus said. "He's in his room."

"Who's with him?"

"Three of my men," Nick cut in. "He's not getting out, at least not until we kick him out."

Orpheus turned toward the half-breed leader. "Nick—"

"What about Titus?" Skyla asked. "How bad is it?"

"Bad enough," Nick answered as the healer placed a bandage on his arm and handed him his shirt. As he pushed off the table and mumbled a thanks to the female who'd stitched him up, he added, "He was barely breathing by the time we subdued Gryphon. Punctured lung, broken ribs, and a wound the length of my arm in his gut. Anyone else would be dead right now."

Maelea swallowed back the bile as she listened. If it had been her or any of the other colonists...

"He didn't mean it, Nick," Orpheus said. "You both got in his way. He thought you were daemons."

Nick swung his attention Orpheus's way, and there was fire in his amber eyes as he tugged on his shirt, not even grimacing at the pain he must have been feeling in his injured shoulder. "He's fucking out of control. If he can't tell the difference between us and daemons, he's got no business being out there. And he's got no business being here either."

Orpheus's face paled. But before he could answer, Skyla asked, "What are you saying, Nick?"

Nick drew a breath, seemed to calm himself for her sake. "I'm saying he can't stay. If I can't trust him around me, I sure as hell won't trust him around my people. Look, I know he's been through shit no one should have to endure, but the colony comes first. He's not getting any better. It's been two months. He still twitches, he still acts like he's hearing things, and he scares most of the colonists on a good day. I won't risk them. Not even for the Argonauts. He has to leave."

Orpheus's back straightened, and from the doorway, Maelea could actually see his defenses come up. She knew Gryphon meant more to Orpheus than a mere brother would. They weren't just linked by blood, they were linked by the horror they'd both experienced and lived through. Except in Orpheus's case, he'd come through unscathed. Gryphon was a changed man because of his time in the Underworld.

"Fine," Orpheus said through his clenched jaw, "then I'll leave with him."

Skyla reached out to him. "Orpheus—"

"Theron won't let you take him back to Argolea," Nick said. "I already talked to him. He's in the other room with Titus as we speak. And he's more pissed than I am. Even he knows Gryphon's become a liability."

"He's not a liability," Orpheus snapped. "He's just…struggling right now. I'll get him through it."

Nick frowned as if he didn't think there was any hope, but his anger waned as he stepped toward the door. "I don't know what the hell you're gonna do for him that you haven't already done. Some things can't be saved, O, no matter how much you want them to be."

Maelea dropped back into the shadows of the hall as Nick rounded the corner. When he caught sight of her, her adrenaline surged, but he didn't acknowledge her presence, just as he never acknowledged her when he passed her in the halls. Instead he turned and headed out the front of the clinic, his boots echoing down the corridor in his wake.

The door on the far side of the exam room opened, drawing Maelea's attention back inside. Both Skyla and Orpheus looked toward the massive blond male Maelea recognized as one of the Argonauts. "O? Theron wants you to come in now. Hey, Skyla."

Skyla offered a weak smile. "Hey, Zander."

The male disappeared again, and as Skyla reached Orpheus's side, Orpheus grasped her hand and kissed it, whispering something Maelea couldn't hear. Skyla brushed her fingers down his cheek. Then the two walked through the door and vanished from sight.

Skyla had obviously forgotten all about Maelea, evidenced by the way she didn't even glance back, but that was okay with Maelea. As the door clicked closed behind them and silence settled over the room, Maelea told herself that being forgotten was something she'd just have to get used to all over again.

Some things can't be saved, no matter how much you want them to be.

As she turned for the front of the clinic, she couldn't help but think that a truer statement had never been uttered.

He was nothing more than a caged animal.

Gryphon paced his bedroom suite. The pale blue walls were closing in on him. The heavy draperies made him want to scream. And every time he looked out through the cathedral-style window toward the glimmering lake below, he had the uncontrollable urge to take a flying leap off the balcony and hurl himself through air and water to smash into the rocks and tree trunks lining the bottom of the lake.

He'd have done it, too, if he thought death would improve his situation. But he knew it wouldn't. Even if his first trip to the Underworld had been a result of magic, he'd done enough shit there and since to know that if he died now, he'd wind up right back in Tartarus. This time to be tortured for all eternity. And he wouldn't go back. The Isles of the Blessed...the resting place of the heroes...it was lost now to him until he found a way to redeem himself. And after what had happened today...

Bile welled in his stomach when he thought of Titus lying on the ground, unconscious from a blow to the head, blood oozing from wounds in his flesh. Even now, Gryphon couldn't quite remember what had happened during that fight. But he remembered Nick gripping his bleeding shoulder, surrounded by mutilated daemons, screaming that Gryphon was nothing more than a fucking menace who needed to be locked away.

Gryphon closed his eyes. Fought the bile rising in his chest. Titus had to live. The guardian was strong. He couldn't die. Not because of what Gryphon had done.

Come to me, doulas. *Come home...*

"No!" He grasped the ends of his hair and pulled so hard, his scalp burned. "Leave me the hell alone!"

The voice chuckled. And inside, Gryphon fought back the urge to listen. To do what it wanted. To draw him toward darkness for good.

A knock sounded at the door. His adrenaline lurched;

he dropped his hands and whipped in that direction. Seconds later, Orpheus stepped into the room, and relief swept through Gryphon. But it was quickly quelled when he noticed Orpheus's drawn features, his tight muscles, and his messy hair, all signs that said he'd been through hell and back in the last hour.

Considering Orpheus hadn't looked this bad when he *had* come back from hell, Gryphon knew something was wrong.

No, gods. Not Titus.

"He's fine," Orpheus said, closing the door at his back before Gryphon could ask. "He came through the surgery okay. Callia had to do some major reconstructive work, but he's going to make a full recovery."

This time, the relief was sweet as wine. Gryphon dropped into a chair and cradled his head in his hands, thanking the Fates for Callia, the Argolean healer and Zander's mate. But even as relief over Titus's prognosis rushed through him, the darkness pressed in, telling him this was not good news. That good news would be to see the guardian die. To see them all die.

He pressed his fingers against his eyes, clenched his jaw to the point of pain. *Skata*, he was going nuts. The urge to claw his way out of his own skin consumed him all over again.

"Listen, Gryph," Orpheus said, his boots scuffing on the floor near the door. "I gotta talk to you. For the time being, I think it's best if you and I take a little trip."

Gryphon's head came up. Orpheus shoved his hands in the front pockets of his jeans and worked to keep his shoulders relaxed, but Gryphon saw the tension coiled beneath the tough exterior. "Just until you're feeling better."

Nick wanted him gone. Gryphon had expected as much—after all, the half-breed leader had never been jazzed about his being here in the first place. "I don't want to go back to Argolea."

"No," Orpheus said, lifting one arm and rubbing the back of his neck. "No, we're not going there."

They didn't want him either. Reality settled in, and the ramifications of what had happened earlier today hit full force. Theron, the leader of the Argonauts, had to be here by now. And even he wasn't willing to give Gryphon the benefit of the doubt anymore.

A space in his chest opened wide as he stared down at his arms, covered in the markings of the Eternal Guardians. Serving with the Argonauts had been his life, his identity, the only thing he'd known since being inducted into the order. He'd bled for them, he'd fought for them, he'd have died for any one of his kin if needed. But even though he still had these markings, he wasn't one of them anymore. His actions today proved he wouldn't be one ever again.

Come to me, doulas.

He closed his eyes. Fought the emptiness creeping over him. And the voice. The wretched, evil, blathering voice.

"Listen, Gryph," Orpheus said. "We'll figure it out. Don't…don't worry about it. The rest of them…they don't understand what you're going through. I do. I'll help you through this. We'll get away from all of this and we'll…we'll find a way to help you."

If anyone could help him overcome the voice, it would be his brother. Orpheus had learned to tame the daemon inside him. He'd fought and he'd won. But

Gryphon wasn't possessed by a daemon. What swirled deep in his core was something else. Something not even Orpheus could tame.

"And what about Skyla?" Gryphon managed to say.

Orpheus shoved his hand back in his pocket and studied the ground. "Skyla will be fine. She understands."

There was no way Orpheus would ever agree to leaving Skyla. The soul mates had only just found each other again. Not unless even he didn't trust Gryphon. That realization cut sharper than knowing the Argonauts were abandoning him.

Silence stretched over the room. Then finally, Orpheus said, "We'll leave first thing in the morning." But there was no excitement in his voice. Only resolve. "Just…try to get some sleep tonight. I'll be back for you at daybreak."

As his brother exited the room, Gryphon caught sight of the three armed guards stationed outside his door. And beyond them, Skyla, her green eyes filling with tears as she rose on her toes and wrapped her arms around Orpheus's shoulders.

The door snapped closed, blocking out the image of the two lovers embracing. And that emptiness swamped Gryphon all over again as he remembered what it had felt like to be trapped in the Underworld.

Helpless. Alone. Forgotten.

He wasn't forgotten now. He was hated. Feared. The enemy. Orpheus had risked his life to save him, and this was the result. Only one thing was clear to him now: he was done being a burden and a responsibility. Done with the Argonauts. The brother Orpheus so desperately wanted to save was never coming back.

He looked toward the windows and the sun setting low over the lake. Tried to find some kind of joy in the view. Couldn't. As the same emptiness he'd gotten used to living with the last few months swamped him, all he could think about was what he had to do next.

Come to me...

He would. All too soon, he would.

—— ∾ ——

The castle was quiet when Maelea slunk out of her room.

Sconces lit the darkened hallway, illuminating the thick carpet runner, the paintings hanging on the walls, and the heavy doors, all closed and likely locked. Twisting her arm around, she pressed the backpack against her spine to keep the contents inside from causing too much noise. Her adrenaline soared as she tiptoed toward the end of the hall, every creaking board sounding like an alarm to her, announcing she was making her escape.

Nothing moved around her. The bedrooms on each side of the hall were silent. She'd been given a room on this floor, made up only of single females, when she'd first come to the colony, and she'd memorized her floormates' sleeping patterns early on. Except for Samara, who liked to stay up to watch Jay Leno, everyone else turned in by ten. And at this hour—just after one a.m.— they were surely all sound asleep.

Under the cover of darkness was her favorite time to roam the castle. When it was quiet, when people were locked away, when she was confident she wouldn't be stopped. Orpheus had called her a ghoul because of it at first, but she didn't care. She'd learned a lot about the people and their rituals by sneaking out during the night. And she'd learned just how to escape when the time was right.

She held her breath when she reached the end of the hall, pushed on the door, and waited for the hinges to squeak. To her surprise, they didn't, and seconds later she was standing in the dimly lit stairwell alone, the door between her and discovery closed at her back.

One obstacle down. She only had about thirty more before she was out of here for good.

She checked her watch, realized she'd wasted too much time waiting for Samara to turn off the TV next door and fall asleep, and picked up her pace. Skipping stairs, she made it to the ground level, then paused to look out the rectangular window in the steel door and scan the courtyard.

This was where it got tricky. She could take the elevator down to the tunnels, but that would create noise that would undoubtedly rouse someone. She could continue down these stairs, but there were guards at the bottom she didn't want to deal with. Her best option was to cross the courtyard and head for the armory on the far side. Weeks ago she'd found a door from the armory down to the tunnels, one seldom used and blocked off so no one would venture into the tunnels unaccounted for and get injured.

The key was to make it across the courtyard unseen. The moon cast a mere sliver of light. But the guards in the towers weren't as dismissive as Hawk. Even with a virtual blanket of darkness, they could still spot her.

Maelea checked her watch again. One twenty-nine. In another minute, the guards would change shifts. She looked up, watched the tower to the south, and waited until she saw a shadow pass in front of the light.

Go time.

She pushed down her nerves, slipped out into the darkness, and darted into shadows as she made her way around the central courtyard. Water gurgled in the fountain to her right. The air was crisp and cool, and her heart pounded in her chest as she eyed the base of the guard's tower looming ahead like a sleeping giant.

Halfway there, her spine tingled, and she had the distinct impression she was being watched. Dashing into a patch of darkness, she looked up toward the tower and saw nothing but light, indicating the next guard had yet to take position. Glancing back toward the castle, she scanned the darkened windows, pausing when she reached the one she knew belonged to Gryphon.

He'd watched her from that window before. Several times she'd been out here in the courtyard, had felt her back tingle just like this and looked up to see him standing behind the glass, peering down at her with a haunted expression. The way he watched her was unnerving. But now that she knew what he was capable of…now it sent sickness sliding up her throat.

Tonight his window was empty, though. Swallowing hard, telling herself she was just jumpy, she picked her way toward the tower. The pack bounced against her spine. The black pants and boots were sleek and made it easy to move—way easier than the long, full skirts she was used to wearing. Perspiration dotted her spine. When she reached the ten-foot-long patch of moonlight between her and the tower, she hesitated.

Once she was on the other side of the tower, she could

easily disappear in the orchard, and from there make her way to the tunnel entrance she'd found on the backside of the armory. She just had to get there first.

This close, she couldn't see the guards above anymore. But it was now or never. Holding her breath, she darted from shadow into light, nearly swallowing her tongue as she skidded to a stop at the base of the structure, her back pressing into the cool stone as she tried to catch her breath.

Her chest rose and fell as she worked to slow her pulse. And she almost laughed when she thought of what she must look like, slinking around in the dark. Two months ago, she wouldn't have been so bold as to try to escape. But she'd changed in the months she'd been at the colony. Maybe more than she'd changed in all the long years she'd spent alone. And she knew the root of that change was spurring her to leave now.

Confident she could breathe again, she pushed away from the stone and took a step toward the orchard to her left, already thinking ahead to what she would do when she was out of the tunnels and on her own in the vast Montana wilderness. She had money. She knew how to blend in with humans. She'd find a place—hundreds, maybe thousands of miles away from here—and start over. And then she'd decide how she was going to make it to Olympus.

Rocks crunched under her boots as she walked. A voice sounded above.

Maelea's heart lurched into her throat. She slammed back against the base of the tower, looked up. Couldn't see anything except shadows and darkness. But she could hear them. Several voices now. Shouting words she couldn't make out. And feet pounding down the stairs inside the tower at her back.

They'd seen her.

Sweat dripped down her back to pool at the base of her spine. If she didn't make a break for it now, she was screwed. Orpheus would never agree to let her go back to her old life.

The pounding footsteps grew in intensity. Drawing one deep breath, she gripped the straps of her backpack and darted for the orchard. The heavy, metal door on the north side of the tower screeched open. And a voice—a clear voice—yelled, "Stop!"

Maclea pushed her muscles to the max. Just as she stepped past the end of the tower, a hand snaked out and wrapped around her mouth. A muffled yelp slipped from her lips, then the air rushed out of her lungs as she was pulled back against a body that felt like it was made of solid steel.

Chapter Three

"DON'T MOVE. DON'T EVEN MAKE A SOUND."

Maelea's heart raced beneath her breast and her adrenaline jumped into the stratosphere. She didn't know who held her, but if she didn't get away from him soon—like *now*—her one shot at freedom would shrivel and die.

She'd never been good with weapons, but over the last few months she'd participated in self-defense classes taught by the colony's guards. She still wasn't any real threat, but she knew enough to defend herself—something she'd never known before.

Her hand slinked down the outside of the black pants, and her fingers found the snap on the holster at her thigh. Even through the pack strapped to her back, she could feel the push and pull of air in his lungs against her spine. The beat of his heart thumped through the canvas, strong, steady, nowhere near as fast as hers. As voices echoed around the front of the tower, her hand trembled, but she flipped the snap anyway and wrapped her fingers around the handle of the blade.

The voices drifted away, and near her ear, the man whispered, "They're leaving."

He seemed relieved. Was he not one of the guards? She didn't care. Whoever he was, he was still an obstacle between her and freedom.

The hand over her mouth dropped, and as soon as he

loosed his grip on her waist, she pulled the knife and whipped around, ready to strike out. But there was just enough moonlight to make out his face. Light hair, a long, straight nose, rugged jawline, and piercing blue eyes. Unfriendly, searching eyes she'd seen peering down at her from a high window too many times to count.

Gryphon. Orpheus's brother. The guardian who'd mutilated those daemons today, who'd nearly killed one of his own in the process. The guardian, rumor ran in the colony, who was psychotic.

Fear burst in the center of her chest. Arm outstretched, she moved backward, her boots echoing off rocks as she stumbled into the moonlight. The blade in her hand shook, and every instinct in her body said run, but she couldn't turn her back on him. This close, she was afraid that if she did, she'd never even reach the trees. She wasn't immortal like her parents, only ageless. And because she'd been cursed by Hades at birth, there was no afterlife for her. If she died now—before finding her way to Olympus—she'd simply cease to exist. No one to even remember who or what she'd been.

"Don't…don't come near me," she managed.

He didn't move a muscle, just stared at her with those haunted eyes, watching her as he'd done for months now from the isolation of his room. Except this time his brow was furrowed as he studied her, and a perplexed expression grew slowly across his features the longer he watched her.

Her heart rate picked up speed. Was he going to kill her? Would she even see him move? Her puny knife was nothing against a warrior as skilled as he was.

Voices grew louder toward the front of the tower

again. As he turned to look, she knew it was her only shot. She tore off toward the darkness of the trees and ran with everything she had in her. If she could reach the passageway she'd found before he did, she could bar the door. She could still get away.

Twenty yards into the darkness of the orchard, he slammed into her from behind, knocking her off her feet. The air whooshed out of her lungs. Her backpack went sailing. The knife flew from her fingers. She hit the ground on her side, her shoulder and hip taking the brunt of the impact. A grunt left her mouth. But even before pain registered, she scrambled to her feet, tried to push herself up, the flight instinct roaring in her blood. He flipped her to her back before she could find her footing, though, and pinned her hands easily with one of his. Then he slapped his free hand over her mouth and used his weight to still her struggling.

"Stop moving, dammit," he whispered. "They'll hear you."

He outweighed her by at least a hundred pounds, and this close, she could feel the corded muscles beneath the thin, long-sleeved shirt he wore. He was warm where she felt cold, hard where she was soft, and his breath, mere millimeters from her ear, heated the skin of her neck and sent shivers of fear racing down her spine.

And yet…the darkness inside her that was a result of her link to the Underworld vibrated with excitement. It pulled on something in her chest, drew her toward him—a pull she'd felt before but resisted because she didn't understand it.

Now she did. Now, the reasons he watched her made sense. Still to be radiating darkness like this, here in the human realm, he had to have been cursed.

Hades had already tried to kill her numerous times. He could very well have let Gryphon free to finish the job. Her need to get away from him shot into the stratosphere.

Her mind was a blur of frenetic activity. But when she realized he was listening to what was happening around them, she tuned in to her surroundings.

The voices had separated. One seemed to be coming from her left, another from her right. From far off in the distance more shouts echoed, more voices heading this way.

There were more than the two tower guards out here. Earlier, when she was with Skyla, she'd heard Nick say Gryphon was locked in his room, under armed guard. They had to be looking for him, not her.

Hope resurged. If she could get away from him, if she could signal the guards as to his location, they'd forget all about her. He'd be locked up and she could still escape in the resulting chaos.

Dogs barked in the distance, and another voice—a voice Maelea recognized as Nick's—boomed from the direction of the castle. "Fucking find him. He couldn't have gotten far."

Gryphon lurched to his feet and hauled her up next to him. "Run."

"But my pack," she started, pulling on the hand wrapped around her bicep, hoping it would be enough to get him to take off without her.

"Forget the damn pack. I said run!"

Maelea gasped as he dragged her forward, a death grip on her arm. Her feet went out from under her, but he yanked her close to his side, kept her from falling. As she found her footing, she tried to pull away, but he wouldn't let go. His legs were longer than hers, and she struggled to keep up with his pace. Her adrenaline surged. Her muscles screamed in protest. She couldn't see a damn thing out here in the darkness of the orchard, only the lights of the towering castle fading in the distance.

He jerked them to a stop and finally released his hold. Maelea's lungs blazed as she bent over, and even though instinct said to keep running, to get as far from him as possible, she couldn't. She needed a second to suck back air.

Hinges groaned.

"Through here," Gryphon said. "Quick."

Hands braced on her knees, Maelea looked up only to realize he'd found her exit, a door hidden behind twisting vines that led into the hillside behind the armory. Hope dropped like a cement block into the bottom of her stomach.

"Go, dammit!" Gryphon pushed her inside the darkened tunnel that led straight down.

"But—"

She stumbled. Her hands slammed into the rock wall of the tunnel. The heavy steel door clanged shut behind them, followed by the groaning of metal against metal and then nothing at all as the tunnel was blanketed in utter darkness.

Fear leaped in Maelea's throat, followed by a heavy weight pressing in from every direction. She twisted around, could hear the dim voices in the orchard and the barking dogs, searching for their trail. She opened her mouth to cry out, but Gryphon's big hand covered her lips, and then his enormous body pressed against hers, pushing her spine into the cold rock wall at her back.

"Don't you dare make a sound," he whispered near her ear.

She froze, unable to see anything but the whites of his eyes. But she heard everything—the pounding of her heart, the rapid pace of his, the push and draw of air from his lungs so close to her own, and the muffled voices in the orchard, the orders being shouted right and left, the boots clomping over soft spring earth.

Tears burned her eyes. There was an army of men searching just beyond that door. An army ready to bring Gryphon down. An army that didn't know she was with him.

A scratching sound echoed against the metal door. Gryphon turned his head, his lips brushing Maelea's cheek as he twisted. Realizing his face was closer than she'd expected, shards of heat—heat she didn't want—ricocheted through her body, followed by a resurgence of the darkness inside her, and finally a jolt of fear that paralyzed her limbs.

"Here!" A muffled voice called from beyond the door.

Gryphon pressed harder against her mouth with his hand.

"Open it!" another said.

"I can't. It's bolted from the inside."

"Sonofabitch." That was Nick's voice. Maybe there was still a chance… "This entrance leads into the tunnels, right?"

"Yeah," someone else said. "I don't know where, though."

"Well, fucking find out," Nick hollered. "Get me blueprints of this damn castle. Keep working on that door And someone wake up Theron and Orpheus. I want this sonofabitch caught before he gets outside the colony's borders."

Gryphon's free hand gripped Maelea's wrist. Without letting loose of her mouth, he pulled her away from the wall and shifted her around so her back was plastered to his front and his big, hard body was pushing her forward.

"Walk," he said in her ear. Hot breath ran under the collar of her jacket. "I know you've been in here before. I've seen you when no one else is watching. You know exactly where this tunnel lets out. We've got minutes before they figure it out too. If you want to live, you'll get me the hell out of here. And you'll do it fast."

—⁓—

Orpheus jolted from the erotically charged dream involving him, Skyla, and a vat of JELL-O he'd just as soon have continued exploring.

Glancing toward the clock on the nightstand, he caught the time. Just after two a.m. Against his chest, Skyla lay softly snoring, her heat warming him where she'd passed out after they'd made love for the third time.

His chest pinched. Gods, he did not want to leave her in the morning. But there was no way around it. Nick wouldn't let Gryphon stay—not after what he'd done—and Orpheus wasn't abandoning his brother to the outside. He ran his fingers through Skyla's long blond hair and remembered the way she'd stood up for him, even knowing all the dumb shit he'd done in this life and the previous one. If Orpheus could be saved, then there *had* to be hope for Gryphon.

She wanted to go with them, but no matter what, he

wasn't letting Gryphon anywhere near her. She'd tried to argue about it last night, but he'd successfully distracted her with his mouth and hands and the rest of his body—several times. In the morning she'd likely try again, and she'd be pissed when she found out he wasn't relenting, but he'd rather have her alive and pissed than dead.

He'd meant it when he said he wasn't losing her. Not again.

A pounding echoed through the room, and lifting his head from the pillow, he realized that was the sound that had woken him.

As he pushed up on his elbows, Skyla stirred. Grunting once, she lifted sleepy, sexy eyes his way. "What's wrong?"

"I don't know." He slid out of bed, pulled on the jeans he'd tossed on the floor earlier, and crossed the room toward the glass door. Embers still burned red in the fireplace, and shards of moonlight shone through the windows on four sides of the hexagonal room in one of the highest towers of the castle. Beyond the glass door, a male figure loomed. A figure Orpheus recognized as one of Nick's men.

Skata. *Please tell me Gryphon didn't attack someone else.*

Orpheus pulled the door open. The guard's face was flushed from running, and he drew a breath before saying, "He's gone. Tower guards spotted him crossing the court-yard, heading for the orchard. If he gets to the tunnels—"

"How in the bloody hell did he get out?" Skyla asked from across the room, already standing near the bed, the sheet wrapped around her luscious body, her hair a wild tangle around her worried face.

The guard glanced toward her, then looked quickly away when he realized she was all but naked. "We think he went out the window and scaled the building."

"Son of a bitch," Orpheus said. "Where's Nick?"

"Already searching. He requested you and Theron join him."

"I'll be right down."

The guard nodded. As he left, Orpheus shut the door and searched for his boots. Near the bed, Skyla dropped the sheet and shimmied into her own clothes. "He can't have gotten far," she said.

It wasn't how far Gryphon could get that worried Orpheus. It was what his brother would do to anyone who got in his way that sent fear racing down his spine. And what Nick's sentries would do if they found him first.

They dressed in record time and made it down to the main hall just as Theron, the leader of the Argonauts, Zander, and Demetrius were stepping off the elevator. With Titus's injury yesterday, all the Argonauts had gathered in a show of solidarity. All except Gryphon, who'd been locked in his room.

"Where are the others?" Orpheus asked.

"Cerek and Phin already went down to start looking," Theron said.

"What about the girls?" Skyla asked. She was dressed in black pants, a black long-sleeved top, and her signature goth boots, which Orpheus knew housed her weapon of choice: a bow and arrow that would expand to full size when used, one patterned after the bow she'd carried when she was a Siren. "They might be able to tell us where he's at."

"The girls" were the queen of Argolea—Isadora—who

was also Demetrius's new mate, and her two sisters, Callia and Casey. As all three shared the same father, the late king, and were descended from the Horae, the ancient Greek goddesses of balance and order, they had the ability to channel their gifts and see into the present. Maybe even see where Gryphon was right this moment.

"I already sent word to Argolea for Acacia and Isadora to join us," Theron said. "Callia's in the clinic seeing to Titus. When they get here, I'll call her up."

Acacia, or Casey as everyone but Theron called her, was Theron's mate, a half-breed, and Callia was Zander's mate, a healer who tended to the queen and the Argonauts when needed. Since Atalanta was hunting the Horae, it was never smart for them to be in the human realm, but in this instance Skyla was right—they might be the Argonauts' best chance at finding Gryphon before Nick's sentries did.

"Zander, D," Theron said, turning toward the guardians, "head down to the tunnels, see what you can find out. Orpheus, Skyla." Theron looked their way as Zander and Demetrius both headed back for the elevator that would take them down. "Why don't you two hit the orchard. Nick's men have probably already messed with Gryphon's trail, but maybe you can use some of those super Siren tracking skills Skyla has left and see what you can find. I'll go try to talk some sense into Nick before one of his men kills Gryphon. He's pissed about what happened yesterday, and in his mood I don't think he'd stop them if they tried."

Orpheus's gut hitched at that thought, but it warmed at the fact that even with the incident yesterday, the Argonauts weren't abandoning his brother. There was a bond there, among all of them, one that couldn't be broken even by the Underworld.

"Okay," Skyla mumbled, already in Siren mode, heading for the hallway and the stairwell that would lead out to the courtyard.

Before Orpheus took two steps to follow her, Theron grasped his sleeve. "O, wait."

When Orpheus turned to face the leader of the Argonauts, Theron glanced toward the elevator doors that were closing, then toward the hallway where Skyla had already disappeared. "I didn't want to say anything to the others, but there's something else."

Orpheus's nerves jumped another notch. "What?"

"Maelea's missing."

"What do you mean, *missing*?"

"No one's seen her since she retired for bed last night, and she's not in her room."

"That's nothing new. She likes to wander at night."

"Right," Theron said, "and that's my concern. If she happened to come across Gryphon while wandering…"

Oh, shit.

"Gryphon's not thinking clearly," Theron went on. "There's no telling if he'd see her as a threat or bargaining chip if he found her while trying to escape. And it's no secret none of us even know what he has planned… even you."

Dread welled in the bottom of Orpheus's stomach. He'd dragged Maelea into all of this. He'd gone looking for her because, with her ability to sense energy shifts on earth, she'd been the one person who could tell him where the Orb of Krónos was being used, which he'd needed to reunite Gryphon's soul with his body after he rescued Gryphon from the Underworld. Hades already hated her simply because she was Persephone's daughter. And now Hades knew she'd helped the Argonauts find the Orb, that she'd played a hand in rescuing Gryphon from Tartarus. Outside these castle walls—if she made it that far—Gryphon wasn't the only threat to her safety.

Guilt seeped in to mingle with the dread. Because of Orpheus, she'd lost her home and her freedom. And because of him, she could very well lose her life now too.

Urgency pushed at Orpheus from all sides as he headed for the doorway at the end of the hall. "We'll find her. We'll find them both."

"Let's just pray they're not together," Theron mumbled at his back.

—∿∿—

As Gryphon guided Maelea forward, her spine pressed against his chest and her ass bumped into his groin every time she hesitated in the darkness. She was smaller than he'd originally thought, but the baggy clothes he'd seen her wear from his window had hid muscles he didn't know were there. Dressed in the slim black pants and long-sleeved shirt so no one would see her making her escape, and plastered tight against him in the dark tunnel, he also realized how many curves she'd kept hidden under all that fabric.

"Which way?" he growled in her ear when she hesitated at the fork in the tunnel. He'd let go of her mouth so she could breathe, but he kept a firm hold around her waist, not for a second risking the chance that she would bolt.

"I…I'm not sure. I—"

Her words cut off and she sucked in a breath as he pressed his fingers into her hip. "Don't lie to me, female. Which way?"

"Right," she managed. "To the right."

He released his hold on her hip, steered her in that direction. "This will go a whole lot smoother if you don't fight me."

She didn't answer as they moved ahead through the tunnel, but he could feel the anger and fear radiating from her. That and the light. The same weird light that had drawn him to the window each and every time she'd been in the courtyard. The same light that had told him she was out tonight, that she might be his ticket out of this place.

A voice echoed from ahead, deeper in the cave. She hitched in a breath. Wrapping his free hand around her mouth, he pulled her back against the cave wall and held her still. The voice grew louder. His adrenaline jumped. Taking a step back the way they'd come, his spine slid from solid rock to air, then rock again, and he realized the wall opened here. Not much, a gap really, but if he turned sideways, enough to squeeze through. As the voice continued to grow in intensity, he knew it was his only shot. He twisted Maelea, shoved her through the gap, then shimmied in after her.

She grunted under his hand. The gap turned to the left. When his body came up flush against hers, he realized she'd reached the end.

"Shh," he whispered, not letting go of her mouth. She'd shifted around so her face was mere millimeters from his. His arm snaked down to her hip to hold her still, his leg pressed between both of hers, and he used his weight to push her into the wall and keep her quiet. They'd been walking for a good ten minutes. They had to be close to the main intersection. In the central space deep below ground, tunnels extended in various directions, several of which would lead him to freedom. He just had to figure out which ones.

Her heart raced beneath her breast, so loud in the quiet he was afraid the guards might hear it. But the *thump, thump, thump* was drowned out by the heat from her body, circling around him in the confined space, and the scent of…jasmine.

The same scent he'd noticed in the orchard. Only this wasn't from any tree or flower, it was coming from her. He looked down. Couldn't see even an inch in front of his face. But she was there. Against his skin, her breasts pushed into his chest as she drew each labored breath, her lips hovered against the palm of his hand, and that intoxicating fragrance mixed with her body heat to leave him light-headed.

Footsteps pounded somewhere close. Gryphon turned his head to listen, held his breath. Against his hand, Maelea drew in a startled breath, the effort forcing her breasts tighter against his chest. Breasts, he couldn't help notice, even now when they were about to be discovered, that were firm and plump and warm against his chilled skin.

Tingles raced over his flesh where they touched, fanning out to spread tiny tendrils of heat all across his body. It had been months since he'd been close to a female. Months since he'd let anyone touch him. Most days he couldn't even stand the feel of cloth against his skin, but this—her body against his, soft where he was hard, warm where he felt frigid—this didn't bother him. It relaxed him. Heat pooled in his stomach, trickled lower, brought every nerve ending to life.

"Nothing," a voice said from the tunnel beyond. A male voice. One Gryphon didn't recognize. "I don't see any sign of them."

"They had to have come this way," another voice said.

Maelea sucked in another breath, held it. Her nipples pressed into his chest, stiff points hardening against the fabric of his shirt. His stomach tightened at the contact, and without thinking, he shifted his hand from her hip to her rib cage, then higher, to the edge of her bra.

A strangled sound echoed in the back of her throat.

"Did you hear that?" the first voice asked.

Gryphon's hand froze. In the darkness his palms grew sweaty. He looked down at where he'd almost touched her, still couldn't see shit.

Skata, what the hell was he doing? He wasn't here to get hot and heavy with the female. He only needed her to get away. Dammit, he really was going bat-shit crazy if he was trying to feel her up out here in the dark, when they could be discovered at any moment.

He lowered his hand back to her hip. Knew if he didn't do something right away, she'd ruin his chance to escape. She stiffened as he leaned close and his lips brushed her ear, but he ignored the reaction. And he fought the shards of heat touching her like this sent ricocheting to his belly when he said, "Make another sound like that and I'll kill them both."

Her body shook against his, a mixture of fear and hatred, but to her credit she didn't utter another sound.

And in the silence, he felt his control resolidify. Several seconds passed before the first voice said, "Whatever it was, it's gone now. Let's split up. You keep on going, I'll double back."

"Sounds good."

Footsteps pounded away. Gryphon waited a good minute before his heart rate slowed enough so he could put some venom in his voice. "Don't test me, female. I guarantee if you do, you'll lose. All I need from you is to get me out of these tunnels and away from the colony. If you do that, no one will get hurt, you included. Do you understand? Nod once if you do."

Silky hair brushed his cheek as her head bobbed. She drew in a breath through her nose, one that lifted her chest all over again and pressed those wicked breasts tighter to him, dimming all other sound until the beat of her heart was all he heard. A sound he was sure he could now pick out in a crowded room, even with drums and trumpets blaring.

It had been months since he'd heard anything as clear as this. The voice usually overrode everything. But right now, the voice was nothing but a dull buzz somewhere far off in the background.

He stepped away from Maelea, stared down at her in the darkness. He still couldn't see her, but his other senses—smell, hearing, touch—were alive and vibrating with the need for…more. More of whatever the hell she was doing to him.

He had no fucking idea what was happening, but since returning from the Underworld, the only constant he'd grown to expect was that when weird shit happened in his head, it meant something bad was about to go

down. Case in point: what he'd done to Titus and Nick
out there in those woods.

Skata...he really was losing his shaky grasp on reality. Before that happened for good, he had to get out of
these fucking caves. And he needed her to get him there.

He pulled her out of their hiding place and back into
the tunnel, harder than necessary. A yelp slipped from
her lips. He turned her around again so her back was
once more plastered against his front and whispered,
"Okay, nice and slow. Your fate and the fates of those
in this tunnel are in your hands now. Understand?"

She nodded again, swallowed beneath his hand, then
cautiously stepped forward.

And in the silence, he told himself that if he was
too hard on her, if she was afraid, it was a good thing.
Because she should be scared shitless. There was no telling what might set him off or what he'd do next.

Gods, please don't let me kill her. Just let me get away.

"Good girl," he managed, reassuring both of them at
the same time. "This will be over soon, Maelea. Just do
as you're told and in a few minutes, we'll both be free."

Chapter Four

HE KNEW HER NAME. THAT SHOULDN'T HAVE SURPRISED Maelea, but it did. And it pushed that frustration and fear even closer to the forefront.

Her body trembled as they moved down the pitch-black tunnel. The voices were gone. She couldn't even hear footsteps anymore. She wanted to scream out for the sentries to come back, to find her, but knew if she did, Gryphon would make good on his promise.

Tears of anger burned the backs of her eyes. Images of what he'd done to Nick, of what Nick had described he'd done to Titus, swam in her mind. She bit her lip beneath his palm, reminded herself that any kind of unexpected reaction from her would only lead to his being trapped...to him doing something drastic, like injuring either her or those sentries. Like killing them all.

There were worse things than being a prisoner, she told herself. He'd said he just needed her to get out of the tunnels. She had to believe he'd hold to that promise. Once he was free, she'd be a burden—something to slow him down. He'd want to get away as fast as possible. There was no other reason for him to keep her.

They turned a corner. Her elbow knocked into rock and she bit down harder on her lip to keep from crying out, tasted blood against her tongue. His hand slid from her hip to her elbow and rubbed until the pain dissipated. And at the soothing and way-too-comforting touch, warning bells went off like giant red flags waving in the wind.

Oh yes, there's a reason he would keep you around.

Every muscle in her body tightened as his hand moved back to her hip, his fingers digging into the pressure points of her groin to direct her movements. She suddenly became aware of his powerful thighs brushing her hamstrings, of his hips pressing up against her backside. And she remembered all too well how his fingers had grazed the underside of her breasts when he had her pinned in that cramped space only moments ago, how heat had radiated from his body to hers, how he'd hardened—even if only slightly—behind the fly of his jeans.

No. He couldn't possibly want her for that.

Why not? He's a monster. Like Hades. You feel the darkness of the Underworld inside him.

Anger and an increased need to escape vibrated within her. Options raced through her mind. Dammit, she'd lost her backpack in the orchard. She had no weapons now. Nothing to use to even attempt to overpower him. How was she going to get away?

She had to get away.

They rounded another corner. A light burned ahead. He jerked her back into the darkness, even tighter against him. Near her ear, he whispered, "Shh…" and his hot breath sent gooseflesh all over the skin of her neck. A sensation that was both terrifying and electric. "Don't move."

Voices echoed ahead—several—in the central opening of the cave where the tunnels all joined together. Hope erupted in her chest. He'd never make it past them.

There were too many. There was no choice for him but to surrender.

"He's got to be in here," a male voice said—Nick's voice. "I want two in every tunnel and the rest of you here when he shows himself."

Boots clomped. Metal clanged. The sounds grew closer. Someone was heading their way.

Yes!

"*Skata*." Gryphon jerked her back down the tunnel they'd just come through. Maelea's foot slipped on the rocks and a muffled yelp fell from her lips as she scrambled for her footing, trying to keep up in the blinding darkness. Back toward the direction of the orchard, which they seemed to be backtracking to, another voice rang out.

A growl emanated from Gryphon. He yanked her around, tight to his side, both of their backs pressing against the cold rocks. Water dripped down from somewhere above to send a chill over Maelea's skin as she worked to catch her breath.

But the anger...it built inside her. Vibrated stronger. Gave her a confidence she didn't know she had.

"You...you can't get out," she rasped, her courage growing. "There are too many. It's over."

"I say when it's over!" His fingers dug into her wrist. He dragged her toward an elbow deeper in the tunnel. Dim voices still echoed from the central space of the cave, but they weren't following. The footsteps ahead echoed louder. Someone was running toward them. A light barreled closer.

The sentry from before. The one who'd gone back to check the orchard door. It had to be. She needed to do something fast before Gryphon killed him.

"Here!" she screamed. "I'm here!"

Gryphon's fingers dug into her wrist with a death grip, and he yanked her so close, the air whooshed out of her lungs. The sentry's boots skidded to a stop.

Whatever fear she'd felt before was replaced with determination. She wasn't going to go willingly this time. She had let Orpheus drag her to this colony. She'd spent her life hiding. But not anymore. This time, she was in control.

She jerked hard on Gryphon's arm. "No! I'm not going any farther with you."

Light from the sentry's lantern ahead curved around the bend, illuminating the cave and Gryphon's enraged eyes. Behind her, toward the main chamber of the caves, voices dimmed as if they'd heard her too. An eerie silence settled over the space, followed by the squawk of a radio from the sentry frozen around the corner.

Fear raced down her spine, but she held her ground. And when Gryphon muttered, "Stupid female," and his grip tightened on her wrist, she didn't even think, she reacted.

She wrenched her arm from his grip. Electricity raced down her arm. The force of it hit the rocks at her feet, vibrated through the floor of the cave. A great cracking sound echoed.

"Dammit," Gryphon muttered, glaring into her eyes, taking one menacing step forward.

She braced herself for his fury, for the first time not afraid of what might happen to her. Energy rippled through her limbs, into the rocks beneath her feet. But before he could reach out and grasp her again, a rumble echoed through the tunnel.

Gryphon stopped. Looked up and around. Voices echoed through the cramped space. And Maelea took the opportunity to strike.

She thrust her arms out full force. "No, you son of a bitch."

Her palms connected with his chest. Energy shot from her into him, from her legs into the floor. He stumbled back a step, lost his footing, started to go down. Then an ear-shattering crack echoed through the cave.

As Gryphon hit the ground with a grunt, dim voices grew stronger. Boots clomped over rock. And Orpheus's voice rang out strong. Calling…her name.

She turned toward the sound. Screamed, "I'm here!"

But her voice was drowned out by the roar of rushing water. Rushing fast.

"Maelea!"

She looked back over her shoulder where Gryphon was pushing up from the ground, trying to come after her. Her eyes flew wide. Another burst of energy rippled through her body. Followed by an earth-shaking roar just as the ceiling opened up and a wave of water poured into the tunnel.

The force knocked him off his feet. He slammed into her, kicked her legs out from under her. She hit his chest hard, gasped as water sprayed her face, filled her lungs. Gryphon's fingers dug into her biceps, dragging her with him down the slippery cave floor, rushing in a river of water right for Orpheus and the others racing in their direction.

She tried to catch her breath, tried to twist away from Gryphon. Through blurry vision, she saw lights ahead. People coming their way. Orpheus's face.

"Hang on to me!" Gryphon yelled over the thunder of water.

No. Never. She fought against him. Lashed out with her arms, tried to kick away with her feet.

Another crack resounded. Her eyes grew wide. Locked on Orpheus and Nick skidding to a stop. Then the rocks gave out beneath them.

She managed one bleating scream. And felt nothing but air.

Atalanta was in a time crunch.

She glanced at the calendar mounted to the wall as her frustration grew exponentially. "Galto!"

The clacking of nails against stone echoed through the room, followed by a raspy voice at her back. "Yes, my queen."

She turned to glare down at the three-foot-tall, scaly, goblinlike creature she'd dragged back from the Underworld when she escaped after following Gryphon and the daemon spawn out. "What news of my *doulas*?"

Galto rubbed his gnarled hands together, his forked tongue licking his dry lips. One pointed ear turned back as if to listen for movement behind him. "Nothing, my queen. It's as if he's vanished from the human realm."

"Imbeciles." Atalanta brushed her long red robe behind her and moved to the window to look out at the sea of snow. She craved the cold. Even her realm in the Underworld—when she'd resided there and had been building her army of daemons—had been a frigid wasteland, so different from the fiery chasm of Tartarus. But as a goddess, she'd had the power to turn her little corner of hell into whatever she wanted. Here in the human realm, she had to resort to locating her base where cold weather persisted. And though she'd have preferred to be somewhere isolated, like Antarctica, her daemons couldn't flash from place to place on earth as she could. They were limited by the same laws of physics as humans—and Argoleans. Which meant she had to set up camp someplace convenient for them and cold enough for her. Since her fortress in northern British Columbia had been destroyed by those bastard Argonauts, she'd been forced here. To sunny, sinfully cold Scandinavia.

Revenge whipped through her. She would not rest until she saw Argolea in ruins and those pompous Argonauts in chains. They'd shunned her. Cast her out because she'd dared question their order. Banished not only her, but her love.

Thoughts of Meleager—the only person who'd ever understood her and who'd died standing up for her—drifted through her mind. So many years alone. So many disappointments. But it all ended now.

I'll make them pay, my love. I promise you they'll burn for what they did to you.

"Perhaps…" Galto started.

She glared over her shoulder at the disgusting creature.

"Perhaps he's in Argolea?"

Atalanta looked back over the snow. And sent out feelers. Searching. Scanning. Drawing on the darkness of the Underworld that had been bestowed on her *doulas*. "No, he's out there somewhere. I can feel him. The pull is too strong for him to be in Argolea. Besides, after what was done to him in the Underworld"—a wicked smile twisted her lips—"he'd never have the nerve to face his fellow warriors in Argolea. His honor would be too strong for that. He's out there, Galto. But he's fighting the darkness."

"He will eventually give in. He can't resist much longer. We just have to wait for that to happen."

Atalanta looked back to the calendar on the wall. Six months. Krónos, the king of the Titans, had given her six months to get the Orb, and more than two had already passed. Even though Krónos was locked in the depths of Tartarus, he still commanded a power like no other. Atalanta didn't doubt for a minute that if the six-month mark hit and she didn't live up to their bargain, he'd drag her back to the Underworld and make good on his threat to turn her into his slave.

"We don't have time to wait," she said, angling back to Galto. "Send a group of daemons to the Pacific Northwest. The half-breeds are likely hiding him."

She'd wasted too much time rounding up her daemons and rebuilding the army those blasted Argonauts had scattered after she'd been sent to the Underworld. But that was rectified now, and her army was growing in strength *and* number, thanks to her new breed of daemons—hybrids who looked human but could shift into daemon form at any time.

"But, my queen. We haven't been able to locate the half-breed colony yet."

"Then step up attacks in the area. That'll draw those bloody Argonauts out. Torture humans, half-breeds…I don't care which. Just find out where that half-breed colony is located. I guarantee my *doulas* is hiding there."

Her *doulas* was the key to everything. As an Argonaut, he could infiltrate Argolea. He could gain the other Argonauts' trust, slip into the Argolean castle, take the Orb their queen had hidden there. And then he could bring it—and one of the Horae, the descendants of the ancient goddesses of balance and justice, whom Atalanta needed to control the Orb—to her. Gryphon was tied to Atalanta now, thanks to Krónos's help. When he finally gave in and came to her, he'd be bound to do her will. And once she had the Orb, she could negotiate more time with Krónos. Without all four sacred elements— earth, air, water, and fire—the Orb couldn't be used to its full power. And Krónos needed the Orb at maximum power to be able to escape the Underworld. Once she had the Orb in her possession, Krónos would be cornered into giving her more time to find the remaining elements. And when she did…

When she did, well, he'd bow to *her*. Not the other way around.

"Yes, my queen," Galto said, backing out of the room, his long, clawlike nails clicking against the stone-cold floor as he moved.

Alone, Atalanta looked back out the window. A storm was moving in. Dark gray clouds on the edge of the horizon waited to unleash their frigid fury. Being back in the human realm was both a blessing and a curse. Here she once more commanded her army, but she was mortal. If it weren't for that one limitation, she'd be out hunting Gryphon herself. But even with her goddess powers, she couldn't take the risk. However, once she had the Orb…

One corner of her lips curled as she watched the first snowflake drift to the ground. Once she had the Orb in her hands again, she'd be close to achieving her ultimate goal: seeing every single Argonaut destroyed.

Once they were wiped from the cosmos and she had the power to command the human realm, only then would she rest.

—∿∿∿—

The air was bitter cold, but the water cut with the bone-chilling frigidity of a thousand knives stabbing into every inch of his skin.

Gryphon plunged beneath the surface, kicked hard to come back up. They'd fallen for at least fifteen seconds before hitting this ice-cold pool of water. He gasped when he reached the surface, gulped in air, opened his eyes, and tried to get his bearings.

Dooouulaaaas…

He shook the water from his ears. *Not fucking now!*

He turned in the water. No, not a pool. An underground river. The current was swift, already rushing him downstream. The voices of Nick's men—of Orpheus—hollering from above were long gone, and he couldn't see shit in the dark.

"Mae—" He sputtered water. Coughed as he tried to keep the current from sucking him back under. "Maelea!"

No cry for help met his ears. Nothing but the increasing roar of water crashing close. He swiveled in the dark, tried to squint to see ahead. Saw nothing but pitch-black darkness in every direction. "Maelea!"

Dooouulaaaas…

He ground his teeth. Worked like hell to ignore the voice. The churn of water grew in intensity. Something brushed his leg beneath the surface. He tried to swim back the way he'd come, but the current was too swift. Panic pushed in as he was forced downstream. "Maelea!"

A splash echoed to his right. Then a gasp. And a cough. He twisted in that direction, kicked hard to reach the noise. "Maelea?"

Maelea sputtered somewhere close.

His hands pushed through water, passed over flesh, tightened around muscle and bone to tug her close. "Grab on to me."

"What's that"—she coughed, dug her fingers into his flesh—"noise?"

He shifted toward the roar. Realized it was a water-fall. Shit. They were going over. "Don't let go of me!"

Her scream met his ears just as they rocketed off what had to be an enormous drop-off. Water sprayed into his eyes, messed with his vision. For a second he thought he saw something glowing green beneath them, but it was so dark in here, that couldn't be right. Air rushed up his back, but he didn't let go of Maelea's forearm. Not as they sailed through the frigid air, not as they hit—thank gods—another pool of water, not as they submerged beneath the surface and his breath rushed out of his lungs like air from a popped balloon.

He kicked as if Hades himself were after them, gripped her arm tighter so he didn't lose her. And gasped when he finally came back up. Musty, damp, bone-chilling air filled his chest. Beside him, Maelea broke the surface and drew large gulps of air.

Realizing she was okay, that they'd both survived, his heart rate began to slow and he let go of her as he treaded water and tried to figure out where the hell they were.

To his surprise, the pool of water they'd dropped into was indeed glowing green, the light enough to illuminate the giant cavern around them, the underground lake they'd fallen into, even the small stream leading out at the far end, which continued like a phosphorescent trail toward freedom.

He looked up at the forty-foot waterfall they'd just come down. No other bodies sailed over the edge, which meant no one had been stupid enough to follow them. Nick and his men...and Orpheus...probably all thought he and Maelea were dead by now.

Beside him, Maelea's teeth knocked together. He looked her way as she shivered in the cold water, her long black hair a wet mess plastered to her head, her normally pale skin even whiter in the glow of the lake.

He didn't know what was making the water glow, but he was thankful for it. Especially since he didn't have a flashlight. "We need to get out of this water."

"I..." Her teeth clattered together and her body shook, but she didn't fight him when he pulled her toward the rocky edge of the pool. "I...d-d-d-don't...l-l-l-like you."

"You wouldn't be the first."

He climbed out of the water, hauled her out next to him. Chilled air rushed over his already wet and cold skin, sent a shiver down his spine. Maelea wrapped her hands around her waist and trembled harder.

Shit, he was totally unprepared for this. No matches, no blankets, not even any supplies. They weren't going back out the way they'd come in, and looking around the cavern lit by the eerie green glow, their only hope was to follow the river and see where it came out. But they couldn't do that until they got warm.

"Take off your clothes."

"Wh-*what*?" Her shocked and enraged eyes shot to

his. Eyes, he noticed up close, that weren't just dark, as he'd guessed from the hours he'd watched her from his room at the colony. They were black. Jet-black. The same color as her hair. The same color as the vileness of the Underworld that lived inside him.

He reached for the hem of her long-sleeved top. "It's either that or freeze to death."

She swatted at his hand and moved back an enormous step, those dark eyes growing wide as saucers. "D-d-d-don't touch me!"

"It's not my first choice, female, but it's either that or die. And I'm not about to die down here."

He reached for her shirt again. She smacked at his hand, stumbled back a step. "I said don't t-t-t-touch me. I'll scream!"

His own anger ramped up. "Go ahead. There's no one to hear you. Do you think they're coming after us? They think we're dead. And even if Nick and the others figure out a way to climb down safely, it'll be hours before they reach us. That river brought us at least a couple of miles underground. In hours, I plan to be long gone."

He grasped the hem of her shirt before she could think of words to match her shocked expression, and yanked it up to her head. She let out a muffled scream, threw her arms up to push him away, but her limbs weren't working yet because of the cold and it did little good. When she stumbled, he didn't try to catch her, knowing the rock wall of the cavern would do that soon enough.

A crack echoed as her head hit stone. In her dazed yelp, he ripped the rest of her shirt off, dropped it on the ground. Then he went to work on the buttons of her slim black pants. "Hold still, dammit."

She struggled against him, tried to kick him with her foot. He moved down, barely missed getting cracked in the nose by her knee. While she pushed against his shoulders, he braced one arm across her hips to hold her tight to the rocks and used the other to unzip her boots then drag her pants down her legs.

"You s-s-s-son of a bitch! If you so much as t-t-t-touch me, I'll—"

She was still shivering, likely in shock. He tugged off one boot, then the other, dragged her pants the rest of the way from her legs. "You'll what?"

She slammed her fist against his spine. "I'll k-k-k-kill you! I swear I w-will!"

"With what? Your fingernails? I don't think so, female." He pushed back up to his feet, pressed his hips into hers to hold her still, and let go long enough to strip his own dripping shirt over his head.

Anger erupted in those obsidian eyes. But her pupils were dilated, and he wasn't averse to taking advantage of her disorientation in any way he could.

She raked her fingernails down his chest. Fire burned across his skin where she gouged his flesh.

"Son of a bitch." He captured her hands easily in one of his. Pinned them over her head and glared down at her. "Stop fucking around. I'm not going to rape you, dammit. I couldn't even if I wanted to."

She struggled against his hold, finally realized she was trapped, and slowed her flailing. But when he reached down with his free hand to unbutton his jeans, her gaze shot to his waistband and her eyes flew wide all over again. "D...don't."

The tremble that ran through her body had nothing to

do with the temperature and everything to do with fear. His gaze strayed to the cream-colored bra against her much paler flesh, then lower to the bit of nude lace at her hip peeking out where he wasn't pressing into her. And against his groin, her stomach tightened. Followed by a rush of heat. A whole lot of heat he wasn't sure came from only her.

He looked back into her eyes as something sharp stabbed his chest. Not her fingers this time, since they were still bound above her head, but…an emotion? No, definitely couldn't be that. He hadn't felt a damn thing other than empty since returning from the Underworld. It had to be something else. Leftover adrenaline from nearly being discovered or even a muscle spasm from almost drowning.

Cool air washed down his spine, spread beneath the waistband of his jeans, sent a shiver over his skin. Enough dicking around. If they didn't warm up soon, they were both going to die from hypothermia, and then this argument would be nothing but a past-tense waste of time.

Eyes still locked on hers, he toed off his boots, kicked them across the rocks. A buzz echoed in his head, but it wasn't like the screaming voice he was used to. This, at least, was manageable. He popped the button on his jeans.

Against him, she sucked in a breath and went still as stone.

People were afraid of him. He was used to that reaction. But hers pissed him off more than most. Why, he didn't know.

"I told you before, I'm not going to hurt you," he said, working not to yell as he pushed his pants down and wrestled his way out of them, leaving him in nothing but soaking-wet boxer briefs. "If you cooperate, that still holds true."

He let go of her hands, pushed her arms to her sides, and wrapped his around hers, crushing her to his chest. She drew in another startled breath but was smart enough—this time—not to fight back. He turned them both around and sank down to sit on the rocks, holding her close as another shiver racked his body.

"Wh-why are you d-d-doing this to m-m-me?"

Now that the fight had left her body, the shock was crashing in hard. He loosed his hold, rubbed his hands up and down her arms to stimulate circulation. "I'm not doing anything but trying to break free. Just like you."

"You d-did that." She bent her elbows, drew her forearms up against his chest. "You d-d-don't need me now."

He didn't, technically, that was true. At least not after he got warm. Keeping her around wasn't an entirely ludicrous idea, though. There was no telling where this cavern let out, or who'd be waiting for them when they finally made it back to the surface. Any hostage was better than no hostage.

But dragging her along…he hadn't planned for that, and it created a whole other set of problems. Problems he needed to work through in his head. And right now, though he didn't understand why, the voice wasn't screaming at him, so it was his best chance to think. "Shut up already and just"—he wrapped his arms back around her, tugged her head so it fit under his chin—"try to generate body heat."

She shivered against him for several minutes, then

finally drew in a shuddering breath and relaxed a few muscles at a time. But she kept her hands pressed against his chest, ready and waiting to push away as soon as she could.

Her warmth seeped into his skin as they sat in silence. Water gurgled nearby, and the green glow from the bottom of the lake gave the entire cavern an eerie feel. His mind drifted to where he'd go after he got out of this cave. If he let the voice guide him, he had no doubt he'd find his target. The question was…could he fight the voice? If he let it take hold, could he keep the darkness from consuming him?

Sensation came back to his toes, his knees, his arms and legs. Gradually, he became aware of Maelea against him, not only as a heat source, but as a woman. Warm breath brushed against his collarbone, slid lower to tighten his nipples. Soft breasts pressed against the underside of his pecs, making him wonder what they felt like without that bra. And everywhere her bare skin touched, heat erupted. Against his chest, his stomach, especially in his hips, where she was straddling him, nothing but her damp panties and his wet boxers separating their flesh.

His mind drifted to sweaty, wet, steaming flesh. Skin moving against skin. Eyes half-closed, hungry mouths, hands and lips and tongues touching, sucking, tasting…

Skata. Definitely not what he needed to be thinking about right now. Avoiding hypothermia. Escaping. Finding that fucking voice that had been haunting him for months.

The voice…

He hadn't heard it since…the river. Since before he'd

found Maelea. It was still there—he could hear the dull buzz—but it wasn't the incessant screaming he was used to. Come to think of it, in the tunnels, before the ground had given out—something he still didn't understand—when he'd pressed Maelea up against the rock wall and covered her mouth with his hand to keep her quiet, the voice had dimmed then too.

He thought back to Maelea's curves locked tight against him. To the feel of her lips beneath his palm. Tried to remember if she'd done or said anything that could be messing with his concentration. But nothing came to mind. And though he fought it, he couldn't help but compare how she'd felt then—completely clothed and trembling—to how she felt now. Half-naked, relaxed, all but melting into his skin, warming him in a way that left him burning.

Tingles started in his stomach, spread lower. He was suddenly aware of every detail. The jasmine scent of her skin, the way her nearly dry hair curled around her shoulders and brushed his arms, every curve and subtle softness. And how incredibly warm she was. Everywhere. Reawakening his body in ways he didn't expect.

Her breath caught. She went still against him. And he realized, *skata*, she felt that reawakening too. *Fucking fabulous*. While he had no remorse about scaring the crap out of her to get what he wanted, he'd finally just settled her down by promising he wasn't about to rape her. And here he was with a massive hard-on she definitely couldn't miss.

In a minute she was gonna freak. He'd lose the heat they'd generated. Unless he did something quick to change her mind.

He slid his hands down to her hips and lifted her from his lap. But his fingers slipped on her silky skin and she dropped back down, right on his erection. And just that little bit of friction sent blood screaming to his cock and a roaring need rushing through his veins.

She gasped. Dug her fingers into his chest. But this time the clawing motion didn't hurt. It felt good. And where they were locked together at the hips, heat erupted. A volcano of want and need and lust. A lust he'd gone way too long without. A lust he could sate, right here and now.

All he had to do was take.

Chapter Five

"*SKATA*. THIS ISN'T WORKING. YOU NEED TO MOVE."

Maelea nearly choked as Gryphon positioned his hands at her hips and lifted her from his lap only to drop her again on a monster erection she'd have had to be dead to miss. Her fingers dug into his chest and she tried to push away, but he held her too tightly. Fear rushed in on a wave, swamped her chest. She'd been stupid to think he wouldn't take advantage of her just because she was cold. Stupid to trust him.

"Don't. I—"

He lifted her from his lap, dropped her on her butt on the rocks. Words died on her lips as pain ricocheted up her spine. Still disoriented from that fall, she scrambled back against the cave wall, drew her knees up to her chest, and wrapped her arms around herself, scanning the ground for anything she could use as a weapon, but there was nothing. She blinked several times, tried to clear her vision. Couldn't see even a rock to hurl at him when he came after her.

He pushed to his feet, and in the green glow from the water, her vision faded and blurred on muscles in his massive arms, his powerful back, his thick legs. She scooted farther down the wall. Gave her head a swift shake. Glanced right and left. Gods, she must have hit her head when they went over those falls. She wasn't thinking clearly. She could run, but where? Every muscle in her body tensed. She was ready to fight to the death if she had to, but was smart enough to know if she tried to stand, she'd probably fall over.

But instead of turning and coming after her as she expected, he reached down and picked up her pants. Shook them out. Laid them over a boulder. Then he did the same with her shirt and finally his clothes.

When he turned and stepped toward her, her gaze shot to his groin, and even through her blurry vision, she noticed whatever she'd felt before had definitely deflated. He didn't make eye contact, and she pressed her palms flat to the ground, ready to push up if he lunged for her, but he didn't. He just sat on the rocks at her side and said, "We need those clothes to dry out if we're going to get the hell out of here."

Every muscle in Maelea's body stayed rigid as he lifted an arm, slung it over her shoulder, and tugged her tight to his side. Warmth immediately replaced the chill, and though she didn't want to, she felt herself giving in, sinking against him. A shiver racked her body again, knocked her teeth together.

He wrapped his other arm around her front, pulled her even closer into his chest. Then he shifted onto his side and pulled his knees up next to hers, creating a blanket of warmth around her with his body. This time he didn't hold her so tight she couldn't move, and she had the strangest sensation he was letting her know that if she wanted to get away, she could. "That's better."

Maelea wasn't so sure. She couldn't read him. Didn't know what he was thinking or planning next. That dead look she'd seen when she caught him watching her in the courtyard from his bedroom window still lingered in his light blue eyes, but this didn't seem like the action of a monster. At least not the one who'd mutilated those daemons or attacked his own kin. And the warmth that immediately enveloped her threw her totally off-kilter.

His hand moved up and down her arm, rubbing her muscles back to life. "A blanket would be nice. You didn't happen to have one of those in that backpack you were carrying, did you?"

"I...I did." She'd also had a flashlight, food, and a handgun she'd lifted from the colony late one night when she was out roaming. Not that it would do her any good now.

"Damn. Well, we should rest for a few minutes. I don't know how long it's going to take us to get out of here. If our clothes dry."

Maelea didn't know either. But she was as determined as ever to get far, far away from the colony, and especially him. So he hadn't hurt her yet. That didn't mean he wasn't going to soon. For the moment, he needed her warmth as much as she needed his. But she wasn't about to let down her guard. She'd learned long ago not to trust. And the dark energy vibrating from his chest, calling to her, told her never to trust him.

Someone was singing a really bad version of AC/DC's "Highway to Hell."

Titus cracked his eyelids open and turned his head to figure out where the incessant noise was coming from. Bright light burned his retinas, forced his eyes shut, drew a curse from his lips. Lips that were dry and chapped and as crackly as the singer's caterwauling voice.

The song cut off midline, and a voice called, "Hey, I think he's coming around."

Footsteps echoed close, and Titus cracked his lids again, this time squinting up at a very familiar face.

"*Skata*," he managed, his voice raspy, his throat dry as a cotton ball. "I should have known it was you. You sound like a dying cat when you sing, and you've got the fucking mug to match."

Phineus, his warrior kin, grinned down at him. "I wasn't singing, smart guy, I was humming. And you should watch your language in front of the kid."

Titus looked to the left where Phin nodded and saw Max, Zander's son, sitting in the chair on his other side. "Hey, kid."

Max shrugged the mop of blond hair out of his eyes, looking way too much like his dad, his bored expression screaming, *I'd rather be anywhere but here*. "Hey."

"And I know you're secretly jealous of this face," Phineus added. "It's a chick magnet. Hollywood's got nothing on me."

Titus chuckled, then swore as blinding pain radiated through his torso and up into his rib cage.

"Uh…Callia?" Phin's voice took on a note of concern. Seconds later, Callia, the queen's personal healer and Max's mother, moved into Titus's line of sight.

"Hey there, stranger," she said with a smile. Auburn hair fell over her shoulder as she peered down at him. "How are you feeling?"

"Like I got run over by a truck."

"That's not far off the mark, actually," she said. "How does your throat feel?"

"Like sandpaper."

"I'll get you some juice."

As Callia moved away, Titus took a look around. The white walls, blinking machines, and uncomfortable bed told him he was in a medical facility. His memory was foggy, but as he looked from face to face, then around the room, bits and pieces of what had landed him here spiraled through his mind.

Shit. Gryphon.

Titus closed his eyes. Pain pulsed along his skull as the scene replayed behind his eyelids. "Where is he?"

"Who?" Phin asked.

"The king of fucking France," Titus said sarcastically. "Gryphon, you dumbass."

"Um...*k-i-d.*" Phineus lifted his eyebrows, pointed across the bed. "Remember?"

"I've heard it before," Max muttered. *And I can spell that word, moron.*

Shit...what the hell do I say?

Whatever you do, don't tell him the truth.

Thoughts spun out of control in the room. The first from Max—full of attitude and animosity. The second from Phineus, frazzled and desperate for a way not to answer. And the third from Callia across the room, clear and calm, the only one of the three who was obviously totally with it.

Oh, fucking fantastic. The blow to the head Titus had taken when Gryphon had knocked him into that concrete wall hadn't done shit to alter his gift.

Irritation edged Titus's already dwindling mood, kicked up his headache. He ignored Max and focused on Phin—whom he could see—and Callia—whom he couldn't. "Stop pussyfooting around me, you two. You can't block me from your thoughts, so you might as well just tell me what the hell happened to Gryphon. Nick didn't kill him, did he? What happened out there wasn't Gryphon's fault."

"Considering what he did to you," Phin muttered, "that's pretty generous."

Titus remembered all too well Gryphon's crazed eyes and the things that had been running through his mind when he charged those daemons. "Yeah, well, you don't know what's going on in his head. We'd already have you locked in the loony bin if it were you, pretty boy."

Phineus grinned again, his brown eyes crinkling at the edges. "I knew you were jealous of this gorgeous face. Admit it."

Titus snorted, then swore as another shot of pain rushed through his torso.

"Okay, enough," Callia said, coming back to the right side of his bed and holding out a cup with a straw. "Drink this."

As Titus took the cup from her hand, careful not to touch her, she turned to Phin and added, "Why don't you take Max to get something to eat." She looked at her son on the other side of the bed. "Are you hungry, honey?"

Max shrugged, crossed his arms over his chest, and deliberately didn't meet her gaze. "I guess."

The kid dropped to his feet and shuffled toward the door. While Titus sipped the juice, which tasted like heaven, he watched Callia watch her son. He didn't need to read minds to know what she was thinking. Her *I love you and I don't know what to do to help you* expression was written clearly on her face.

"I'll be back to sing to you later, smart guy," Phin

said as he pushed up on his long legs and scrubbed a hand through his short dark hair. "And this time I'll serenade you with my pristine tenor. You want 'T.N.T.' or 'You Shook Me All Night Long'?"

"If you're gonna come back here and sing, I want a lobotomy."

Phin winked at Callia. "He's delirious with excitement."

Titus's head fell back against the pillow as Phin headed out the door. "I'm gonna need more drugs. Preferably whatever you gave me before that knocked me out."

Callia turned and looked down at him, her hands on her slim hips, her eyebrows lifted in amusement. A stethoscope was slung around her neck and a pen was tucked behind her left ear. One he bet she probably forgot she'd put there. "I only gave you enough to keep you asleep during the surgery. With that head wound, I'd prefer not to give you more than you need."

Surgery. Shit. It really had been bad. No wonder his ribs hurt like hell. "What did you have to do?"

She sat on the side of his bed. He shifted his legs out of the way so she wouldn't accidentally touch him. "You had a punctured lung, couple of broken ribs, and I had to stitch you up from the inside out. It wasn't pretty, but the last time I checked, the wounds were healing well. Your superhero Argonaut genes come in handy in a crisis."

Yeah, no shit. "What about my head?"

"There was some pressure on the left side of your brain. I didn't want to drain it if I didn't have to. Now that you're awake, I think it's going to be okay."

Titus nodded and rubbed his fingers through the long

hair over the back of his scalp, cringing when he felt the tender bump.

One corner of Callia's mouth turned up at the edge. "Zander said you'd be pissed if I had to shave your head. You have him to thank that I didn't."

Titus lowered his hand. "How'd you get Zander to agree to bring Max to the Misos colony? That's where we are, right?"

Callia sighed, but this time was careful to guard her thoughts. "He's not happy with me about that, actually. We argued about it as I was rushing to get here to help you."

Because Callia was a descendent of the ancient Horae, the goddesses of balance and justice, her son, Max, was a valuable asset in the war between good and evil. While it was a risk for even Callia to be in the human realm, it was an even bigger risk for Max. He'd been taken from Callia and Zander as a baby and raised by Atalanta, the vengeful goddess who had only one goal: to see Argolea and the Argonauts destroyed. The Argonauts had successfully rescued Max from Atalanta's clutches months ago, and since then he'd been kept safe in Argolea, which was the one realm Atalanta couldn't access. But Titus knew from being around Zander that things weren't all rosy at home these days. Max was struggling with the adjustment. And the strain was evident on Callia's face.

"Zander's just worried," Titus said, hoping to ease a little of her anxiety.

"Zander's right to be worried," she said. "Every day that goes by, Max is slipping farther and farther away from us. I hoped coming to the colony, where we can keep him safe and he could feel like he was a part of things, would help." She looked toward the door with longing. "But I guess that was a pipe dream, huh?"

"Callia, I—"

"Don't worry about it," she said, pushing to her feet and reaching out to squeeze his bare arm. "We'll all survive."

A jolt of emotions rippled through Titus, drew him forward on the bed with a gasp, and hurled him back against the mattress with a crack. The cup flew from his hand. Air whooshed out of his lungs as pain encircled his chest and tightened with the force of a boa constrictor.

"Oh my gods, Titus." Callia immediately let go, stepped back.

The pain dissipated as soon as she released him, and he breathed through clenched teeth as the emotions followed suit.

"You feel, don't you?" Callia asked in small voice. "I suspected, but I wasn't sure. That's why you wear gloves all the time. I am so sorry. I didn't…"

"It's okay," he managed to say, even as the residual effects of the transfer left him feeling like a limp noodle. "I'm used to it."

"All the time?" she asked. "Has there ever been a time when you've touched someone and not felt what they feel?"

There had been. Feeling others' emotions wasn't part of his gift. It was a curse. A hundred-year-old curse he'd been damned with because of what he'd done.

"Not that I can remember," he lied, not wanting to talk about it, let alone remember. "Lucky me, huh?"

"Oh, Titus."

He could handle just about anything except pity. He

pushed himself up in the bed. "It's okay, really. Just"—he managed a weak smile—"don't do that again."

"I won't. I'll put a sign on the door that anyone who comes in has to wear gloves. Will that do the trick?"

"Yeah, that'll work. And I'm sure it'll raise all kinds of questions regarding what sort of contagious disease I have."

Screw what anyone thinks.

Titus couldn't help it. He chuckled at her thought, then regretted it when pain stabbed his cracked ribs again. He pressed a hand against his side, breathed through the burn. "Zander's one lucky SOB, you know that?"

"Remind him of that when you see him. He's still mad at me about Max. Do the others know? The Argonauts? About touching you?"

"We're guys, Callia. We don't go around getting touchy-feely with each other." When she frowned, he added, "You think I need them looking at me as more of a freak than they already do?"

That would never happen.

He leaned his head back against the pillow. "Trust me. It would."

She was silent for several seconds, and though thoughts ran through her mind, he tried to ignore them. But words got through: *awful, sad, lonely.* Words he definitely didn't need to hear.

Just when he was about to tell her he didn't want or need her pity, she turned for the door. "Don't worry, I won't mention it to any of them. Try to get some rest while I get that sign up."

He trusted her to keep his secret. But he knew when she was playing the avoidance card. And no matter what weird shit was happening with him, what was going on outside these clinic walls was a thousand times more important.

"Callia." When she glanced over her shoulder, he asked, "Where's Gryphon?"

She was careful not to meet his eyes. *You don't need to hear this right now.*

"Yeah, I do. Where is he?"

She hesitated, then finally sighed in defeat. "No one knows. The Argonauts are all out looking for him. It appears he climbed out his window, scaled the castle wall…No one's entirely sure how he got out, but he did, and he got by Nick's guards without anyone noticing."

Skata. "Nick's gotta be pissed."

"He is. His healer had to put twenty-four stitches in his arm. He was going to kick Gryphon out of the colony tomorrow. Orpheus was going to go with him. I'm guessing Gryphon figured that out and ran before it could happen."

"Gryphon wouldn't want O sacrificing anymore for him. What about Theron?"

"Theron wasn't sure what to do about the situation and he didn't have time to decide. Before he could come up with a solution, Gryphon bolted."

"Shit. Nick's men will kill him if they find him first."

"I know," she said quietly. "Which is why the Argonauts are out looking for him right this minute. Theron left Phineus here to make sure we were okay, but the others…they'll find him, Titus."

Titus ground his teeth and pushed the covers off his legs. "It wasn't his fault. I should be helping to look for him."

Callia rushed back to his side of the bed. "No way. You're in no condition to move yet. Even superhero genes need time to work."

"Get out of my way, female."

Callia held her bare hands up. "Don't make me use these again."

Titus glared up at her, then remembered the way her emotional transfer had knocked him on his ass. Dammit, he hated the fact he was so freakin' weak. Not physically—at least not normally—but emotionally. Just the slightest touch from another person could cripple him.

He clenched his teeth in frustration, but eased back against the bed again, not wanting a repeat of the I'm-a-giant-pussy ordeal. Especially in front of Callia. "Maybe I'll just rest for a few more minutes."

"Smart *ándras*," Callia said, lowering her hands. *I really didn't want to zap you again.* "I'll be right on the other side of that door if you need anything. And don't worry, I'll be sure to keep you updated as I hear news."

That didn't leave him feeling all reassured. It only pissed him off even more.

She moved to the door, paused, and looked back. "Phineus was right. Most people wouldn't be nearly as forgiving after what Gryphon did. You're a special man, Titus."

No, he wasn't. He was cursed. And not only did he know why, he also knew he deserved it.

"Save your praise for someone who's worthy." He closed his eyes, blocking out her way-too-gentle eyes as he tried like hell not to hear her thoughts. "I just know what it's like to be tormented by voices. And trust me, yours and everyone else's are nothing compared to the voice that's haunting Gryphon. I wouldn't wish that shit on anyone."

——~~——

A shiver racked Maelea's body. Startled, she jolted awake. Confusion hit as her eyes adjusted to the weird glow. Something hard pressed against her face. Bracing one hand beneath her, she pushed up and looked around.

The cavern. The underground waterfall. The river. Trying to escape the half-breed colony. Gryphon.

Memories rushed in on a wave and doused her spirits. It hadn't been a dream after all.

She moved to sitting, swallowed down the panic. Something fell from her shoulder. Looking down, she realized it was her shirt. She was wearing nothing but her bra and underwear, but her pants and shirt—still slightly damp—had been draped over her like a blanket.

She reached for the garments and scanned the dark cavern illuminated only by the green glow coming from the bottom of the lake. Nothing moved around her. No sound echoed except that of rushing water. No sign anyone else had ever been here besides her.

She had no idea how much time had passed or how long she'd been asleep, but the fact that her clothes were still damp told her it hadn't been that long.

Rising on unsteady legs, she tugged on her long-sleeved black shirt and noticed Gryphon's clothes were missing.

A clicking sound echoed somewhere to her right before she could wonder where he'd gone. She swiveled in that direction on bare feet, hands stilling in the process of tugging her shirt down. Listening carefully, she waited, but the sound didn't repeat.

Her imagination. It had to be. Logic told her Gryphon had likely ditched her when she was asleep. Now that they were away from the half-breed sentries and he was warm, he didn't need her anymore. She should have been relieved by that fact—she wanted away from him too—so why wasn't she? Irritation brewing, she reached for her pants and shoved her foot in the right leg. A click echoed somewhere close again.

Her head came up. Her hands froze on the garment. "Gryphon?"

More clicks echoed in the shadows. Maelea's heart rate kicked up as she frantically scanned the eerily illuminated darkness, searching for the source of the noise.

"It's scared," a raspy voice whispered.

Maelea's adrenaline surged. That definitely wasn't Gryphon's voice. They weren't alone down here after all. She tugged her pants the rest of the way on, hastily buttoned them.

"Scared is fine so long as it's tasty," another voice said, this one just as raspy, but deeper.

Oh, shit. Maelea scrambled for her boots. Shoved one foot in, then the other, the whole time scanning the dim cavern for signs of whoever or *what*ever was out there.

A sniffing sound echoed. Then, "It's female."

"We haven't had a *female* in ages!"

Pulse racing, Maelea looked all around her for something to use as a weapon. Only, shit, there was nothing. No loose rocks, no twigs, nothing to grab on to and swing or hurl to defend herself.

She eyed the river. Even though it was freakin'

freezing, if she had to, she'd jump back in and let it carry her downstream.

Shuffling echoed, followed by more clicks. Maelea moved for the river just as a three-foot-high gnomish creature peeked out from behind a boulder and blinked at her with wide, catlike eyes.

She hesitated, because what stared back at her was not the monster she expected. If anything, it was cute. Pointy ears, a long chin, and a nose that twitched from side to side. Yeah, it had scales and long claws, but the way it gripped the rock, the way those eyes seemed to grow bigger the longer it looked at her, it was as if it was more afraid of her than she was of it.

"Don't antagonize it!" a voice hissed from behind the rock.

A little of her adrenaline waned. She tried to look around the creature to the voice behind. Still couldn't see anything else. "Who...who are you?"

"It's talking to me," the one gripping the rock whispered, his knuckles turning white. "What do I do?"

"Don't answer it!"

Oh yeah, they were definitely scared. Maelea let out a relieved breath. She was otherworldly herself. She knew there were creatures in the world not often seen by humans. That didn't automatically mean they were evil. Look at her.

"I'm not going to hurt you," she said. "Why don't you come into the light so I can see you both better?"

The creature stared at her for long seconds. Then the clicking echoed again, and cautiously, the other one moved out to stand next to the first.

Oh, man. They really were cute. The second even had

a tuft of white hair on the top of his head between his pointy ears.

A thought occurred. Maybe they knew the way out. "Where did you both come from?"

"It's talking to us," the first said, leaning toward the second. "What should we do?"

The one with the white fur tipped his head, regarded her with narrowed eyes. Then licked his lips, baring yellow-stained, razor-sharp teeth. "Let's eat it. Boys!"

A flurry of movement sounded from the boulders at their backs. Then at least ten more of the scaly creatures popped out of the shadows. All showcasing the same sharp teeth, all staring at her as if she were lunch.

Maelea gasped and stumbled backward.

"Get it!" the one with the white hair called.

Maelea screamed. Her adrenaline in the out-of-this-world range, she turned and ran. Darting around boulders and small pools full of murky green liquid, she tried not to think about how many were following her. The clicking of hundreds of nails on rocks echoed at her back, shot her anxiety into the stratosphere. She ran faster, tried not to slip on the smooth rocks beneath her feet, rounded a corner, and smacked headfirst into something hard.

This wasn't rock. It was solid, warm, and very male. She bounced off and hit the ground on her ass. Before she could pick herself up, a large hand wrapped around her bicep, hauled her up, and thrust her behind him.

"Stay back!" Gryphon yelled.

The creatures raced toward them, their claws clicking across the rocks, echoing in the vast space. Gryphon arced out with a sword and sliced the chest of the first—the one with the tuft of white hair. It hissed and jumped back, then screamed as if were burning and crumpled to the ground. Green blood oozed all around it. The others skidded to a stop and hissed in Gryphon's direction. But instead of advancing, they rushed back into the shadows and disappeared, leaving the injured creature to writhe on the ground.

Hands braced against the rock wall at her back, eyes wide, Maelea stared at Gryphon, unable to believe what she'd just witnessed. He turned and grasped her at the upper arm again with his free hand, dragging her away from the body. "We need to make tracks."

"Wh-what the hell was that?"

"Kobaloi," he said as he moved.

His pace was quicker than hers, and she struggled to keep up. "Koba-*what*?"

"Gnome-dwarfs. They live underground. Damn, I should have expected them when I saw the therillium in the water."

They rounded a bend, followed the river as it swept through the cavern. Her eyes darted right and left, her mind trying to make sense of what was going on. "What's therillium?"

"An ore. Responsible for the green glow you see in the water. This." He let go of her arm, fished out a rock from his pocket. It glowed green in his palm as he handed it to her. It was cool to the touch, and heaver than she expected. "The metal used to make Hades's invisibility cap."

Maelea stopped dead in her tracks. Stared at the glowing green rock in her hand. When Gryphon turned to look at her, her eyes met his, and trepidation raced down her spine. "How do you know that?"

"Because when it heats up, anything it touches becomes invisible. And those things back there? The kobaloi? Legend says they guard Hades's reserves and mine it for him."

Maelea turned and stared down the darkened cavern they'd just passed through. Swallowed hard. They were likely a mile underground. As close to the Underworld as she'd ever been. And now they'd killed one of Hades's minions.

Panic consumed her. She dropped the ore. Pushed past Gryphon and ran. Where she was headed, she didn't know. She just had to get out. She'd thought Gryphon's using her as a hostage to get away was the worst thing to happen to her? This topped that by ten miles.

"Maelea! Son of a bitch."

She ignored Gryphon's voice at her back, pumped her arms as she darted past boulders, around corners, following the green glow of the river. It had to lead out. It had to reach the surface. Dear gods, she had to get there before Hades found her.

She rounded a corner, tripped over a rock, hit the ground with a grunt. Cringing, she pushed herself up and came face-to-face with a blackened skull.

Her eyes grew wide. And a scream ripped from her mouth before she could stop it.

Metal clanged behind her. Hands grabbed her at the arms, hauled her up, twisted her around until her scream was muffled by a broad chest covered by a damp shirt, and large, male hands tugged her in to hold her close. "Quiet. Quiet, dammit. They're gonna hear you."

They.

The one word killed the scream, brought every muscle in her body to a complete standstill.

"That's better," Gryphon said, massaging her scalp. "Breathe. Just like that. *Skata*, you are one hellfire female."

He ran his big hand up and down her back, used the thick fingers of his other hand to tangle in her hair and slide across her scalp. Tingles ignited everywhere he touched, and heat enveloped her. The same heat she'd felt when he held her before. She knew she should push away, that she was down here, close to hell, because of him, but she couldn't. His hard, warm body was solid and real. Comforting in a way she didn't expect and right now didn't want to question. And his hands...they were like magic. Drawing out her fear one tiny inch at a time.

Insane. They were likely being followed, and at any moment Hades could pop out of the ground and annihilate her. Not to mention the fact that everything she knew about Gryphon screamed nut job. But he didn't feel like a crazy man to her at the moment. In fact, she was acting more psychotic than he. And the longer he held her, the more she didn't want him to let go. With her hands pressed against his muscular chest, she closed her eyes, sank in just a touch. Worked to slow her pulse. Tried to find control.

The hand on her spine slipped lower, to the curve of her lower back, to trace tiny circles along the pressure points above her buttocks. It relaxed her, made her limbs feel like jelly. His scent—leather, musk, the slightest hint of citrus—assailed her nostrils, smelled way too damn good. And when his chest brushed the fabric of her thin shirt, her nipples hardened.

Heat spread lower before she could stop it. To her abdomen, cradling his groin. To that space between her legs. Memories of his body, half-naked in the green light, rushed through her mind. She couldn't help but remember what he'd felt like as she'd straddled his lap. How aroused he'd been then. How hard. How big.

She swallowed. Tried to stop her frantic mind from imagining what he'd look like completely naked. Couldn't. He'd be thick, dominating, mouth-watering, she bet. Though she didn't like the desire suddenly rushing through her body, she knew it came from the center of her. From the darkness of the Underworld that resided within her. It was attracted to the vile and wicked and seemed to be drawing her to him, and it, combined with the panic and anxiety she was already feeling, was so strong. She'd always been able to fight the pull before, but this…the way she reacted to him, her kidnapper, for crying out loud…was different. This burned her. Consumed her. Taunted her to take and sample and, for once, let go.

Gods, she wanted to. Suddenly, it was all she could think about. Letting go with him. Being as depraved and selfish as her parents. Acting out every X-rated fantasy she'd ever had over the long, lonely, pathetically empty years of her life.

A moan slipped from her lips before she even realized she'd made a noise. Against her stomach, his erection swelled and hardened just as it had done before. Only this time she wasn't scared. She felt energized. Excited. Alive. And when she sucked in a breath and held it, his hand paused just above the cleft of her ass.

What would he do if she touched him? If she slid her

hand down his rock-hard abs and brushed her fingers over his cock? If she gripped him there? If she stroked his shaft?

A thousand fantasies played through her mind, each more wicked and erotic than the last. And though she knew this wasn't the time, that *he* wasn't anywhere near the male she should be reacting to, she couldn't stop her body from wanting. From craving. From needing. Too many years of self-denial were coalescing to loose her shaky hold on control. And that darkness inside—the darkness that was drawn to him—was winning where common sense was supposed to prevail.

"Um...Maelea..."

His voice, dark, raspy, so damn sexy, slid over her skin with his breath, bringing to life places inside she hadn't known were dead. She closed her eyes, moved into him, and knew she was about to lose the battle.

Chapter Six

GRYPHON WENT STILL AS STONE, UNSURE WHAT TO SAY or do.

The voice that had been taunting him again as he'd searched for a way out was suddenly gone. Replaced by only that low buzz, the one that was irritating as hell but manageable. And oh, gods, right now he didn't even mind the buzz, because Maelea's hot body was pressing into his, lighting up his groin, distracting him from everything but her.

Skata, he didn't dare move, because then it'd be painfully obvious he had a hard-on the size of Mount Etna—not that she couldn't already feel that damn thing pushing into her stomach—but he also knew if he moved right now, the friction against his dick might just be too much. He swallowed hard. Tried like hell to fight the need. But only one thought prevailed.

Bloody hell, he wanted her. Any way he could get her. Wanted to shove her up against the rock wall at her back and ravage every inch of her body until she screamed. Then he wanted to do it all over again.

Fantasies swam in his head. Followed by the harsh slap of reality.

This was not a good idea. She was afraid of him, dammit, had wanted nothing but to get away from him earlier. He wasn't stupid. There was something about her that was interfering with that voice. Anytime she got close, it dimmed, gave him the chance to think. Except, man, when she was *this* close, there was only one thing he could think about.

He told himself to stop thinking with his dick. She could be the key to his finding Atalanta. He could use her to keep his sanity while he hunted. But the only way he was going to get her to cooperate was to give her the impression she was safe with him, even if that wasn't the truth.

He stepped back, intent on putting distance between them, but her hand slid from his chest to his abdomen, and he froze again. Her fingers were warm, her touch sure. And as she trailed a hot, needy line down his stomach, lighting up ever nerve ending in his body, all that "common sense" shit flew out of his head.

Need circumvented control. He grasped her hand at the wrist, pushed her back until her spine hit the rocks. Her eyes flew wide. Her breath hitched. But there was no fear in her features, only excitement. The same blinding excitement consuming him. A dim voice in his head yelled *No!* but he ignored it. He was dying to know what she tasted like. Needed to know if she was as good as she smelled.

He lowered his mouth to hers. Felt her draw in a surprised breath. But she didn't push him away as he expected. Her lips were soft. Her heat, intoxicating. He kissed her, feeling that pressure in his chest ease for the first time in months. Kissed her again, this time more insistent. And then she opened her mouth to his, slipped her tongue along his, moaned against him—something he never in a million years would have expected.

Whatever restraint he'd had snapped just that fast.

Her tongue was slick and wet and tangling with his before he could find his footing on the rocks. Her nipples brushed his chest. Hard, stiff, begging for attention. Her fingers dug into his biceps, pulling him closer. He answered by shifting into her, pressing her against the rocks, pushing his already hard dick against her stomach.

A clatter echoed through the cave. He pulled away from her mouth and looked down to see the blackened skull rolling across the rocks, where he'd accidentally kicked it with his boot.

She went rigid against him, stared at the skull with wide eyes as her chest rose and fell with her quick breaths. Then muttered, "Oh gods."

Her face paled. She lifted a hand to her mouth as if she were about to be sick.

And his stomach rolled. Shit, what was he doing?

He let go of her. Immediately stepped back. Swiped the sweat from his forehead and tried to calm his racing pulse. *Skata*, he'd been about to take her against the rocks, just as he'd imagined. Just as he'd promised he *wouldn't* do. He turned away, gripped his hair, pulled hard with both hands until the burn was all he felt. Until it killed whatever asinine desire had been toying with him and he was no longer tempted to touch her.

"Wh-what was that?" she asked in a quiet voice.

Stupidity. Lack of self-control. The monster he'd become not caring whom he hurt, so long as he got what he wanted.

He cleared his throat. "I'm not sure. I didn't plan to—"

"No," she said quickly, her boots clicking on the rocks at his back. "The skeleton. Was it…? Is it human?"

Her question cut through the self-deprecating thoughts. Wondering what the hell he'd missed, he turned, studied her from a good five feet back. She wasn't looking at him. She was staring down at the remains, her dark hair falling across her shoulder to partially shield her face. But she didn't look scared—at least not of him. If anything, she looked...wigged-out at what they'd found.

"Yeah, it's human," he said, still watching her for any indication he'd scared the living daylights out of her. Couldn't see it.

She knelt, one hand on her knee, and studied the charred remains, careful, he noticed, not to touch them. "They look...burned. But down here? How is that possible?"

He didn't have an answer that made sense. Only knew the poor guy had been more unlucky than them.

"He probably wound up here the same way we did." Happy she wasn't going to bring up the kiss that was still ringing in his toes, he leaned over and lifted the sword he'd dropped. "I found the remains earlier, when I was looking around. It's where I got this."

She glanced over her shoulder, eyed the sword in his hand. Her hair was a dark, wild tangle around her face, her lips still swollen and pink from his mouth, and her eyes were clear. Clear and mesmerizing and utterly hypnotic, teasing him to slip close all over again.

"There's a satchel. Did you look inside?"

His gaze slid from her eyes to her straight, regal nose, then to her mouth. Plump, soft, so damn erotic. He imagined that mouth making a trek down his body, kissing his belly button, sliding lower to open and—

"Gryphon?"

He blinked. Realized his mind was getting away from him again. *Skata*, if he wasn't hearing voices, he was living in a freakin' fantasy world. He gave his head a swift shake. Slammed the heel of his hand against his forehead, hoping to knock something loose. He needed to get a grip, like *now*. "No, I heard you scream and went back for you."

She eyed him as if he had a third eye. But that was okay. That he could deal with. That, at least, was normal for him. It was when she looked at him as if he were a real person that things went straight into the shitter.

Her gaze skipped past him to the darkness of the cavern they'd come through, and she shuddered. When she turned back to the remains and reached for the satchel hanging off one side of the skeleton, he saw her hand shake. "Do you think they're gone?"

She was talking about the kobaloi. He looked behind him, didn't see any sign they'd been followed. But that didn't mean they were safe. "Yeah," he lied, not entirely sure why he cared if she was scared or not. *She* was not his problem. "I think we proved they shouldn't mess with us. They're tricksy gnome-elves. They like to cause trouble, taunt people, but that's it. I doubt they're violent."

She didn't look so convinced, but as she turned to glance over the remains, he noticed the way she tucked her dark hair behind her ear, the way the light caught the delicate line of her jaw, the way—even dressed in all that black and those ridiculous boots—she was soft and feminine and tempting as hell.

Skata. He was losing his ever-loving mind. What the

hell was he doing? She was a means to an end, nothing more. The sooner he remembered that, the better off he'd be. What he should have been focused on was the fact he'd been so swept up in some insane psycho lust because of her, he'd nearly forgotten they weren't alone in this cavern.

He slid the sword into the scabbard draped across his back and was silent as she pawed through the satchel, pulled out a wallet. Tried like hell to remember what Orpheus had said about her during those miserable hours his brother had sat in his room trying to cheer him up while he stared out the window wishing he could stab out his eardrums. Somehow she was linked to the gods, but he couldn't remember which ones. She wasn't a goddess herself, but she'd been the one to tell Orpheus where the Orb of Krónos was located.

What if she was casting some kind of magic over him? What if she was playing head games? She'd been trying to escape from the colony herself tonight. He didn't put it past her to use whatever means she could to get free of him. She'd gone from scared shitless to queen of irate to completely turned on faster than he could flash in Argolea. Something was off with this female. Something that sent a shiver of foreboding down his spine.

She opened the wallet. It too was blackened and crusty, as if it had been burned, but the contents inside were still readable. She turned it so he could see. "Vladimir Aristov. That sounds Russian."

Cautiously, he took the wallet from her, ignored the way heat arced from her fingers into his. Ignored the fact that just that little contact reminded him what she'd felt like, all hot and bothered between him and those rocks. "It is. Aristov…That name's familiar."

She pushed to her feet next to him, and he smelled jasmine. Remembered the rush of heat that had sent him into a tailspin only moments before. He wanted to move back, but there was nowhere to go except into the freezing river. And he wasn't risking that again.

"Wasn't Aristov the name of the Misos who built the castle?" she asked. "The one the colony is housed in? I'm sure there's a plaque in the library about him."

Gryphon's gaze slid to the blackened skeletal remains, and understanding dawned. "That's why no one's ever found the colony."

"What are you—?"

He pulled the ore from his pocket. The one she'd dropped earlier when she wigged out and left his ass behind. "He must have come down here and taken samples back up. When the ore is warmed, whatever it's touching becomes invisible. I bet you ten bucks there's a room in that castle full of these." He looked up and around, a new tingle sliding down his spine, one that had nothing to do with arousal and everything to do with urgency. "It's not the mountains and the lake protecting the colony, it's the ore. And that means there's some kind of access from the castle down here to this cavern. One a whole lot easier to access than the way we came through."

Sonofabitch. They needed to make tracks before Nick and his men caught up with them. They'd wasted precious time getting warm, drying out their clothes, kissing.

No more fucking kissing. Not with her. Not now. Not ever. He was not going back to the hell of that colony.

Not because of her. Whatever she was doing to him, it ended here.

He turned to tell her just that, when trepidation slid over her face, and she looked at the body near her feet. "Then what about him? All the stories I heard said Aristov never actually lived here. If he did—"

"Then they were covering up his death."

Maelea's worried gaze shot to him, then slowly slid back to the remains. "What else is down here that they want to keep secret?"

A clicking sound echoed behind them. Followed by hushed whispers wafting on the air. Lots of them.

Maelea tensed, looked past him into the dark. And froze.

Fuck.

Slowly, Gryphon turned too. Then swore again when dozens of beady eyes stared back at them from the dark.

He'd thought they needed to get out of this damn cavern to get away from Nick's men? Think again. Right now they needed to find a way out so they didn't get eaten by the forty or fifty kobaloi waiting to devour them alive.

"What do we do?" Maelea whispered at his side.

"Run like hell."

Maelea's heart pounded hard in her chest as she pumped her arms and pushed her legs forward. Her boots slipped on the wet rocks, but she caught herself at the last second and kept from going down. Behind her, Gryphon yelled, "Haul ass, female!"

Clicks and scratching sounds echoed in every

direction. It sounded as if they were being pursued by at least a hundred kobaloi, maybe more. Panic swamped her chest. The green glow from the river lit up the steadily shrinking cavern. Ahead, the river wound to the right, disappearing in darkness. The cave narrowed to only an archway over the river, nothing but sheer rock walls rising straight up on each side.

They were running out of ground. There was nowhere else to go.

Her feet slowed. That panic tightened her chest until she could barely breathe. Before she could turn to look back, Gryphon grasped her arm and hollered, "Jump!"

He yanked her with him into the frigid water. Her head submerged. She came up sputtering, grasping for Gryphon's arm, as the current caught hold and whisked them downstream.

His arm encircled her waist, and the long, hard line of his body came up against hers. Shrieks sounded from the shoreline. One look over his shoulder confirmed the kobaloi were pissed, jumping up and down, waving their scaly arms, hissing toward the river. But they made no effort to jump in and follow.

Relief was bittersweet. A shiver racked her body as they passed under the archway and were drawn into the low-ceilinged tunnel. She grabbed on tighter to Gryphon in the hope his body heat would keep her from freezing to death. "Wh-what now?" she managed through chattering teeth.

"I don't know."

He grasped the sword in one hand. The other was wrapped tight around her body, holding her close. As he studied the tunnel for some escape route, she eased back and took a good look at his face. Maybe the first good look she'd taken since this nightmare began.

Water dripped down the sandy blond hair plastered to his head, slid over his temples and along his chiseled cheekbones. His skin was pale—not as white as hers, but it clearly hadn't seen sunshine in months—and a hint of blond stubble ran along his strong jawline. He had a straight nose and a small mole near his left temple, and his irises…they were the most mesmerizing blue she'd ever seen. Light, not rich—like the summer sky on a clear morning.

Handsome. The word came out of nowhere. Ricocheted in her head. If he didn't have that dead look to his eyes, she'd think him good-looking. And if she'd seen him anywhere else—like on the street back at her home in Seattle—she'd likely have been attracted to him for purely physical reasons.

His head swiveled in her direction, and his gaze pinned hers with an intensity that pierced the core of her. She sucked in a breath even as the pull toward him intensified. The one that stirred the darkness inside with excitement.

"You're staring at me."

"I just…" But she didn't have a valid comeback, because she was. And who was she kidding? She was attracted to him now, regardless of the vile things she knew about him. *Because* of the vile things she knew about him.

She looked quickly away, but didn't let go. Not even she was that stupid. Another shiver raced over her skin. "Where do you think this goes?"

"I don't know," he said again as they bounced along with the current. "But until it opens up, all we've got is each other."

That wasn't exactly a comforting thought. But that darkness inside her leaped again just the same.

They floated downstream in silence. If he was cold, he didn't show it, didn't even shiver, but every time she did, he dragged her even closer, as if trying to warm her. Below their feet, the ore on the bottom of the river glowed bright, illuminating the small tunnel around them like daylight awash in a blinding green. There was more ore here, she noted, as if the kobaloi hadn't mined this area.

The rock ceiling was only a foot above their heads. And for the first time Maelea wondered how the hell the tunnel back at the colony had given way in the first place, landing them here. But before she could ponder too much, a crashing sound echoed from ahead, dragging her from her musings.

Gripping Gryphon's shoulders, she shifted in his arms to look. The river seemed to pick up speed, and the ceiling was gradually climbing.

"*Skata*," Gryphon muttered.

"What?" It wasn't his curse that brought every muscle in her body to attention, it was the way he tightened his arms around her that told her something was coming.

"Don't let go of me."

"Why would I…?"

Her voice trailed off when she saw the rapids. A flurry of undulating whitecaps broken only by the occasional green glow from the riverbed. The current grew faster, the sound of rushing water louder. Maelea tightened her arms around Gryphon's neck and held on as they passed through the first rapids, grunting when her body smashed into a rock and pain shot up her spine

"Hold on!" Gryphon yelled above the roar of the water, gripping her around the waist with one arm, pushing away from the rocks with the other.

They bounced downstream, slamming into rocks with their backs, their sides, fighting to keep their heads above water. Gryphon grunted, loosed his hold on her waist. And then he slipped beneath the water with a gasp.

"Gryphon!"

Maelea floundered in the water as he let go, sputtered and kicked as hard as she could so she wouldn't go down too. Just when she was sure he'd drown, his head popped up three feet in front of her.

He twisted back her way, held out his arm. "Grab on!"

She didn't miss the blood trickling down his forehead, but she didn't have time to think much of it. A roar grew louder in the distance. The green glow that had illuminated their way so far faded to nothing. Darkness closed in as she kicked and finally reached his hand. His solid body slammed against hers then he pulled her tight.

"What is that?" she asked, heart pounding, body shaking from both adrenaline and the bitter cold.

He listened for a second, gritted his teeth, and pushed away from boulders with his feet to keep them from smacking into them again. "*Skata*, it's another waterfall."

Dread filled Maelea's chest. They'd been lucky to survive what they'd already come through. With the amount of rocks here and the rapids, they'd never make it through another sharp drop.

She frantically scanned the new cave they'd moved into. It was nearly pitch-black—only a few glowing stones were spaced unevenly on the bottom of the river. She squinted, tried to make out their surroundings. The ceiling was higher. A small shelf ran along the edge of the water. Not much, but enough that maybe, if they could reach it, they could get out of this water before they went over that waterfall. "Look. Over there."

His head swiveled in the direction she pointed, and she watched his eyes grow wide like hers.

Daylight. Coming from the ceiling far off to the right.

"Come on!" He was already dragging her in that direction. "Swim hard!"

She thought her legs might fall off from the effort it took to swim against the current. Her arms ached, and her chest was so cold it was hard to draw air, but when she reached the ledge, when she realized daylight was only ten feet above, up a jagged hill they could easily climb, hope and a resurgence of energy spurred her on.

Gryphon hauled himself out of the water, dropped the sword at his feet, and turned to reach for her. Her hand slid into his. She braced her boots against the rocks along the edge and tightened every muscle, helping him as best she could. "Come on," he said. "We're almost there."

She could barely believe it. In a few minutes they'd be out of this cave. And even though they'd shared that crazy, never-should-have-happened kiss, she was thankful she'd be free from him as well. Because that darkness inside him, those handsome good looks, and the way he felt so deliciously perfect against her skin? They were all a temptation she didn't need. Not if she was going to get to Olympus. Not if she wanted to stay alive.

She levered herself up. Grunted at the effort. Halfway out of the river, with her torso perched on the rocks and her legs still dangling in the frigid liquid, a hiss echoed in the darkness

Chapter Seven

CROUCHED BY THE SIDE OF THE RIVER, WITH WATER dripping from his body and both hands wrapped around Maelea's arms to haul her out, Gryphon froze. He didn't have to turn, because he knew what was behind him. The only question was where. And how many.

Maelea must have read his mind, because her gaze strayed over his right shoulder, and her eyes grew even wider.

Okay, that meant more than one. Their luck was not improving. He squeezed her hand to get her attention. When her fear-filled eyes darted back to his, he glanced down at the rocks, silently telling her not to make any quick moves when he let go.

The tiniest nod of her head was all the confirmation he needed. At his back, another hiss echoed, followed by the clicking of dozens of nails against stone.

He let go of her, grasped the sword, and swiveled, arcing out before the first kobalos could attack. A shriek sounded as he caught one across the chest, followed by another series of hisses and growls as they charged.

He swung out with the blade, kicked and knocked one creature into another. A grunt sounded as they went down. It was darker in here, with very little light coming through from above, and he wasn't sure how many he took down, but when Maelea screamed at his back, he knew the longer they lingered, the more would arrive.

"Grab on to me!"

She'd climbed all the way out of the water already. Her fingers grasped the back of his shirt. She grunted as he continued to fight and move forward, drawing them closer to the light. Her grip tightened on his shirt, and she nearly lost her balance before righting herself. Bones cracking against rock echoed in the darkness along with more grunts and hisses, and the feel of Maelea slipping. She was fighting too, he realized. Kicking, punching, doing whatever she could to get them through as well.

They reached the incline. He turned, pushed her between him and the rocks. Yelled, "Climb!"

A roar rocked the cavern, the vibration nearly knocking Gryphon off his feet. Maelea gripped his back to steady herself. The kobaloi stopped their attack, their heads swiveling in the direction of the sound. With the sword gripped in two hands, Gryphon looked to the right too, toward a darkened tunnel coming alive with a fiery red glow that seemed to be growing in intensity.

Vibrations shook the floor. Another roar echoed through the cave. The kobaloi shrieked as if in fear, hissed, and jumped back.

"Wh-what is that?" Maelea asked at his back, her fingers shaking against his spine.

"I don't know." But whatever it was, it was big. And coming right for them.

They didn't have time to dick around. And Gryphon wasn't waiting around to see what the fuck it was. "Go!" he hollered, pushing her up the incline.

Rocks clattered together as she dug her feet into the loose pile and scrambled up the side, heading for the sliver of light only five feet away now. He followed,

tried not to twist his ankle on the rocks and slide back
down the hill. Three kobaloi close by realized they were
about to get away, shrieked, and charged, even as the
rest of the creatures scrambled away from the oncoming
threat. Gryphon twisted, arced out with the blade, caught
one across the throat. The creature went down. Another
hissed and charged.

"Maelea!"

"I'm there!" she screamed.

More rocks tumbled down the incline, smacked him
in the face as he battled. He kicked out, knocked the
closest kobalos down the hill to land with a crack on his
back. On the other side of the river, the red glow erupted
in flames ten feet high. And then light flooded the cavern, blinding Gryphon with its intensity. He blinked several times, opened his eyes, and saw the twenty-foot-tall
fire demon, surrounded by a vortex of swirling black
smoke and fiery flames.

Holy shit.

The hundreds of kobaloi along the banks of the river
shrieked and rushed away from the demon, crawling like
spiders along the walls, rushing for a hole in the ceiling
and their only chance for escape. The demon roared,
vomiting a steady stream of fire that singed kobaloi, sent
screams of agony ringing through the cavern, and kicked
the temperature up at least twenty degrees.

"I'm through!" Maelea yelled.

Sword gripped in one hand, the other arm out for balance, Gryphon scrambled up the wall of rock after her.

His lungs burned, but he reached the opening.
Squinted into the bright sunlight. Maelea grasped his
arm and pulled. Halfway out, something grabbed his leg,

then blinding pain shot across his nerve endings as nails
or claws or teeth slashed through his calf.

Max knew he wasn't supposed to be in the tunnels, but
he was tired of being told what to do. And the way his
mother kept watching him with those eagle eyes of hers
was driving him freakin' nuts.

He shoved his hands into the front pockets of his
jeans. Scowled as the elevator doors opened at the low-
est level of the colony's castle, the level that led into the
tunnels. His mother hovered over him as if she expected
him to freak out or something. As if she was just waiting
for the moment he was gonna go all "Atalanta" on her.

His mood grew darker with each step. The walls
seemed to close in around him. He wasn't a baby, dammit. He'd killed daemons before. And no one had more
reason to see Atalanta dead than he had. He was sick and
tired of being told what he could and couldn't do. Of
being treated as if he were a kid. He was an Argonaut,
dammit. Didn't he have the markings?

As he rounded a corner, voices echoed ahead. His
high-tops slipped on a wet section of rock, and he
reached out to grasp the wall to steady himself. The
trickle of water echoed, followed by his dad's voice.

"Whoa! Hold on," Zander yelled. "That's not working. Someone's gonna slip and fall into that crevice
and die."

"*Skata*," Theron's voice echoed. "The flow's still too
strong. We're not going to be able to rappel in until we
get this water dammed up."

Other voices murmured in agreement. Max picked

out Cerek and Orpheus. He'd seen Demetrius in the castle talking with Queen Isadora, giving her an update on the search for Gryphon, and since Phineus was still helping Max's mom with Titus in the clinic, it meant the other voices had to be Nick and some of his Misos sentries.

Max pushed forward, hesitated at the bend in the tunnel. Light burned ahead. He could see far enough around the corner to pick out the bodies blocking his view, the water seeping around their boots. But he couldn't see the crevice they were talking about.

"Theron," Zander said, "Nick's gone."

Silence descended, and Max leaned forward to hear better.

"*Skata*," Theron finally said again. "That's not good. How long's he been missing?"

"I don't know. He was here while we were all trying to stem the flow, but as soon as it became manageable, he disappeared."

"Why do I have a feeling he knows something we don't?" Theron asked.

Zander didn't answer, and Max's interest was piqued in the resulting silence. What was down there in that crevice?

He was so lost in his thoughts he didn't hear the boots clomping his way until it was too late. He took one step back just as his father rounded the corner and drew to a stop, staring down at him with surprised silver eyes. "What are you doing in here?"

"I—"

"Does your mother know you left the castle?"

"She—"

His dad grasped him by the arm before he could

answer and turned him back through the tunnel, pushing him toward the castle. "*Skata*, Phin is supposed to be
keeping an eye on you."

Max's feet shuffled to keep up. His dad had a temper,
thanks to his link with the legendary hero Achilles, and
Max had learned quickly after coming to live with him
and his mom not to push the Argonaut. But his curiosity
had gotten the better of him this time.

"Dad, I—"

Zander yanked him from the tunnel into the receiving
room lined with lockers, then pulled him to a stop at the
elevator doors and pushed the call button.

"Take it easy on the kid, Zander," Theron said at
his back.

"Stay out of this." Zander shot Theron a look, then
glared back down at Max with stormy, swirling gray
eyes. "It's not safe for you to be in the tunnels. You're
to remain in the castle with your mother or I'll send you
back to Argolea, you got it?"

"I wasn't trying to—"

"I knew this was a bad freakin' idea," Zander muttered, staring at the elevator doors. "I told your mother
you wouldn't stay put."

Max's mouth slammed shut. And that anger boiled hot
in his veins all over again. But instead of arguing, he stood
still and silently fumed as they waited for the elevator.

This was how it was always going to be. Them
treating him like a kid, sending him away when all
he wanted to do was be included. Why had they even
rescued him from Atalanta? They'd all be happier if he
just left, like Gryphon.

As his dad pulled him onto the elevator and the door

closed behind Theron, Max couldn't help but wonder where Gryphon was right now.

Lucky bastard. At least he was free.

—◦◦◦—

A roar ripped from Gryphon's mouth. Maelea pulled harder, fell with a grunt on her butt, but didn't let go. Gryphon kicked out as hard as he could, and when the kobalos released, scrambled the rest of the way out of the cave.

Heart racing, he crawled on hands and knees as far from the cave as he could get, dropped back on his ass, tried to suck in air. The sword was still in his hands, and he waited for the creatures or that demon to burst from the hole they'd just climbed out of, but nothing happened. From inside the cave, the sounds of hundreds of hissing monsters was drowned out by the roar of a fire demon that shouldn't be real.

Gryphon pushed to his feet, grasped Maelea by the arm, and yanked her up, the whole time still watching that opening. "Come on. We need to get the hell out of here before they decide to come through."

"They or it?" she asked with wide eyes.

"Either."

She kept pace with him as he ran through the woods, dodging trees, trying to avoid twisting an ankle, focusing on putting as much space between them and that cave as they could. Judging from the sunlight shining through the canopy, he guessed it was midafternoon. The air was warm, the scents of pine and moss strong. Out here in the late-spring air, their clothes dried quickly, and before long he grew damp not from the water of that underground river, but from sweat.

He didn't slow until the trees thinned and opened near the edge of a cliff that looked down over a valley of green. A small river wound through the valley, sparkled in the sunlight, ran through what looked to be a human settlement. The sun had now dropped and was heading for the mountains on the far side.

Maelea huffed and leaned forward, bracing her hands against her knees as she worked to suck back air. Black hair fell over her shoulders, shielded her face from his view, but her features were branded into his brain—those dark eyes, that pale skin, the plump, pink lips he now knew were meant for kissing and a whole lot more. With the danger passed, memories of those lips, of that kiss that had rocked his world, rushed to the forefront of his mind. Followed by a dark desire that seemed to strengthen every second he was near her, pulling him toward her like a magnet.

Who the hell was she?

"Do you think…?" She swallowed, turned to look behind them, drew in another gulp of air. "Do you think we lost them?"

"I don't think they followed us. I don't think they see well in sunlight."

He slid the sword into its scabbard at his back, perched his hands on his hips, studied her as she nodded and regulated her breathing. Tried not to be impressed but failed. She'd held her own back there. She hadn't had a weapon, but she'd fought against the kobaloi just the same. And she'd saved his ass on the way out. If she hadn't been pulling him, he'd have slipped back down when that beast bit into his leg. He'd likely be lunch right now.

He looked down at his leg, for the first time taking stock of the damage. His pants were ripped at the calf and five large puncture wounds in the shape of a half circle oozed blood. Pain immediately registered in his leg, but he ground his teeth and ignored it. He'd heal, he didn't doubt that. Argonauts healed faster than most. His gaze strayed to his arms, and the ancient Greek text that ran across his skin, marking him as a guardian of his race. Disgust rolled through him. Not that he was an Argonaut anymore—or deserved to be. Not after the things he'd done.

Forcing back the memories that threatened to creep in and consume him, he looked out over the valley and realized night was coming fast. They needed to find shelter before that happened. Needed to rest and regroup. And he needed to figure out how he was going to find Atalanta, now that he was free.

"Where do you think we are?"

Her soft voice brought his head around again. Her sleeve was ripped at the shoulder, and her clothes were dirty, but he didn't see blood anywhere, which was a good thing. Since he'd decided to keep her with him, he didn't need anything slowing them down.

"No idea." He scanned the valley again, didn't recognize it. "A ways from the colony, that's for sure."

Thank the Fates for that little blessing. He had no doubt Nick and his men would be looking for them. But if they ventured into those tunnels, the kobaloi would slow them down. It wasn't as if anyone in the colony wanted Gryphon to stick around. With any luck, Nick and Orpheus and the others would just give up searching for them altogether.

Orpheus.

Thoughts of his brother spiraled in. Of the sacrifice Orpheus had made going into the Underworld to rescue him. Of the sacrifice Orpheus had been willing to make to leave the colony with him after the mess yesterday. Gryphon's chest pinched tight as he pictured Orpheus and Skyla together, and he rubbed a hand over the spot, wondering what the hell was causing the pain. It hurt like a son of a bitch, but Gryphon had been dead inside so long, he couldn't imagine it was an emotion. He didn't have emotions anymore. Likely it was nothing more than a muscle spasm from running. Like before.

Maelea pushed up to her full height, and the movement dragged at his attention, pulled his mind away from Orpheus and back to her. In the sunlight she looked taller than she had in the tunnels.

She wasn't Misos. He couldn't sense even a drop of hero blood running through her veins. What had she been doing at the colony these last few months? Residents of the colony could come and go as they pleased—they weren't prisoners, not like him. So long as they took measures to make sure they weren't followed, they were free to do as they pleased. But she'd clearly been escaping. What was the female hiding? Or what had she been hiding *from*?

"Well," she said, looking out over the valley herself. "I guess that's it then. Good luck wherever you're heading."

He grasped her by the sleeve before she made it a step away, and tugged her back to face him. "Where do you think you're going?"

"You said if I cooperated and helped you get out of the tunnels, I'd be free to go. I did that."

"That was before."

Her eyes narrowed with distrust. "Before what?"

"Before I realized I need you." He didn't miss the flash of fear in her eyes at his words, followed by the quick burst of anger. Anger that told him keeping her with him might not be the smartest idea he'd ever had, but it didn't do a thing to change his mind.

"But you said—"

"Forget what I said before, female." His hand tightened around her upper arm. "Focus on what I'm saying now. You're not going anywhere. Not without me."

Chapter Eight

"MY LORD, WE HAVE...A PROBLEM."

Seated on his blackened throne in the heart of the Underworld, Hades turned his attention from the view of the boiling red sky he'd been gazing out at to Orcus, the four-foot-tall gnomelike troll whose one and only job was to monitor that fucking stain Maelea.

"Be careful in how you present this *problem*, Orcus, or it will be the last you ever voice." Hades was in a piss-poor mood already. Not only had his wife, Persephone, been summoned back to Olympus for the miserable summer, but Maelea hadn't shown herself in months. The stain knew he was hunting her, so she was hiding somewhere, likely with those pathetic Misos. Only no one knew where their precious colony was located. He'd had hellhounds searching for Maelea for months, and they'd come up empty. Not even Orcus, who always knew where she was, could find her.

Hatred brewed hot in Hades's veins. Because Maelea had not only helped Orpheus find the Orb of Krónos, but had helped the Argonauts, she had to pay. Fuck the Fates and their so-called rules that said he couldn't touch her unless she ventured into the Underworld. Fuck his wife's inevitable reaction. He didn't care what it cost him. He wanted Maelea dead and gone once and for all. It had become his obsession.

Orcus, knowing the extent of Hades's fury, swallowed,

tapped his long clawlike fingernails together. "Yes, my lord. It seems Maelea is on the move."

Hades pushed himself forward in his throne, excitement bubbling in his chest, the first he'd felt in months. "That's not a problem, you moron. It's what we've been hoping for."

"Yes, my lord, I know. It's just…"

Hades rose out of his chair and glared down at the pathetic creature, his patience at its breaking point. "Spit it out already, Orcus."

"Somehow she ended up in a tunnel. She and…an Argonaut."

Those fucking miserable Argonauts. Always interfering. Orpheus—the son of a bitch who'd become a good-for-nothing Argonaut, thanks to Lachesis the Fate—obviously had a soft spot for the stain. "They left together?"

"It looks that way," Orcus answered.

An Argonaut would be of use getting her settled somewhere, but out in the open, Hades's minions would be able to track her. One measly Argonaut was not a detriment to Hades's goal. And if Orpheus was killed in the process? Even better. "I'm still not seeing the problem, Orcus."

Orcus wrung his scaly hands together, looked right and left. "My lord, the tunnel they were in…" He swallowed, finally looked up at Hades. "It was the Tunnel of Arima."

Hades stiffened. "She found the therillium? Is that what you're telling me?"

Orcus nodded. "Yes, my lord. She and the Argonaut… They found it and…and it's possible they took pieces with them."

"Do you know this for certain?"

Orcus looked to the left and motioned with his hand. A kobalos, a distant cousin of Orcus, hobbled into the room, his long nails clicking along the black stone floor.

"My lord Hades." The kobalos bowed. "It is with great pleasure I meet you, my king."

"Dispense with the pleasantries," Hades snapped. "Tell me what you know of the stain."

The kobalos lifted large, round eyes to peer up at Hades. "She and the male escaped the tunnels before we could catch them."

That anger morphed to fury. "How the hell did they get there in the first place?"

"I don't know, my lord. Perhaps the river. We had no warning. They escaped through a crack in the rocks just before Typhaon arrived, hindering our pursuit. A few tried to follow, but the sunlight…"

Son of a fucking bitch. Hades barely resisted the urge to backhand the kobalos across the room. One more reason to despise his brother Zeus. The King of the Gods had banished the monster Typhaon to the bowels of the earth, and the beast had discovered Hades's therillium supply. It guarded the ore now, making it nearly impossible for the kobaloi to mine. Typhaon was a problem Hades was constantly trying to work around, but Hades adapted because it was imperative the therillium supply *not* be found. If any of the other gods—especially Zeus—got their hands on it, Hades would no longer be the only god who possessed the power of invisibility.

He started down the steps. Both Orcus and the kobalos backed up quickly, eyes wide with fear.

"You"—Hades pointed at the kobalos—"seal the

holes, do you hear me? And you find out where she came from. If anyone else discovers our mine I will hold you personally responsible, and I will torture you until you are begging for death. And you." He rounded on Orcus. Orcus's eyes flew even wider. "Send hellhounds. I want Maelea dead. Her and that fucking Argonaut who helped her. You find them and you kill them, or I'll make his"—he nodded toward the kobalos—"torture seem like nothing."

Both creatures nodded quickly and stared up with enormous, frightened eyes.

"Go!" Hades bellowed.

They scurried off like rats.

Alone, he pressed his fingers against his temples, drew two calming breaths. He was juggling too many balls, trying to keep too many from stealing his power, from taking what was rightfully his. His wife would be pissed when she returned from Olympus and discovered he'd killed her precious child, but Hades didn't give a fuck. Aside from his own bitter need for revenge, there was more at stake here than just one mere mortal's life. Atalanta, the bitch, was still scheming for a way to get the Orb and control the human realm. And if she somehow found his therillium mines because of Maelea or that miserable Argonaut, she might just have a chance.

His hounds would pick up Maelea's scent and kill her. With one problem solved, he needed to stop worrying about the stain and focus on the Orb. Once he had that, everyone would bow to him, even the monster Typhaon.

He crossed to the window. An acrid burst of hot air swept across his face and he breathed in the misery floating on the wind. Somehow, Atalanta planned to use the Argonaut who'd been freed from the Underworld to get her that Orb. Since the Orb now resided in Argolea, that plan made sense, especially since Atalanta couldn't cross into that realm—no Olympian god could.

But Hades could.

A plan began to form in his mind, and his anger slowly dissipated one agonizing moan at a time. He knew just who in Argolea he could use.

—⁓—

"You bastard," Maelea sputtered as Gryphon hauled her through the woods next to him.

"I've heard that before." He didn't loosen his hold on her arm, all but dragging her as he skirted the cliff and headed down the hillside in the direction of the valley.

Dusk was rushing in fast, and that fact only made Maelea more determined to get away. She wasn't spending the night with him. Not after what had happened in those tunnels. "That's because you are one. We had a deal."

"The deal changed."

She tried to wrench her elbow from his grip, only he held her too tightly. "I didn't agree to this."

He jerked her to a stop. Glared down with those dead, light blue eyes. Eyes, she noticed out here in the daylight, that were more piercing than they'd been in the tunnels. And much more unfriendly. "Get this through your head, female. I don't care if you agreed or not. You're not leaving me. Not until I'm done with you."

He yanked her forward again. And as she struggled to keep up with his long legs, her mind spun. What if he really was crazy, just as those females had said? She'd seen the way he twitched and looked around as if he were hearing things. It didn't matter that he'd saved her life back there in the caves. He'd nearly gotten her killed too. If she stayed with him, only bad things would happen. She felt it in her gut.

And the darkness inside her...it was too attracted to him. Too tempted by him. She had to get away.

Escape plans tumbled through her mind as he dragged her around pine trees and over downed logs. The forest grew darker with every step they took, and her arm ached where he held her bicep with a death grip. She couldn't break free until he loosened his grasp. But when he did...

"Where are you taking me?" she asked when she couldn't stand it anymore.

"Into that town. We need wheels."

She nearly choked. "I have no money. I know you have no money. How do you plan to find *wheels*?"

"That's not something you need to know."

Maelea's temper skyrocketed. She wasn't a helpless female. She'd lived for thousands of years by keeping to herself and never relying on another. She wasn't about to change that philosophy now.

Stay calm, she told herself as they reached the bottom of the hillside and headed for the river. When they got to the town, when he was distracted looking for *wheels*, then she'd make her break.

At the first opportunity, she was gone.

———

Titus had reached his limit with the coddling shit. Much to Callia's disapproval, he'd showered, dressed, and was now riding an elevator up to the main floor to find out what the hell was happening with Gryphon.

At his side, Callia crossed her arms and frowned. "I still think you need more rest."

"I'm sick of that freakin' bed. If you like it so much, you go lie in it."

"You're the worst patient ever," she mumbled.

"No, that'd be your mate."

At the mention of Zander, Callia's face softened, and a wistful smile tugged at one corner of her mouth. "He is a horrid patient, you're right." She shot him a look. "But you're not far behind."

Titus didn't answer. Sweat broke out on his forehead, but he didn't dare look Callia's way and give her any reason to order him back to bed. He was weaker than he should be and knew he could use at least a few more hours of rest, but he'd had it with the clinic and the strange looks he'd been getting ever since Callia put up that damn Do Not Touch sign. And though he liked Callia, he couldn't stomach being around her much longer. She thought about Zander constantly, and every time she did, she'd get that sappy newlybound look on her face. The one that screamed *happiness* and reminded Titus of everything he was never going to have.

He put that thought out of his head, refocused on Gryphon. Shit, he seriously hoped Nick's men hadn't found the dumbass yet.

The elevator door pinged open and he stepped off onto the main floor. Night had settled over the lake, and the tall arching windows stared out at nothing but darkness. Seated on a couch in the middle of the room, Max glanced their way. At Titus's side, relief whipped through Callia, and she stepped around him, heading for her son. "What are you doing out here?" she asked.

Max shrugged. Picked at a thread on the arm of the sofa. "Zander told me to wait out here."

Zander. Not *Dad*. Titus didn't need to read minds to pick up the animosity.

"Where is he?" Callia asked in a stiff voice as she sat next to her son, obviously picking up on it too.

Max nodded toward a cracked door across the room. "In there. With Theron and Nick."

Happy for any reason to get away from Callia and her son, Titus turned in that direction, pushed the door open, and stepped into the space. Nick sat behind an intricately carved Russian desk, dwarfing the piece of furniture as he flipped papers. Theron and Zander stood in front of him, hands on hips, shoulders tense. No one looked up when Titus stepped into the room. No one even noticed him.

"You're not going," Nick said. "End of story."

"I have an Argonaut down there," Theron said.

"I don't care if the queen of fucking England's down there," Nick snapped, "The hole's being sealed as we speak."

"You can't do that—" Zander started.

"I can do whatever the hell I want," Nick tossed back.

Theron braced his hands on the desk and leaned forward. "You son of a bitch."

Nick glanced up at Theron, and his amber eyes were as steely as Titus had ever seen them when he said, "Let me make something clear to you, Theron. You don't have any authority here. I allow you and your Argonauts to use the colony as a stopping ground when you're in the human realm out of simple courtesy, but I don't have to. You have no say in how the colony is handled or maintained. The tunnel's being filled in for security reasons, and that's that. You don't like it, you can poof back to the mother ship for all I care."

Nick cast a glare Zander's way, then pushed back from his chair and rose to his full height. At six and a half feet and close to two hundred and eighty pounds, he was a force to be reckoned with, but then so was Theron. And as a descendent of Heracles, there wasn't much that made Theron back down.

"My guardians and I are going into that cavern to look for Gryphon," Theron said. "That, my friend, is the end of the story. Come on, Z." He signaled Zander, turned for the door, caught Titus's gaze, and clenched his jaw. Behind him, Zander's thoughts were easy to pick up. *This is so fucked*.

Titus had rarely seen the leader of the Argonauts so worked up. Something big was going down here. His gaze jumped from face to face, trying to read each of their thoughts, but emotions were too close to the surface to get an accurate picture of what was happening.

"If you do that," Nick answered before Theron and Zander reached the door, "you're signing your death certificates. We'll close up the cavern whether you're in there or not."

Nick wasn't lying. Titus's adrenaline inched up a notch as he read the *Come on, challenge me, I dare you* thought coming from Nick.

Zander's eyes narrowed. He looked Nick's way again. "What's down there in that cavern?"

Nick clenched his jaw but didn't answer. But Titus

heard the lies racing across the half-breed's mind as he fished for something to get them to back off.

"Where the hell did Gryphon and Maelea end up?" Theron asked in an accusing tone. "There's something you're not telling us."

They'll find out soon enough. Or they'll make things worse for the colony. You don't have a choice here.

Nick's thoughts echoed in Titus's mind, piquing his own curiosity. This was about more than just Gryphon and—oh, great—Maelea now.

The half-breed leader clenched his jaw once, twice, then finally muttered, "Fuck," followed by "Get in here and close that damn door."

Titus closed the doors at his back. Caught Theron's *Read his mind and tell me if he's telling the truth* thought.

Nick moved in front of his desk and rubbed his hand across his forehead as if he had the mother of all migraines. "I told Isadora there were extenuating circumstances to relocating the colony here after our location in Oregon was destroyed."

"I remember," Theron said. "The Russian Misos colony loaned you the property."

"Right. This place had been sitting empty for quite some time. It wasn't being used as a residence. Turns out, there's a reason for that."

"What reason?" Zander asked.

Tell them, don't tell them. Nick's thoughts bounced around as he debated his options. *Shit, if I don't tell them, they'll just go down there and fuck things up.*

Nick scowled and motioned them to follow as he stepped toward the wall at the back of his office. "This way."

He touched the molding high on the right side of a bookshelf. The entire unit swung out, revealing a secret passageway.

"Sweet," Zander muttered. "Where the hell does it go?"

"Just shut it and keep up," Nick said, stepping through the open doorway and into a steel-walled tunnel. Titus followed Zander and Theron inside. At his back, the massive bookcase snapped closed with a clack. Titus was too far back to read Nick's thoughts, but he picked up Zander's and Theron's, and both were wondering what the hell was going on.

No one spoke as they reached a circular staircase that seemed to go on forever. Nick started down without a word. Theron followed. Zander turned back to Titus and whispered, "You okay? You're sweating. Maybe we should go find Callia."

Titus wasn't missing this. He needed to know where Gryphon had gone. He stepped past Zander. "I'm fine."

Before Zander could press him for more, they reached the bottom of the stairs. The floor was concrete, the walls cinder block.

Titus wiped the sweat from his brow, ignored the pain in his side. "What does this place have to with Gryphon?"

"You'll see in a minute," Nick answered.

The panel lights flicked green, then the steel door hissed open and disappeared into the wall. He stepped into the dark room, lit by only a glowing orange lamp somewhere in the center of the space. The rest of them followed.

"*Skata*," Theron muttered when he came to a stop.

Titus read his *No fucking way* thought before he moved out from behind Theron's massive body and stopped next to him. Shock registered first as he stared ahead at the glowing orange rocks rotating on a pedestal in the center of the room with what looked like a heat lamp hovering above. "Is that—?"

"Therillium," Nick answered, dragging a hand over his close-shaved head. "It glows orange when heated. In its normal state it's green."

"*Skata*," Theron muttered again. "You're housing your people over Hades's personal stash of invisibility ore?"

Nick shot him a look. "Trust me, it wasn't my first choice. But when our colony in Oregon was destroyed, we didn't have many options. The Russian Misos colony agreed to loan us this location with the provision that we keep the therillium mines secret and continue to provide their colony with enough ore so their location remains hidden. I had my doubts at first, but Hades doesn't know we're here. He doesn't even know this castle exists."

"How the hell not?" Theron asked.

"Because the therillium"—Nick motioned toward the slowly turning chunk of glowing orange rock—"keeps the castle invisible. The tunnels are sealed with only one way in or out, which is known only by me and one other person. Hades uses kobaloi to mine his therillium, but they can't come out into the sunlight, so they're no threat to us. As for Hades himself, he doesn't dare venture into the mines."

"Why not?" Zander asked.

"Because there's something darker and fouler down there than just kobaloi. Something even Hades won't mess with."

The pain in his side forgotten, Titus shifted his gaze from the ore to Nick when he read the leader of the half-breed's thoughts. "Typhaon. Shit. Are you telling us the most deadly creature in all of ancient Greece is down there?"

Nick nodded. "Yeah. The ore lets him take on a smoldering fire-demon form. And as he's found something the gods all want—"

"He's not about to let it go," Theron finished for him. Of course all of the gods would like to get their hands on a substance that could make them invisible, but Typhaon wasn't just any monster. Even Hades feared the legendary beast that had been trapped underground by Zeus thousands of years ago. "*Skata*. How the hell do you get more if and when you need it?"

Nick perched his hands on his hips, stared at the glowing ore. In the orange glow the cuts on his scarred face from his run-in with Gryphon looked deeper and angrier than before. "Very carefully."

It was clear the half-breed wasn't going to elaborate. And in the silence, Theron's *We need to get Gryphon the hell out of there NOW* thought slammed into Titus.

"I'm going in," Theron announced.

"No, you're not," Nick said quickly. "We're not giving Hades any reason to look twice at this location."

"Gryphon and Maelea—"

"Are dead by now," Nick said bluntly. "If they even made it out of that river, and I seriously doubt they did. Trust me. If the freezing cold didn't get them, the kobaloi certainly did. And on the off chance they somehow survived all that, if they ran into Typhaon…"

Then they're nothing but dust now, Zander thought.

"The tunnel's getting sealed, Theron," Nick said. "I want to kick Gryphon's ass because of what he did, but this decision isn't a personal one. I won't risk my people

to kobaloi, Typhaon, or Hades just so you can save one
rogue warrior. It's well past time you accepted facts and
let the guardian go."

———

The cover of darkness made it easy to hide in the shadows.

Crouched behind a rusted Ford pickup that had seen
better days, Gryphon scanned the building to his right
and waited.

The town was small, just one main street and a couple
of shops. They'd waited until late, until the measly handful of stores had already closed for the day. Beside him,
Maelea breathed slowly, and her pulse raced beneath
the skin of her wrist, which he hadn't dared let go of
since they stopped on that cliff. The female was pissed,
but he didn't care. He was thinking clearer than before
and he knew it had something to do with her. Whatever
she was, however she was linked to the gods, he wasn't
above using her to get to his ultimate goal.

Even now, Atalanta's draw was strong. Her voice
was a dim vibration in the back of his head—tolerable
when he was near Maelea—but inside there was always
that desire to find her. A desire he would eventually use
to his advantage.

A man exited the small A-frame building on the
end of town Gryphon had scouted out earlier, locked
the door behind him, then headed for his car across the
parking lot, tossing his keys in the air and catching them
again as he whistled. Gryphon shifted on the asphalt to
look around the other side of the pickup, watched as
the man climbed in his SUV and closed the door, then
started the ignition and backed out of the lot.

"What now?" Maelea asked.

The parking lot light above was burned out, draping the area in darkness. Without answering, he tugged Maelea toward the door, continuing to stay close to the building so no one could see them.

He already knew the store didn't have a security system, but that didn't mean a night guard wouldn't be driving by sometime tonight.

He used his elbow to break the glass on the door. It shattered and sprayed across the floor inside. Reaching in, he unlocked the dead bolt, then pushed the door open and dragged Maelea in after him.

Glass crunched under their boots. The shop was dark. Tables were laid out with clothing and supplies. Coats hung on one wall, boots were lined up against another. To the right, a long counter ran the length of the room, and behind it, another glass case was filled with weapons.

He went there first, tugging Maelea along with him. Grabbing a military-grade flashlight from a table, he smashed in the glass, then opened the cabinet door and stared at the knives and daggers.

"What is this place?" Maelea asked.

"Army surplus store." He chose three knives, each with a different blade, knew it had been too much to hope for guns—those would have come in handy if Nick and his men found them. He turned and looked at the cash register.

It was old style, with push buttons and a locked drawer, not new and high-tech electronic. Using the tip of a knife, he fiddled with the lock, jimmied the drawer open. No money sat inside. The owner had obviously emptied the drawer before closing up shop.

Petty cash. The guy had to keep some kind of money around for emergencies.

Gryphon rifled through drawers until he found a zippered pouch. Inside he counted at least three hundred dollars in different bills. Not ideal, but enough to get them the hell out of here. He tucked the envelope into the waistband of his jeans, then turned and scanned the store for a thigh holster for his knife.

He moved through the shop quickly, grabbing supplies they'd need, pulling Maelea along behind him, handing her coats and blankets to hold with her free arm while she continued to protest his every move. "Why do you need this? What's that for? You can't carry all this stuff, you know."

Skata, she never stopped talking. It was beginning to grate on his nerves. He grabbed a length of rope, tossed it on the pile she was carrying, turned, and scanned the room one more time.

"Someone's going to find us," she said. "It's only a matter of time. I bet police are on their way right now."

His gaze zeroed in on what he'd been looking for and he smiled.

He reached across the table, picked up a set of handcuffs.

"What are those for?" she asked in a startled breath.

Gryphon's grin widened.

Before she could sputter off another protest, he tugged her toward the door. "Come on, we're done."

They went out the way they'd come in. Maelea nearly tripped and dropped the load she was carrying, but Gryphon caught her at the last second. The heat of her body warmed his side, slid across his arm. And that flare of desire burned hot all over again. A desire he knew—now that he was thinking clearly—would only distract him from his goal.

A siren rang out down the street. Gryphon's head swiveled that way, and he didn't miss the burst of hope in Maelea's eyes or the way her pulse picked up speed against his fingers. "Come on."

He stopped at the rusted pickup truck he'd checked earlier, pulled the Ford's door open, and pushed Maelea inside. She grunted as the supplies fell out of her arms and splayed across the seat and floor. "Hey!"

He climbed in after her. Tugged the door shut, looked all around for keys.

Come on. This was a small town in the middle of nowhere. There had to be keys in here some—

He pulled the visor down. A set of keys dropped into his lap.

Victory pulsed in his veins. He slid the key into the ignition and felt the motor hum beneath his feet. When the passenger door creaked open, he threw out a hand and grabbed Maelea by the wrist before she could get away.

"Let me go!" she hollered.

"Not a chance, female."

He snapped a cuff around her left wrist. She gasped in surprise and outrage. Then he snapped the other cuff to the grab handle on the dashboard.

"You son of a—"

"You need to come up with new curse words, female. Yours are getting old." He shoved the truck into reverse, backed out of the lot, and shifted into drive. The passenger door slammed shut.

Maelea struggled to free her wrist from the cuffs. "You're not keeping me here, you bastard!"

He swerved around a dog in the road on their way out of town. Glancing in the rearview mirror, he spotted a cop car pulling into the lot they'd just exited, lights flaring, siren roaring.

Too late, boys.

A smile twined its way across his face as they left the town behind. He ignored Maelea's thrashing and string of curses, instead breathed in the fresh air sailing through the open window. For the first time since he'd come back from the Underworld, he truly felt free.

They made it five miles up the winding mountain road before he slammed on the brakes.

Maelea, still struggling to free her arm from the handcuffs, flew forward, hit the dashboard, and bounced back. She groaned at the impact. "What the hell…?"

"*Skata.*"

She gave up fighting long enough to rub her forehead with her free hand, but her words died off as she stared ahead at what blocked the road.

Three sets of eyes glowing green in the darkness peered back at them. Three sets of eyes that were definitely not human.

Chapter Nine

MAELEA STARED AT THE MONSTERS MOVING TOWARD them in the dark—daemons from Atalanta's army—with the bodies of men, faces of cats, horns of a goat, and ears of a lion. They were dressed all in black, each at least seven feet tall, carrying lethal blades as long as her forearm. But their hands…She didn't miss the claws wrapped around the handles of those swords or the way they gripped the blades with the intent to swing and annihilate.

"Why—why are you stopping?" she asked. They should be flooring it right now, not stopping!

Gryphon shoved the truck in park, reached back for the blade he'd tossed into the extended cab. "Stay here. Don't move. Lock the doors."

Lock the doors? Was he serious? As if that was going to stop those things if they came after her?

She jerked on the handcuff wrapped around her wrist, panic building in her chest. He'd not only *almost* gotten her killed in those caves, he was about to get her killed now. "Let me go!"

He popped the driver-side door, stepped out of the old truck with his weapon. "I'll be right back."

No. *No!* "Gryphon!"

He ignored her scream, slammed the door, and stepped in front of the truck, its headlights hitting his back to highlight the muscles in his shoulders and torso and down through his butt and thighs.

Through the window she heard the daemon in the middle—the one she could no longer see—sniff and growl, "Argonaut."

"Yes, I am," Gryphon said in a clear voice. "And I'm wondering which one of you wants to die first."

As a unit, all three daemons moved forward.

Oh, gods. Oh, *gods*, this was not about to happen.

Maelea cranked on the handcuffs, gritted her teeth, and tried to pry her hand loose, but the cuffs were too tight, and all she was doing was bruising her hand and tearing up her skin. Damn Gryphon for handcuffing her to this stupid truck. Damn him for slipping the key in his pocket. If he got killed out there, she'd never get to the key before those monsters devoured her.

Panic consumed her as the first daemon arced out with his blade and Gryphon's sword clanked against metal. The floor of the truck vibrated. She watched in horror as Gryphon shifted, turned, kicked a second daemon in the stomach, sending that one sailing backward. He sliced the third across the shoulder. Blood sprayed over Gryphon and the ground. Gryphon swiveled, ducked, barely missing a blade to the chest, then sliced out and around again and again, forcing the monsters back from the truck, pushing them deeper into the shadows and away from her.

He was mesmerizing. The panic slowly dissipated and the vibrating stopped until a strange calm came over her. Even though she wanted nothing more than to run, she couldn't take her eyes off him. Memories of what she'd heard in the colony flashed in her mind, the way he'd gone berserk and annihilated those daemons in that village. How he'd turned on his own kin. But this didn't look like a warrior who was losing control. If anything, he was the perfect combination of danger and strength… and very clear, very focused, intent.

Minutes later it was over. Three dead daemons lay in the middle of the road, steam rising from their bloodied bodies. The truck's headlights illuminated Gryphon's heaving chest as he stood over them, his skin covered in streaks of red and other things Maelea didn't want to acknowledge. She watched as he reached down and lifted the head of the closest daemon by the scalp, but when he used his blade to decapitate the beast, bile rose in Maelea's stomach and she quickly looked away.

Adrenaline coursed through her system. She swallowed hard, tried to ignore the scraping sounds coming from the road. A mixture of relief and dread whipped through her as she waited…for what, she wasn't sure. Would he turn on her now? Even though he seemed calm, that was no guarantee she wasn't next.

Her anxiety peaked as footsteps echoed close. She finally looked up. The monsters' bodies were gone. The headlights now glowed bright against nothing but empty, bloody pavement. The door to her left creaked open, and she looked in that direction, pulling on the cuff around her wrist, wishing she had some kind of weapon to defend herself.

Gryphon tossed his blade behind the seat, then climbed into the vehicle, barely sparing her a glance. "We need to get the hell out of here."

The door slammed, and he shifted into drive. As they moved forward, leaving the sights and sounds and smells of the battle behind them, Maelea couldn't help but stare at the man beside her who suddenly looked less like a maniac and more like the warrior he'd once been.

That last thought stayed fresh and foremost in Maelea's mind as she settled back against the seat, careful not to say anything, thankful she wasn't close enough to touch him, because this new Gryphon was even more enticing than the last. Attractive to her in ways that had nothing to do with the darkness inside him. To keep from focusing on that fact, she tried to understand what he could possibly want from her. Now that he was free of the colony, had weapons and cash and supplies he'd need for wherever he planned to go next, why would he possibly want to keep her around?

You're female. Why do you think he wants to keep you around?

Her gaze strayed in his direction. With both hands gripping the wheel, he remained focused ahead, but the dashboard's lights illuminated a muscle twitching in his strong jaw, his thick arms, his broad, warrior chest. Heat burst in her stomach as she remembered that body pressed against hers in the tunnels. And she heard his voice on that cliff when he'd held her tightly and announced he wasn't letting her go after all.

I need you.

The heat burst to a full-blown flame. She averted her eyes, swallowed hard. Told herself it was the darkness making her think differently of him. So afraid it could be something more. Something that would eventually hinder her goal of getting to Olympus.

Olympus. That's what she needed to stay focused on. *That's* what she needed to remember. Not how heroic he looked. Not how he'd saved her—again. Not how freaking amazing he looked right now, sitting across from her, bruised and scratched and incredibly sexy.

Dear gods. At the next stop, as *soon* as he uncuffed her, she had to get away. She didn't trust herself around him any longer.

She looked out the side window into the darkness of night as she narrowed her strategy. But her mind came to a screeching halt when she saw the glowing red orbs of light flickering off behind the trees. Orbs of light she knew without a doubt were searching for her.

A heavy weight pressed down on Titus's chest as he made his way up to the fifth floor of the castle. Thoughts of what Nick had told them about the tunnels still echoed through his mind. As did Nick's unspoken words. *He deserves this. He's not been right in the head since he came back from the Underworld. It was only a matter of time before something happened…*

Guilt slithered in, glommed on tight. Titus had backed Orpheus and encouraged Nick to let Gryphon join them on that scouting trip. He'd assured Orpheus he'd help keep Gryphon contained in case anything happened. Had promised Nick nothing would go wrong.

Yeah, he'd done his fucking job there, hadn't he?

Shit. Orpheus. Titus rubbed a hand over his forehead and thanked the Fates Orpheus was with Skyla now, searching beyond the colony's borders, looking for an outlet from the caves. Nick's men had already sealed the tunnel, and Orpheus was frantic for a way to reach Gryphon. So frantic, Theron had to restrain him from doing bodily harm to Nick when he heard the news.

Titus was thankful he couldn't hear the thoughts going through Orpheus's mind right now. If he felt guilty, Orpheus had to feel like pure crap.

He stopped outside Maelea's room and drew a deep breath. He didn't expect to find anything, but he had to look. He'd already been through Gryphon's room, searching for any shred of evidence that would tell him where Gryphon planned to go after leaving the colony, and had found nothing. If there was a chance Gryphon and Maelea had escaped the tunnels alive, Titus wasn't giving up hope. He braced a hand on the door and was just about to push when a sound like drawers closing echoed inside the room, followed by springs on a bed.

Excitement burst in Titus's chest. Maelea was back? If she'd gotten out of the tunnels, then Gryphon had to be somewhere close as well. He pushed the door open and stepped into the room, then faltered when the woman near the windows looked up sharply and pinned him with the greenest eyes he'd ever seen.

Not Maelea. Not even close. This female's hair was a fire red tangle of curls that fell to her shoulders, her skin as white as alabaster, and those eyes…they were mesmerizing. Sharp, polished, gleaming emeralds he was sure couldn't be real.

She rose quickly off the bed where she'd been sitting, shifted what looked like a book behind her back. She was dressed in jeans and a black sweater, and at eleven o'clock at night didn't look the least bit tired. "Who are you? What are you doing in here?"

He scanned her thoughts, and only picked up a few filtered words: *Whoa. Big. Careful.* Confusion hit, because Misos couldn't block his gift. Which meant she wasn't Misos. Wasn't strictly human either, if his senses were at all working.

"I could ask you the same question." He moved into the room, let the door slap shut behind him. The muscles in her shoulders tightened in response, sending his wariness up another degree.

"I'm a friend of Maelea's."

He still couldn't totally read her thoughts, but he knew that was a lie. The way she glanced around the room spoke volumes. As did the way she kept looking past him to the door as if contemplating her chances of escaping unscathed. "Then you've heard the news."

She hesitated just long enough to tell him she hadn't heard any such thing, then said, "Of course."

Definitely lying. Who the hell was this female? And what did she want with Maelea?

She cleared her throat and moved forward. "I have to be going."

She was still hiding something behind her back. Something she'd found in this room? Something that might help him figure out where Maelea had been heading? It was a long shot, but any shot was better than nothing at all.

The female stepped around him, reached for the door. Before she could get away, he grasped her wrist to stop her, then realized—belatedly—that he wasn't wearing his gloves.

No emotions flowed from her into him. And though he still couldn't read her thoughts exactly, the few he was picking up—*Run. Go. Bad idea*—barely even registered, because the room spun, leaving him light-headed and woozy as shit.

He braced a hand against the wall to keep from falling over. Warmth rushed over every inch of his skin, sent fire burning along his nerve endings. He looked down where he touched her, then up to her face. Saw no surprise, no awareness in her gemlike eyes. Only suspicion.

He blinked twice. Gave his head a swift shake. Knew he still had to be tripped out on those drugs Callia had given him earlier. But then why had he been able to hear his kins' thoughts so clearly? And why had he felt Callia's emotions when she'd touched him?

The female clenched her hand into a fist, tried to pull her arm free. "Let me go."

He didn't loosen his grasp. "*What* are you?"

Her face blanched. And in the resulting silence, he knew, oh, yeah. She was definitely hiding something. But of more importance was the fact that this was the first person in almost two hundred years whose touch didn't send a tidal wave of transferred emotions zinging through his body.

"No one important," she said.

"You're not Misos."

"Neither are you."

She was definitely otherworldly, that much he could tell, but just what, exactly, he didn't know. "What do you want with Maelea?"

She glanced at his hand, still wrapped tight around her wrist. "Are you going to release me?"

Not a chance. He was enjoying the sensation of her skin against his too much to let go just yet. Even with that light-headed wooziness making him feel as if his head might spin off at any second. "Answer the question."

She heaved out a breath. "Maelea is an old friend. I'm just trying to find her."

Another lie. Maelea was a loner. Though she'd warmed up since being at the colony, she didn't have friends in the true sense of the word. And he'd remember if this woman had ever been with her.

"For what reason?"

"My reasons are my own. Now unhand me." She jerked her arm back, and this time the motion was strong enough to snap her wrist from his grip.

The room stopped spinning. The fog seemed to clear from Titus's mind. And cool air trickled over skin that moments ago had been flushed and heated. Wondering what the heck was going on, he took a step toward her, ready to reach for her again, when the door to the room burst open and Phineus barreled in.

"T," Phin said, "there you are." His head swiveled toward the female, and he did a double take. "Um…whoa. Am I interrupting?"

"No," the female answered.

"Yes," Titus said, not ready to let her go just yet.

Phin looked back at Titus. "Sorry, man. Theron needs you. The queen and her sisters used their woo-woo magic and caught a glimpse of Gryphon and Maelea. And they're not in the tunnels anymore."

The first inkling of hope ricocheted through Titus's chest. "Where?"

"Not sure yet." Phin glanced at the redhead again, who was listening intently—too intently—then back at Titus. "But, Titus, man…there are daemons after them. And hellhounds."

The redhead drew in a sharp breath.

Oh yeah, she was definitely otherworldly, and very clearly more than a simple Misos,

Phineus turned to leave, and the redhead started out the door, but Titus gripped her by the upper arm, careful this time to make sure he closed his hand around her shirt and not bare skin. Heat pulsed through his palm again, but no emotions, no pain, nothing like what he was used to.

"What are you—?"

"You're coming with me," he said, dragging her after Phineus down the hall. "Something tells me you've got a stake in what we find out about Maelea. And you might just be of use to us."

Maelea's arm ached from holding it out. She'd finally given up and leaned forward to brace both hands on the dashboard and rest her head against them so she could get some rest. The fact that Gryphon had seen those hell-hounds and pressed down on the accelerator was good, but it didn't ease her anxiety any.

The truck jolted, and she startled from the light sleep she'd managed to slip into. Groggy, she glanced out at the dark forest around her, then across the bench seat to Gryphon, his jaw tight, his eyes intense, his face both familiar and too damn sexy at the same time.

"What time is it?" she asked.

Gryphon glanced at the dashboard, which didn't have a clock. "I don't know. Late. We've gone a little over a hundred miles."

She wanted to ask in which direction but thought better of it. She didn't really want to know what he had planned. She just wanted to get away.

"I'm tired," she said, thinking of a way to make him stop. "I can't sleep like this."

"I'm not uncuffing you."

Bastard.

She bit her tongue so as not to antagonize him. "I'm starving as well. And I need to pee. Can't we stop somewhere? You have to be hungry and exhausted too."

His jaw clenched again. He didn't look at her. As his hands flexed around the wheel, she knew he was debating.

"You have enough money for a motel, don't you? I'm dying for a shower. And at least a couple hours of sleep. I've been awake for nearly thirty-six. If I don't get some sleep soon, I'm going to turn into a zombie, and then I'll seriously slow you down."

"Fine," he said as the truck slowed. They were coming into some sort of small town. Lights shone in from outside. "We'll rest for a few hours, but don't get any ideas. This doesn't change anything. You're not going anywhere but where I want you to go."

That's what you think.

Maelea bit her lip as they rolled through the town, which consisted of one stoplight, a bank, a grocery store, a fast-food joint, and a truck stop. On the far end, Gryphon parked the truck in front of an eight-unit, one-story motel set back from the other businesses, with a flashing vacancy light in the office window.

Definitely a far cry from the mansion she'd lived in on Lake Washington, but she didn't need fancy. She just needed him distracted. "I'll wait here while you check in."

"Not even." He unlocked her from the dashboard then snapped the free cuff on his own wrist. Anger burning in her gut, she bit her tongue so as not to antagonize him and slid across the seat to climb out the driver's side door.

Cool air rushed over her face as she stepped from the truck. Her muscles ached from sitting so long. Before she could catch her breath, Gryphon hooked their joined wrists around her back, tugging her body tight to his side so he could lean down and whisper, "If you say or do anything that upsets me, you won't be the only one I hurt."

Her stomach tightened. He was talking about the clerk in the office. Maelea nodded once, ignoring the heat radiating from his body and the blood and gore still fresh on his clothes. How did he plan to get by the clerk looking like that? The man would undoubtedly notice Gryphon had been through a massacre.

Her pulse sped up as they walked across the dark parking lot, the only sound their boots clicking on the pavement. Maybe that was her way out. If she could get the clerk to notice the blood and gore on Gryphon's clothing, he could alert someone. Call for help. She could escape in the chaos.

The door to the office was locked, but a sign over a call button next to the night window read Press After Hours. Gryphon pushed the button, moved close to the window. Through the glass, Maelea watched as a door at the back of the office opened, and a teenager, probably no more than fifteen, ambled out.

Her spirits dropped. The teen barely even glanced their way. Through the grate in the window he said, "You need a room?"

"One," Gryphon answered.

The kid slid a form and pen across the counter through the opening in the window. "Fill that out. You got a car?"

Gryphon pointed behind him with the pen, then scribbled info on the form with his free hand. As he wrote, Maelea watched the kid, hoping, praying he'd notice what the hell was happening on the other side of the glass.

Almost as if he'd heard her prayer, the teen looked up. Curious eyes gave way to horror.

Yes, yes! Call the police. Call anyone!

"How much?" Gryphon asked as he set the pen down and slid it and the paper back through the narrow opening in the window.

The kid didn't answer. His face went ashen.

Hope burst in Maelea's chest.

"I...uh..." The kid reached for the paper, started to move back.

Gryphon's free hand sprang through the gap in the window and gripped the teen's arm at the wrist.

The teen tensed, tried to pull back. "Hey! Let me..."

His voice trailed off as he locked eyes with Gryphon, then slowly, the fight rushed out of his body, and he eased a step closer to the window.

No. *No!* Maelea's muscles tensed. She tried to pull away but Gryphon held her too tight.

"That's right," Gryphon said in a gentle voice. "Nothing here out of the ordinary. Just a couple passing through, needing a room for the night, right?"

"Yeah," the kid repeated in a monotone voice. "Nothing out of the ordinary."

Maelea's gaze shot to the teen's wrist, where Gryphon's finger was running a slow circle over the boy's pulse point. *Élencho.* He was using a mind-numbing technique on the boy. What little hope she'd had for help faded with every muscle the boy relaxed.

"Now," Gryphon said calmly. "How much for the room?"

"Thirty...eight dollars."

"We also need some food. Little lady here can't wait to get me alone, but she's hungry. Think you can run to the fast-food joint down the road and get us something to eat?"

"S-sure."

Slowly, Gryphon released the kid's wrist, pulled money from his pocket, and slid it across the counter. The kid pocketed the cash, then reached for a key hanging from a hook to his right, moving as if in a trance. He slid the key across to Gryphon. "Number eight. Last door. Will take me about a half hour to get the food."

"That's fine," Gryphon said, looking down at Maelea. "Gives us time to get...comfortable. Right, honey?"

Sickness rolled through Maelea's stomach. This kid was her only hope, and Gryphon had easily turned his brain to butter. She didn't answer, but her stomach turned when Gryphon leaned down and kissed her cheek.

I need you.

She hadn't lived nearly three thousand years to have her life come down to this. If she was to prove her worth to the gods and earn her way to Olympus, she had to get away from him. She had to beat him at his own game and come out the winner in the end.

She didn't fight him when he grasped the key and turned her toward the motel room. She was already thinking three steps ahead as their boots echoed across the sidewalk.

He leaned close and whispered, "You did well. As long as you cooperate, nothing bad will happen."

She didn't answer. His warm breath rushing across her chilled skin set off a rush of tremors deep in her body. Ones she didn't like and were at complete odds with the sickness brewing in her stomach.

He stopped at the truck, yanked open the door, and grasped the clothes they'd taken from that army surplus store. Then he ushered her toward the last door at the end of the motel and handed her the key.

Her pulse raced as she unlocked the door. The smell of bleach assailed her nostrils as they stepped inside. A filthy green shag carpet covered the floor. A narrow hallway opened to a bathroom on the right. Ahead, a double bed sat flanked by two nightstands holding wood lamps with stained yellow shades. Across the room, an old, beat-up armoire housed a TV, and next to the sliding glass door on the far side, a mismatched table and chairs was pushed up against the wall.

Gryphon dumped the clothes on the floor near the armoire and jerked on the cuffs linking them together before she caught her bearings. "Come here."

Her anxiety shot up as he pulled her into the bathroom and flipped on the light. Carpet gave way to dirty linoleum. She blinked twice under the fluorescent beam. A bathtub reflected in the mirror that ran along the wall above a counter and single sink. Gryphon closed the door at her back. From his pocket he produced a key and unhooked the cuff from his arm, freeing his hand and breaking the bond between them.

The cuffs clanked against her wrist where one was still locked tight. Freedom burst inside her as Gryphon slid the key back into his pocket, then peeled off his shirt, tossing it on the toilet lid behind him. But that

freedom turned to unease as he unsnapped his jeans and
pushed the denim down his legs.

Maelea stepped back until she hit the wall. "Wh-what
are you doing?"

"We both need a shower."

Her eyes grew wide. "I'm not showering with you."

He kicked off his pants, leaving him clothed in nothing but gray boxer briefs—briefs he filled out really,
really well—then reached for her. "You smell like a
pond. It's either with me or not at all."

She swatted at his hand when he gripped the bottom
of her shirt. "I'll stay dirty."

"You're not staying out here alone while I shower."
He easily grabbed her hand. "Stop fighting me or I'll
handcuff you again."

Her pulse picked up speed. And she wasn't sure,
but she thought she felt his finger moving against the
pulse point of her wrist. "*Élencho* doesn't work on me,
you bastard."

A ghost of a smile made him look devastatingly handsome. She didn't doubt that this was a male who knew
how to get what he wanted from a female. "I didn't think
it would, but it was worth a shot."

He moved a fraction of an inch closer. Just enough so
his body brushed hers. That darkness inside jolted with
excitement. "I have no intentions toward you except
keeping you within my sight. If you cooperate, we'll be
in and out of this shower before our food arrives."

Liar. He'd made it clear over and over that he needed
her for something. She wasn't stupid when it came to
men, especially this one. Not after the way he'd kissed
her in that cave.

Or had she kissed him? The entire moment was jumbled in her mind. But she remembered the heat. The slide of his tongue against hers. How wet and tantalizing he'd been. How tempting.

Her cheeks heated with the remembered lust and embarrassment. "I don't believe you."

His smile faded, and something dark crept into his light blue eyes. Something that made her catch her breath. A haunted look that spoke of pain and…torment. "I only want a shower. I won't force you into anything else. I won't do to you what was done to me."

Maelea's pulse raced beneath her breast as she stared into his eyes. He was talking about the Underworld. What had happened to him there? All sorts of scenarios raced through her mind, but she couldn't imagine him the focus of any single one. Not the strong, commanding warrior who'd escaped the colony, battled both kobaloi and daemons, and won.

But it was the Underworld. Hell. The land of the depraved. Not Disneyland, for crap's sake. Hades could have done any number of things to him there, and even he wouldn't have been able to stop them from happening.

Don't trust him.

"I promise," he whispered, his gaze still locked with hers. "I won't hurt you."

That darkness inside bubbled with exhilaration, and the fight slid out of her muscles even though she willed it to stay. As if he sensed her wavering resistance, he grabbed his pants from the floor, fished the key from the pocket, reached for her wrist, and unlocked the cuff. The metal clanged against the floor. And in the echo that followed, he tugged her shirt up and over her head before she could stop him, leaving her standing in nothing but her pants and thin bra.

Her nipples tightened under his heated gaze. She crossed her arms over her stomach so he couldn't see her inner forearms. This was a bad idea. This was not something she should be letting him do. Why wasn't she fighting him?

Warmth unfurled in her stomach as he moved closer. And oh, gods, she had to put a stop to this. But before she could find the words, he dropped to his knees and reached for the button at her waistband.

Chapter Ten

BESIDE GRYPHON, MAELEA TENSED. HER HANDS landed against his bare shoulders, but she didn't push him away. And when he unzipped her boots and slid her pants down her legs, tugging both off in one fluid motion, she didn't try to stop him.

His gaze traveled up her bare legs as he tossed her clothes on the ground at his side, hovered on the nude-colored panties she wore, which weren't sexy in the least but made his blood pulse hot in his veins. Then traveled over her flat stomach to the swell of her breasts hidden behind the plain nude fabric of her bra.

He cringed at the bruises he saw on her skin, but in the light couldn't help but notice curves he'd felt in the tunnels. Her stomach quivered and memories of that kiss, of how warm and alive she'd been against him, rushed through his mind, reigniting an arousal he hadn't felt in months.

Except with her.

He pushed to his feet, looked down at her face, and saw the unease in her eyes. Then ground his teeth against the desire burning in his veins. He hadn't lied to her. Even though he was keeping her with him against her will, he wouldn't force her to do something she didn't want to do. He'd never give her the nightmares he lived with on a daily basis.

Grasping her hand, he tugged her toward the tub. He

pushed the curtain aside, flipped on the water, waited for it to warm, then turned on the shower.

Steam filled the room. Maelea grew tense all over again as he stepped beneath the spray and pulled her in after him, drawing the curtain closed behind her. Water soaked the boxer briefs he still wore, plastered them to his body. As he moved aside to make room for her under the spray, he forced himself not to look at her bra. Instead he let go of her hand and reached for the soap.

He rubbed the bar between his hands until it created a lather, then brushed his fingers over her shoulders.

She jumped, tried to move back, but the shower wall stopped her momentum. "Wh-what are you doing?"

"Washing you." He trailed soap down her biceps, back up again. Bubbles formed a frothy path along her skin that shimmered under the fluorescent lights.

"I can wash myself."

"Relax."

Her mouth snapped shut. She didn't fight him, only stood rigid with her arms wrapped around her middle as he moved the bar down her chest and over to her side. Though he knew he shouldn't be touching her, knew she was throwing off every *I don't like this or you* sign in the book, he didn't stop himself because any kind of distraction was better than waiting for the bloody voice to come back. And taking charge also guaranteed they'd be in and out of this shower as fast as possible, which was all he wanted right now.

He soaped her neck, her collarbone, moved his hands in quick, clinical sweeps. And managed to remain somewhat detached until his gaze hovered on a path of bubbles sliding down her pale skin. The soapy mass disappeared beneath the edge of her bra, and before he could stop them, his eyes dropped to her dark pink areolas, easily discernible behind the now-translucent fabric, then finally lingered on the hard nubs of her nipples.

Blood rushed to his groin. That arousal roared in his veins. Without thinking, he trailed his hands down the outsides of her breasts, pushed her arms aside and rubbed the soapy lather all over her soft, silky abdomen and down to her perfectly flared hips.

She drew in a startled breath but he didn't look at her face, was suddenly too entranced by her body. His gaze slid farther south, to her wet panties, to the dark vee of hair now easily seen behind the thin satin fabric. To that place he desperately wanted to see more of.

His cock grew thick and hard as he studied each gorgeous inch of her body. As he remembered what she'd felt like in that cave, how she'd tasted against his tongue. And in the silent steam circling his head, he knew without a doubt that he wanted her. More than he had before. More than he'd fathomed possible when he'd decided to pull her into this shower in the first place.

Common sense told him to *get the hell out right now*, but he ignored it, wanting only to prolong this moment. He dropped to his knees, dragged the bar of soap across one hip and down her thigh. She sucked in another breath and held it, then gently rested her hands against his shoulders as if trying to balance. And this close, with the only sound the rush of water from above, he caught her scent. Jasmine and…the sharp tang of her own arousal.

His gaze darted up in surprise. Her eyes were closed. Her lips tightly compressed. Against his shoulders, her hands tensed as he continued to rub soap all over her legs, but she didn't push him away. And when his fingers brushed her inner thighs, she *moaned*.

Holy hell. She was as turned on as he was. The realization made his balls tingle; shot an image of him sliding off her panties, brushing his fingers against her most sensitive flesh ricocheting through his mind until it was all he could focus on.

No. *No*. He couldn't do that. He'd promised her he wouldn't.

Swallowing against the urge, he pushed to his feet. Knew he needed to finish this and refocus. "Turn around."

She let go of his shoulders, did as he said without a word. And then it was his turn to groan. It had been too dim to see well in the caves but in the fluorescent glow of the bathroom he got his first good look at what he'd only barely had his hands on earlier. Strong toned shoulders, a slim waist, and a firm, tight ass he definitely shouldn't be staring at now.

Shower…shower…think about showering. Not sex. Definitely not sex. This is about getting clean. Not getting off.

Heat seared his skin, sent sweat slicking his forehead. He swept the soap over her spine harsher than he intended, and only barely brushed her backside before turning her around again. And though he tried not to notice the pink tinge to her cheeks that said she knew exactly what he'd been thinking, he couldn't ignore the way her eyes remained tightly shut as if she couldn't stand to face him. As if she were repulsed by him. As if he were every bit the monster she believed him to be.

The arousal he'd felt before swept out on a wave. A mixture of disappointment and anger rushed in to fill the void. What did he expect? That she'd *like* his touch? That she'd *want* him after everything he'd done? He really was psychotic if he thought she'd ever see him as a man. Clenching his jaw, he ran the soap down her arms to her fingers, all the while calling himself a fucking idiot, then faltered when he caught sight of the fine white lines all over the soft skin of her inner arms.

Scars? He couldn't tell. But a glance at her face told him now—when she clearly only wanted to get as far away from him as possible—was not the time to ask.

He slapped the bar in her hands. "Hold this."

Large, onyx eyes peered up at him as he poured shampoo from the travel bottle on the side of the shower into his palm and lathered her hair. Eyes he tried like hell to ignore. Eyes that dragged at his attention because they were so damn mesmerizing.

He ground his teeth together, focused on his task. But when her hands landed against his forearms, heat ricocheted through his body all over again. And the groan that slipped from her lips nearly made him come out of his skin.

Gods, the sounds she made. His hands stilled in her soapy hair. He chanced a look at her face, saw her eyes were closed once more. But this time pleasure, not pain, coated her features. And his cock grew hard once more with the prospect of hearing her moan like that when he was touching her elsewhere. When he was kissing her. When he was inside her.

No sex. No sex. Nooooooo sex.

"Tip your head back," he said between clenched teeth.

He quickly rinsed the lather from her hair. Took the soap from her hand and turned away so she couldn't see the erection pushing against his soaked boxer briefs. As rapidly as he could, he lathered his chest and stomach. Told himself to remember why the hell he was keeping her with him. Not for his own perverse pleasure, but so he could think.

He leaned forward, cringed at the pain in his dick and scrubbed the grime from his legs. After lathering his face, he set the bar in the dish, then stepped sideways around her to reach the spray. Water sluiced over his cheeks, did shit to cool him down. He rubbed his eyes, then froze when small hands landed softly against his back.

She was touching him. Holy gods she was touching him and he hadn't asked. Or ordered. Or even begged. Soap slid over his skin, ran up his spine, then across his shoulders. Her fingers were small and dainty, her touch gentle. Gooseflesh jumped out all over his skin while his pulse pumped hard and that erection he'd worked to deflate came roaring back.

"Wh—what are you doing?" he asked.

"Helping." She set the soap down, reached for the shampoo he'd used on her. "Turn around and lean forward. I can't reach your hair."

His pulse turned to a roar in his ears. He knew he shouldn't, that it was a bad idea to let her touch him any more than she already had, but he couldn't seem to stop himself from turning. At the last second some sense of decency shot through him, and he bent forward at the hips so she couldn't see the effect she had on him. Her fingers slid into his hair. His curled into his palms so he wouldn't react to her. But when her nails raked his scalp, tingles rushed all down his spine, sending a shiver over his skin he couldn't contain.

"Am I hurting you?"

Gods, no. Her hands felt good. So good, he had to bite his lip to keep from moaning. He managed a quick shake of his head, braced one hand against the wall so he wouldn't fall. Tried not to lose it from so little contact. But damn, she looked like a wet dream, smelled like a fantasy. And her hands…they were pure heaven.

"Tip your head back," she said.

His eyes slid closed at the husky timbre of her voice. He didn't care anymore if she saw he had the mother of all hard-ons. He was lost in an erotic fantasy he didn't want to wake up from. Of this beautiful creature touching, lathering, caressing every inch of his skin. Water ran down his face and dribbled across his back. Her delicate fingers landed on his shoulders, his chest, his abdomen. His skin tingled with the need for her touch elsewhere…everywhere. As he imagined those hands sliding down his stomach and into his boxers. Wrapping about his—

Her gasp jolted him out of his fantasy. He shook the water from his eyes, moved out from under the spray and looked down. Then nearly groaned all over again when he found her eyes wide, her mouth open in a small O, and her gaze locked solidly on his hips.

Electrical currents rushed under his skin, made his blood hotter, his cock harder. The draw to her was so strong that the urge to reach for her overwhelmed him. But something held him back. It wasn't just that he'd promised he wouldn't, it was the knowledge that as soon as he did he wouldn't be able to stop, whether she begged him to or not.

Fire sizzled along his skin as water ran over his

body, left him achy and hot. But he couldn't leave yet either. Feet firmly rooted against the base of the tub, he watched her throat work as she swallowed, as she licked her kiss-me lips and continued to slide her electric gaze over his body. His balls tightened as that gaze lifted, as it hovered on his lips. And he held his breath and waited, expecting the worst, hoping it would be what he needed to cool him out. But he didn't see fear in their dark depths when they locked with his. He saw desire. And hunger. And the same damn heat that was scorching him from the inside out.

"Maelea…" Her name left his lips before he could stop it. His hand lifted to touch her as if it had a mind of its own.

A knock sounded at the outer door. His hand froze halfway to her hip. Her head swiveled toward the sound and her eyes widened as if she'd just remembered where they were. And before Gryphon could figure out a way to draw her attention back to him, a voice called, "I've got your food."

Maelea's shocked gaze shot back to his. She took a step back, quickly crossed her arms over her body as if the sound had broken some trance. And in the steam and silence that remained, disappointment rushed through Gryphon all over again, followed by the sharp, swift slap of reality.

Skata. What the hell was he doing? He'd been about to touch her, about to kiss her as he'd stupidly done in that cave. He really was losing his ever-loving mind if he'd so easily been entranced by her in the timespan of one measly shower.

He jerked the curtain open harder than necessary,

stepped out, then yanked the plastic closed behind him, leaving her alone in the running shower. No protest echoed from the tub. And the fact that she didn't seem to care if he came or went pissed him off more than if she'd flat out rejected him.

"Finish up," he snapped as he wrapped a towel around his hips, cursing himself and that darkness that still lingered inside him. The darkness that was controlling him, even now. "You've got five minutes before I haul you out myself."

What in all the gods' names was she doing?

Maelea scrubbed the wet hair back from her face and closed her eyes tight. Good gods, she'd touched him. She'd rubbed his back. When he'd turned around and she'd seen that monster erection, she'd almost...

Nope. Not going there. Not even remembering it.

She flipped the water to cold and stood under the stream until her skin chilled and a scream built in her throat. She was not falling for her kidnapper. What did the news call it? Stockholm syndrome. That was it. When hostages twist events around in their minds until they have empathy for their captors. Gods, she was not that stupid. It didn't matter that he'd saved her life in that tunnel...or that he'd killed those daemons before they had a chance to get to her. Or even that he'd gotten them away from those hellhounds. He hadn't done that for any noble reason other than the fact he *needed* her for something.

A shiver ran down her back, so she turned the water back to warm. She could hear Gryphon talking to the kid out in the hall. He was probably mind-washing the boy again. Now *there* was a noble and heroic act if she ever saw one.

She picked up the soap and washed her entire body, needing to clean away Gryphon's touch, to wash away any memory of his fingers brushing her skin. Relief bubbled through her at the knowledge he wasn't going to rape her. He'd had ample time in the shower and hadn't made a move. In fact, he hadn't been aroused at all until she took the soap and started washing his back. Calling herself ten kinds of stupid all over again for that brilliant move, she scrubbed harder, cursing that miserable darkness inside that was so obviously attracted to him. He was psychotic, unbalanced, and he'd kidnapped her, for crying out loud. She had the bruises to prove it. Needed her? Bullshit. What he needed was a good, swift kick to the head. Preferably from steel-toed boots. He needed—

Her fingers stilled.

Did it really matter what he needed from her? As long as it wasn't sexual, she was safe—for the time being. But between that kiss in the caves and this shower, it was obvious he was attracted to her as much as—no, *more* than—she was attracted to him. Why, she didn't know. Whether it was her or just the fact she was the first female to get close to him in months didn't matter. She could use that attraction to her advantage, if she was careful.

But…damn. She bit her lip as the warm water beat down on her body. She was so not good at the seduction game. It'd been years—way too many—since she tried to seduce a man. She'd given up sex when she realized relationships—even the short ones—caused too many complications and put her and those she even remotely tried to care about at too much risk. Keeping to herself had served her far better over the years than a few mind-shattering orgasms ever could.

But *he* didn't know she sucked at seduction. After all, he'd been hard as stone after just a few minutes in the shower with her. And the way he'd kissed her in the tunnels like a man starved…well, hell. He was one, technically. He'd been in the Underworld for three months—no sexual pleasure there—then locked in his room at the colony for the two after that. She seriously doubted he'd had any kind of female contact of late. The females at the colony were too scared of him even to go near his door.

Which meant…she could do this.

Her pulse picked up speed as the idea took root. So long as she gave him just enough so he didn't handcuff her again, she could trick him. It didn't necessarily mean she had to have sex with him. She just had to…satiate him. Then she could figure out a way to escape.

All kinds of images flashed in her mind. Ways she could pleasure him. What he'd look like in the moment of release. What he'd sound like. What he'd *feel* like. And they all started with him naked, as he'd been moments before in this shower. Except this time without those soaking-wet boxer briefs.

Her blood ran hot, and her own arousal trickled from her stomach lower to spread between her thighs. Still remembering what Gryphon had looked like, how hard and hot and turned on he'd been from so very little contact, she brushed a hand against her aching breast, then lower to her stomach, her fingers heading for the spot that was now throbbing with the need for her own release.

The shower curtain jerked open. Maelea jumped and dropped the soap. Gryphon glared at her from the other side of the tub. "What the hell are you still doing in here? Time's up. Rinse and get out."

Her adrenaline surged. He stared at her with heated, knowing eyes. Eyes that seemed to sense what she'd been about to do. Eyes, she noticed as she looked closer, that were filled with frustration.

"I...Okay," she managed.

He frowned, then his gaze traveled the length of her body, and when they lingered on her breasts and she saw the heat that erupted in his light blue eyes, she knew that frustration was purely sexual.

He wanted her, and that wanting pissed him off. He might not force her into anything, but he craved her touch as much as she craved his.

Maelea's heart thumped hard as he turned and left. In the silence, her body tingled with a mixture of anticipation and nervousness. And that darkness inside—the darkness that was drawn to him—vibrated with excitement. She could do this. So long as she remembered what was at stake here, she could do this and win. For the first time in her life, she held the power.

Freedom was at her fingertips. All she had to do was reach out and grasp it.

Chapter Eleven

FRESH CLOTHES WERE SITTING ON THE BATHROOM counter when Maelea yanked the shower curtain open. The door was ajar. Faint sounds of a TV echoed in the next room, but Gryphon was nowhere to be seen. Tugging the towel tighter to her dripping body, she stepped out of the tub and fingered the drab brown T-shirt and khaki pants Gryphon had picked out for her in that army surplus store.

Not exactly the sexy bedroom look she was going for, but she wasn't ready to go out there in her birthday suit. She had to ease into this whole seductive siren role. She wasn't Skyla, for crying out loud.

She tossed her wet undergarments over the shower rod to dry, then tugged on the pants, which were a good size too big, and pulled on the top. Her nipples hardened in the cool air, pressing against the rough cotton, but there wasn't much she could do about that. And if he found it sexy, well, that was the goal, right? After all, it'd be the only sexy part of this whole ensemble. After towel-drying her hair, she finger-combed her long locks as best she could, then drew in a deep breath.

Showtime.

Her nerves hummed as the stained, worn strands of the carpet brushed her bare feet. She turned the corner, then stilled as she caught sight of him standing in front of the TV, the remote in his hand, his gaze locked on the

screen as he flipped channels, looking for...she didn't
know what.

Blue-green light flickered off his bare chest, highlighted the tight muscles in his stomach and the dan-
gerously low camo pants hanging loosely on his hips.
Her gaze traveled down his legs to his bare toes, peeking from beneath the cuffs of his pants. And she was
startled to realize that for the first time since she'd met
him, he looked more human than monster. More man
than warrior.

What would she think of him if she'd met him in a
bar? In a restaurant? At the theater? She dragged her
attention from his rock-hard body, up his torso to his
face. His jaw was set in a hard line, covered in a dusting
of stubble that matched his blond hair. Even she could
see he was movie-star handsome, even with the smatter-
ing of scars from battles fought over the years. Yeah, if
she'd met him anywhere else, she'd have been intrigued.
She'd have wondered who he was and whom he went
home to. And she'd likely have gone back to her house
on Lake Washington and fantasized about him for at
least one night, probably more.

That realization sent a tremor of awareness through
her body, heating her blood, igniting electric tingles all
along her skin. As if he'd just realized he wasn't alone,
he looked her way, and those eyes, those Caribbean blue
eyes that reminded her of paradise, focused in on her,
latched on tight, and tugged at something deep inside.
Her breath caught. Even before she realized it, she was
taking a step in his direction, moving as if someone else
or some*thing* else was controlling her.

IIis eyes slid over her body, from the top of her wet

head to the bottom of her bare toes, and the heat of his
stare washed over every inch of her skin, stirring those
tingles to full-on vibrations she couldn't stop.

"I thought you might have drowned in there."

His voice was rough, bringing nerve endings to life
that ramped up her awareness and teased her to states of
arousal she shouldn't be feeling. Oh, man. Maybe she
should go back and flip that shower to cold. Was seduction really a good idea, when she was having so much
trouble controlling her body's reaction to him?

"What's wrong with you?" he asked.

"N-nothing."

His scrutinizing gaze said he didn't believe her. But
he nodded toward the table instead of pressing for more.
"The kid brought food. You should eat."

Happy for the distraction—*any* distraction—she
moved to the table and sat in the scuffed chair. He pulled
a box from the bag, set it in front of her. Added a car-
ton of fries, then stripped the paper off a straw and
stuck it in the drink next to her hand. "If cheeseburgers
won't do—"

"That's fine," she said, opening the box and lifting
the burger. It was already cool, but her stomach rumbled
at the sight.

He sat across from her. They ate in silence, with the
muted TV flickering behind her. As her stomach filled,
and one need was slaked, her mind drifted to what she
needed to do next. And excitement and worry warred
hot all over again.

She swallowed a bite, set down her burger, and wiped
her hands on a napkin. Gods, she really didn't know how
the hell to start this, but he'd never believe her intentions

if she came out and jumped him, so she needed to try to ease the tension in the room first.

"I bet the others are worried about you," she said, deciding to go with small talk first.

"They're not." He picked up a french fry, popped it in his mouth, didn't look at her while he chewed.

"I'm sure Orpheus is."

The mention of his brother stilled his hand against his drink, but he didn't answer. As he lifted his cup, she wondered if he felt any guilt for running out on the brother who'd rescued him from the Underworld. Orpheus had to be going crazy right now, not knowing where Gryphon was or what he was doing.

He took a drink, set the cup back down, and went back to eating. In the low light, the Argonaut markings on his arms stood out in dark contrast to his light skin.

She studied the ancient Greek text that made up the markings. Realized the other Argonauts had to be mad at him after what had happened to Titus. She wanted to ask why he'd turned on one of his own, but knew that was small talk that would only lead her away from her goal. So she tried a different line of attack.

"What do you think of Skyla?"

"I don't think about her."

"No, I mean for Orpheus. It must have been quite a shocker to know he'd fallen for one of Zeus's Sirens."

He looked up…finally. And gods, those eyes were captivating. "Are you always full of so many questions?"

"Depends on the situation. Normally I'm not around people much, so I keep to myself. But since you're forcing me to stay with you, there's no sense ignoring each other, is there?"

He stared at her with those piercing light blue eyes

so long, she was sure he was going to tell her to shut the fuck up. Then he looked back down at his burger and resumed eating. But before he did, he said, "As long as he's happy, I don't care."

The comment surprised her. There was love there. But then, there had to be, if Orpheus had been willing to go into the Underworld—again—to rescue Gryphon. For the first time, she wondered what Gryphon had been like before he was sent to Hades. She remembered the females at the colony whispering that he'd been a playboy. Sought after by Argolean females. She could see why, with his looks. But his mood must have been a hell of a lot better then. She couldn't imagine a bunch of women throwing themselves at him if he'd been as dark and brooding then as he was now.

You're about to throw yourself at him, aren't you?

Yes, but I have a reason.

She shook off the thought, not wanting to argue with herself over this decision. Looking down, she fingered a fry. "Did you know? About Orpheus? That he was Perseus's son reincarnated?"

"No," he said, swallowing a bite, his focus still on the food, not her. "But it makes sense. I always knew he belonged with the Argonauts. Now I know why."

Maelea dropped her hands in her lap. Yeah, Orpheus did belong with them. In fact, he'd proved himself a hero probably more than any of the others. "I still can't believe I didn't realize he was my nephew right off the bat. All that time I spent with him, and I didn't even know. I guess I'm not as perceptive as my father."

He finally looked up, his eyebrows drawn in question. "Orpheus is your nephew?"

"You didn't know?"

"No. Who are your parents?"

"Zeus and Persephone."

He set down what was left of his burger and leaned back in his chair. "Holy shit."

Unease rippled through her. "I thought you knew that. I though that was part of the reason you were keeping me with you."

"No, I…" He rubbed a hand over his head. "Holy fucking shit."

Her stomach clenched as he pushed to stand and paced the room. He really didn't know? Then what the hell was he doing, keeping her?

Think. Think, dammit. Now that she'd opened her big mouth and blabbed who she really was, she didn't need to give him any reason to hold her any longer than he'd originally planned. Or to get rid of her, so no one would know what he'd done.

"Neither one of them care about me," she said quickly. "I don't see them. In fact, I'm in the human world because I'm not allowed in either of their realms."

He stopped pacing. "Maelea." His wide-eyed gaze shot to her. "You're Melinoe?"

She ground her teeth at the mention of that name. Oh, how she hated that blasted name Hades had branded her with, the one that meant "dark thought." She crossed her arms and glared in his direction. "I stopped using that a long time ago."

"*Skata.*" He rubbed a hand down his face. "You're, like…three thousand years old."

"Three thousand one hundred and forty-two years, thanks for reminding me. And I think I look pretty damn good for being that age. You try living through wars and plagues, and we'll see how you look."

He stopped and stared at her. "How the hell…? What are you…? What the *fuck* were you doing at the half-breed colony?"

Her temper flared, and she pursed her lips as she stared at her half-eaten food, wishing she hadn't traveled down this revelation road. "I wasn't there by choice. Orpheus came looking for me because he needed… help…finding the Orb. In the process he alerted Hades to my location, which, thank you very much, I've kept hidden from him for years. It's no secret Hades hates me and wouldn't mind seeing me wiped off the planet."

"Yeah, but—"

"Orpheus is the one who took me to the half-breed colony. He felt guilty and thought I'd be safe there. But I'm not. No one's safe, so long as I'm around."

Her mouth snapped shut. Holy hell. Had she really just told him why she'd left? That was stupid. There was no reason he'd care. All she was doing was making things worse.

Refocus, Maelea.

"That's why you were sneaking out the night I found you."

She didn't answer. Didn't want to dig herself an even bigger hole.

"Holy shit," he said again from across the room. "I kidnapped Zeus and Persephone's daughter. If they find out—"

"They won't," she said quickly, jumping on the opportunity. "Not if you let me go tonight."

He stared at her. Electricity crackled in the air

between them. Her pulse beat frantically as she waited. As he considered. As she hoped.

Please, just let me go.

"I can't do that," he finally said in a quiet voice.

"Can't or won't?"

"Can't. Not yet at least. I still need you."

Anger flared inside her. Her muscles bunched, and something in her head screamed, *Run, now, he won't stop you!* But then she saw his eyes. Eyes that weren't as dead as she'd thought all along. Eyes that were filled with...pain. The same sort of pain she lived with every day.

Something in her chest tightened, a reaction she wasn't prepared for. Something that tugged on her soul and refused to let go.

What had been done to him in the Underworld? Just what had he seen and been subjected to?

Her pulse picked up speed. And for the first time, a place inside her understood at least a little of where he was coming from. They weren't all that dissimilar, after all. They were both misunderstood, both outcasts in a world neither knew how to navigate. But while she was running from a hurt that had festered for thousands of years, he was running from one that was more recent and likely a hundred times worse.

She swallowed hard. Slowly pushed to her feet. Tried like hell to slow her racing heart. Nothing worked. She still didn't know what he needed from her, but now that she knew he wasn't keeping her to use as a pawn against her parents, and that he didn't plan to rape her, everything seemed different. Whatever he wanted from her, it was more personal. It was unique. It was—the darkness inside her vibrated all over again—it was something only she could give him.

Her pulse pounded. All she could focus on was the male in front of her. The one who had rescued her from kobaloi, who had kept her safe from those daemons, who was now looking at her as if he felt a kinship with her as strongly as she suddenly felt with him.

She stepped close. He drew in a surprised breath, but it didn't deter her. Heat from his body seeped into her own, giving her strength. How long had it been since she'd found someone who shared her pain, who knew what it was like to be alone, who craved a connection with another person as much as she? Never, she realized. She'd never found anyone like her in all her long years. Until now.

Carefully, because her hands were suddenly shaking, she lifted a finger and traced it across his bicep where a jagged scab ran down his arm.

"What are you doing?" he asked in a thick voice. A sexy voice. One laden with the same desire rushing through her veins.

"This healed fast." He'd gotten it in the caves, when a kobalos launched itself at him as he was protecting her. She'd seen it bleeding. Had tried to ignore it. Now, couldn't.

He tensed, and she watched muscles in his stomach tighten. He liked her touch. As much as she'd liked his in the shower. The knowledge sent power skipping through her veins. "Maelea—"

"I never thanked you," she said, stepping even closer, drawing in a deep whiff of his intoxicating scent. "For saving me. In the tunnels. For keeping me from freezing, for fighting back those kobaloi. You didn't have to do any of that, but you did."

"I—"

His entire body trembled when she slid her hand from his arm to his ribs, to another scratch that had already healed and was nothing more than a thin red line. Her fingers traced the puckered ridge, and his body jerked, a movement that multiplied tenfold the power she was feeling.

He captured both her hands before she could touch him more. "Maelea, stop."

She lifted her eyes to his, searched his face for proof that's what he really wanted. Didn't see it. She saw want and need and hunger. The same hunger overwhelming her.

The knowledge electrified her. Thrilled her. Empowered her. This suddenly wasn't about seducing him to get away. This was about easing a need she'd sensed since he first touched her in the caves beneath the colony.

"I'm not going to hurt you, Gryphon. I just want to say thank you. I haven't been very nice to you so far and…and I'm trying to tell you now…I'm sorry. Just relax and let me thank you."

She rose up on her toes, brought her mouth close to his. He drew in a sharp breath again, one that told her yes…*yes*, this was what they both needed. She didn't know why, but an uncontrollable urge to prove that and so much more to him consumed her.

Just before she kissed him, he blocked her by bracing his hands against her shoulders. "Maelea, don't. You don't know what you're doing. You don't know what I'm capable of."

"Yes, I do," she whispered. "And trust me, Gryphon, we both need it."

He went still as stone as she pressed her lips to his. His hands fell from her shoulders. She eased in closer, until the tips of her breasts brushed his skin. Skimming her lips over his again, she laid her hands against his hard, warm chest, her body growing more needy with each long, silent second that ticked by. Growing more frustrated too, because he wasn't kissing her back the way she wanted.

Was he not as attracted to her as she thought? She'd been so sure this was what he wanted too. She lowered her heels to the floor, stared up at him in the dim light. Searched his eyes for what was holding him back.

Fear. Stark and raw. But not of her. He couldn't be afraid of her, could he? No one had ever been scared of her.

"Gryphon," she whispered.

A strangled groan rumbled from his chest. Then he snagged her at the waist and jerked her tight against his body before she could gasp.

And just as he lowered his mouth to hers, he whispered, "*Skata*. I do need you."

Her mouth was everything he'd remembered and had been afraid to taste again. Warm, wet, inviting. She opened for him on reflex and drew his tongue inside without hesitation. Her fingers slid to his shoulders, dug into his skin as he kissed her. She tasted of darkness. Of hunger. Of need. Of heaven and hell and everything in between.

He groaned, changed the angle of the kiss so he could taste her deeper, pulled her tighter so he could feel her closer. His hardening erection pressed against the soft indent of her belly, sending shards of heat ricocheting through his groin. She moaned, and the darkness inside him hummed in pleasure. Vibrations that echoed through every inch of his skin, even as that place inside that had been broken since the Underworld lurched toward her, as if she were a magnet. As if she were the antidote to his pain. As if she were his very last chance for salvation.

Which she was. She was all that stood between him and insanity. Between him and the voice that had been calling to him since he'd left the Underworld. The one that made him twitch, made him want to claw his skin off, made him want to scream. And now he knew why. Because of the light inside her. The light that was counteracting the darkness simmering inside him. The light that was interfering with Atalanta's hold on him. With her ability to summon him.

"Gryphon," she whispered against his lips.

The sound of her voice drew him back. He stared down at her swollen lips, at her wide and aroused eyes, at that tangle of damp, dark hair around her face. Did it matter why he was attracted to her? Did it matter if it was the darkness of the Underworld pushing him? If he'd met her in his old life, would he have wanted her as much as he did right this second?

She brushed her thumb against his bottom lip. And everything inside him tightened as her eyes hovered on his mouth. Gods, she was beautiful, with her pale skin, the mole near her eye, that small button nose. His cock swelled against his zipper as he gazed at her, as her small breasts pressed into his chest. Desire stoked the roaring need already building to explosive levels.

Yes, he realized as she skimmed her mouth against his again, as she slipped her arms around his neck and kissed him with more urgency, more intensity. He'd have wanted her. He fisted the fabric of her shirt at the base of her spine and opened to her, drawing her wet, tempting tongue into his mouth and kissing her the way she was kissing him. He'd noticed her months ago in the courtyard of the colony. From the confines of his room, staring out at her through the window, he hadn't been able to feel the light inside her. He'd been attracted to her simply because of her beauty, her secrets, and the way she'd looked up at him with the same longing he felt deep in his soul.

He turned her, slid his hands over the soft globes of her ass, lowered her to the bed. The mattress dipped. She gasped, then moaned and opened her legs, making room for him, drawing him even closer to her heat. He slanted his mouth over hers and stroked his tongue across hers, found the hem of her shirt, and ran his fingers along her smooth, enticing skin. And when he trailed his fingers up her rib cage and finally found her breast, he groaned all over again.

No bra. She was naked beneath the thin cotton. She must have taken off her undergarments when she got out of the shower. The thought of her wearing nothing beneath those pants made him kiss her even harder.

He squeezed her breast, then pinched her nipple with his fingers. She shivered and moaned against his mouth, lifted her hips, ground against his throbbing erection. "Yes, gods, yes, Gryphon. I want you." Her hands shifted down his back to his ass. She gripped and pulled, grinding his cock against the heat between her legs, making him that much harder. "I need you."

Her last three words filtered through his mind. They were the same ones he'd said to her numerous times. As she continued to kiss him, awareness trickled in. She was Persephone's daughter, the offspring of the Queen of the Underworld, which meant she had the same darkness inside her that he did. The same darkness that had been gifted to him by Krónos, that son of a bitch. She likely felt the same draw toward him that he felt toward her. The same pull. And that meant her reaction to him now was likely a result of that darkness and not her attraction to him, the person.

She knew how crazy he was. Everyone at the colony did. He'd seen the stark fear in her eyes when he captured her in that orchard, when he dragged her into the tunnels, when they were trapped near that river. And he'd seen the anger erupt inside her when they escaped those tunnels and he told her he wasn't letting her go.

Her mother was a manipulator, her father a righteous prick. She'd lived over three thousand years, no doubt knew exactly how to get what she wanted. And up until just a few minutes ago, what she wanted was to get away from him.

I kidnapped Zeus and Persephone's daughter. If they find out—

They won't. Not if you let me go tonight.

I can't.

Can't or won't?

She was playing him. Reality settled in hard, latched

on tight. This wasn't about her wanting him. This was about her distracting him. Did she have a weapon on her? Was she planning to strike out when he was so overcome with lust, he dropped his defenses? Or was she going to take things all the way, fuck him until he passed out, then run when he was sound asleep?

Anger replaced desire. Disgust rolled through his stomach instead of heat. As she continued to kiss him like a lust-driven slut, he pulled the cuffs from his pocket. Slowly, he slid his hand from under her shirt, grasped her wrist, and pushed it over her head. She lifted her hips again, tilted her head and licked into his mouth. And before she could work the fingers of her other hand beneath the waistband of his pants, he slapped the cold metal over her wrist.

She pulled back from his lips. "What the…?"

He climbed off her, slapped the other cuff around the metal railing of the headboard, and snapped it closed.

"Gryphon!" She jerked upright. Pulled hard on her arm. Metal jangled against metal. "What the hell do you think you're doing?"

"Wising up, she-devil."

She yanked on the cuffs. The headboard rattled against the wall. "Let me go."

"So you can run? Or murder me in my sleep? I don't think so. You're good, female, but you're not irresistible. Should have asked Mommy Dearest for more pointers."

"You asshole." Fiery, jet-black eyes shot to his. "I'll scream."

"Go ahead. I'll just kill any human who tries to rescue you." He leaned close to her ear, so close he could feel the heat still radiating from her skin. "Get used to the fact that you're mine. I'm the one calling the shots here, not you."

"You bastard." The nails of her left hand caught him across the cheek before he moved out of her reach.

A burn rushed over his skin as he straightened. He dabbed at his cheek, looked down at the blood on his knuckles. "Maybe you did learn something from that bitch of a mother."

He glanced at her on the bed, her black hair a wild tangle around her face, her lips still swollen from his mouth. But the lust was gone from her black-as-sin eyes, replaced with a fury that made those obsidian irises blaze, made her chest heave, made her look every bit the daughter of the Queen of the Underworld.

Needed her? He only needed her for one thing—to calm the voice. The sooner he realized that, the better off he'd be.

"Get some rest," he said as he headed for the door. "We've a long trip in the morning."

Chapter Twelve

MAELEA JERKED ON THE HANDCUFF FOR THE UMPTEENTH time. All her efforts did were rattle the headboard against the wall and send pain lancing through her wrist.

Anger rolled through her, followed by a hum that echoed all the way to her toes. If she hadn't known better, she'd have thought the bed was vibrating, but that was ludicrous. As ludicrous as what she'd just let happen in this dive of a motel room.

She glared toward the door. Gryphon had been gone at least ten minutes. She wanted to scream, but didn't dare. His mood changed so drastically from one minute to the next, she didn't trust him not to follow through on his threat to kill anyone who tried to help her. And whether he was bluffing or not, she didn't want to be responsible for an innocent's death. Even if it might be her only chance at freedom.

She yanked on the cuff one more time. Clenched her jaw. She'd kissed him? She'd felt something for him? She'd obviously been *out* of her fucking mind. What the hell had she been thinking?

Bitterness brewed in her chest and hummed through her legs as she remembered the way she'd offered herself to him like a meal. But before she could get all the way worked up, a sliver of guilt crept in. One that took hold and grew little by little until it lodged in the center of her chest and wouldn't let go.

Okay, so maybe he had a valid reason to be pissed. Maybe she *had* set out to seduce him. And maybe distracting him *had* been her original plan. But that wasn't what had pushed her to kiss him, dammit. Something had changed during their conversation. Something even she didn't totally understand.

Whatever. It didn't matter. The bottom line was simple: no more kissing. None. Obviously, whatever humanity she thought she'd seen in him was long gone, if he could so easily turn on her. The first chance she had, she was out of here.

Olympus. That was what she needed to stay focused on. That was all that mattered anymore.

Plans she'd made back at the colony reformed in her mind. The only way for her to be granted access to Olympus, a home that would forever be safe from Hades's wrath, was to prove her allegiance to the gods. To turn her back on the Underworld for good.

And she would. But first she had to break free. Everything hinged on that. She jerked on the chain again, grasped the metal with her free hand, and tried to pry the cuff off. Pain shot up her arm, and a burn ignited all around her wrist.

"Padded handcuffs are nicer. There's nothing better than being strapped down and used by a male when you can't fight back."

Maelea jerked around at the sound of the voice so close, then froze. Her mother sat in the chair beside her bed, wearing a black gown cinched at the waist with a red belt. Her long legs were crossed at the knees. A red sandal dangled from her toes.

"I ―"

"Speechless? You wouldn't be the first, my child."
Persephone shrugged her straight black hair over her
shoulder. Hair that was just like Maelea's. "Now, I don't
have a lot of time, daughter, so I need you to focus. My
husband doesn't know I'm here, and if he did, we'd both
be in deep shit. Plus my mother's going to be looking
for me soon. She's always worried I'm ditching her to
find Hades when I'm spending my allotted time of the
year with her."

Maelea's eyes grew wide. Her *mother* was sitting next
to her, for the first time in hundreds—no, thousands—of
years. Her mother, Queen of the Underworld. Wife to
Hades, the one god who couldn't wait to see Maelea
ground to dust.

"You look pale, child." Persephone's dark eyebrows
drew low. "Are you all right?"

"No. I…" She swallowed hard. "What…? You…?"

"I wish I had more time, but I don't, so I'll make this
quick. I know you're searching for a way to Olympus.
For a way to prove your allegiance to Zeus. I can make
that happen."

"You can?"

"I can," Persephone said with a grin. "And trust me,
it's much better than what you've been planning. The
guardian who has kidnapped you has given us the perfect opportunity. Convince him to take you to Argolea.
The Argolean queen has something that I want. A small
orb with four chambers. When you have it, bring it
to me, and I will make sure the gates of Olympus are
finally opened to you."

Maelea's skin chilled. Her mother wanted her to steal
the Orb of Krónos for her. The relic that held the power

to release the Titans from Tartarus and bring about the war to end all wars. The talisman every god was searching for, including her father, Zeus, and her mother's sadistic husband.

No...way.

"Why...why me? Why can't you get it yourself? You're not technically an Olympian. You can cross into Argolea."

"True, but I cannot get into the castle, which is undoubtedly where the queen has hidden my gem. But she will let your guardian in. In fact, her Argonauts are searching for him now, trying to bring him back. He has ulterior motives, child. Motives that will lead to your demise, if you are not careful. Convince him to go back to Argolea and get help. Then when you're there, find the Orb and bring it to me. Once you do, Olympus will be yours."

Wariness crept through Maelea. "Why are you offering me this deal now? Why did you never offer it before?"

"Because I couldn't when I was in the Underworld. Hades would have known what I was up to. And before that...the Orb had not been located."

"You're not planning to give it to Hades?"

A wicked smile spread across Persephone's ruby red lips. "Of course not. Do I look stupid? I may love the son of a bitch, but I will not let him control something that should be mine."

Persephone wanted power. All the gods did. The fact Maelea thought her mother would be different just because she was *her mother* proved just what a fantasy she'd been living all these years.

"I don't need your help," she said. "I found Hades's therillium mines. Once I tell Zeus where they are, he'll grant me access to Olympus."

"You found the mines?" Interest sparked in Persephone's eyes. And too late, Maelea realized she should have held her tongue. Even if her mother plotted against Hades, she was ultimately loyal to him, and there was no guarantee the secret Maelea had just revealed wouldn't make its way back to his ears. A secret that would only inflame his hatred for her. "Oh, now that is an interesting turn of events. One that might yet become useful to me."

A smile slinked across Persephone's face while Maelea cursed her quick tongue and held her breath, waiting…for what, she didn't know.

"It is of no matter to you, though," Persephone finally said. "The therillium mines will not be enough to prove your allegiance to the gods. A good start, but not enough. The gods require sacrifice. One made in blood. Proving the risk you take is worthy of the reward." Her smile grew wider. "Which is why you need me. With me, there is no risk. No blood. Get me the Orb and I will grant you the freedom from this world you have long sought."

Persephone pushed to her feet, crossed the space between them, and slid a small vial filled with clear liquid into Maelea's pocket. "This will help you lure the Argonaut to your way of thinking."

Maelea knew her mother was right. The location of the mines wouldn't be enough. Disappointment flowed even as she looked down at the vial disappearing into her pocket. "What is it?"

"A concoction of ancient herbs guaranteed to grant you control. Seduction is a powerful aphrodisiac, and no male can resist a woman's wants when he's under her spell. If you play him right, he'll take you to Argolea. Then it's up to you."

She stepped back. Began to fade.

"Wait!" Maelea jerked on the cuffs. The headboard rattled again. "Release me first!"

Persephone's lips turned up at the corners. "You have to continue to let him think he holds power over you, even if he doesn't. Only then will he be unguarded long enough for you to get what I need. Don't forget our deal, child."

She left as quickly as she'd arrived. Maelea stared at the empty chair as the room swirled around her. Her mother wanted her to steal the Orb of Krónos? Dread filled Maelea's chest as she thought of the consequences. If she did that—even if Persephone did grant her access to Olympus—Zeus would be pissed. All the gods would be pissed. Life there would be no better than it was here. Worse, in fact. And if Hades ever found out…

She shuddered at the thought. No, that was most definitely *not* an option. No matter how much she wanted to get to Olympus, even that wasn't a risk she was willing to—

A growl echoed near the door. Maelea jerked around, listened. A clicking sound echoed, followed by the door handle rattling.

Her heart rate skyrocketed.

"I smell her," a voice echoed from the other side of the door. A nonhuman voice. A monster voice. "And she's alone."

―᠁―

Titus's brain was running a mile a minute trying to figure out who the redhead with the emerald eyes could possibly be, and how the hell she was messing with his gift—and curse.

As she stood rooted in place in Nick's office, staring wide-eyed at Theron and Nick engaged in a heated argument about Gryphon, he tried again to tap into her thoughts. But just the same as in Maelea's room and again in the elevator, he wasn't getting enough to read her.

Who the hell is this?

I don't remember seeing her around here before.

Wow, she is hot.

Thoughts from his Argonaut kin swirled in the room, several of whom had finally noticed he'd dragged some unknown female into the office. The last came from Cerek, which not only shocked the hell out of Titus, because Cerek never paid females any kind of attention, but set off some protective instinct inside him he didn't know was there. He stepped in front of her and shot Cerek a warning look.

Then realized, belatedly, that he could hear his kin clear as day, but still not her.

Okay, freakin' weird. She was definitely screwing with his powers. And yeah, it was juvenile and totally not like him, but he didn't want anyone else touching her until he figured out just what was going on.

Nick finally looked past Theron and caught sight of her, then narrowed his eyes in suspicion. Silence settled over the room. Theron turned, noticed her standing behind and to the right of Titus, and narrowed his own eyes. "Who is this?"

"I found her snooping in Maelea's room," Titus said. "I don't know who she is, but she says she's a friend of Maelea's."

"What do you want with Maelea?" Theron asked her.

She moved back a step until she bumped into the windows that looked down over the lake. "N-nothing."

"She had this." Titus held out the book she'd been holding. The one that he'd taken from her in the elevator. The one she'd found in Maelea's room. The one that was a diary of sorts, giving a detailed listing of the gods and their offspring.

Theron took the book and flipped it open. The redhead drew in a sharp breath and held it as he scanned pages. And even though Titus couldn't read her mind, he knew panic when he saw it. Something important was in that book. Something she didn't want them to see.

Theron lifted his head, focused on her eyes. But only one thought reached Titus's mind: *This is all we fucking need*.

Before he could read more, footsteps echoed near the door, drawing Theron's attention. Noticing the queen and her sisters, Titus reached for the sleeve of the redhead's sweater to tug her out of the way. She stumbled, reached out to steady herself. Her fingers landed against his bare forearm, and just as before when he'd touched her bare skin, the room spun, and warm tingles rushed all over his skin.

She drew in a quick breath, tensed against him. The sweet scent of her perfume—or maybe it was just her—bombarded him. A scent as sweet as roses he'd never smelled before, one that hit him on the most basic of levels and sent his already overly aware hormones into overdrive.

Holy hell. Who was this chick?

She let go of him quickly. Pushed back. But in her eyes, he saw the same awareness he was suddenly feeling.

Theron's eyes lit when he caught sight of Casey, but ever the leader of the Argonauts, he bowed in Isadora's direction before moving toward his wife. "Your Highness."

Isadora frowned, rubbed a hand over her pregnant belly. "Am I ever going to get you to stop that, Theron? It's bad enough I get it in Argolea. Here, at least, I'd like you to treat me as you do everyone else."

Casey moved up on Theron's left, smiled, then rose on her toes to kiss his cheek. "He treats everyone but me like a bear, Isadora. I'm not sure you want him barking orders at you the way he does at them."

At his side, the redhead watched the conversation with careful eyes, but Titus recognized the moment she realized who the females were. Every muscle in her body tightened all over again and worry crept into her emerald eyes.

Oh yeah, definitely otherworldly. And she was definitely somehow linked to the gods, if this reaction was any sort of indication.

"Careful, *meli*," Theron said to Casey, "or I'll start barking at *you*."

"Promises, promises," Casey answered with a grin.

Titus watched in more than a little awe as Theron's face softened while he looked down at his mate with longing and love. He tried to block out the sappy thoughts rushing through both their minds but couldn't, not entirely. He'd served with Theron for over a hundred years, and it still amazed him that a hard-ass, honor-bound Argonaut like Theron could change so much all because of a female. But then, that's what a soul mate did to an Argonaut. They changed everything.

Not that he was looking for a soul mate. Considering his gift—and his curse—he didn't want one. And he definitely didn't need the responsibility or worry. Demetrius's harried thoughts about Isadora simply being in the human realm pinged around the room as he stood next to the queen, as did Zander's, regarding not only Callia but their son Max—neither of which were things Titus wanted to know, let alone stress over. He didn't want to be responsible for anyone else, not if this was the result. But that didn't lessen his interest in the redhead standing at his side.

The redhead radiating warmth, even inches away from him, who was suddenly breathing like a racehorse in heat.

He looked down at her. And noticed her face was turning quickly from pink to red. "What's wrong with you?"

Air. Tight. Can't… She waved her hand as if she were having trouble breathing.

Confusion morphed to concern, and Titus pushed away from the window, grasped her by the sleeve again. "Uh, Callia?"

Callia's footsteps echoed across the floor. "Let go of her, Titus."

"Who is she?" Zander asked as Callia took her from Titus and led her toward a chair.

"Have a seat here." Callia eased her into a chair Phin had pulled out for her. Titus watched as she bent forward and put her head between her knees, weird, raspy breathing sounds coming from her lips.

Callia knelt at her feet. "Look at me. That's it. Slow breaths. I want you to draw in a breath then let it out while I count, not stopping until I get to four. Ready? Breathe in. Good, now let it out…one, two, three, four… Good. Again."

The redhead focused on Callia's eyes. Tried to follow directions. Her hands shook against her knees, and concern for her well-being—a concern that came out of nowhere—shot through Titus as he watched.

"Should I get a paper bag?" Isadora asked, coming to stand on Callia's right.

"No. This is better. Sure and steady," Callia said to the redhead. "One, two, three, four. Again." Then to the rest of the group, "She's having a panic attack. We just have to rebalance her oxygen and carbon dioxide levels. Good, you're doing great. Now slow. In through the nose, out through the mouth."

Slowly, the female's breathing regulated and the pink tinge to her cheeks began to fade. Relief swept through Titus.

Callia smiled. "Better. Much better. Keep breathing, just like that."

"Is she okay?" Casey asked.

The Argonauts were as quiet as Titus, watching and wondering who the hell she could be. And all seemed to be in awe of Callia's calm handling of a situation none of them knew how to manage. Put them in a field full of daemons, and they knew exactly what needed to be done. Give them a hysterical female, and each one froze in fear.

"Yes, she's going to be fine," Callia said. "She just needs some space. It's no wonder she had a panic attack in a room full of you guys. I've felt like freaking out while surrounded by the Argonauts myself on more than one occasion. Good, keep breathing. You're doing perfect."

Argonauts? The redhead lifted her eyes, looked around the room with wariness. But no other thoughts got through to Titus.

"Who is she?" Phin asked.

"That's the question of the day," Titus answered, shoving his hands into the pockets of his jeans and staring at her.

Her gaze shot in his direction, and though he couldn't be sure, he thought he saw a spark there. A flare of...was that interest?

His blood warmed even as his brain screamed, *Not a good idea. You don't even know who or what she really is.*

Theron looked his way, and Titus read the *What are you picking up from her?* thought in the Argonaut leader's mind.

He tore his gaze from hers and looked to his guardian kin. "She wouldn't answer any of my questions, just said she was a friend of Maelea's. And I'm not getting anything to confirm one way or another."

"I thought Maelea didn't have any friends," Demetrius said near the door.

"Yeah, bingo," Titus answered, looking back at her.

Her breaths picked up speed. She didn't break his gaze.

Callia pushed out of the crouch she'd been in and rested a reassuring hand on the female's back. "You boys aren't helping the situation. Theron, I need to take her down to the clinic. I want someone to check her out."

"Titus will take her," Theron answered. "Nick's healers are good. You can check on her in a little while, Callia, but we need you here for a few minutes."

That didn't seem to appease Callia, but she nodded.

"T?" Theron asked.

"Yo."

"You up to staying with her until we're done here? I want to ask her a few questions, but first we need to figure out where the hell Gryphon is."

"Sure. I'm up for it." He was more than up for it. He had his own questions he wanted answered.

Callia helped the redhead out of the chair. When Titus reached for her other arm and his fingers pressed against her bare flesh, his head spun all over again. A hazy feeling settled in, leaving him loose and relaxed. Callia looked down at where he touched her, and concern dawned in her eyes before they shot to his.

Titus shook his head as the two helped the redhead toward the door, and conversation picked back up behind them. "Don't ask," he said. "I don't have a clue what it means either."

Casey turned toward Nick and Theron. "So we think we narrowed down where they might be—or at least where they were as of an hour ago. But Callia and I are both in agreement. It's too much stress on Isadora to look again. It's not good for her health or the health of the baby."

"You guys," Isadora protested, "I'm fine. Demetrius, tell them I'm fine."

"Don't look at me, *kardia*," Demetrius said with a

frown. "I'm with them. If it were up to me, you wouldn't even be in the human realm right now."

Callia glanced over the redhead's curls toward Titus. "I'll be down as soon as I can,"

He slipped an arm around the redhead's waist to hold her up, liking the feel of her body against his way more than he expected. Really liking that high he was experiencing just from touching her. "Go. I've got her. I think this is an argument you need to be in on."

"Thank you," Callia whispered.

Callia let go, and the redhead leaned into Titus for support. Whether it was because she wanted to or needed him, he didn't know. But man, that felt good. The heat of her body, the slide of her skin. And that sweet, floral scent mixing with his already foggy mind…Heaven.

As he led her through the massive gathering room with its soaring ceiling and gigantic fireplace toward the elevator, and the voices behind him dimmed with distance, he told himself this was a slippery slope to traverse. A female he could touch and who left him feeling high? Combined with the fact she was hotter than hell? If ever there was a temptation, she was it.

She balked when they neared the elevator.

"What's wrong?" he asked.

"I…no elevator. I can't…"

Claustrophobic? That worked out good for him. It meant he got to enjoy the feel of her body pressed up to his even longer.

"Okay," he said, his arm tightening around her, the heat of her body seeping deeper into his skin, igniting a burn in his flesh he'd missed more than he ever thought possible. "No elevator. We'll take the stairs."

He steered her toward a doorway at the end of the hall. "I'm Titus, by the way. I can either call you Thief or Panic Attack, unless you've got a name you'd rather I use."

"Na-Natasa."

He pushed the door to the stairwell open with his shoulder. "Natasa. That means 'resurrection' in Old Greek, doesn't it?"

She didn't answer. But one thought got through: *Fuck*.

Not that he wouldn't like to. But there was a story there. One he needed to discover first. One some deep-buried instinct told him was going to mean something important. Soon.

———

Gryphon stood on the small dock and listened to the water slapping gently against the pilings beneath his feet. The lake looked like a black, oily slick, reflecting the motel lights across the road behind him. No moon shone, and there were no other lights around the perimeter of the small lake, which meant if there was any civilization out there, it was hidden in the densely forested mountains beyond. He hadn't even known there was water out here until he left the motel and went for a walk to try to clear his head.

Dooooulas. Come to me…

He scrubbed at his scalp, pressed his fingers against his ears, knew he needed to go back to Maelea so the voice wouldn't torment him, but he couldn't. Not yet. Not until he knew he was in control. His body still hummed with a mixture of arousal and anger that left him on edge. He wanted her, dammit, but he wasn't about to let some female—some daughter of Zeus, for shit's sake—get in the way of what he needed to do next.

Dooooulas…

He raked his hands through his hair and dug his fingernails into his scalp until pain shot through his skin. The voice was so much louder out here. So much more insistent.

Come to me, doulas. *You know you can't resist for long…*

He pulled hard on his hair. "Leave me the fuck alone!"

"Not usually the reaction I get when I come calling."

His head snapped up. The petite, elderly female dressed in diaphanous white seemed to hover over the surface of the water. *Skata*, was he hallucinating now too? That shouldn't surprise him. After the shit he'd been through, nothing should fucking surprise him. But it did. "What…? How…?"

"Now *that's* the reaction I usually get," she said with a grin.

A Fate. Before she even leveled those white irises on him, he realized she was Lachesis, the Fate who spins the thread of life. And though he tried to contain it, he just couldn't stop the anger and rage from spilling over. "You're here now? I could have used you five fucking months ago. Not *now*."

Her features softened. She floated toward the end of the dock and stopped. Not, he noticed, close enough for him to touch her. Or grab her. Or drown her for abandoning him when he needed her most.

"The choices were not yours to make in the Underworld," she said. "Hence I would have been of no use to you there. Now is when you need guidance, Guardian."

Fuck guidance. He needed a lobotomy so he could forget the hell of the Underworld. So he could stop hearing that damn voice. He leveled his steely gaze on her. "I don't need you or any of the gods. Go screw over someone else's life."

He turned for the shore, vibrating with a fury that came from the core of him. A fury—an *emotion*—he realized he hadn't felt before Maelea came into his life. But the Fate appeared in front of him before he could step off the dock. And the depths of her white irises stilled his feet. "Choice was taken away from you, Guardian, and it was wrong, but you endured. You will endure now because you are strong. Maelea is more important than you know. Keep her safe."

Wariness crept in. "What's so important about Maelea? She herself said no one wants her."

Mystery swam in the glow of the Fate's blinding eyes. "I cannot answer that. But I can tell you this. There is a reason you are together now. A reason you were sent to the Underworld. A reason that will someday make sense to you."

She faded before he could ask what the hell she was smoking.

Shaking his head at her vague advice, he headed for the road. Gravel crunched under the soles of his boots. Like he needed more voices telling him what to do? And what the hell was she telling him anyway? To be nice to Maelea? The princess of the fucking Underworld? Screw that.

He reached the road, his temper bubbling with each

step. Where had the Fate been when he was being tortured in the Underworld? Where were the rest of the
Argonauts? Orpheus was the only one who'd cared to
come after him, and then only because he'd felt guilty.
And Maelea? Too fucking bad if she was an innocent
victim in all of this. So the hell was he.

A roar sounded from the direction of the motel. He
narrowed his eyes to see through the darkness. And
spotted two, three…no, four daemons rounding the corner of the building.

His adrenaline surged. He grasped the knife he'd
strapped to his thigh before heading to the lake. That
was exactly what he needed. A knock-down, drag-out,
shit-kicking fight to remind him he was alive. That he
wasn't in hell anymore. That the only hell around him
now was the result of one vindictive brunette locked in
his motel room.

Maelea…

He'd left her chained to the bed. Without a weapon.
While he'd walked away to clear his head. Panic closed
in and choked the air in his lungs. Glass shattered across
the parking lot. A scream ripped through the darkness.

Fear pushed Gryphon's legs forward. His lungs
burned as he raced across the pavement to reach her in
time. He didn't bother with the doorknob, just threw his
shoulder against the wood and crashed into the motel
room, tearing the door from the frame, sending splin-
tered wood flying across the ground.

One daemon had already come through the broken
window. Another was on its heels. Maelea stood on the
bed, throwing lamps and pillows and anything she could
reach at the monsters with her free hand.

He hurled himself in front of her, arced out with the blade, caught the first daemon across the chest. Blood streamed. The daemon roared. His claws connected with Gryphon's shoulder, knocking him back into Maelea. She screamed, jumped back as far as her cuffed arm would let her go. Gryphon's head cracked against the headboard, but he slashed out again with his knife, this time connecting with the daemon's thigh, slicing right into its femoral artery.

The daemon screamed a deafening sound, dropped to its knee. Blood gushed over the bed and floor. The second daemon knocked the first out of the way and charged. At the window, three more were scrambling to get into the room.

They were outnumbered and about to be overrun. And he had no idea where he'd left his sword.

He swung out, but the charging daemon plowed into him, knocked him off the mattress and into the wall. His shoulder and head hit with a crack. Pain raced along his limbs. He kicked out, swung with the puny knife in his hand. Caught the daemon across the neck. Blood spurted. The daemon howled and staggered back. Gryphon tried to push up to his feet, but a vibration knocked him back into the wall. One that seemed to come from the ground and made the other daemons in the room stumble, grab on to whatever piece of furniture was close, and steady themselves.

"Get up!" Maelea cried. "Do something!

He scanned the room, took in the seething monsters ready to annihilate, Maelea standing on the mattress, cuffed to the headboard, her face alight with fear and horror. And knew there wasn't time to free her. No time to mount a defense. No suitable weapons to protect them.

Keep her safe.

Gryphon was down to his last option. And using it—the gift he'd gotten from his forefather Perseus—meant losing Maelea forever.

Chapter Thirteen

GRYPHON DUG THE KEY FROM THE FRONT POCKET OF his pants and tossed it toward Maelea. "Here!"

She caught it with her free hand and tried to get it into the lock on her cuffs. Her fingers shook. She missed the hole. Three more daemons poured into the room through the broken window while Gryphon scrambled to his feet and kicked the injured beast in front of him to the ground, then arced out with his blade, catching another in its arm.

"Come on, come on, come on," she muttered, fumbling with the key. There! The key slipped in, turned. The cuff sprang from her wrist.

"You," the closest daemon growled, advancing on Gryphon. "Atalanta is looking for you."

"Tell her to go back to hell," Gryphon yelled.

The daemon growled. Maelea looked up just as it lifted its arm and swung out.

"No!" Maelea watched in horror as the daemon's claws raked across Gryphon's chest. His body sailed back into her from the blow, shoving her off the bed and into the wall. The knife flew from his hand. She grunted as she dropped to the floor, as Gryphon landed on top of her. Panic welled as she looked up at the three daemons advancing quickly.

"Gryphon!" She wrestled her way out from under him, shook his shoulders. His eyes were closed. Blood welled from deep gashes across his abdomen. For a minute, she thought he was dead, and fear spread to the center of her soul. Then she realized he was still breathing and the muscles around his eyes were tightening as if he were concentrating. Or dreaming. Or freakin' hallucinating.

"Gryphon, wake up." She grasped his shoulders, shook harder. He still didn't open his eyes. Belatedly, as she worked like crazy to revive him, she realized the growls had stopped. The room was quiet. She looked across the bed toward the five daemons, four of whom stood frozen midstep. The other lay on the floor where Gryphon had kicked it, still as a statue, blood pulsing from its wounds.

Panic and fear intermixed with confusion. She didn't have a clue what was going on, why the monsters weren't already killing them, but for whatever reason, they had a chance now. She shook Gryphon again. "Wake up, dammit!"

His eyes fluttered open. A dazed look passed over his face. "What are you…waiting for? Run!"

Run. Yes. Run. Fear morphed to urgency as Maelea scrambled to her feet. She knew how to run. She was good at it. She'd been running from Hades her whole life. Twenty minutes ago, all she'd wanted was to run from Gryphon.

"Run!" Gryphon hollered in a hoarse voice.

She turned for the door, stumbled down the hallway. Saw the sword Gryphon had taken from that skeleton in the tunnels below the colony, leaning in the corner.

Her feet stilled. Her mind swam. She sensed he'd done something to those daemons, though what or how, she didn't know. They weren't dead. For some reason they were frozen. And the urgency in Gryphon's voice—a voice that had recently whispered how much he needed her—brought her back to reality.

He was lying on the floor in there bleeding because he'd stepped in front of her...because he'd protected her. And he no longer had a weapon. If she ran now... If she left him, he'd be killed.

Her pulse raced and her heart beat so hard she was sure it had to be bruising her ribs. All these years she'd been hiding. All these years she'd done her best to stay off Hades's radar. Even though the daemons were technically Atalanta's creation, they were from the Underworld, from his darkness. If she turned against them, it would eventually reach Hades's ears.

But if she walked away and Gryphon died, she knew she'd never be able to live with herself. She'd stayed hidden not only to protect herself, but to protect those she cared about. And she cared about Gryphon, even after the things he'd done and said to her. Cared more than she should. Because she understood him. Likely in a way no one else ever could.

Her hand shook as she wrapped her fingers around the hilt of the sword. But her determination had never been stronger.

She rushed back into the room before she could change her mind. Gryphon lay on the far side of the bed, where she'd left him, his torso at an odd angle, his head against the wall, blood welling from the cuts across his chest. His eyelids fluttered when he saw her, that dazed look telling her he was more injured than she'd first thought.

"What are you doing?" he managed. "You have to run. You have to get away before they…wake up…"

She'd been right. Whatever he'd done to freeze them was only temporary. Gripping the sword in both hands, she turned to stare at the grotesque monsters. Vibrations ran down her legs, into her feet. Into the floor, making the bed rattle against the wall. But that wasn't right. It couldn't be coming from her. She had no power other than sensing energy shifts, which this most definitely was not.

She ignored the ludicrous, refocused on what she had to do next. Her stomach rolled, but she swallowed hard and said, "What do I have to do to kill them?"

"Maelea—"

"There's only one way to kill them, right? Otherwise they heal and bounce back. Isn't that right?"

"Maelea—"

"Tell me what to do, Gryphon! Before they wake up! I'm not leaving you here."

"You…" He hesitated, and she looked to him, saw the way he pressed a hand over his wounds, tried to sit up but couldn't. Blood oozed between his fingers, dripped down to this stomach. "You…you have to…decapitate them."

Oh…*gods*. Her attention shifted back to the monsters. And this time she had to swallow back bile and what little dinner she'd eaten earlier to keep from losing it. They were each at least seven feet tall. She was only about five six. She'd never be able to do this.

"Push…push them over," Gryphon managed, as if reading her thoughts. "It'll give you a better angle. We've only got minutes before they start to…wake up."

Maelea forced back the sickness, moved to the first

daemon. Its body was hard as stone, and reeked of a foul stench. When she pushed against it, the skin burned her hand. She jerked her arm back, then realized she needed leverage. Stepping away for momentum, she rammed the beast with her shoulder, putting her weight behind the blow.

It toppled to the floor like a tree falling in the woods. Maelea stumbled when its weight shifted, almost dropped on top of it before she caught her footing. Breathing heavily, she looked down at its body lying still on the carpet, eyes wide, fangs dripping something vile. Then she swallowed hard and lifted the blade.

Vibrations arced through her body, ricocheted through her feet. Shook the room. She didn't look when she brought the sword down. Couldn't. She turned her head and closed her eyes. But she felt the blood and slime splash across her clothing when the blade connected, and she heard the horrific squelch of tissue and the crack of bones breaking as the steel sliced through its neck.

"Maelea…"

She couldn't look at Gryphon. Couldn't look at what she'd just done either. Knew if she did, she'd lose it. And there were still four other daemons left to deal with before she lost it for good. Swallowing back the bile in her throat, she opened her eyes. And was shocked to see the remaining daemons had all toppled to the ground, all on their own.

Weird. But she wasn't about to question luck. Not right now. She stepped over the decapitated daemon, moved to the next. Lifted the sword in her shaking hands and repeated the movement.

She was dripping sweat by the time she finished. Her clothes were covered in blood and gore. The room looked like something straight out of a slasher movie. She dropped the sword at her feet, moved on shaky legs toward Gryphon, grasped the comforter from the bed, and tossed it over him.

"Maelea…"

She tucked the blanket around him, told herself not to focus on what she'd just done, but on what she needed to do next. "Where are the keys to the truck?"

"Maelea—"

"Gryphon, the keys."

He dropped his head back against the wall. Pain and regret rushed over his features, but she couldn't deal with either of those just yet. She had to get them out of here before more daemons showed up. "In the back-pack," he rasped. "Near the wall."

She scrambled for the pack, found the keys in the front pocket. She also found the money he'd taken from that army surplus store, a handful of knives, and a few clothing items, which would undoubtedly come in handy when they got the heck out of here. Zipping the pack, she threw the strap over her shoulder and pushed to her feet, then reached down and grasped him by the arm, trying to help him up.

"I can't carry you," she said, grunting with the effort when she realized how heavy he was. "I can help, but I'll need you to…help me back."

He groaned and shifted, placed an arm on the bed, tried to push himself up. Fell back on his ass. It took three tries before she was able to slip an arm under his and use the strength in her legs to push them both up. His chest rose and fell as if he was having trouble breathing, and his eyes weren't focusing. As the blanket fell from his body, she caught sight of the slash marks across his chest, bleeding profusely.

He needed stitches. He needed a doctor. Shit, what was she going to do with him?

Just get to the car. Just get to the car.

She turned for the small hall that led to the door, felt as if she was dragging deadweight. Gryphon braced a hand on the wall and tried to help her but did nothing more than shuffle his feet and slow them down. The muscles in her arms and legs screamed in protest as they moved. When she finally reached the threshold, she propped him against the wall and kicked wood and metal aside so he wouldn't trip and drag her down.

"The bodies," he managed. "We can't…leave them like this." His head fell back against the wall. His eyes slid closed. If she let go of him, she was sure he'd slump right to the floor like a rag doll.

"We don't have time to worry about that."

She bent to push a board out of the way. He pulled away from her hand pressing into his chest, holding him up. Startled, she looked back to see him heading into the room again, scrubbing his shoulder against the wall as he used it to keep himself upright. "Can't…leave them for humans to find."

She reached for him. "Gryphon—"

His leg went out from under him. She reached for him. A gasp tore from her mouth when he nearly hit the floor. At the last second, his hand slammed into the wall, and he pushed himself back up, the muscles in his arm straining with the effort.

Dear gods, he was delirious.

She had to stop him. Had to get him to come back this way. Toward the car. She also knew that if he fell, which he'd likely do at any minute, she wouldn't have enough energy to pull him back up. Her adrenaline was waning now that the battle was over. She needed to convince him to cooperate so she could conserve what little strength she had left and get them the hell out of here. As her mind spun with how to get him to do that, she remembered the vial Persephone had slipped in her pocket.

She fished it out, stared at the clear liquid inside. A concoction of ancient herbs guaranteed to grant her control, Persephone had said. Maelea had no idea what it contained, but she knew there were a variety of ancient calming herbs still used today by the gods. It had to be one of those. Persephone wanted the Orb too much to risk harming her or Gryphon, otherwise she wouldn't have bothered to offer Maelea Olympus. And that meant, whatever this was, it was intended to give Maelea exactly what Persephone promised.

Before she could change her mind, Maelea popped the top and reached for Gryphon. She pressed a hand against his shoulder, pushed him back against the wall so he faced her. "Wait."

Sweat slid down his brow. "We have…"

"Drink this." She lifted the vial to his lips. "It'll help."

When he opened his mouth to protest, she poured half the contents over his tongue. His mouth closed. His face scrunched up tight, but, thankfully, he swallowed. "What…?"

She capped the vial and slid it back into her pocket. Waited to see what would happen.

His pupils dilated. The muscles in his face contracted, then relaxed. Then finally his eyes locked on hers. And as they stared at each other, something passed between them. An arc of heat. An emotion she couldn't define. Something totally unrelated to the Underworld darkness that dwelt inside each of them. It burned in the very center of her. Ignited in a rush of flame. And in the silence that remained, it lit off currents of heat that pulsed all through her body.

His eyes rolled back. His body slumped. Maelea gasped and wrapped her arms around his torso, pressing her body into his to try to hold him up. "Gryphon?" Oh, shit. "*Gryphon?*"

Panic swamped her chest. She braced her feet and tried to keep them both from going down. What the hell had she just done? Shit. *Shit!* She never should have trusted her mother. "Gryphon?"

His hands landed on her arms. His head fell forward to bump into her shoulder. "Wh-what?"

Oh, thank you, thank you. She hadn't just killed him. But the relief was bittersweet when she realized he was even more deadweight now than he'd been before. "We need to get outside. Can you help me?"

"Sure." He turned his head so his cheek brushed her shoulder. Drew in a deep breath. Let it out. "Whatever you want. Gods, you smell good."

He blew out another long, sultry breath. Warmth slid along her neck, sent tingles all down her spine. His hands inched down her arms then landed on her waist. And as he tugged her closer with what little strength he had left, she recognized the stirrings of an erection pressing against her stomach.

"Have to help *me*, though," he slurred. "Don' know if I can get it up."

Oh, good gods. That wasn't a calming elixir in that vial, it was an aphrodisiac. Her blood warmed as he drew in another breath and nuzzled her neck. Why the hell hadn't she expected that from her horn dog of a mother?

Okay, this entire situation was so fucked up it wasn't even funny. They were standing in the middle of a gruesome murder scene, he was bleeding all over her, and she'd just drugged him with the ancient Greek equivalent of a bottle of Viagra. And now she was getting turned on by the fact *he* was turned on? They needed to get the hell out of here, *right fucking now*.

She shifted her weight, angled them toward the door, and pulled as hard as she could. "Come on. Let's just get to the truck."

He pressed forward. Stumbled. Banged into the wall with his shoulder. Didn't even seem to notice. "Coming. Come…*coooming*. Would like to be coming."

Holy hell. He was worse off than she thought. Her stomach tightened. She was thankful for the cool evening air when they stepped over the threshold and into the parking lot, which kept the heat burning in her belly from becoming a full-blown inferno as she slid her arm around his waist and he leaned into her side.

Somehow they made it to the truck. She pulled the passenger door open, helped him in, then dropped the backpack at his feet. His head fell against the headrest as she shut the door. A quick glance at the front of the small motel confirmed her fear. The office windows were smashed out, which meant those daemons had hit there first before coming after them.

She wanted to go check to see if anyone else was still alive. Wanted to know if the kid who'd checked them in had made it out, but knew they didn't have time. There was no telling how many other daemons were in the area. Knowing that it was all she could do, she said a quick prayer for the kid, then swallowed the fear and ran for the motel room once more.

The stench hit her even before she stepped into the room. She covered her mouth with her hand. Grabbed towels from the bathroom and forced herself not to look around too much as she went back into the bedroom and grasped the sword. She didn't breathe again until she was back in the parking lot, relieved to see Gryphon still sitting in the truck. His eyes were closed, his face pale, his body covered in blood and other things Maelea didn't want to think about. Anyone walking by might think he was dead, but as she climbed into the driver's seat, she saw his chest rising and falling with his even breaths. Relief spread through her all over again.

She placed a towel against his wounded abdomen, laid his hand over the terry cloth. "Hold this here until I can get you some bandages."

His hand covered hers. Warm. Electric. So very alive. And he tipped his head her way on the seat back but didn't open his eyes. "Like when you touch me, *sotiria*. Dreamed 'bout it for months."

Her pulse picked up speed at the lazy way he called her his salvation. At the memory of the way he'd watched her from the window of his room when they were at the colony. At the slide of his skin over hers. And that connection she'd felt when he kissed her earlier, the one that had amplified when they stood in the hallway minutes ago, flared hot all over again.

She had to force herself to tug her hand away, so she wouldn't be tempted to touch him anywhere else, and started the truck. Her heart raced against her ribs as she pulled out onto the highway. She didn't know which direction they were going. All she knew was she had to get them both as far from this nightmare as she could.

That and the fact that things between them had dramatically changed tonight. And that her life—her future—might never be the same because of it.

Chapter Fourteen

GRYPHON'S HEAD FELT SO LIGHT, FOR A MOMENT HE wondered if it would float off his shoulders and disappear into the clouds.

Of course, he had no idea if there were clouds up there. At the moment he didn't know what the hell was up there. Above him. Below him. Shit, he didn't know much of anything.

His body jostled against…something. A seat? He opened his eyes to see Maelea's face, illuminated by an eerie green glow, one vaguely similar to the glow of the therillium in those caves.

Dashboard lights, he realized as he looked up at her. She was driving, and he was lying across the truck's bench seat, his head pillowed on her thigh. A blanket covered him, but it was her heat—blessed heat—that seeped from her body into his that warmed places inside he hadn't known had been cold.

Her hands were clenched on the wheel, her eyes focused straight ahead. She'd swept that long fall of silky dark hair around her neck to drape down her left shoulder, leaving her throat bare and beautiful from his viewpoint. And man, she had a great jawline—sleek, covered in the creamiest skin he wanted to taste and sample. An angular little chin that led up to soft, supple lips he only craved more of. Desire spread through his abdomen and burned in his groin as his gaze drifted to her breasts, only inches from his face. Small, firm, high. The perfect size to wrap his hands around. The perfect shape to draw into his mouth and suckle.

The truck rolled to a stop. The muscles in her legs flexed as she pressed on the brake. Surprise lit her eyes as she looked down. "You're awake."

"Just." Was that his voice? Damn, it didn't sound like him. It sounded as if he'd swallowed a mixture of sandpaper and gravel. And why the hell weren't his eyes working? He could see her, but everything else was fuzzy. He should be over the effects of freezing those daemons by now.

"I thought I'd have to wake you. How are you feeling?"

"Tired. And sore." Add to that light-headed as hell. And horny.

Shit. He hadn't been horny in months. And after what had happened back in that motel... Yeah. He didn't need a repeat of *that*. What he needed was to get his fucking head on straight and refocus on what was important. And figure out why the hell she was having this strange effect on him.

He tried to sit up and move away from her, but rethought it when the truck spun. Sweat broke out on his forehead. He lay back down.

"Wait here." She popped the driver's door, carefully climbed out of the cab, and threaded her fingers into his hair so she could ease his head onto the seat. The vinyl was warm from her body. And her fingertips...Tingles spread all along his scalp wherever she touched, seemed to shoot sparks straight to his dick, brought every inch of his body to life. And oh, damn, it was good. So good.

It was also gone way too fast. The door closed softly

behind her. Her shoes crunching on gravel echoed through the cab, then faded. His skin chilled, and panic spread through his chest when he couldn't hear her anymore. Darkness pressed into the truck. No streetlights, not even the moon, shone in through the windows. He tried to sit up again to figure out where she'd gone, only his head spun with such ferocity, he was afraid he might pass out.

Doooulas…

Fuck. He closed his eyes tight, pressed the heels of his hands against his eye sockets. He didn't need this right now. Where the hell was Maelea? He breathed deep. Tried to get the damn truck to stop spinning. Tried to block out that fucking voice.

Long minutes later, the passenger door opened, and the darkness inside leaped with excitement, telling him Maelea was close. Followed by a wicked curl of heat through his abdomen and hips when she slid those tantalizing hands under his back and helped him up.

"Easy," she whispered.

Easy. Right. Not the word he was thinking. *Hot. Sultry. X-rated.* All were words more suited to what was flooding his veins. All were words he shouldn't be thinking. Her fingers skimming his bare back were electric. And her scent…sweet jasmine flowers…was way too exotic. She took the bloody towels from his stomach and dropped them on the floorboards of the truck as she helped him out. Cool air washed over his skin, tightened his nipples, did shit to cool him down.

"Where are we?" he managed, trying like hell to stay focused.

"Outside Coeur d'Alene, Idaho. Come on."

He had no idea where they were heading, but he wasn't in the right frame of mind to protest. So long as they weren't going back to the colony, he didn't care.

She wrapped an arm around his waist, propped his over her shoulder so she could help support his weight, then closed the truck door with her hip. Gravel crunched under their feet as they moved at a snail's pace. He had the impression of tall trees in the darkness, a narrow path, a downward slope, and the sound of water lapping a shore somewhere close. But it all swirled together in front of his eyes, making zero sense. And his legs and chest ached as if he'd taken the mother of all beatings, which made walking and focusing at the same time fucking hard.

"Why?" he asked as he kicked up gravel.

"Why what?"

"Why Coeur d'Whatever?"

"We needed to get as far from that motel as we could. I should have stopped sooner but didn't want to risk it. You need bandages."

He had no idea what she was rambling about. The forest swayed. His feet stilled. He reached out to brace himself on the base of a pine tree so he wouldn't go down. Holy Hades, his head was seriously fucked-up and his legs felt like they were about to give out at any second. "I'm just gonna"—he let go of her, eased down onto the ground—"sit here a minute."

He dropped to his butt. The ground was cold but solid. Yeah, that was better. Sitting kept the spinning to a minimum. Maybe he'd just lie here awhile too. He drew in deep breaths of mossy air, rested his head back against the tree trunk.

"Come on, Gryphon. It's just a little farther."

"No, you go. I'm…good." He closed his eyes. Yeah, this was definitely better. With his eyes closed, he didn't feel like he was on a freakin' Tilt-A-Whirl.

"Dammit, it's wearing off," Maelea murmured.

Her hand brushed his side. Heat seeped from her into him, reigniting the arousal he'd experienced before when she touched him. Then her soft and silky fingers grazed his jaw, tipping his face her way. "Here, drink this."

Something small and glass brushed his lips.

He opened his mouth to tell her he didn't want anything, that he just wanted to sleep, but sweet liquid flowed across his tongue, and on instinct, he swallowed.

Warmth immediately spread straight down his chest, exploded in his belly, sent wicked flares of electricity through every limb that bounced back and condensed in his groin. His eyes rolled back in his head. Every muscle in his body relaxed, then surged with anticipation, quadrupling the arousal from before until it was all he could focus on.

He dragged his eyes open, looked up to find Maelea cradling his head in her lap, her shadowed face expectant and worried.

Dark hair fell like a curtain around her face, but he could still see her mesmerizing eyes. And her small nose. And that luscious, kiss-me-crazy mouth.

Gods, he wanted to taste that mouth again.

"Are you okay?" she asked.

"Ss..fine. Better zan fine."

Shit. What was wrong with his lips? He knew what he wanted to say, but it was coming out wrong. He frowned. Or tried. The muscles in his face weren't working either.

Whatever. He didn't even care. He just wanted *her*.

"Let's get you up," she said.

She pushed up on his shoulders, all but dragged him to his feet, then slid her arm around his waist again, wrapping his around her shoulder like before. Only this time, heat exploded everywhere they touched, drawing him to her like a magnet, making him want to curl around her, slide inside her, lose himself in every inch of her sweetly scented skin.

Gravel turned to wood beneath his feet. And through the haze ahead he saw something moving. Something big.

"Step over," Maelea said. "Careful."

The ground rocked, adding confusion to his already messed-up head. She pushed against his chest. His back hit something hard. Water slapped a solid surface nearby.

"Stay here for a second." She eased her hips against his, using her weight to hold him upright. Heat and electricity flared once more in his groin, tightening his dick where she pressed against him. The door directly to his left opened. Her scintillating voice drifted to his ears. "That was easier than I thought it would be."

She pulled him into the darkened room before he could ask what she meant, closed the door at his back, and helped him down a set of steps. As the floor rocked again and he tried to make sense of their surroundings, he realized they had to be on a boat.

"Where...we?"

"Someplace no one will see us." She pulled him forward. A click echoed in the dark, and a steady stream of light illuminated the small cabin. "This way."

He had trouble seeing, especially the way his vision kept coming and going, but it looked like they passed a small galley off to his left, a U-shaped padded bench and table. Ahead was a door that had to lead to a bedroom, and relief flooded through him at the thought of dropping on a soft, supple mattress. But Maelea turned him before they reached it, and pushed open a different door.

She shined the light around the closet-size bathroom. After pushing him in, she pressed down on his shoulder. He dropped onto the closed toilet lid. "Wait right here. And don't fall over."

He didn't have much of a choice. He leaned his head back against the wall and closed his eyes. Gods, he could fall asleep right here, if it weren't for that damn rocking. And the ruckus from the other room.

Drawers rattled. Shuffling echoed. When footsteps sounded close, he opened his eyes to a watery image of Maelea holding what looked like a handful of first-aid supplies.

She set the flashlight on the small sink ledge so light shone straight up, rippled off the ceiling, and illuminated the small space. Then she flipped on the water and ran a hand towel under the flow. "You're not going to get sick, are you?"

Sick? No way. Seeing her kneeling in front of him like that, looking up with those wide eyes and that made-for-sin mouth, blood flowed straight into his cock, making him hard as hell all over again.

She squeezed water from the towel, turned toward him, and leaned close. "This might be cold. I'm not trying to hurt you."

Her stomach brushed his erection as she splayed the cool rag across his abdomen. But it did nothing to cool him down. He closed his eyes, groaned at the wicked sensations running through his body. Fuck, if she touched his dick the way she was touching his chest, he'd let her do whatever she wanted. He wouldn't stop her, wouldn't even try.

"Sorry," she said in a pained voice. "I just need to get the blood off to see how it's... Oh."

His eyes fluttered open. She was staring at his stomach. And oh, hell, her breasts hovered right over his cock, close enough to touch. As she wiped his skin, each brush of her fingers sent shards of desire swelling in his groin.

"This is nearly healed," she said in surprise.

Like he cared about the wounds right now. Like he cared about anything but her skin on his, her mouth, her tongue...any part of her body she wanted to rub against his. He shifted his legs wider to make more room for her. Wished like hell she'd stop talking and fucking *touch* him again. "Heal fast."

The words came out slurred, but when she lifted her gaze to his, she either didn't notice or didn't care. "I see that. I'm glad. I was afraid..." Emotion passed over her face, but he couldn't tell what she was thinking. Couldn't make much sense of anything but his own burning need. Then she shook her head, looked back down at his stomach, and resumed wiping away the blood. "How do you feel?"

"Hot." He eyed her breasts. Noticed for the first time that her T-shirt was covered in dried blood and that streaks of something green marred the skin of her hands. "And dirty."

So dirty. Oh, man. Suddenly all he could think about was getting nasty dirty with her, right here on the bathroom floor.

"I brought extra clothes." She left the washrag on his

stomach, pushed to her feet, and was gone before he could stop her. Disappointment flowed, but she returned seconds later. And as she stood in the dim light of the doorway, he realized she was holding a backpack. The backpack he'd picked up at that army surplus store.

She opened the flap, pulled out new clothes for both of them, set them on the counter. Then she knelt in front of him all over again and reached for the button of his pants. "Here, let me help you get these off."

Holy...*hell*. She wanted to take off his pants. Something way in the back of his mind warned he should stop her, but he was too far gone to care. All he could think about was her touch. About how it would feel. About where it would lead.

Please let it lead somewhere.

His dick throbbed in anticipation. She freed the button. He lifted his hips as she tugged to pull off the stained cotton. Didn't even try to stop his boxers from sliding right down with the pants. When she realized she'd stripped him completely naked, her eyes grew wide and a small gasp escaped her lips.

Her hands froze. But he was suddenly wide awake, even with a spinning head. He toed off his boots, pushed his pants the rest of the way down his legs, and kicked them off. And when she only continued to stare, his erection swelled, growing harder and hotter under her watchful eyes.

He sat up. His cock bobbed against his belly as he reached for her shirt and tugged it up and over her head. She didn't stop him, seemed to be in shock, and he was glad, because he wasn't sure he could call things quits right now, even if she wanted him to.

He groaned when her naked breasts came into view. No bra. Nothing but heavenly, perfect skin. Her nipples hardened as he took her in. Her stomach tightened in the dim light. He flipped on the water in the sink at his side, ran the washcloth under the stream, then brought it dripping back to her chest.

She drew in another gasp as he ran it all over her breasts, down her belly, then back up again, washing away every last bit of that battle. He cupped her left breast with his free hand, ran his wet thumb over her nipple, pinched it gently, and watched it harden into a tight little nub.

"Gryphon," she whispered.

In his foggy head he couldn't tell if the word was a warning or a plea. But he felt the shiver that ran down her spine. And the way it pushed her a fraction of an inch closer.

He took that as his cue. Dropped the washrag on the floor. Slid his wet hand around the nape of her neck and pulled her tight to him as he closed his mouth over hers.

She opened without hesitation, pressed her hands against his bare chest, moaned as his tongue slid into her mouth and he tasted her all over again. Heat and life pulsed through his veins as his erection pressed against her bare belly. As her arms slid around his neck and her breasts brushed his chest. As she tangled her tongue with his and kissed him back with all the urgency and hunger he was showering on her.

Ah, gods. This was what he wanted. More of her heat. More of her skin. More of this feeling in the center of his chest, telling him he was alive. But she wasn't close enough. He needed to get inside her. Needed to feel *her*.

It was all he could think about. All he could focus on. He tried to drag her up onto his lap, but her knee knocked into the counter and she pulled back from his mouth, cringing at the pain.

He surged to his feet, lifted her around the waist before she could find her footing. The room spun but he ignored it. Couldn't see anything but her. "Wrap your legs around me."

She gasped as his hands slid down to cup her ass. He closed his mouth over hers again, stumbled through the door. She kissed him back. Harder. With more insistence. Her tongue slid along his, and the silky, sultry feel of her mouth made his balls tighten to near painful levels.

He pressed against her mound, only to groan when another shudder rushed through her body. But it wasn't enough. He wanted more. Wanted all of her. He made it as far as the table before he lost his footing.

She landed on her ass on the hard surface with a grunt. Her arms came around his shoulders to keep him from falling on top of her. "Gryphon. Are you okay?"

Okay? *Okay?* The room spun again. But the throbbing ache between his legs was all he could think about. The ache only she had the power to ease.

He leaned down, brushed his mouth over hers. Couldn't wait any longer. He needed her. More than he'd ever needed anyone before.

He reached for her hand and brought it to his cock. Then shuddered as her fingers brushed his shaft. "Not okay. Not even close. Just touch me, dammit. Touch me like I've been wanting you to for months."

—⁂—

Maelea's heart raced beneath her breast. She knew she shouldn't. She knew this wasn't the time or place, that they were trespassing on a private dock, on someone's boat, in the middle of the night, and could be caught at any moment. She also knew that Gryphon likely wasn't even aware of what he was doing, thanks to that concoction her mother had given her. Not to mention there could be daemons out there searching for their trail. But…

She didn't want to stop. The ache between her legs was too strong. The pull toward him too great. And the fact that he'd said he'd been dreaming about her for months and wishing for her touch was the tipping point that sent her right over the edge.

She brushed her fingers over his cock again, reveled in the way he groaned. He was hard and hot, smooth skin over a rock-solid center, and bigger than she expected. Oh, she wasn't a virgin, not by a long shot, but it had been quite a while for her. She'd pretty much given up on sex when she'd given up on the notion of falling in love. What was the point, after all? But right now, she didn't care about a future or about what would happen next. All she cared about was touching him. About the fact none of the human men she'd been with over the years came close to having the power and strength pulsing in the palm of her hand right this very second.

Her thighs ached. She tightened her muscles to ease the throb. It didn't work. If anything, it made her need greater. Wrapping her hand around his length, she slowly slid her fingers up to the tip, squeezed the head, used her thumb to brush a bead of fluid over his tip. He moaned, pressed into her hand. She answered by sliding her fingers down, stroking him from tip to base.

"*Sotiria*. Gods, that feels so good." His hand slid into her hair, his fingers playing with her long locks as he eased even closer, drawing her toward him.

She knew what he wanted. The same thing she suddenly wanted. She moved her hand up his length again, licked her lips, leaned close. And as she lifted her gaze to his, she flicked her tongue over the tip and watched in awe as his eyes rolled back in his head.

"Ah, gods." He threaded his other hand in her hair, massaged the back of her scalp as she drew him into her mouth. He didn't pull her forward or force her to take more. Just stood there while she ran her tongue against the underside of his cock, while she closed her mouth around his shaft, while she tasted him deeper.

He was salty and sweet. So hard and hot against her tongue. As she sucked, she wrapped her hands around his thighs, partly to draw him closer, partly to hold him up. He responded by pressing into her mouth, groaning long and low. At any minute she expected his legs to give out, but she didn't stop. Because he tasted too good. He felt too incredible. And because for once she didn't want to think. Didn't want to worry. She just wanted to *feel*.

"*Sotiria*," he groaned again.

My salvation.

Did he even know what he was saying? Her chest warmed, and the space around her heart filled. He'd called her that in the car. She wasn't anyone's salvation, since she couldn't even save herself—but she loved the word. Loved the way it sounded on his lips. Loved that he thought of her like that, even if it was only part of some drug-induced dream

She stroked her tongue around the flared head of his cock, then drew him all the way back in her throat. He groaned, gripped the back of her head, then released her and pulled away.

She looked up in surprise. His eyes were as blue as she'd ever seen them when he leaned over her, forcing her back on the table.

He gripped her pants at the waistband and yanked them all the way off. "Have to see if you're wet. Need to know…"

Cool air rushed over her bare skin. She tried to sit up. Tried to tell him she wasn't done tasting him. But he dropped to his knees between her legs, pressed her thighs open before she could stop him. Then his fingers slid along her sex, and a groan tore from her throat at the first touch.

Her head fell back against the table. She lifted her hips as his finger brushed her folds, then slid lower, inside. She moaned, nearly came out of her skin when he stroked her, when he slid out and back in again, this time with two fingers. And when his thumb circled her clit, electricity raced down her spine.

"Gryphon—"

"Gods, *sotiria*, you're so wet. So swollen. You want to come, don't you?"

Yes. *Yes*. Just that.

He kissed her lower belly, her belly button, trailed his mouth higher and closed it over her breast. Sparks shot from her nipples to her sex, amped her need even more. She groaned as he continued to drive her mad with his fingers, with his mouth, as she ran her hands through his short hair and pressed into his wicked touch.

"Oh, Gryphon. Yes, there. Right there."

Electricity gathered in her pelvis, a firestorm of sensations about to explode. But just before the orgasm reached her, he pulled free, let go with his mouth.

She cried out in frustration, but he leaned over her again before she could ask why he'd stopped, captured the sound with his mouth. Then his tongue was stroking hers, his chest brushing her nipples, the tip of his cock sliding along her sex. So hot. So hard. So very close to where she needed him.

"I want to feel you come around me," he said against her lips.

"Yes." *Yes*.

She tasted desire and hunger, so much hunger it stole her breath. Wanted only to go on kissing him forever. But he pulled back from her mouth before she was anywhere near satisfied. He braced one hand on the table next to her. Used the other to grip his cock and slide it along her wetness.

A moan slipped from her lips as she looked up into lust-filled eyes fixated on only her, as she rocked against his touch. Water lapped against the hull, and in the silence between them, staring at each other as if they were the only two people in the world, that space around her heart filled even more.

"Gryphon…"

"Tell me, *sotiria*." He looked down, watched as his erection slid along her wetness, circled her clit with the tip, dipped down to her opening.

Pleasure rushed through her core. She knew he was teasing her, wanting her even closer to the edge before he pressed inside. She lifted her hips, tried to show him what she wanted. When he didn't take the cue, a groan echoed from her throat. "Gryphon, gods, I want you."

His lips lowered to hers. His tongue slid inside her mouth just as he pushed into her body. She tightened around him, kissed him harder, and gripped his shoulders, pulling him deeper when he tried to ease away.

Not going anywhere. Not now.

She stroked her tongue against his. Lifted her hips. Moaned when his thickness pressed deeper inside.

Yes, yes, yes.

His mouth broke free of hers. "So tight," he breathed against her cheek. "So hot and wet." He drew back a fraction of an inch, pressed in again. "Don't want to hurt you."

"You can't." She dug her fingers into the firm skin of his shoulders, lifted again, wanting all of him. "Don't stop. Don't stop now."

He kissed her once more, slid out and back in. Did it over and over, until long seconds later his hips were flush with hers and her sex contracted around his length, all the way inside her.

He dropped his head to her shoulder. His whole body trembled. While he breathed heavily against her neck as if trying to slow himself down, she closed her eyes and let her body adjust to his size. It had been so long, and he was big. But gods, he felt good. So very, very good.

But not good enough.

She lifted her hips, tried to get him to move. "Gryphon." Kissing his ear, his jaw, anything she could reach, she hoped like hell he hadn't just passed out. "More."

"It's gone," he whispered against her neck. "I can't even hear the buzz. Ah, gods, it's been so long and now it's finally gone. All because of you."

He pushed up on his hand, and for the first time since she'd known him, his eyes were clear. Clear and beautiful and focused on her. Surprise flickered in those blue pools. Surprise, mixed with relief and need. So much need, it shot straight to her heart.

"*Sotiria…*"

His mouth closed over hers with such force, it drew a gasp from her lips. She lifted to meet him, wrapped her arms around his shoulders as he drove into her again and again, as his thrusts picked up speed. As her release barreled closer with every glide and pull and stroke and plunge.

She had no idea what he was talking about. Didn't know what was gone or what buzz he could no longer hear. All she knew was that he needed her. That whatever had scared her in that statement before now rocketed through her chest and clamped onto her heart like a vise.

He dragged her up from the table so she was sitting on the edge. She wrapped her legs around his hips, took him deeper. He cradled the back of her head with one hand and slid his arm around her waist with the other as if trying to get even closer.

"*Sotiria…*" he mouthed against her lips.

She answered by kissing him with all she had in her, tightening every muscle. And when he groaned, when he grew impossibly hard, when she knew his release was consuming him, then she let go. Electricity raced down her spine, exploded in her pelvis, arced out to every nerve ending in her body, blurring her vision, stealing her breath, draining the strength from every single muscle.

Her body quaked against his as she held on, as she struggled to breathe through the aftershocks. Against her, he began to relax, but his heart still raced just as fast as hers. And she loved the strong, steady thump so close to her own.

It had never been like that for her. Never as good. Never as hot. Never as soul-shattering as this had just been. She closed her eyes and rested her head in the curve between his neck and shoulder, tried not to read too much into what that meant. Tried not to laugh at how quickly things had changed.

"I…" he managed in a raspy voice, his sweaty chest rising and falling with his fast breaths. "Gods, that was so much better than I imagined."

A smile twined across her lips. Just the fact he'd imagined, that he thought of her…No one else ever did.

His legs buckled. He slipped from her grip. She tried to grab him but was too limp to stop him from going down. "Gryphon!"

"Mae—"

His arms tightened around her, but all that did was drag her down with him. She landed with a grunt against his chest. His head cracked the bench on the opposite side of the small space. Panic replaced pleasure as she quickly pushed up. "Gryphon?"

He blinked twice. A dazed look passed over his face. One that definitely wasn't rooted in drugs. Or sexual gratification.

Oh shit. "Gryphon?"

His eyes rolled back in his head. His hands fell from her waist, landed against the floor of the boat with a thwack. Then his head lolled to the side and stilled.

And in the silence that remained, all she could think was *Holy gods, I just killed him.*

Chapter Fifteen

TITUS CROSSED HIS ARMS OVER HIS CHEST AND WATCHED as Lena, one of Nick's healers, flashed a light in the redhead's eyes where she sat on the exam table.

"Do you have panic attacks often?" Lena asked, studying the female's pupils, then feeling her throat.

"Sometimes," Natasa answered, those green eyes of hers flicking in Titus's direction, then quickly away. "I'm claustrophobic."

A trickle of irritation rushed through Titus. It was more than claustrophobia that had sent her into a panic attack. But just what, he didn't know. All he'd managed to get out of her on the way down to the colony's clinic were more lies that she'd known Maelea before, from Seattle.

Who the hell was she? What did she want with Maelea? And why the hell couldn't he read her?

"Well." Lena dropped her hands, stepped back. "You look pretty good now. Heart rate's normal, lungs sound okay. You have a slight temperature, but it's not high enough to worry me. If I were you, I'd take it easy for the rest of the day and try to avoid confined spaces."

A weak smile spread across Natasa's face. Her lips were plump and pink, her teeth white and very straight. A blush ran up her cheeks, making that flame red hair of hers look even redder. "Okay."

Lena moved to the sink, washed her hands, and

reached for paper towels as she turned. "And you, big guy. How are you feeling?"

Titus dragged his attention away from Natasa and looked toward the healer.

"Yes, you," Lena said with a chuckle when he didn't answer. "You're sweating."

Titus swiped at his brow, looked at the moisture on his fingers. Yeah, he was sweating, but not from his injury anymore. He could feel his body healing. In another day he'd be totally back to normal, thanks to a blessing from the gods. All the Argonauts healed fast. But this sweat had nothing to do with what had happened to him. His gaze cut to Natasa again, who was now watching him with careful and very interested eyes.

No, right now he was sweating because the red-head was throwing off heat waves he'd have had to be blind, dumb, and deaf to miss. All of which he was definitely not.

"I'm fine," he said, dropping his hands, eager to change the subject. Whatever she was, he didn't want to discuss it in front of Lena. "So she's good to go?"

"Yes." Lena tossed the towels in a recycle bin. "If anything else happens, Natasa, just come right back down and we'll take a look."

"Thank you," Natasa said.

Lena cast a speculative glance between the two, then stepped out of the room and closed the door at her back.

The paper on the table crinkled as Natasa began to climb down. "Well, I guess that's that."

"Not so fast, female."

Her hand froze against the table. Her eyes lifted to his. A curly lock of hair fell over her brow just before fire flashed in her emerald eyes. "I already told you why I was looking for Maelea. I think we're done here."

Feisty. Now that the panic attack had passed and she was no longer surrounded by the Argonauts—who, Titus knew, were designed to be damn intimidating—she was regaining some of her spunk. Which he liked. Way too much.

"Not quite." He took a step closer. Watched as she leaned back and her eyes widened with surprise and… awareness. "You still haven't told me what you are."

Her gaze slid from his eyes to his lips, where it hovered. And if he hadn't known better, he'd have thought she was holding her breath. "I'm no one you need to concern yourself with."

"Oh, I think you are." He moved a fraction of an inch closer. "I think there's something about you that very much concerns me."

She pressed a hand against his shirt. A hand that was warm and soft and sent tingles all across the flesh beneath the thin fabric. A hand he suddenly wished was pushing against his bare skin, so he could feel that high all over again.

"Move back, Argonaut."

Her push had no power to it. Didn't even budge him. And her eyes couldn't seem to leave the vicinity of his mouth.

"Or what?"

"Or—"

His cell phone rang, and the sharp shrill dragged his attention away from her and down to his pants pocket. Her hand immediately dropped from his chest, chill air replacing the warmth of her skin, irritating him more than he liked. More than was rational.

"*Skata.*" He pulled his phone out, pressed it to his

ear, but didn't move far enough back that she could get away. "What?"

"T? It's Orpheus."

"O?" *Shit*. "Where are you? Did you find them?"

Reading thoughts over wireless cell-phone signals was a hell of a lot harder than in person, so he had to wait for Orpheus to tell him whatever was up.

"No, but what we found isn't good."

"He wouldn't have left it like this," Skyla said in a muffled voice somewhere in the background.

Titus's brow lowered. "What's going on? Why are you calling me and not Theron?"

"Because I don't want Theron to know what we found. Titus, man, someone killed a handful of daemons. Clean cuts. Knew what they were doing. Looks like a pro job. But they left the bodies on the side of a road here in western Montana."

"Decapitated?"

"Yeah."

"Shit. It has to be Gryphon."

"If I call this in to Theron or Nick, they're going to assume it was Gryphon. And if the Council finds out he's not covering his tracks…"

Titus didn't want to think about what the Council of Elders would do if they found out Gryphon was violating every Argonaut code ever established. They already hated the Argonauts. This wouldn't go over well politically in their realm. Especially not when the Council already thought Gryphon was damaged goods thanks to his stint in the Underworld.

"Gryphon would have covered his tracks," Skyla said in the background, louder this time.

Titus wasn't so sure. He'd seen what Gryphon had done to those daemons in that village. Skyla hadn't been there, but Orpheus had, which was why O was calling him now. O knew Gryphon wasn't thinking clearly. And if he called this in to Theron, Nick would catch wind of it. And then their chances of getting to Gryphon before Nick's men would drop from slim to fucked.

"I'll come to you. What are your coordinates?"

He waited while Orpheus gave him their location. "It'll take me a few minutes to bounce back to Argolea and then to you. Any sign of them?"

"No. But someone knocked over an army surplus store in the town behind us. Took both men's and women's clothing, weapons, handcuffs, and survival gear. And they stole a car."

Shit.

"They could be anywhere by now," Orpheus added.

And therein lay the problem. Along with what the hell Gryphon planned to do with Maelea whenever he got wherever the fuck it was he was going.

"Stay put. I'll be there in a minute."

He clicked off the phone and moved back from the table.

"What's happening?" Natasa asked.

He looked her way as he shoved the phone back in his pocket and noticed the curiosity and concern across her face. If she did really know Maelea, he didn't want to be the one to tell her her friend was likely being held hostage by a psychotic Argonaut.

"How did you know Maelea was here? You said you knew her from Seattle."

"I…" When she looked away from his eyes, he knew she was about to lie. Forget reading minds, he was a pro at reading basic body language, and hers was suddenly screaming *Busted!* "A friend told me."

"What friend?"

"No one you know."

She wasn't going to cough it up. And he didn't have time to try to pry it out of her. "Where would Maelea go if she wanted to disappear?"

Natasa's eyes finally met his. Shimmering, gemlike eyes he knew he was going to have a hard time forgetting. "I thought that's why she came here."

"No, she was brought here, and not willingly. Where would she choose to go if she could?"

"I don't know. She has property in Seattle and up on Vancouver Island. But I looked in both places before coming here. She wasn't at either location."

No, she hadn't been. She'd been here at that point. But if Gryphon was using her to escape, he could force her to take him anywhere. Both locations were long shots, but they were options, if Gryphon's trail kept leading west.

"Stay put in the colony," he said as he moved for the door. "We'll finish this when I get back."

Fire flashed in her eyes as she climbed off the table. "We won't be finishing anything, Argonaut. This conversation's over."

Humor curled one side of his mouth as he turned the knob. "I don't think so, female. I have a feeling this, whatever it is, is long from over."

An hour later, Titus stared down at the bloodbath beneath his feet. The motel room was something straight out of a Fright Night movie marathon. Five beheaded daemons, blood sprayed along the walls and floor, a bed torn to pieces.

Skata. Gryphon knew better than this. He knew to cover his tracks. Humans were not to know about the war between the Argonauts and Atalanta's daemons. Bodies were always to be destroyed. But this…he'd left this here for anyone to find.

"Orpheus wiped the last cop's mind," Skyla said at his side. He hadn't even heard her come back into the room. "That *élencho* comes in handy. We lucked out; this motel is in the middle of nowhere and there weren't any other guests staying here."

"What about the hysterical kid?" Titus kicked a daemon sword to the side. After meeting Orpheus and Skyla at the site of those daemon bodies, they'd disposed of the remains, then continued west and come across a pack of dead hellhounds. They'd cleaned up that mess as well, and finally found this.

Police lights swirling, an ambulance waiting. A handful of small-town cops who'd looked shocked to hell and back, mingling around outside. It was still night, but dawn would be breaking soon, and they had to clean up this disaster before anyone else arrived. Like the FBI special-crimes unit or some paranormal-obsessed freaks.

"Orpheus wiped his mind as well," Skyla said. "Kid was lucky. The daemons destroyed that office. I'm not sure how he hid from them."

Dammit. Gryphon should have wiped the kid's mind, then torched the place after he killed these fuckers. If

humans knew daemons roamed their world, pandemo-
nium would break out. And there was no telling who or
what Atalanta would target if that happened. Or what
the gods would do in retaliation. It was the Argonauts'
responsibility to clean up Atalanta's mess.

Orpheus's boots crunched over broken glass as he
came back into the room. "They're gone. For now. But
we don't have much time before others show up."

From the corner of his eye, Titus saw the way Skyla
reached for Orpheus, wrapped her hand around his, and
squeezed, giving him a little of her strength. And he
thought back to the redhead at the colony. About how
he could touch her like that if he wanted. About the
light-headed, way-too-enticing feeling he'd experienced
when his skin had brushed hers. About the fact she was
the first person in over a hundred years he'd wanted to
touch again.

Orpheus swiped a hand over his brow, let go of Skyla,
and stepped farther into the room. He looked like shit.
Worry lines creased his face and dark circles marred
the skin under his eyes. He probably hadn't slept since
Gryphon went missing, but then Titus couldn't blame
him. To bring his brother all the way back from the
Underworld, only to have it result in this...

"We'll find him," Skyla said softly.

"I know," Orpheus answered, turning a slow circle
as he stood in the middle of the devastation. "That's not
what I'm worried about. I'm worried about what the
fuck he's doing in the meantime. He's obviously not
thinking right." He eyed the handcuffs hanging from
the bedframe. A sick look crossed his face, and Titus
picked up the memory rushing through his mind, one

of seeing those female undergarments on the floor in the bathroom.

Skyla moved back to reach for his arm. "Maelea's strong."

Orpheus huffed. "Maelea's not strong. She's a pincushion."

"She's lived for thousands of years—"

"In hiding. She's not you, Skyla. You know the shit Gryphon went through. You know what it did to him. You saw it firsthand. If he…" He closed his eyes. Swallowed. When he opened his mouth to speak again, his voice was pained. "She wouldn't know how to fight back. She wouldn't know how to stop him."

Skyla wrapped her arms around Orpheus's waist. His face slid into the hollow between her shoulder and neck, and he held on as if she really was his strength. Right there in the middle of a nightmare.

Titus watched, more than a little in awe. Orpheus had spent hundreds of years on his own. Hadn't needed anyone. Had been a thorn in the Argonauts' sides as long as he could remember. But this woman…she'd changed all of that. Not only was he now serving with the Argonauts, he was different. Yeah, he was still a smart-mouthed sonofabitch, but he was now an utterly devoted, softer around the edges, cooperative, smart-mouthed sonofabitch.

Titus turned away, knew in the bottom of his heart he didn't want a soul mate. Didn't want to be left open to the pain losing one could cause. Or the responsibility of protecting someone else. And that meant he probably shouldn't go back to the colony with the intention of finishing anything with Natasa

He wasn't convinced she was his soul mate, but there was obviously some kind of connection between them. Something drawing him to her. Something that could get him into serious trouble if he wasn't careful.

And he'd had more than enough of that kind of trouble. Had been cursed because of it. Had vowed never to dabble in it ever again.

"We need to go," he said, more harshly than he intended. "I say we torch the place, then keep heading west. They can't be far ahead of us. Wherever they're going, we'll catch up sooner or later."

Orpheus finally let go of Skyla. And before he even asked the question, Titus knew what he was going to say. "What about Theron and the others?"

All the Argonauts wanted Gryphon back in one piece, but if they called this in now, Theron would have to report it to both Nick and the queen back in Argolea. And though Titus trusted Isadora, he knew the Council had spies in the castle, waiting for any reason to undermine the Argonauts. No, if they called this in, they wouldn't be the only ones hunting Gryphon. For Gryphon's sake— and Maelea's—it was better to keep this quiet for the time being. "We'll call Theron when we've found him."

Skyla slid her hand into Orpheus's, turned to face Titus too. "Then let's stop dicking around and find him."

Titus's thoughts exactly.

―――

Dooooooouuuulas… Come to me. Come…

Gryphon sat straight up, cringed when pain ignited behind his eyelids. Grasping his head with both hands, he closed his eyes tight, breathed through the throb in his skull.

He felt as if he'd cracked his head through a plate-glass window. His fingers passed over a knot on the back of his scalp, and he tried to remember where he'd gotten it. Couldn't.

Prying his eyes open, he glanced around the room. Sunlight filtered through windows covered in sheer white curtains. A slight breeze blew through the screen door. He was in a bed. White sheets were tangled around his legs, and whitewashed furniture sat against the wall on both sides of him. An open door led into a dark room to his left, and ahead, a white wicker chair held neatly folded clothing. At the base sat his boots.

A quick look down confirmed he was naked, but he couldn't remember how he'd ended up like this or where the blazes *here* was. But as he tried to clear his hazy mind, he had fuzzy flashes of skin, of heat, of the sweetest mouth he'd ever tasted. Of a blinding orgasm that even now made his dick hard.

Doooooouuuuulas…

He shook his head. Ignored the voice. It was there, but not as strong as before. And always in the back was that damn buzz he'd grown accustomed to.

He pushed to his feet, gripped the dresser at his side when he wobbled. The sheet fell to the floor. On shaky legs, he made his way over to the chair, lifted a pair of jeans that definitely weren't his. Since they were better than walking around naked, he tugged them on, was relieved when they fit. As he zipped the fly, he turned for the window, then pulled back the sheer curtain and looked out at…an ocean of blue.

Surprise rippled through him. A balcony over-looked a beach. Rock walls created a sheltered cove on both sides. Trees rose up all around, offering privacy. And down below, waves lapped gently against the shore, where a female with long dark hair, wearing a thin white dress, frolicked in the sand near a cluster of seagulls.

Something in his chest cinched down tight. He knew it wasn't his heart, because he was pretty sure he didn't have one anymore, but as he stared out at the female, something stirred inside him. A feeling. A calling. Something pulling him toward her. Something that wasn't related to the darkness that still lingered from the Underworld.

She turned and looked his way, almost as if she'd sensed him watching her. And as their eyes met, he remembered the hundreds of times he'd stared out at Maelea like this from his room at the colony.

Sotiria…

Images flashed in his mind. A boat rocking. A closet-sized bathroom. Closing his mouth over hers. Dragging her up his body. Laying her out over a table like an offering and all but devouring her whole.

His skin grew hot. He turned away from the window, tried to slow his racing pulse. He didn't know where they were, but he was pretty damn sure the images flitting through his mind weren't fantasies. They were real. Which meant that sometime between the motel where those daemons had attacked them and here, he'd done something horrible. Something he never ever should have done.

Fuck. *Fuck!* He gripped his hair and pulled until pain shot across his scalp. Why couldn't he remember? Why did his brain feel like it was short-circuiting?

Dooooouuulas…

Why the hell was that voice suddenly the least of his worries?

His skin tingled with the intensity of a thousand needles stabbing into him over and over. His pulse was a roar in his ears. He didn't bother with a shirt or shoes, had only one thought in mind as he pulled the bedroom door open and headed out into the hall in bare feet. He had to see for himself that he hadn't hurt her. But shit...would he know if he had? That kind of pain, the kind he lived with every damn day, was on the inside. It couldn't be seen, only felt. Sickness brewed in his stomach, threatened to push up into his chest at the thought that he'd done that to her.

He stopped at the bottom of the stairs, gripped the newel post, and breathed deep, forcing back the bile. When he was sure he wasn't about to lose it, he scanned the wide family room with white beadboard trim, comfy oversized furnishings grouped around a fireplace, the adjacent open kitchen alight with an orange glow, and the wide windows that looked out over the serene beach.

Serenity was the farthest thing from his mind. His nerves kicked up as he crossed the room, pushed the screen open, and stepped out onto another deck, this one with stairs that led down to the sand.

Maelea stood ankle deep in the gentle waves, throwing breadcrumbs up into the air for the seagulls to catch, her dark hair flowing in the breeze behind her. The birds squawked and fluttered over her head. The gauzy white, long-sleeved gown with the wide cuffs hit at her calves, cinched in at her waist, and was open just enough at the neckline to showcase her breasts. Tight, firm, high breasts he remembered closing his mouth over, drawing deep, licking to stiff peaks

Skata. He was every bit the monster Nick and all the other colonists thought he was. Orpheus never should have rescued him from the Underworld. The Argonauts shouldn't have let him stay in the human realm. They all should have left him in Tartarus to rot. He deserved that. Deserved more than that now.

His skin felt three times too small. He swiped a hand over his brow. Forced his feet forward. If Maelea heard him, she didn't show it, and that only increased his guilt and nausea. As he moved down the stairs and crossed the beach toward her, all the shitty things he'd done and said to her since the day he took her hostage at the colony rolled through his mind. But none of them—not even all of them combined—compared to what he'd done to her on that boat.

He stopped several feet away, shoved his hands into his pockets so as not to scare her. Didn't know what the hell to say. What *could* he say?

She threw up the last piece of bread, dusted off her hands, then turned his way. No surprise rushed over her features in the sunlight, and he couldn't read her dark eyes. Wasn't sure he wanted to know what she was thinking.

"I thought you'd sleep longer," she said. "How are you feeling?"

How are you feeling? Seriously? She was asking him how *he* felt? He searched her face for any signs of injury, didn't see it. But that didn't mean there weren't internal injuries…emotional injuries.

"Maelea…" His throat grew thick. Words dried up on his lips. Now that he was out here, now that he was staring at her face-to-face, he didn't know what the hell to say. What the hell to do, for that matter. His stomach rolled, and that bile pushed right back up his throat.

She stared at him for several seconds, waiting, he knew, for him to say something. Anything. When he didn't, she looked past him to the house. "You were out most of the trip. I thought it was best to let you sleep. After all, it was my fault you were hurt in the first place."

Her fault? Confusion seeped into his already hazy mind.

"It's mine, by the way." She gestured behind him. Still not sure what the hell was going on, he turned to look at the two-story beach house with wide decks, nestled into a private bay. No other houses could be seen. No other people, either. Just trees and cliffs and the one little house. "I bought it over a hundred years ago. It's been remodeled once. Probably about due for another update, but I don't get up here very often."

He looked back at her. She was talking about a stupid house, when inside he wanted to die over what he'd done.

The wind blew a lock of hair across her face, the contrast between the dark of her hair and the light of her skin reminding him of her lineage. Of who she was and how long she'd lived. She tugged the lock away from her eyes, shook out her hair. He remembered her doing that in the caves, when her hair had been wet and plastered to her face. Remembered sliding his fingers in those thick locks as he'd kissed her again and again on that boat.

He swallowed hard, forced himself to find his voice. "Maelea—"

"No one will find us here, in case that's what you're worried about," she said. "I paid cash for it. Didn't put my real name on the deed. And it was so long ago, it'd be hard to track this place to me. Plus, I used the ore."

"The what?"

"The mineral? The one you picked up in the caves? I found it in your backpack when we got here. I did some research on therillium while you were asleep, and you were right. When heated, it makes the area around it invisible from the outside. The invisibility factor seems to spread out at least a quarter mile from the source. Or at least that's what I found from my unscientific tests. I have it under a heat lamp inside. From the road up on the hill, you can't even see the house anymore."

He wasn't sure whether he should be impressed or way the fuck confused.

Confusion won out. "Maelea—"

"Let's go inside," she said, moving out of the waves and up on the beach. The bottom of her skirt was wet when she stepped onto the sand and moved by him. She didn't touch him, but her heat warmed the air nearby. Stirred a memory of their bodies locked tight together on that boat. "It may be July up here on Vancouver Island, but that doesn't mean its beach-weather warm. You look cold."

For the first time, he noticed the temperature. Brisk. The slight wind puckering his nipples. Likely only in the upper sixties, even with the sun.

"Vancouver Island?" he asked as she headed for the house. Why the hell wasn't she screaming at him? Why didn't she look…hurt and upset? What the *fuck* was going on? "How did you get us all the way from that motel in Montana to here?"

"I drove."

"Drove? The whole way?" No, that wasn't right. He

remembered water, a boat. He remembered bending her over a table, closing his mouth over hers, pushing—

She stopped at the base of the steps and looked back as she gripped the banister. "Okay, I didn't drive the whole way. When we got to Coeur d'Alene, I had to stop. We needed a place to get cleaned up, and you were injured, so…"

Coeur d'Alene. There was a lake there. A big one. That's where he remembered the boat. Guilt seeped back in to tighten his stomach to painful levels as he crossed the sand. "Maelea, about the boat—"

Her eyes snapped to his, but he didn't see anger there. Or fear. He saw…heat.

His feet faltered. No, that wasn't right either. She couldn't possibly have enjoyed what he'd done to her.

A rose tinge spread up her cheeks. "Yeah, about that. I'm…I'm sorry."

She was sorry? His head spun. What could she possibly be sorry for?

She looked at a spot on the banister. Wouldn't meet his eyes. "I…I shouldn't have taken advantage of you when you were…injured…like that. I should have stopped it. I think it was the adrenaline rush from killing those daemons and being on the run. And then when you kissed me on that boat, I…" Those cheeks turned even pinker. "Yeah, I…that was a stupid idea. But you don't have to worry. I won't get pregnant or anything. I mean, I can't. Hades's curse and all that."

She blew out a breath, and her cheeks turned a full-blown red. "Oh boy, that was more than I needed to share, huh? How about food? Are you hungry? Because I'm starving all of a sudden."

She jogged up the steps in her bare feet before he could stop her. Before he could figure out what the hell was going on.

She'd taken advantage of *him*? Images ran back through his mind. Maelea unbuttoning his pants. Her small hand stroking his cock. Her fingernails digging into his shoulders and holding on tight.

His blood ran hot, and that sickness that had been churning in his stomach since he awoke slowly morphed to arousal.

Oh, Gryphon. Yes, there. Right there. Don't stop.

He grew rock hard when her words drifted back into his mind. And even in the cool breeze, sweat broke out all over his body.

He hadn't forced her. He hadn't hurt her. He looked up at the house as his pulse roared in his ears. She'd wanted him.

Him. The guy who'd kidnapped her. Said cruel things to her. Used her so he could think straight. Not to mention handcuffed her to a bed, nearly gotten her killed multiple times, and made her decapitate those daemons back at that motel.

There was something seriously wrong with her. There had to be.

His hands shook as he moved up the steps, as he pulled the screen door open, as he stepped back into the airy, light family room and looked toward the kitchen. Her back was to him. She was pulling items from the refrigerator, setting out food he couldn't imagine eating. An orange light from somewhere in the kitchen made the room glow, but he didn't give a rip where it came from right now. He only cared about her.

"Why didn't you run?"

She froze, one hand on the refrigerator door, the other inside. Light from the appliance shimmered over her in waves of gold. "What do you mean?"

"At the motel. When those daemons were attacking and I freed you. Why didn't you run? Why did you come back?"

She turned slowly, set a block of cheese on the granite counter, pushed the refrigerator door closed with her spine. Then bit her lip and stared down at her feet. "I was going to run."

"So why didn't you?"

"I knew if I left, you would have died."

"Why would that matter to you?"

"Because I didn't want to be responsible for that. And because...you saved my life. Several times before that."

He couldn't believe what he was hearing. "If it weren't for me you wouldn't have needed saving."

"True, I guess," she said with a ghost of a smile. "But..."

"But what?"

Her smile faded. "But...in the motel? When we were having dinner? And we were talking? I realized we weren't all that different. We were both running from the colony, both running from our pasts and who everyone thinks we are or should be. I don't know. I guess I just realized you weren't the monster I'd pegged you to be."

He remembered that moment. How she'd asked him to let her go, and when he told her that he couldn't because he needed her, instead of lashing out at him as he'd expected, her eyes had softened. He'd already told

her several times that he needed her, but that time…
that time, he'd been racked with guilt over the fact he
couldn't let her go. And she'd obviously seen it. Then
she'd pushed to her feet, crossed to him, given him
his first taste of something sacred he'd been craving
for months.

His nerves vibrated at the memory. And then he
remembered how he'd accused her of trying to seduce
him to get away.

Shit. His eyes slid closed at that doozy of a memory.
"Then I handcuffed you to the bed and left you."

His voice was gruff. That guilt slithered in and
grabbed on tight. He opened his eyes, forced himself
to meet her expression. Didn't deserve to hide from it.

"Yeah," she said with a smug smile, her dark eyes lifting to his. "I was pissed about that. But…I can't really
blame you. I mean, I *was* planning to seduce you so I
could try to get away. But then we talked and I started to
understand you better and…everything changed."

He didn't know what to say. Wasn't sure what to
make of this. Not only was she admitting something she
didn't have to, she was doing so staring at him across
the small space as if…he were nothing more than a man.

He'd never been *just* a man. The entirety of his life
was wrapped up in being an Argonaut, a warrior, a
fighter trained in honor and duty. Females had come on
to him, but they'd never wanted him for who he was
inside. They'd only wanted him because of his status,
because screwing an Argonaut was akin to banging a
celebrity in the human realm. And then…then, after he'd
been sent to the Underworld, he'd lost even that. He'd
become everything he despised. Someone so desperate

to avoid torture, he'd sacrificed everything he'd ever believed in and done things that would horrify even the sickest bastard, all in an attempt to save his sorry ass. No one had wanted him after that. No one *should* want him after that.

Gryphon, gods, I want you.

No one except her.

She could have seduced him without those words, but hearing them… Reality slammed into him as he stood there staring at her. She'd wanted him. The *real* him. Even knowing all that other shit.

Then she'd saved his life. Brought him here. Tended his wounds.

The hole around his heart slowly started to close in. And air choked in his lungs until it was hard to draw a breath.

"Do you like grilled cheese?" she asked. "It's my favorite comfort food." She glanced toward the cupboards on the opposite wall of the kitchen. "I think I have tomato soup somewhere. I did some shopping while you were asleep."

"Maelea." His heart—a heart he was starting to think he might still have—pounded hard as he moved into the kitchen, as he stepped up behind her, as he gently turned her to face him.

She didn't flinch at his touch, but her muscles tensed, and a shudder ran through her. Not one born of fear but rooted in…awareness.

She stared at his chest, didn't make any move to reach for him. Didn't make any move to pull away either. He wanted to kiss her, wanted to taste her again. Didn't know if he should. She'd said her reaction on the

boat had been the result of adrenaline, of nearly dying.
He knew all too well how amped up a fight could leave
a person.

Skata, he didn't know what to do. Only knew…that
he wanted her. That what was pulling him to her now
had nothing to do with the darkness inside him and
everything to do with her as a woman and him as a man
and this roaring desire he hadn't felt for…anyone. Ever.

"I…ah…I have a proposition for you," she said
before he could decide what to do. What to say.

Surprise lifted his brows. "A proposition?"

"Yeah. I was thinking about it on the drive out here
when you were asleep. I know why you need me. I know
it's my link to the Underworld and the light inside me
that…balances you. I've watched you, and I can tell that
when I'm close you seem calmer, more relaxed. So I
have a trade I'm willing to make."

His eyes narrowed. "What kind of trade?"

"I want you to teach me how to fight. Really fight
and protect myself. I learned a little at the colony, but
after you grabbed me in the orchard, I discovered I
don't know nearly as much as I should. And truthfully,
I haven't needed to know all these years, because I've
been hiding. But when I was fighting those daemons, I
felt something. Some strength I didn't know I had. The
ground rumbled, just like it did in the caves before we
fell into that river. And looking back, I'm not entirely
sure—maybe—somehow, that didn't come from me."

She drew in a breath. Straightened her spine. "I know
it sounds silly. My only gift has been the ability to sense
energy shifts on the planet, but what if there's more?
What if I just wasn't strong enough before to use it? I'm

not the same person I was before I went to the colony.
And the last few days with you—as much as I hated it at
first—it taught me that I'm a heck of a lot tougher than
I thought. And the truth is, Gryphon, I'm tired of hiding. I would do anything to get to Olympus. Sitting back
waiting isn't going to get me there, and being afraid to
go after what I want isn't doing anything but prolonging
my measly existence. But I can't even try, until I hone
my skills."

She pushed a lock of hair behind her ear. Met his
gaze with such determination and strength, he couldn't
help but be awed. "So I'm willing to make you a deal. If
you'll stay here for a few days, if you'll teach me what
I need to know, then when I'm ready, I'll go anywhere
you want me to go. And I promise I won't try to run until
you've done what you need me to help you do."

He'd been floored before, but now…shock and disbelief and wonder rippled through him. She didn't know
him. Didn't know what he had planned. But she trusted
him. And that meant more to him than anything she'd
said or done to this point. The space in his chest filled
in until that emptiness he'd lived with since his soul had
been condemned to the Underworld—since before that,
really, when he'd been an Argonaut wondering what
kind of difference he was really making in the world—
was gone.

When was the last time someone had trusted him…
really trusted him? When was the last time someone
had been willing to put their life on the line for him? His
Argonaut brothers didn't count, because for them, protection wasn't even a thought. It was a duty. But this…this
was different. She could find anyone to teach her how to

protect herself. She didn't need him the way he needed her. And yet, she was offering. Looking up at him with those big eyes. Making him *feel* after all this time.

"Why would you want to do that?" he whispered.

"Do what?"

"Stay with me."

"Do you really have to ask?"

He swallowed hard, almost afraid to hear her answer. Somehow found the strength to nod.

"Because you didn't ask for what happened to you any more than I asked to be born between worlds. Because if somehow in the middle of this craziness we can each help the other get what we need, then it'll make all of this—what we've been through—worth it. And because…"

"Because what?" he asked when she bit her lip and her gaze dropped to his mouth.

She drew in a deep breath. "Because I care about you, Gryphon."

He couldn't breathe. She cared about him. Really cared. Not because she had to, not because some warped sense of duty or honor said she should. She cared simply because she could.

His heart beat so hard, he was sure she had to hear it. And when her gaze slowly lifted to his, he saw all the things he'd dreamed of seeing on her face for months. Desire. Hunger. The same damn yearning he felt in the depths of his soul.

"Gryphon?" she whispered.

"Yeah?" he managed, still unable to believe what was happening was real.

"What do you think? Do we have a deal?"

Chapter Sixteen

"WELL?" MAELEA ASKED.

As she held her hand out to him, the doubt he'd struggled with before melted away. Ignoring the offering, Gryphon slid his fingers into her luxurious hair instead. Then reveled at the spark of lust that flared in her eyes as he drew her mouth toward his. "I can think of a much better way to seal this deal, *sotiria*."

A tiny gasp slipped from her lips when his mouth closed over hers. But it turned to a groan that supercharged his blood as his tongue dipped into her mouth and he kissed her the way he'd wanted to kiss her ever since he'd awoken with the mother of all hard-ons.

Her arms closed around his neck, and she pressed those tantalizing breasts against his bare chest as she kissed him back. Her nipples hardened through the thin cotton dress, and he knew from the sensations rushing through his skin that she couldn't possibly be wearing a bra. His jeans grew even tighter as he wrapped his arms around her, as he tugged her hips toward his. As the heat of her pelvis seeped into his own.

He changed the angle of the kiss, nipped at her bottom lip. Shivered at the sweet, erotic taste of her on his tongue.

"Gryphon?" she said against his lips.

"Mm, yeah?" He fisted the cotton dress at her lower back, wanted so bad to lift her up on the counter, push inside her body, take her hard and fast. But he wasn't going to do that. Because this time he needed to make sure she enjoyed the experience. Wanted to remember each and every time she came apart. Which would be way more than once. Guaranteed.

Her hands slid to each side of his face. She kissed him. Eased back and licked her lips as she stared at his mouth. Kissed him again until he thought he'd go mad. Finally stopped long enough to say, "Are you hungry?"

"Starving." But not for food. Just for her.

"Me too. Take me upstairs."

Relief whipped through him like a tornado.

He lifted her around the waist. Her mouth closed over his and she wrapped her legs around him without his asking, stroked her tongue against his as his hands slid down to cup her ass.

He carried her out of the kitchen toward the stairs. His brain was nothing but mush. He had no idea how this had happened. How she'd gone from hating and fearing him to wanting him with the same desperation he wanted her, but he wasn't about to question the whys of it all. He only wanted more. More of her sweetness. More of her body. More of this fullness in the center of his chest that felt way too damn good.

He made it halfway up the rickety stairs before his bare feet slipped on the carpet runner. He was still wobbly, not totally healed from whatever had happened to him, but he didn't want to let go of her. Grunting against her mouth, he turned so he wouldn't drop her. Her spine hit the wall. She pulled back from his mouth for only a second, then kissed him harder, pushing her sex against his erection and tangling her tongue with his until he saw stars.

He groaned, hitched her over onto his thigh so he could balance her weight, and pulled her dress up the backs of her thighs. The hem was damp from the ocean. She smelled like jasmine and salt. She rocked against him, tore her mouth from his, nipped his ear, then offered her throat. He answered by kissing her jaw, the soft skin behind her ear, drawing her lobe into his mouth and suckling as his hands finally found skin.

"Oh, yes, Gryphon." She rocked against him again, the heat of her mound so close to his cock, he hurt.

He gripped the backs of her thighs, kneaded the tight muscles, slid his hands higher, and shuddered when he realized she wasn't wearing panties. "Maclea…"

She found his mouth again, dropped her hand from his shoulder, slid it down his bare chest. Her fingers brushed his lower abs, sending jolts of electricity through his pelvis. Then she pressed her hand right between her legs and gripped his cock through the denim of his jeans.

His legs buckled. He gasped. Tried to push her against the wall so she didn't go down with him. He hit the stairs on his back. Pain echoed up his spine, but it was fleeting. Because as soon as Maelea's feet touched the ground, she lowered herself and kissed him again. Hard, hot, needy kisses he felt everywhere. Then her mouth slid to his ear and she straddled him, rubbing her breasts against his chest, her sex against his erection, her hands anywhere she could reach.

He threaded his fingers in her long hair, drew her mouth back to his, lifted his hips to meet hers as he kissed her. As he tasted the wetness of her mouth, as he felt the fire from her body, everywhere. He didn't even care that the stairs were digging into his spine. She broke the kiss, trailed her mouth down his throat. Shivers rushed over his skin, and he groaned. Then nearly came when her tongue circled his nipple and she nipped at the very tip.

Pleasure arced from his nipples to his cock. His vision blurred. He needed to get her upstairs. Wanted her in that big white bed. Couldn't think of anything else. He tried to find the words to tell her to stop, but her mouth moved from his nipple down the center of his stomach. Her tongue circled his belly button. Then every muscle in his body tensed when she gripped the waistband of his jeans and popped the button, finally freeing him.

His cock sprang up, hard, hot, pulsing. She wrapped her small hand around his shaft, looked up at him with lust-filled eyes as she caressed him. Long, teasing strokes that made him burn with the fire of a thousand suns.

"I love the way you feel," she whispered. "I love the way you taste. I want to feel you come against my tongue."

Oh, holy gods. If she kept up that kind of talk, he was going to lose control. And he didn't want this to be about him. He wanted it to be about her. He wanted to feel *her* pleasure. Taste *her* release. Make *her* as crazy as she'd made him.

Before she could take him into her mouth, he gripped her arms, dragged her up his body, and kissed her again. She moaned into his mouth, stroked his length one more time before letting go and bracing her knees on each side of his body. He gripped the hem of her dress, pulled it up her thighs and around her waist. Her naked sex brushed his cock, and she shivered. It would be so easy to pull her hips down to his, slide inside her right here, take what he desperately craved. But not yet. First he wanted her dizzy with need.

He tugged the dress higher up her rib cage, over her breasts, and finally broke the kiss to pull it over her head.

She was completely naked. And so damn gorgeous. He dropped the dress on the stairs, took in every curve and angle and the way the morning light highlighted soft skin, the lines of her ribs, the gentle indent of her belly button. Her nipples hardened as he stared at her, and he watched her stomach muscles cave in and quiver, watched her eyes grow wide as he palmed her breast, as he brought her nipple to his lips and ran his tongue over the tight, stiff peak.

She braced her hands on the stairs on each side of his head, leaned forward to give him better access, moaned long and low as he suckled her. With his free hand, he pressed against her lower spine, pushing her higher up his chest as he trailed his lips down her stomach. She took the cue easily, lifted one knee, then the other, and moved her hands up the steps until she was finally straddling his face.

He could smell her. That sweet, tangy scent of her arousal. Remembered the unique aroma from their night on that boat. When he breathed hot against her sex, she moaned and pushed up so her torso was perpendicular to the stairs, then gripped the spindles of the banister on one side and braced her hand against the wall on the other. "Gryphon…"

He looked up, reveled in the way her eyes darkened with arousal as she watched him. "My turn to taste you."

He lifted his head and made one long, lingering sweep up her cleft with the flat of his tongue. She groaned.

Dropped her head back and shivered. He did it again, loving the way her whole body shook. Loving the way she tasted.

He licked her again and again, trailed his tongue up to her clit and circled. Gripping her ass with one hand, he brushed the finger of his other hand against her opening and was rewarded with a guttural sound from her throat as he pressed inside and stroked.

"Gryphon…I love that. Oh, gods, you're going to make me come."

Exactly what he wanted. All he wanted. He slid his finger out, pressed inside again with two, and closed his lips around her clit to suckle. She lifted her hips, lowered, rocked against his face while he drove her closer to the edge. He stroked deeper with his fingers, circled and swirled with his tongue. And when she tightened around him, when she cried out and he tasted her release on his tongue, his entire body spasmed, as if he were coming too.

He continued to lick her, to gently caress her, as the aftershocks rocked her body. As they echoed through his. He knew he hadn't ejaculated, but he felt her orgasm as strongly as if it were his own. In his skin. In his veins. In the very bottom of his soul.

She shuddered one last time, dropped forward to brace her hands against the stairs over his head. While she tried to catch her breath, he looked up her body. Noticed—in the morning sunlight spilling over them— faint white lines on the skin of her inner arms.

He'd seen those scars in that shower they'd taken together at the motel. But then he'd been too distracted to wonder about them.

Like he wasn't distracted now? *Skata*, he'd worry about them later. Right now he needed her.

He eased out from under her. His balls were so tight, he knew it wasn't going to take much. But he wasn't about to let go until he felt her come again. This time when he was deep inside her.

He slid his arms around her waist, lifted her off the steps. She was so light, he turned her easily. She gasped when his mouth found hers again, but then she was kissing him with urgency, wrapping her arms tight around his neck and her legs even tighter around his waist.

Gods, this was what he wanted. All he wanted. All he'd dreamed about since the first moment he saw her at the colony. Couldn't believe she was here with him now. He palmed her ass, rubbed the length of his shaft up and down her wetness as he carried her the rest of the way up the stairs. Even though it brought him within degrees of boiling, he luxuriated in the vibrations that echoed through his chest when she groaned.

He dropped her on her back on the bed. Eased away just long enough to push down his jeans and kick them off. She reached for him when he came back. Kissed his forehead, his cheek, his jaw, then finally found his lips again. Shivers rushed over his spine as he settled in the vee of her body. As his cock brushed her wetness and the tip barely pressed inside.

"Gryphon…" She dropped her head back against the mattress, tightened around him.

"*Sotiria*, look at me." He wanted to see her eyes when he filled her. Wanted to know what she was feeling.

She blinked several times, then finally opened those dark orbs to focus on him. And as he pressed into her, he watched those eyes widen, watched them haze over with pure lust. Watched her give herself to him.

No fear. No pain. Just trust.

Warmth unfurled inside his chest as he eased out, as he pushed into her again. As she trembled beneath him. And for the first time in his life, he felt completely whole. Not empty. Not the shell of the man he'd always yearned to be. Not the broken soul he'd been since the Underworld. With her, here, he felt…complete.

Emotions rolled through him. Ones he couldn't define and was afraid to try to. So many, the combined power slammed against his ribs. The connection he felt to her now…it was different from before. It wasn't bathed in darkness. It radiated light. A light that warmed him from the inside out. A light that shoved aside the voice until he couldn't hear it anymore. Until the buzz he'd lived with the last four months was gone too. Until there was nothing but the two of them, rocking together on this bed, losing themselves in each other over and over and over again.

"Gryphon." She lifted her head, kissed him, slid her hands down to his ass and pulled him closer.

He knew what she wanted. The same thing he wanted. He braced his hands against the mattress and drove into her deeper, kissed her harder, pushed her to the edge with every thrust. And when her climax rocketed through her, when she broke free of his mouth and groaned long and low, he didn't let up. He plunged harder, faster, drawing out every last spasm and shudder and ounce of pleasure from her that he could.

Only when he knew she was spent, that he'd given her ecstasy no one else ever had…then he finally let go. And shook from the sheer force of his orgasm as it exploded through every nerve ending in his body.

He was shaking when he finally collapsed against her. She wrapped her arms around his sweaty shoulders, her legs around his damp back. His head fell into the hollow between her shoulder and neck, and her warm breath washed over his temple as she pressed her lips against his forehead. Her heart raced next to his, and he knew he had to be crushing her, but he couldn't move. His body wasn't working yet. He thought that orgasm on the boat had been the best of his life? It hadn't even come close to this.

Aftershocks rippled across his body, sent electrical jolts through his muscles, keeping him immobilized.

Her chest rose against his as she drew in a deep breath. Lowered as she blew it out. "Gryphon?"

"Yeah." His brain was slowly coming back online, even if his limbs still weren't responding. "I…I'm hurting you. I'll move."

"No, it's not that."

He braced his hand against the mattress, started to push off her, but she tightened her pelvic muscles, stopping him.

He grew hard all over again.

She smiled against his temple. "Mm…that's what I was hoping for."

Arousal and desire and need rushed through him. A need more demanding than before, because now he knew how to sate it.

He eased up on his arm and looked down at her. She tightened her legs around his back and clenched her sex, drawing him back deep inside her, then smiled up at him with a wicked, sinful grin that made his blood run hot.

Her cheeks were flushed, her lips swollen from his kisses, her eyes filled with the same hunger coursing through him. But there was something else. Something more. Something…

His chest cinched tight as she shifted her weight and rolled him over, as she flexed her hips, as she claimed his mouth all over again.

He slid his hands down to her slim hips and helped her ride. Dark hair fell in a curtain around their faces. He brushed it back. Let her take control. And gave himself over to her the way she'd done to him.

It wasn't a mystery anymore. He knew what that connection he felt to her was. Could read it so easily, now that his mind was clear and the voice was gone. Would have known the first time he'd tasted her if it weren't for that damn interference.

She was his soul mate. Everything he'd ever wanted. The only person who could calm him, who could make him feel again. The woman he would eventually lose when she finally got her dream and was accepted into Olympus.

"Touch me, Gryphon," she whispered against his lips. "Anywhere. Everywhere. I just want you."

He was wrong. He did have a heart. A heart that had reawakened, all because of her. And after everything he'd been through, after all the torture and agony and bitter misery he'd endured, he knew none of it was going to compare with what would happen to that heart when he finally lost her for good.

Emotions closed his throat. All he could do was wrap

his arms around her, drag her as close as possible, and take what little she could give him now.

And give the same back to her tenfold.

~~~

The wind rustling the thin curtains through the open window brought Maelea's eyes open.

Darkness pressed in, shards of moonlight illuminating the room in ribbons of white. As waves lapped gently at the shore outside, she glanced down at Gryphon, draped over her, his head pillowed on her chest as he slept, his legs tangled with hers beneath the sheet, his arm wrapped around her waist as if he never wanted to let go.

Warmth spread through her chest when she remembered how he'd touched her with those big hands, how he'd pleasured her so completely, how he'd looked at her not with dead eyes, as he had before, but with emotion-filled pools of blue, as if she was the only thing in the world he needed.

She ran her fingers through his blond hair, traced the puckered edge of a scar near his temple that she hadn't noticed before. In sleep the lines on his face relaxed, the stress and anxiety he carried with him eased. He looked more childlike than warrior, more human than Argonaut. Cocooned here with him in this secluded house, in the quiet of the early summer evening, she wondered how she could *ever* have been afraid of him.

He was not at all what she'd thought. He wasn't cold and unfeeling. Wasn't the monster those females at the half-breed colony had talked about. Wasn't anything but lost and alone, just like her.

Her chest tightened, and she drew in a breath to ease the ache around her heart. She'd accepted her lot in life long ago. Knew that being alone was part of the hand she'd been dealt. She just hadn't expected to find someone who shared her feelings, who understood her, now of all times, when she was finally ready to make her move to Olympus.

Carefully, so as not to wake him, she eased out from under his weight. He grunted, shifted to his belly, tucked the pillow under his head, then resumed the steady draw and push of air as he relaxed back into sleep.

He was really gorgeous, asleep in her bed, looking so big and masculine against the feminine furnishings. The sheet lay angled low across his muscular back, the white of the cotton such a stark contrast to his olive skin and thick blond hair. In the moonlight the Argonaut markings on his forearms stood out, reminding her he was more than just a man who'd brought her to four—no, make that five—blistering climaxes in the last few hours. He was a hero, regardless of what had been done to him in the Underworld. One of Zeus's appointed heroes.

Zeus.

There was a mood buster, if ever she thought of one. Her father. The King of the Gods. The male who'd sired her but had done nothing to help her over the long years of her life. The god who hadn't once even acknowledged her presence. She knew why—because doing so would break the agreement he'd made with Hades, thereby ensuring Hades wouldn't retaliate against her mother's treachery—but it still stung. And now she was trying to get to his realm. Trying to prove herself to someone who obviously didn't care about her. Was she completely insane or just slightly fucked in the head?

Scowling at her obvious stupidity, she moved into the closet, quietly pulled out her thin robe, belted it around her waist, and headed for the stairs.

It was close to midnight, but she was wide awake. They'd spent all day in bed, pleasuring each other, drifting off to sleep only to reawaken and start all over again. And while her body was exhausted and she knew she should sleep, she couldn't, because her mind was racing. Night was her time. When she felt most alive. She supposed she had her mother to thank for that too.

She grabbed a blanket from the back of the couch, pushed the screen door open, and wrapped the cotton around her shoulders. Night, even in summer, was cool on Vancouver Island, but not freezing. As she headed down the rickety steps, she stared out at the water glistening like a million diamonds under the light of the moon and drew in a deep breath that immediately calmed her.

She loved the ocean. Loved the water. The gentle lap of waves against shore always relaxed her, especially in times of confusion, of which this definitely was one. She found a spot midway to the water and dropped down in the sand as she tugged the blanket tighter to her chest, the silky granules like heaven beneath her bare feet.

For the first time in forever she felt torn. She'd finally decided what she wanted, was finally brave enough to go after her goal, and now had found…what? Her soul mate? She frowned. She didn't believe in soul mates, but she did believe in love.

Was that what she was feeling for Gryphon? So soon?

That idea was even more ludicrous than her earlier ones. No, she wasn't convinced this was love, but she found it damn inconvenient that after all these years of being alone, she'd finally found someone who needed her to fill a void no one else had been able to fill. Not a single person—mortal or immortal—had ever needed her like that. Not even the few men she'd loved and lost along the way.

She wasn't delusional. She knew Gryphon hadn't made her any kind of promise. He hadn't said much of anything, for that matter. He'd been too busy making love to her. But she knew he felt something for her. Could see it in his eyes every time he touched her. This connection they shared was deeper than the darkness that resided inside each of them. The question was, if she had the choice to stay with him or go to Olympus, which would she choose?

"What are you doing out here in the dark?"

She jumped at Gryphon's voice so close behind her, whipped around to look up at him. He was wearing nothing but those low-slung faded jeans, his hands shoved into the front pockets, his hair mussed, his eyes sleepy. Moonlight glinted off his bare chest, highlighted his strong stomach muscles, the thin red lines of his wound, which was already healing, and the dusting of hair that led from his belly button and disappeared beneath the waistband of his jeans.

A wicked burst of heat unfurled in her stomach as she stared at him. A heat that told her the question she'd posed to herself was not one she could answer when he was anywhere close. "I couldn't sleep."

He stared at her for several seconds as if she might

jump out and bite him, then finally nodded her way. "You got room in there for one more?"

She smiled and opened the blanket.

He eased in behind her, angled one leg on each side of her body, pulled her back tight to his chest so she leaned against him, then wrapped the blanket around his back so it cocooned them both. Then he slid his arms around her waist as she closed the blanket again at her front.

His breath ran down her neck, heated her skin. His arms around her were snug and secure, and when the stirrings of an erection pressed against her lower back, she remembered all the erotic, amazing things he'd done to her in that bed.

Her eyes slid closed. She drew in a breath, let it out slowly. Told herself to enjoy this, just being close to him. Everything else…her future, his future, what would happen in a few days…none of it mattered.

"You like the night, don't you?" His voice was gruff near her ear. And so damn sexy, a shiver of arousal rushed through her when she remembered that voice whispering to her as they'd made love. "I used to watch you from my window. You always went out at night."

"You watched me?"

"Does that creep you out?"

She looked out over the sparkling water. It used to— when she was at the colony and she'd look up to see him in the window. But now…now it electrified her. "No."

"I thought you were beautiful."

Her pulse picked up speed. "You did?"

His thumb brushed the underside of her breast. "I did. I do. Your skin glows under the moonlight. Did you know that? As white as snow. Every hour in that room alone…" His throat worked against her as he swallowed. "It was dark and depressing. Seeing you outside at night…it gave me something bright to look forward to."

Her heart bumped. She didn't know what to say. Holding the blanket closed with one hand, she slid the other down to his at her waist and closed her fingers around it.

He nuzzled her neck. "That's how you found the entrance to the tunnels, isn't it? When you were out exploring at night?"

She smiled, because watching her was obviously how he'd known where to intercept her. "It is. Orpheus wasn't going to let me leave any other way."

"Orpheus worries about you. Now I understand why. He feels guilty for exposing you to Hades so he could rescue me."

She ran her fingers along the backs of his and remembered her perfect house on Lake Washington. Remembered those hellhounds destroying it. "I know he does. I was upset when he first brought me to the colony, but when I found out he'd come after me to save you… well, not much you can be angry about there anymore, you know?"

"I'd still have been angry. Orpheus has always done shit without thinking of the consequences."

She chuckled, because that sounded a lot like Orpheus to her. But she also knew what Orpheus had done had been for good, not selfishness. "He loves you, you know."

Gryphon rested his chin against her shoulder. "I know."

They sat for several minutes in silence, just looking out over the water, his warm breath heating her body, his fingers against her waist slowly stoking the fire in her blood.

"I've been meaning to ask you something," he said into her hair.

"What?"

"How did we get from that boat here? I mean, I know you said we drove, but…how the hell did you get me off that boat? I must have passed out, because I don't remember anything except…"

She smiled. "Except sex?"

His lips curled against her neck. "Yeah. That. Really hot sex."

Desire slid back through her veins. She shouldn't be turned on again, not after the numerous times they'd already ravaged each other, but she was. "Well, when your legs buckled and you fell and hit your head then passed out, I knew I wasn't going to be able to get you off that boat before someone found us, so I untied it from the dock and we sailed across to the other side of the lake."

"So that's how I got that bump on my head."

She cringed. "Yeah. Sorry. I tried to stop you from falling, but you're a little heavier than I am. I couldn't hold you up."

He chuckled. "So you stole someone's boat."

"I didn't *steal* it. I *borrowed* it. And I'll have you know I left it tied to a dock on the other side of the lake in pristine condition along with a note apologizing for the owner's inconvenience. Then I stole a car."

His laughter echoed all through her torso, and she

found herself smiling all over again. "My woman, the thief. No wonder Orpheus likes you."

Her pulse sped up at his words. *My woman*. She wasn't his woman. Didn't think she ever could be. But hearing him say it… It touched her in a way she hadn't expected.

He hugged her tighter as they sat in the sand looking out over the moonlit water. "Why aren't you with someone? Why are you alone? Why hasn't some male snatched you up already?"

The questions caught her off guard. "You know why I'm alone."

"Because you're hiding from Hades? You can hide *with* someone. You don't have to hide alone."

"I haven't always been alone. When I was younger— much younger—I didn't particularly like being alone. But I learned early on that relationships with humans lead to nothing but heartbreak. Their lives only last a maximum of a hundred years, and mine…well, my existence is ageless, so long as I don't do anything to draw attention and get myself killed."

"Were you ever in love?" he asked quietly.

She thought back. Remembered the joy. And the pain. The heartbreak lingered longer than the love. Funny that now it was all she could really remember. "Three times. The first was a Spartan warrior. That was dumb. He died before we'd really even gotten to know each other. But he was kind and gentle, and back then I had delusions that a warrior could take on a god. I was wrong."

When he didn't say anything, she went on. "The second was many years later. I was older, thought I was wiser and more prepared. He was a gladiator who'd won his freedom, and he was as sick of war and fighting as

I was. We had a small house on the coast in Spain. He only lived to be about sixty. Died in his sleep."

Theodosius. That had been his name. His gentle face flashed in her mind. It had been so long ago, it was as if all the love and pain and heartbreak had happened to someone else.

She drew in a breath. "And the last…well, it was over a thousand years later. He was a Spanish explorer. Let me sail with him. That's how I ended up in the new world. Liked it so much I stayed. But he died of malaria." Her heart pinched at the memory. "Since then… Well, since then, let's just say it's just been easier to keep to myself. Safer, too."

His arms tightened around her. "What about half-breeds? Their life spans are longer. As long as Argoleans. And there are Titans living in the human realm."

She nearly laughed. "Half-breeds? Are you serious? The ones at the colony looked at me like I'm a freak. No, someone who knows Hades's fury definitely wouldn't want to be with me. As for Titans…that would be like condemning myself to this realm forever. If Zeus ever found out I shacked up with a Titan, he'd make sure I never got to Olympus."

"I guess I can see your point. Still…you shouldn't have to be alone."

Just the fact he cared touched her heart. "I'm used to being alone, Gryphon. I've been alone a long time. Love is nice, but it's fleeting. I know for a fact it doesn't last. Heartache and pain? They last. They're the only things that endure."

He turned her hand over. Pushed her sleeve up and ran his fingers down the scars on the inside of her forearm. "And what about these?" he asked quietly. "Do these last?"

She drew in a breath and held it. She knew he'd seen her scars, but part of her had hoped he wouldn't bring it up. She knew now she'd been foolish to think that.

"They…" Unease rippled through her. "No one hurt me, if that's what you're thinking."

He ran his fingers over the thin lines again, and she fought the urge to pull her arm back. "Then how did you get them?"

"I…I went through a phase."

"A phase?"

She cringed. "Yeah. A phase. It was stupid. But after Theodosius died—he was the gladiator—I wasn't coping well. I can't explain what it's like to be ageless to you. To watch the ones you love die. To remain when they're gone. I was alive, but I felt dead inside. And then one day I accidentally cut myself in the kitchen, and for the first time in months I felt something. It was pain, but even pain was better than feeling dead. And it was freeing." She looked down at her feet in the sand, knew he'd never understand this. "So yeah, I went through a phase. Every time I felt dead inside, the pain reminded me I was still alive."

"So you still…are you still in that phase?"

"No," she said on a breath. "It was hundreds of years ago. Anytime I feel dead inside now, I just look at the scars and I remember. It's enough. Learning to keep to myself helped tremendously, too. If you don't put yourself out there, you can't get hurt." She tried to add some humor into her voice, because this was getting way too serious. "Plus I was never very good with a knife—as you know from seeing me wield a weapon. I was too afraid I was going to kill myself to do any real damage."

He didn't chuckle. In fact, he was silent so long, she wondered if *she'd* creeped *him* out. Then he said, "When Zander lost Callia, it nearly killed him. He lost the will to live. I can't imagine what that was like for you, not once, but three times."

Surprise registered. That he understood. And his reaction tightened her heart. "It was lonely." And so very painful. So painful she didn't want to repeat it if she didn't have to. But something told her she was already on the road to love and might already be too far gone to stop it. She swallowed hard. Tried not to think of that. "But I adapted. Now I have these ugly scars to remind me about the price of love."

His fingertips brushed her scars again, and warmth curled through her skin under his touch, shot straight to her heart. "They're not ugly. Nothing about you is ugly. And not all love has to be painful."

Her chest pinched down tight. Gods, if he kept up the sympathy and understanding, she'd fall head over heels in love with him before the moon set.

Water lapped at the shore as they sat in silence. She didn't know what to say. And then a thought occurred. One she knew she probably shouldn't ask but suddenly needed to know. "Have you ever been in love?"

He was silent so long, she knew the answer had to be yes. Knew he was likely thinking of some other female right now. And the knowledge of that…it depressed her.

"No," he finally said. "Never before."

Her pulse picked up speed. And if it was possible for her heart to skip, it did. She tried not to read too much into his words. Knew it would only lead her to more pain and heartache down the line, but she couldn't stop herself.

Never before.

She had been in love. She hadn't lied. But it had never been like this. Never as fast. Never as all-consuming. Never as deep. And now she knew why. Because none of the humans she'd loved had been Gryphon. None had understood her the way he did. None could.

Her heart beat hard against her ribs. Would she stay with him if she could? Would she sacrifice Olympus for him? She didn't know. She only knew that, right now, she wanted him. Wanted him more than she'd ever wanted anyone else, ever before.

He pressed his lips to her neck, then to her ear. And shivers of delight rushed over her skin wherever he touched. "I'm getting cold out here," he whispered.

"You are?"

"Mm-hmm. Was wondering if maybe you'd like to take me inside and warm me up. I saw a claw-foot tub in your bathroom."

Relief and desire rushed through her. He still wanted her. She leaned her head back against his shoulder, offering more of her neck. "You did, huh?"

"Big enough for two, I'm almost certain."

Heat spread between her legs when he nipped at her earlobe. "It's only ever held one before."

His hands slid up her rib cage to cup her breasts. And shards of arousal ricocheted through her veins at the intimate touch. She tipped her head to the side and glanced over her shoulder so she could see his tantalizing mouth.

"I'm glad to hear that," he said with a wicked turn of

his lips. "Because I don't want to think about anyone else doing to you what I'm about to do to you in that tub."

Fire exploded in her veins.

Neither did she. She just wanted to think about him. She wrapped her hand around the back of his head and dragged his mouth toward hers.

Chapter Seventeen

TITUS WAITED FOR TRAFFIC TO CLEAR ON THE SMALL Coeur d'Alene street, then crossed the road and ducked into the Internet café. The few humans scattered throughout the space cast curious expressions his way, but he ignored them and moved toward Skyla and Orpheus at a table in the back.

They both looked up from the computer they were using. "Well?" Skyla asked.

Titus pulled up a chair at the Siren's side and looked past her to Orpheus, whose thoughts screamed, *What the hell are you waiting for?* "Got it. It's an Idaho license plate."

He recited the numbers for Skyla, who quickly typed them into the search engine for the Idaho Division of Motor Vehicles, which she'd hacked into. After tracking the truck Gryphon had stolen in Montana here to Coeur d'Alene, they'd run into a wall. Titus had spent all morning hanging out around the police station, trying to pick up any tidbits about the stolen vehicle, and had finally struck gold.

"The truck was found abandoned on a side road near the water. A sailboat was missing. Cops found it all the way across the lake."

"Are we sure it was them?" Orpheus asked.

Titus looked around the café, then lowered his voice. "There was no damage to the inside of the boat, but cops found a bloody towel onboard. Blood of an 'unknown origin.' Matched bloody rags they found in the truck. It was all the talk—and thoughts—at the station."

"That's Gryphon," Orpheus breathed.

Titus agreed. And no damage meant it couldn't be daemon blood. Argonaut blood, while partly human, contained unidentified alleles, and couldn't easily be tracked.

"Here it is," Skyla said. "Black, 2010 Nissan Pathfinder."

"It was stolen from the marina where the boat ended up," Titus told them while Skyla jotted the info on a piece of paper. "And get this. There was a note left on board. Apologizing for borrowing the vessel."

"Oh, that's so Maelea," Skyla said as she looked up. "Which is good," she added, glancing toward Orpheus. "It means she's still alive."

"For now," Orpheus said with a frown.

Titus rubbed his forehead. "This would be a helluva lot easier if Gryphon were wearing his damn Argos medallion. We could track *that*." He gestured toward the computer screen. "We've got the make and model but no fucking clue which way they're headed."

Skyla leaned back, crossed her arms, and stared at the computer screen. "I say we focus on Maelea. If she's still alive—which she is," she added, glancing toward Orpheus again—"then my guess is, Gryphon's likely keeping her alive for a reason. She lived in the Seattle area for over a hundred years, right? Orpheus, you saw that huge house she had. The woman has money. Hell, she's been alive for three thousand years, she's probably got money coming out her ears. It's highly likely she's got more residences than just that one."

"You're thinking Gryphon might have forced her to take him to one of her other properties?" Orpheus asked.

"I'm thinking he needs a place to regroup. To figure out what to do next. He can't do that when they're on the run. They're moving west. Toward where Maelea used to live. It's worth checking, isn't it?"

Thoughts of the redhead who'd been snooping in Maelea's room at the colony pinged around in Titus's brain, but this time the thoughts weren't personal. Or so he told himself.

He pulled out his phone and dialed.

"What's the story?" Theron said as soon as he answered the call.

"The redhead," Titus said, looking at Orpheus and Skyla, who were watching him with curious eyes. "She was looking for Maelea. I need to talk to her. She might be able to help us figure out where Gryphon is taking Maelea."

"I let her go."

Disbelief and panic rushed through Titus before he could stop it. "You *what*?"

"She wasn't here for Maelea," Theron said matter-of-factly. "She was here for something else. Something we don't need or want to get involved with. Where are you? What's the line on Gryphon?"

Titus's vision swam. Theron had let the female go. The first person ever whose thoughts he couldn't hear. Though he knew she was someone he was better off leaving alone, he couldn't stop the panic rushing through him.

Where would she go? How will I find her? Why the hell did Theron let her go?

"Titus?" Theron said in his ear. "Where are you?"

His mind snapped back to the present. "Um…Idaho."

"You've got a lead on Gryphon?"

"Yeah, we think so. Maybe." Holy hell. What was he going to do about the redhead?

"Is Maelea still with him?"

He needed to pull his head out of his ass. He needed to focus on the here and now. He swiped a hand across his forehead. "It seems that way."

"Tell me where you are and I'll have Nick send men your way to help you search. There's been a rash of daemon activity in the area, and the rest of the Argonauts are dealing with that."

No way. Titus didn't want Nick's men in on their search. Not ever, if he could help it. Nick was still out for blood, after what Gryphon had done. "I'll call when we know more."

"Titu—"

He clicked off the phone and shoved it into his pocket before Theron could tell him what the hell to do.

"Who's this redhead?" Skyla asked.

"A female who showed up at the colony looking for Maelea. Said she was a friend."

"Maelea doesn't have any friends," Orpheus pointed out, his brow drawn low.

"Yeah, that was my thought," Titus told him. "But she wanted to find her. For whatever reason. I didn't get much out of her except that Maelea has property both in Seattle and up on Vancouver Island."

Excitement flared in Skyla's green eyes. "Where on Vancouver Island?"

"I don't know," Titus answered.

Skyla turned to the computer and pulled up a new search screen. "This might be our first break."

Titus wasn't so sure. Vancouver Island was a big place, and the redhead—Natasa—could just have been fucking with him to get him to back off.

The redhead…shit. He had to stop thinking of her. She was not his priority now. Gryphon was.

Or so he told himself.

Pushing aside thoughts of her that would only get him into trouble, he looked toward the computer screen. And prayed they found Gryphon before the jackass did something they couldn't undo. "Let's hope you're right, Siren. Because if you're wrong, the time we waste looking could just mean Maelea's life."

——◆——

Atalanta paced the length of her hall. Outside, snow swirled and spit against the side of her ancient fortress, but she barely cared. The cold lived inside her. It was the only thing of comfort to her these days.

"This should not take so fucking long! I'm losing my patience with all of you."

The archdaemon at the front of the pack—Stolas—bowed. "My queen, we will find him."

"When?" she asked, stalking down the three steps to glare into his hideous eyes. "He's killed all the daemons you've sent after him."

"He'll make a mistake."

She ground her teeth, fought the urge to yank the sword from his scabbard and decapitate the bastard. Killing him wouldn't help her find her *doulas*. If she didn't get Gryphon soon, they'd run out of time to find the Orb before the six months Krónos had given her was up.

"Send more daemons." She grasped the sides of

her long, red robe and climbed back up to her throne, refusing to believe even for a second that she wouldn't succeed. She would not go back to the Underworld. Not to be his slave. She was a god. And she was destined to command all. "Gather hybrids to join in the search."

"My queen," Stolas said, "the hybrids are unpredictable."

She turned to glare at him. "Then make them predictable. I will have your head if you fail me here, Stolas." Fear filled his eyes. She averted her gaze and looked out over the ten daemons behind him. "I will have all your heads."

"My queen," a daemon to the back of the pack said. "There is one avenue we have not investigated."

Atalanta's eyes narrowed. "Who said that? Come forward."

The pack parted, and a daemon dressed in a long black trench coat moved to stand next to Stolas. One whose body and eyes looked…vaguely familiar.

"What is your name?" Atalanta asked. Where had she seen him before? And who had he been in the human realm before trading his soul for a second shot at life in the Fields of Asphodel?

"Naberus, my queen."

Naberus…the name meant nothing to her. But then, daemons rarely took on names that resembled those they'd used as humans.

She didn't miss the glare Stolas sent the newcomer. Or the smug expression Naberus shot back. He was challenging the archdaemon, and they both knew it. Something very few daemons even thought about, let alone attempted.

"Tell me what you know," Atalanta said, shaking

off the strange feeling that she knew this daemon from somewhere. "Or I'll have your head now."

"My queen," Naberus said, "the Argonaut travels with a female."

Atalanta cut her gaze to Stolas, whose eyes flew wide. "Why did you not tell me this?"

"I...I did not know for certain. I—"

"It is your job to know all." She looked back to Naberus. "Who is she?"

Naberus shot a wicked smile Stolas's way, then looked toward Atalanta. "Zeus and Persephone's daughter. She goes by Maelea. The one who led the Argonauts to the Underworld to free your *doulas* in the first place. Sources confirmed this to me."

Fire rushed through Atalanta's veins. "What sources?"

Naberus shrugged. "Hellhounds I tortured."

Fury raged through Atalanta. She flew down the steps.

Naberus didn't move, but Stolas lurched backward and held up his hands. "My queen! Hellhounds lie. We're not sure it's her."

She grasped his sword by the hilt, pulled it out of its scabbard, and stabbed him straight through the heart.

His eyes flew wide. He dropped to his knees at her feet. She pulled the blade free, arced back and decapitated the useless beast. His body slumped forward.

Looking toward Naberus, Atalanta barked, "Kneel. Quickly."

Naberus did so without even an inkling of fear.

Atalanta tapped the sword against his shoulder and uttered the magical words that infused him with her powers as archdaemon. When she was done and he pushed to his feet, he'd grown at least a foot. And something in the way his glowing green eyes sparked hit her square in the center of the chest.

Slowly, still trying to figure out who he was, she handed him the sword. "Find her and you will find my *doulas*. And do it quickly. Or you will be my next victim."

Naberus bowed with a sinister grin. "As you wish, my queen."

——*****——

The door slamming brought Max's eyes open.

As footsteps echoed down the hall, he lay on his stomach in the dark of his bedroom, listening carefully. He'd been home in Tiyrns for several days. His dad came and went, as always, and his mom...she was freaking out, worried about what was happening in the human realm at the Misos colony. But because of him, she wouldn't go back. Because his dad had ordered her to take him home.

Anger simmered under his skin. He wasn't a baby. He didn't need to be protected like one.

The door to his room creaked open. He slammed his eyes shut and lay still as stone, trying not to move a single muscle so they wouldn't know he was awake.

"Zander," his mother whispered from the doorway. "He's asleep."

Silence met his ears. He knew his parents were watching him. They were always watching, checking up on him. They didn't trust him.

"Come on," Callia whispered. "Let him sleep."

The door creaked closed, but when he peeked, he saw they hadn't closed it all the way. Light from the hall spilled into the room from a crack.

"Any luck finding Gryphon?" his mother asked in a low voice.

They'd moved away from his door, but Max could still hear them. And because they were talking about Gryphon, he listened closer.

"No, none," Zander answered in a frustrated voice. "It's like they all but disappeared."

"He'll turn up," Callia said softly.

"When?" Zander asked. "He's not stable, *thea*. Whatever the hell they did to him in the Underworld changed him. Every time I think about Max being there…"

"Max is fine," his mother said.

"He's not fine," Zander tossed back, louder this time. When Callia shushed him, he lowered his voice. "He's not fine and we both know it. Every day he grows more defiant. I can't even talk to him anymore, and he's angry all the time."

"He's struggling, Zander. We knew the transition wouldn't be easy. We have to give him time."

"And what if time doesn't work? What if he gets worse? What if he ends up like Gryphon?"

"He won't."

"How do you know?"

"Because I do," his mother said firmly. "Don't even think that, Zander."

Silence echoed like a hollow vat of nothingness from the hall, and Max's heart rate shot up as he strained to listen.

"I never wanted this," his father finally whispered from the hallway. "It's not supposed to be this way."

"I know," his mother whispered back. Cloth rustled, and even without seeing them, Max knew they were hugging. His dad was always touching his mom one way or another. But not him. The only time his dad touched him was when he was mad, the way he'd been when he found Max in the tunnels of the colony. "We'll make it work, Zander. Believe in that. Believe in us."

A heavy sigh, followed by footsteps echoing down the hall, told Max his parents had finally moved away.

But in the darkness of his room, his heart rate didn't slow. *I never wanted this*. The words echoed in his head. Along with the ones his father hadn't said: *I never wanted him*.

He swallowed hard and forced back the tears. His father thought Gryphon had become a monster because of his time in the Underworld. And now he was beginning to question whether Max was one too. He wanted to prove to his parents he wasn't, but he didn't know how.

He didn't know anything except that he suddenly felt more alone than he ever had, even when he was in the Underworld. Because then, at least, he'd had the fantasy of a family who loved him to keep him company. Now he knew he didn't even have that.

"*Delator* is not a word." Gryphon stared down at the Scrabble board on the coffee table between him and Maelea, then shot her a look. Seated on the floor with the fireplace roaring at her back, she flicked him a *what on earth do you mean?* expression that was so damn cute, he itched to wipe it from her mouth with his own.

It was hard to believe this was the same female who'd glared and scowled and plotted her escape every moment he wasn't yelling at her. But things were different now.

Ever since they arrived here a week ago, ever since that morning when he awoke and realized she cared for him, there'd been no more fear, no more animosity, no more anger. In its place there was nothing but heat and desire and need. A whole lot of need neither of them seemed to be able to sate.

"Yes, it is," she said with a sexy little pout. "It's Latin. A delator is an informant. All the Roman emperors used them." She reached for letters from the table, flipped them over, and set them on her stand. "I met a few. Commodus had a special fondness for them. Used them to spy on his senators. Not a nice man, that Commodus. But he didn't even totally trust his delators, and with good reason. They were a slimy, bloodsucking, greedy group of scum. That's forty-three points for me."

He stared at her in bewilderment from the couch, where he sat with his elbows braced on his knees.

When he didn't write down her score, she looked up. "What?"

"Latin? Uh-uh. No way. I'm officially protesting this game. We pick one language and one era. Period. And we stick to it. I'm getting my ass kicked here because I'm nowhere near as worldly as you. And what the hell were you doing, hanging out with delators and emperors in the first place?"

She smiled. Really smiled. And was so damn beautiful, staring at him with that stupid grin, his chest constricted until it was tight as a drum. "Why are you grinning at me like that?"

"Because you're gorgeous when you look at me like I'm nuts."

"You've handed me my ass on a Scrabble board, *sotiria*. I don't think you're nuts. I think you're smart as shit."

She laughed but kept right on smiling up at him. A warm, wide grin that made one corner of his lips curl all on its own. "What now?"

"Nothing. It's just…your face has totally changed in the last week."

He brushed a hand against his jaw. "It's too scruffy for you, isn't it? I'll shave—"

"Not that, silly," she said. "I like the scruff. It's sexy. No, I mean your face. It's different. A week ago your eyes were still haunted. When I'd look at you, I could see the weight of the Underworld on your soul and everything you'd been through. Now, it's barely there."

His smile faded, and he looked away. Memories of his torture in Hades's realm rushed back through his mind, sent sickness brewing in his stomach. And shame. A truckload of shame over what he'd done. What had been done to him. What Maelea would think if she even had an inkling of what had gone down in Tartarus when he was there.

"Hey. Don't." Her soft voice somewhere close brought him around. That and her hand, pressing gently against his shoulder. Soft. Warm. Alive. He eased back while she climbed onto his lap and took his face in her hands, stroking her thumbs over his cheeks, reminding him he was alive too. "Don't go back there. I didn't mean to bring it up for you again. I was just pointing out how different you are. How relaxed. That's a good thing, Gryphon, not a bad one."

He closed his eyes, forced back the bile threatening its way up. "Maelea—"

She leaned in and brushed her lips against his. Lips that shot sparks of heat and desire straight to his belly, warming him from the outside in. Lips he could lose himself in. Lips that were keeping him here, tucked into this isolated house in this tiny corner of the world where no one could find them. Where daemons and hellhounds and gods and the Underworld didn't exist. Where he was losing his desire for vengeance with every passing day.

He wrapped his arms around her back, opened when she slid her tongue along his bottom lip, and let her dip inside his mouth to tempt and tease in that way he'd learned she liked to do. She tasted like the wine she'd been sipping as they played Scrabble, like the sin he knew he could coax out of her with just a little push. She was more than his soul mate, he'd realized over the last few days. She was funny and smart and so damn sexy, she took his breath away. Everything he'd been looking for his whole life. Everything he hadn't realized he was missing. And when he was with her, he barely heard that buzz anymore. Barely heard Atalanta's voice. Never heard either when he was inside her, which was his very favorite place to be.

She drew back from his mouth, stared into his eyes. And in her dark, onyx irises, he saw all the same emotions he felt reflected back at him. Who would ever have thought it? She, the daughter of the King of the Gods, and he a broken, tortured soul.

He tucked a lock of hair behind her ear. Remembered how she'd told him she'd been in love before. How she'd said love wasn't worth it because it didn't last. He knew regardless of who he was and what he'd been through, she cared for him. Even if he couldn't see it, he could feel it. Would she be willing to take another chance if she knew she could be happy for more than fifty or sixty years? Would she put off her dream of Olympus to stay here with him?

His stomach churned, this time with nerves, not sickness, and as she slid down on his lap to rest her head against his chest, he stared into the fire and stroked her hair. She was warm against him. So soft. And they fit together as if they were made for each other. But then that was the point of the whole soul-mate thing, wasn't it? He didn't have a lot to offer her, but he knew he could keep her safe. And he had at least another five hundred years in him, assuming he lived through his face-off with Atalanta. If Maelea knew there was a chance they could be together that long, that he could protect her from Hades, would she be willing to try again?

"Why do you want to go to Olympus?" he asked while they sat staring into the fire, the Scrabble game they'd been playing all but forgotten.

"You know why," she said against his chest.

He ran his hand down her hair, loved how silky soft it was against his fingers. "So you can be safe from Hades."

"It's more than that. Olympus is home for me."

"How do you know it's home if you've never been there before?"

"Because it's where my father is. Where my mother is half the year. Where the other immortals live and where there's no death. I'm so tired of death and dying."

His hope faded. He couldn't give her eternity. Not like the gods. He couldn't even give her half that. And with him there would eventually be death. "You said you had to prove your allegiance to get there. How are you planning to do that?"

She pushed against his chest, eased off his lap, and sat on the couch at his side. He tried not to be disappointed she wasn't touching him anymore. Couldn't help it. "Well, that's where the training I asked you to teach me comes in. Which, by the way," she added with a frown as she glanced over her shoulder, "you haven't done a very good job with."

No, he hadn't. Fighting and defensive techniques were the last things on his mind. Every time Maelea had suggested they go outside to the beach and he show her some moves, he'd distracted her with his hands and mouth and body until they'd both been too worn out to do anything but drop into each other's arms and sleep.

"I thought you needed to know how to protect yourself from Hades," he said with narrowed eyes. "How will that help you get to Olympus?"

She wrung her hands together in her lap. Wouldn't meet his eyes. "Remember I told you Orpheus came looking for me? The truth is, I was looking for him. Or, well, someone like him. See, the only way to prove myself to the gods is to turn my back on my Underworld heritage. By killing someone powerful and important to Hades."

"Killing someone," he said, watching her carefully. "You, who doesn't even like to kill spiders." While he despised spiders with a passion, thanks to his time in the Underworld, he'd watched her rescue two from the bottom of his boot before he could smash them, and release them outside. She hated death. And even though she hadn't had much of a choice, he knew she was still wrestling with the fact she'd had to kill those daemons back at that motel. Daemons she'd killed to save him.

"I know, right?" A weak smile ran across her face before she looked back at the fire. "Which is part of the reason I've put it off so long."

She drew in a breath, let it out. "For a while now I've been keeping my eye out for the dark one. You know, just waiting to see if I ever even had the opportunity, not that I had to follow through on it or anything. When I first saw Orpheus in that concert crowd, I thought he might be the one. His daemon was very strong then. He radiated darkness. And I thought if I killed him, I might finally prove my worth. But things didn't turn out like I'd planned, and by the time he came to find me, his daemon had already faded. Then everything happened with Hades's hellhounds finding me and Orpheus and Skyla taking me to the colony and then you coming back from the Underworld, and...and I realized I'd been thinking too small. I finally figured out who I have to kill to get home."

His lungs squeezed tight. Before she even said the words, he knew she'd realized the darkness in him was so strong, he was the one she had to kill to prove her allegiance to the gods.

She ran her hands through her hair, pushed off the couch. "The reason I asked you to teach me to fight is because I know I'm not ready yet. I still need time to develop whatever gift is inside me. So before I go and face Hades's son, I need to make sure I'm not only stronger but way more skilled."

She picked up their empty wine glasses from the coffee table and turned for the kitchen. "I'm going to open another bottle. Do you want a glass?"

The air whooshed out of his lungs. Was replaced with a fear that shot straight down his spine. *Hades's son?* That's who she was planning to try to kill? Zagreus? The prince of the fucking Underworld?

Slowly, because his legs were shaking, he pushed from the couch and turned to look at her standing at the island, pouring more wine into both their glasses. "Um, no."

She looked at the label on the bottle. "Did you not like this year?"

He raked a hand through his hair. She was talking about the wine when he felt as if he'd just been sucker punched in the gut. "Um, no, you're not going after Zagreus."

Her hand stilled. Her eyes lifted to his. "What?"

"You're not going after Zagreus," he said again. "*I* wouldn't even go after Zagreus, and I think most of the Argonauts would agree I'm a fucking loose cannon right now. None of the Argonauts would dare go after him. We leave him the hell alone."

She frowned, poured more wine in a dismissive move, as if he were talking out his left earlobe or something.

He took a step closer to the kitchen, his chest vibrating with worry and fear and panic. "Maelea, did you hear me?"

"I'm not going after him *now*, Gryphon. I already told you I'm not ready yet."

"Not ever," he said with conviction.

She looked up again. Except this time her eyes weren't warm and soft, as they'd been on the couch. They were cold and hard. And very, very determined. "What does it matter what I do in the future? By the time I'm ready to confront Zagreus, you won't be here anymore."

"What does that mean?"

"It means, this," she waved her hand around. "Us, here, this is only temporary. I know you've been enjoying relaxing and having a little downtime here with me this last week, where no one can find us, and that you needed that, after everything you've been through, but as soon as you decide to go after whatever it is you were planning to go after before I brought you here, you're not going to care where I am or what I'm doing."

"Maybe I've changed my mind."

"About what?"

"About what I do after I confront Atalanta."

Her hand shook as she set the bottle of wine on the counter. "Atalanta? That's who you're trying to find?"

The darkness inside him vibrated with revenge. "Not find. I could find her anytime I want. All I have to do is get away from you and listen to her fucking voice calling me, and it'll lead me right to her. No, I intend to kill her, Maelca. It's why I left the colony. It's the only way I'm going to be free of her for good."

"Atalanta received her power from Hades in the Underworld," she said to herself as she stared at the counter. "That's why you needed me. Why you kept me with you. Because the light in me…what?" She looked up. "It loosed her hold on you somehow?"

He hadn't planned to tell her any of this, but now that it was out there, he wasn't going to lie. He owed her more than that. And he could see her thinking back, remembering what he'd been like when they first met. Twitchy, paranoid, frenetic. All the things he hated being. All the things he'd be again as soon as she left him. "At first? Yeah. When I was near you, I didn't hear her voice as strongly. I could think.

That's why I didn't let you go after we came out of the caves."

Understanding dawned in her eyes, followed by hurt. A hurt that told him she thought that was the only reason he was with her now. He wanted to tell her that wasn't the case, that things had changed, but before he could, she said, "How? How did that happen? Has she always had a hold on you like that?"

His stomach tightened. "No. She was in the Underworld. With me."

Horror seeped into her eyes. Horror and revulsion. "What happened?" she whispered.

Sickness rolled through his stomach. He didn't want to tell her the truth, because he knew as soon as he did, she'd look at him differently. As half a man. As a weakling. And he didn't want that. What he wanted was to go back to the way things had been moments before he'd started this stupid conversation. When they'd been snuggled together on the couch and he was everything she wanted. But he knew now there was no going back. Their little bubble of happiness had exploded, all thanks to him.

His heart cinched down tight. The heart he'd realized he did still have, all thanks to her. There was no way she'd stay here with him now, no way she'd wait for him to get back from his quest to find Atalanta. Not even if he asked. He could see it in her eyes. She was already looking at him differently. But maybe by telling her just what kind of shit he'd done down there in the Underworld, he could somehow convince her Zagreus—Hades's son, the prince of darkness who was as horrific as any in hell—wasn't someone she should even consider tangling with. Maybe, if he shocked her enough, she'd stay away—far away—from the sick son of a bitch. Because he knew if she went ahead with this idiotic plan, she'd lose. She'd lose big.

His heart pinched so hard, pain lanced through every cell in his body. He'd do anything to keep her safe. Even confess his darkest, most gruesome secrets. At this point, that was the only choice he had left.

"You wanna know what happened?" he said in a low voice. "Really know?"

She nodded slowly. Didn't dare look away from him.

He narrowed his eyes. And steeled himself against her reaction. A reaction that was going to change their relationship forever. And likely break him for good in the process.

"I fucked her," he said, watching the shock and repulsion rush across her smooth, perfect features. "And I got fucked. By something a thousand times worse than her. But since I'd agreed to be her *doulas*, there wasn't a damn thing I could do about either one. At least not until now."

Chapter Eighteen

MAELEA'S STOMACH CHURNED WITH SO MUCH FORCE, she was afraid she was going to be sick.

She stared at Gryphon across the granite island where he stood behind the couch, his eyes hard, cold, light blue orbs, so like the icy eyes she'd looked into from the first. Dead. Haunted. Not a bit like the soft, caring eyes she'd peered into this last week as they'd sat together in front of the fireplace, played on the beach, teased each other in the kitchen, and made love in her bed upstairs.

I won't do to you what was done to me.

His words from the motel, before they took that shower together, when he'd convinced her he wouldn't hurt her, came back with a vengeance.

He was telling the truth. She could see it in his hard face. Bile rushed up her throat. She swallowed hard to keep it down.

"Wh-who?" she managed to ask. "Who did that to you?"

"Krónos."

Oh gods. *Oh gods*. The King of the Elder Gods. The most horrific god imaginable. Trapped in the bowels of Tartarus for all eternity by her father, Zeus. And thanks to her twisted family tree, technically, her grandfather. She gripped the edge of the counter. "Y-you saw Krónos?"

"Atalanta took me to him." His voice was callous, unfeeling, as cold as the ice suddenly rushing through her veins. "She knew the Argonauts were going to try to rescue me, and she was desperate for a way out of the prison Orpheus and Demetrius had locked her in with their witchcraft. So she asked Krónos to tether us together. And he did. Gifted me with the darkness of the Underworld so she could call on me whenever she fucking wanted."

As Maelea's stomach churned again, everything—all his twitching and wild eyes and paranoia and haunted looks—finally made sense.

"He made her a deal," he said when Maelea finally looked up. "Gave her six months to find the Orb of Krónos or he'd bring her back to the Underworld. Bring me back."

Her pulse picked up speed. His jaw hardened until it was nothing but a slice of steel beneath his skin, and for a moment, she wasn't sure she wanted to hear the rest. Knew she had to.

"And then," he said in that same emotionless tone, "he sealed the deal by having his way with both of us."

Shock rippled through her. But it was quickly followed by a wave of emotion that rolled like thunder through her blood. Her heart went out to him right there, in the middle of her kitchen. She'd suffered over the long years of her life, but it didn't even come close to what he'd been through. What he must be reliving every single day. She wanted to cry for him. Wanted to hold him. Wanted to do anything to take that haunted, dead look out of his eyes.

She stepped out from behind the counter. "Gryphon—"

"You think that's bad?" Her feet stilled at the rage in his eyes. "If you go after Zagreus, it'll be a thousand

times worse, I guarantee it. He's as sick as his grandfather, and Hades has unleashed him on the human realm
to do whatever the fuck he wants. And he will fuck you,
Maelea. Make no mistake. If you get near him, he'll fuck
you and he'll kill you. In whatever twisted, gruesome,
new way he can. You won't even last a day."

She reached for him. "Gryphon—"

He jerked out of her hand and stepped away, putting
the coffee table between them. "Don't touch me."

Her heart raced. He didn't think she wanted him anymore. He couldn't possibly know she wanted him more.
"Gryphon, just let me—"

"Don't you get it?" he said with such venom, she drew
up short. "I agreed to it. I agreed to be Atalanta's slave to
stop the torture. I did every vile thing she asked me to do,
just to save my ass. And I didn't fight. Not when she took
me to see Krónos, not when she traded away my freedom,
not even when he put his hands on me."

"Y-you did what you had to do to stay alive," she said.

"I was already dead," he snapped.

She took a step closer. "It wasn't your fault, Gryphon."

He scrambled backward, around a chair. "The others…they wouldn't have agreed to any deal. They would
have fought."

He was talking about the Argonauts. And as she
stared at him, she realized where the dead look came
from. It was shame. That he hadn't lived up to his guardian class, to his kin. That somehow, he'd failed them.

Even though she knew she shouldn't, that eventually she'd get hurt because he wasn't ageless like
her, her heart filled. She took a step around the chair.
"You're wrong."

He moved back again. Hit the wall. Panic filled his eyes when he realized he was trapped. Panic and fear that speared her heart.

"They would have done whatever they had to in order to stay sane, too, Gryphon."

He pressed his hands against the wall. Looked toward the door as if judging the distance to freedom. "Don't touch me," he said in a strangled voice. "Just…don't."

Her heart broke all over again for him. She didn't want to push, but she needed to touch him. Needed to show him just how much he meant to her. Needed him to believe it.

She moved in close, slid her hands up his chest. Every muscle in his body tensed as he drew in a ragged breath. "I'm not going to hurt you, Gryphon. I would never hurt you."

"Ah, gods," he whispered, pressing himself even farther into the wall. His head hit the drywall. "Please don't. Not right now."

She wrapped her arms around his neck, eased up on her toes, was just about to brush her lips against his stubbled jaw when his head snapped her way.

"Didn't you hear a fucking thing I told you?"

She stilled, because there was such rage in his eyes. But she wasn't afraid, because she knew no matter what, he'd never harm her. "I heard everything. Every word you said. And if you think any of it makes me love you any less than I already do, then you really are insane. Which I know you are definitely not."

"You *what*?" Disbelief widened his eyes. "No, you don't. You can't. What…what the hell is *wrong* with you?"

A weak smile curled her lips. "Where do you want me to start? I could come up with a whole list."

He stared at her so long her skin tingled. She couldn't read him. Didn't know what he was thinking. Feared she'd just put herself out on the ledge again, taken a chance on loving someone, even knowing how bad it was going to hurt in the end, all for nothing. But he needed to know, needed to understand that what he'd been through didn't change how she felt. It never could.

"You should be running from me. You should be repulsed by me. You shouldn't want to be in the same room with me. You should be—"

"I should be kissing you." She brushed her hand against his jaw, eased up on her toes, and pressed her lips to his cheek.

He froze. A strangled sound echoed from his throat as he closed his eyes. As he whispered, "Maelea—"

She kissed his temple, ran her fingers through the silky hair at the nape of his neck. "I love that you watched me from your window. I love that you protected me in those caves. I love that you were willing to let me go when those daemons found us, even knowing you might die in the process. I love that you did whatever you had to in the Underworld in order to survive so you could be here with me now. That you're willing to do whatever you can to keep me safe, even share this horror with me. Because that's what it is, Gryphon. It's horrible, awful, wretched, and vile what they did to you. And it wasn't your fault. None of it was your fault."

A tear slipped from the corner of his eye, one she captured with her lips. One laced with pain and heartache she felt all the way to the depths of her soul. "And if you think, for even one second, that you aren't brave enough, aren't strong enough, aren't everything any woman would want and need, then you're wrong. You're so very wrong. I want you. I need you." Her voice dropped to a whisper. "I love you, Gryphon."

His arms closed around her with such force, it drew a gasp from her lips. He buried his head against her neck while she wrapped one arm around his shoulder, the other around the back of his head, and held him close, sifting her fingers through his hair, feeling the beat of his heart against her own. He didn't make a sound, but she felt the tears on her skin, felt his big, strong body shake with the power of so many pent-up emotions. And in the silence between them, she closed her eyes and just held on while he let them out. While she gave him what strength there was inside her.

All her life she'd been alone. Even the few times she'd been in love, she'd still been alone, because she'd never opened herself all the way. She'd never admitted who she really was, never confessed her hopes and dreams, never shared her soul. This time, she would. This time, everything was different.

"I won't go after Zagreus," she whispered. "I'll go wherever you want me to go. Do whatever you need me to do. All I want is you, Gryphon. For a few years, for as long as we've got together. If, that is, you want me too."

He lifted his head from her shoulder. Tear streaks ran down his cheeks. His eyes were damp and bloodshot. But the haunted look, the dead look, was finally gone. In its place were the softest, bluest, sweetest eyes she'd ever seen.

"*Sotiria*," he whispered, framing her face with his hands, brushing his thumb over her own tear to wipe it away. "I used to dream of you. Of the one person who would touch my heart and make me whole. I just didn't expect her to show up when I was half the man I used to be. Orpheus may have saved my soul from the Underworld, but you...you saved me from myself. I will always, *always* just want you."

His mouth closed over hers before she could draw another breath. And though he kissed her with those sweet and tempting lips just as he had before, she felt the hesitation, felt the worry lingering beneath.

She needed to *show* him nothing had changed. She needed to prove to him just how much everything he'd told her only made her love him more.

Her hands slid down to his arms, then gently she eased away from his mouth, moved out of his grasp, and stepped back toward the couch, the whole time keeping her eyes locked on his.

He watched her with longing and fear. A fear she wanted to erase forever.

She gripped her long-sleeved T-shirt at the hem, pulled it over her head, dropped it on the floor at her feet. Then she flicked the button of her jeans, slid down the zipper, pushed them partway down her hips.

Desire flared in his damp eyes. A desire she wanted to stoke to a full-blown flame.

She turned, bent over at the waist, shimmied out of her jeans so he had a nice, clear view of her backside. They hit the floor near her shirt. Then she unclasped her bra, let it fall in her hands, looked over her shoulder as she held it out so he could see, and dropped it as well. His eyes were locked right where she wanted them—on her body. His face was flushed with desire and need. She slid her fingers into the lace at her hips, started to push them down. His gruff voice stopped her.

"Don't."

Her heart pounded hard as he moved close. His gaze ran over her, from the top of her head, down her back, hovered on her ass. But she couldn't read his expression from this angle. Didn't know what he was thinking. He barely moved, barely breathed as he continued to study her in the firelight.

"Gryphon…"

He slid to his knees. Pushed her hands away from her hips. Finally whispered, "Let me."

Relief rippled through every cell in her body. Her chest rose and fell with her labored breaths as he ran his palm down her right buttock. As he trailed the fingers of his other hand across her lower back. As he hooked his fingers in the sides of her thong and slowly pulled it down.

This close he could smell her—jasmine and need and hunger. And all of it—the way she felt, the scent of her arousal, the things she'd said—it all coalesced to leave him light-headed.

She loved him. No one had ever loved him. After the Underworld, he didn't think anyone ever could.

His heart—a heart she had reawakened—filled as he brushed his fingers against her inner thigh. As she trembled all over again. "Put your knee on the couch. And lean forward."

She hesitated the briefest of seconds, then stepped out of her panties, braced one knee on the couch, and rested her elbows on the arm of the sofa. He pressed against her other leg, telling her without words to widen her stance. And as she slowly opened herself to him, his heart pounded hard against his ribs.

She trusted him. Not just with her heart, but with her body too. The impact of that nearly stole his breath.

"You are gorgeous," he whispered.

She shuddered. And before she could turn and look at him, he leaned forward and ran his tongue over her clit. She sucked in a breath. He slid between her folds, then finally found the opening of her sex and tasted all of her.

She groaned, dropped her head against the armrest. Gods, he loved the sounds she made. Loved the way she tasted. He slid his tongue back down to her swollen clit, circled the tight knot, flicked it again and again, delighted in the way she moved against him. Sweat broke out on his skin as he listened to her moan, as she pushed back against him. He wanted to slide inside her, to take what she was so obviously offering, but this wasn't about him. This was about her. About showing her how much what she'd said meant to him.

How much *she* meant to him.

She dug her fingers into the fabric of the couch. "Gryphon, I—"

She gasped again, then moaned when his finger slid down her backside and finally into her sex.

"Oh, gods." She tightened around him.

He pushed deep, drew back out, thrust in again. She was so wet. Wet and hot and perfect. She moved against him while he pumped into her sex, while he licked her. Tried to force him deeper. Tried to urge him faster.

He knew she was close. Needed to make her go over. Wanted to taste her release. He closed his lips over her clit and suckled. And was rewarded with a tremor that shook her whole body.

"Gryphon," she gasped. Her arm gave out and her face hit the sofa as her orgasm consumed her. She tightened around his fingers, and his dick twitched in response, as if the same electrical shots rushing through her body were exploding in his.

He'd never known giving pleasure could be enjoyable until her. Hadn't realized what he was missing in life these last few months. Not just sex in general but…love. Her love, her trust, her faith in him… together it sealed the hole in his chest he'd been living with since the Underworld. It brought back the man he once was.

No, that wasn't right. It made him into the man he'd always wanted to be.

He continued to tease her, continued to caress from the inside, slower with each stroke until the aftershocks left her body. Then he squeezed her right cheek and pressed a gentle kiss to her loft.

She breathed deep, seemed to have trouble focusing. As she blinked several times and stared into the flames dancing in the fireplace, a thrill rushed through him at the knowledge he'd done that to her. He'd left her breathless and foggy. As breathless and foggy as he'd been since the first moment he touched her.

She turned quickly, found her footing, gripped his shoulders, and pulled him to his feet.

"Maelea—"

Then she closed her lips over his, licked into his mouth, ripped open his jeans, and pushed them down his hips.

Desire rushed through his body, so much more insistent than ever before. He groaned, pulled her close.

She tore her mouth from his. "Sit."

The cushions dipped under his weight as she pushed him down. She immediately dropped to her knees, tugged the jeans the rest of the way down his legs, and dropped them on the floor. She stripped him of his shirt, and when she had him naked, when he was so hard he hurt, she finally bent and took him into her mouth.

Ah, gods. He dropped his head back against the couch. Threaded the fingers of one hand into her hair as her lips closed around his shaft and her tongue ran along the underside his cock. After a week alone together, she knew exactly what he liked. Which strokes made him shiver. How much suction could leave him weak. Just how deep he liked to press into her mouth.

She took him as deep as she'd ever done, cupped his balls, raked her nails across the sensitive flesh until the wicked sensations erupted in every inch of his skin. He groaned again, thrust up to meet her. And just when the first twitch of his orgasm barreled close, she let go with her mouth, climbed over him, straddled his hips and slowly lowered.

They both groaned as he filled her. His eyes opened, locked on hers. He closed his arms around her hips as she took him as deep as possible. "Maelea—"

She leaned forward until the tips of her breasts brushed his chest, wrapped her arms around his shoulders and flexed her hips, rocking slowly on his lap, grinding against him until he saw stars. "I love you, Gryphon. Nothing else matters to me. Nothing from before can change that. This…you and me together now…this is all that matters."

Emotions overwhelmed him. So many he couldn't speak. He cupped the back of her head with one hand, closed his mouth over hers, kissed her with all the urgency inside him.

A groan fell from her lips as his tongue swept into her mouth. And when his other arm tightened around her waist, when he turned her on the couch and pushed her to her back, then braced one knee on the floor, she dug her fingers into his shoulders, kissed him as if she couldn't get enough.

"Maelea…"

He wanted to tell her what was in his heart. Couldn't seem to get the words out. His thrusts picked up speed. His fingers gripped her thigh and hip. And his cock grew even longer and thicker inside her.

She pushed up on her hands, thrust back against him, and tightened everything. "Take me, Gryphon. I'm yours. Only yours."

His release consumed him, overwhelmed him, shook his body so hard he gasped. She shuddered with her own release, and before he realized what was happening, electricity shot down his spine and exploded in his hips as he came all over again. Something he never thought he could do so soon.

Electrical shocks still rippled through his cells as he groaned and fell against her. She wrapped her arms around his sweaty shoulders, kissed his temple, ran her fingers through his hair, and just held on.

Love—*her* love—was more than he'd ever expected. More than he'd dreamed of. More than he deserved. But he wasn't about to waste it.

Long minutes passed before his muscles came back

to life, but when they did, he lifted his head, looked up at her dark, mesmerizing eyes, at her face flushed from her orgasm, at her skin slick with sweat. And knew from the bottom of his heart that even if she wasn't his soul mate, she was worth living for. She was everything he was fighting for.

He brushed a lock of hair away from her face then skimmed his thumb over her cheek. "I don't deserve you."

"Gryph—"

"But I want you," he said before she could protest. "I'll always want you. You are the heart that beats inside my chest. That gives me life." His throat grew thick. "I love you too, Maelea. Without you, I am nothing."

Tears filled her eyes, and she kissed him. His lips, his nose, his cheeks. "Show me," she whispered, lifting her hips and drawing him deep all over again. "One more time."

With lips that devoured hers, he did.

———

Hades knew how to bide his time. He was a patient god. One who'd spent thousands of years waiting for his moment to shine. This, like so many others, was just one more step along the road to ultimate control.

He waited in the trees outside the city of Tiyrns in the Argolean realm. Because he wasn't an Olympian, he could cross into the blessed realm, wasn't limited to the same rules Zeus had saddled the other Olympians with. Which was lucky for him.

Unlucky for him, though, was the fact he couldn't enter the queen's castle. Some power there kept him out. Even when he used his cap of invisibility. Life would be so much easier if people didn't fuck with the laws of nature.

Of course, then it might not be as fun.

Twigs cracked, and he looked through the dark trees toward the sound. Silently rejoiced when he saw the source. The boy was just as Hades's spies had told him. Young, naïve, as blond as his father, and with those Argonaut markings on his forearms, the perfect prey.

He waited until young Maximus grew closer. Then finally called out, "Do they know you're out here alone?"

Max's head darted up, and his silver eyes narrowed. "Wh-who's there?"

Hades smiled. Any of the Argonauts would know him for who he was, but young Maximus was too green. He might sense power, but because his father, in an attempt to *protect* the youth, had yet to begin his Argonaut training, he couldn't distinguish one god from another. And thanks to Hades's very clever disguise, that was another point in Hades's favor.

"I think you know exactly who I am," Hades said without rising.

Max stepped through the trees, his eyes widening. "Oh my gods, you're a Fate."

Hades smiled, and a sick thrill rushed through him at this little ruse. "Call me"—*the bitch*—"Lachesis."

"What are you doing here?"

"Waiting for you, boy. I know why you wander in these trees alone. Why you don't tell your mother where you've gone. Why you distance yourself from others your age. I know about your time in the Underworld."

Sickness spread over the boy's face. He looked down at his feet, kicked a twig with his sneaker.

"I also know," Hades went on, "that your parents

don't understand you. That they think you're nothing but a weak child."

Max's head darted up, and his eyes flashed a stormy gray. "I'm not weak. And I'm not a child."

Oh, he was, though. Only eleven, maybe twelve. And though he had powers yet untapped, he was still nothing but an inexperienced, albeit haunted, child.

Hades's smile widened, the diaphanous robe like the one Lachesis normally wore all but glowing around him. "There is a way to prove them wrong."

"How?" Max asked with curiosity.

"Oh, I think you know, child. Whom do they protect you from? Whom do they think you're not strong enough to face? Who holds power over you, even here?"

Max's eyes darkened, and his jaw clenched under his smooth skin. "Atalanta," he whispered.

Children were so fucking predictable.

"So face her," Hades said, fighting the smile. "Prove yourself to them."

"I—I can't. I'm not strong enough."

"You were strong enough to escape. You were strong enough to stay alive. How did you do that, if you were nothing but weak?"

Max stared at the base of a tree, and Hades could practically see the wheels turning in his blond head. "The Orb of Krónos."

Bingo.

Hades smiled, careful not to give too much away. "With it you can do anything."

"But how—?"

A little nudge was all the kid needed. Hades faded into nothing. "Good luck, child."

Back in the Underworld, Hades grinned from ear to ear. *Take that, you fucking Fate.*

He looked down at the inventory list on his desk that he'd put off too long. He had to keep close tabs on which souls went where. His father, Krónos, was continuously sucking souls into Sin City, promising them things he could never follow through on. If he ever got out…

Hades's jaw clenched at that thought. Krónos could never get out. No matter what. Which was all the more reason it was so important he got his hands on the Orb. If one of the other gods—if Atalanta, that bitch— released Krónos, then not only the human realm but the Underworld as well would forever be altered.

Altered? Forget that. It'd be fucking ruined.

No, Krónos would not get out. Because Hades was absolutely sure the boy—Max—would do exactly what he wanted him to do. Within a matter of days, the Orb would belong to Hades for good.

A shuffling sound echoed from the hall. Feeling better than he had in days, Hades turned from the desk and called, "Orcus! Just the troll I've been looking for. Where's the stain?"

Now that he had one issue dealt with, it was time to refocus on another.

Orcus dragged his limp leg into the room, his pointy ears twitching forward and back. "I—I bring news, my lord. About the stain."

"And?"

Orcus rang his scaly green hands together. "She— the hellhounds picked up her scent. Somewhere on Vancouver Island."

"Well then, have them kill her," Hades said between

clenched teeth, trying not to let Orcus's incompetence ruin his good mood.

"There's a problem, my lord."

"What problem?"

"They…they can't find her. It's like she disappeared. Even though her scent is still strong."

Hades looked out the open window to the swirling red sky beyond. So Maelea was using the therillium to hide after all, thinking it would protect her. "How many pieces of ore did that kobalos say they took from the tunnels?"

"He thinks only one, my lord."

One…

"And how long has she had it?"

"A week. Slightly more."

Depending on the size of the piece, its power could begin to drain or it could last several more weeks. Until she either came out of hiding or the ore finally failed, she'd be invisible.

He turned back to Orcus. "Send hellhounds to the area her scent is strongest. She can't stay hidden forever. As soon as she shows herself, have her killed. And the Argonaut, if he's still with her."

Orcus bowed and backed out of the room. "Yes, my lord."

Things were finally starting to go his way. As he rocked back on his heels and enjoyed the view, Hades clasped his hands behind his back and smiled. He couldn't wait until his wife returned from Olympus. Couldn't wait to tell her he'd finally killed that fucking stain of hers and that he had the Orb.

Couldn't wait to enjoy her reaction.

———~~~———

Morning light streamed over Gryphon where he lay with his head propped against the headboard, one leg kicked out of the covers, the other pinned to the mattress. He hadn't slept. His chest still vibrated with too many emotions, his head with a thousand thoughts and memories. Some he didn't want to remember. Some he wanted to experience all over again.

He glanced down at Maelea tucked tight to his side, sound asleep, her legs intertwined with his under the blanket. Her head lay pillowed on his chest, her warm breath heating his skin. Her features were relaxed, her dark hair a fall of black silk around her face. In the hazy light, her skin all but glowed, so soft, so perfect, like the smoothest porcelain. Every time he looked at her, he remembered the way she'd held him yesterday. The things she'd said. He still couldn't believe, after everything he'd told her, that she wanted to be with him.

He wanted to roll her over, wake her up with his mouth, with his hands, with his body. Knew he wouldn't, because he'd worn her out last night making love to her and she needed to rest. But it didn't stop him from wanting, from needing, from dreaming about forever with her.

All I want is you, Gryphon. For a few years, for as long as we've got together.

He intended to give her more than a few years. He planned to give her at least five hundred. He'd leave the Argonauts. They could settle anywhere. As long as they were together, that was all that mattered. But first he had to deal with Atalanta.

He tipped his head back against the headboard, closed

his eyes. His heart pinched at the thought of leaving her so soon after this bond they'd created had solidified. But he didn't have another option. He was running out of time. He'd already wasted two months at the colony trying to get his head to work right, a week and a half tucked away in this house here with her. He'd never wanted the Argonauts to know his shame, which is why he'd never told any of them—even Orpheus—about his tie to Atalanta. But now that he was stronger, now that he knew he could fight her voice, he was confident he could find the demigod and destroy her before Krónos's allotted six months were up. And when he had, when that tie between them was severed for good, then he could come back here. He and Maelea could pick up where they left off. His life could finally start.

He ignored the tingle of doubt that rushed over his spine. Told himself he could handle it. That he'd win. There wasn't another option. Not when he finally had something to live for.

He pressed a gentle kiss to her forehead, slipped out from under her, and made his way to the shower. Floorboards creaked under his feet. He flipped on the water to heat, then looked in the mirror.

For months he'd avoided his reflection. Couldn't stand to see that dead look in his eyes. But this morning...it was like looking at the old him. Before the Underworld. Before all the pain and suffering and hopelessness. This morning, he looked like himself again. All thanks to Maelea.

The water was warm and invigorating. And strength seeped back into his bones. A strength he'd lacked these last few months. He showered, dressed, and was surprised when he stepped into the bedroom to see the bed empty.

He moved to the curtains, pulled them back, and looked out over the beach. Maelea stood ankle deep in the surf, wearing a thin white robe, staring out at the water while her hair floated behind her in the gentle breeze. And watching her in the early morning sunlight, that heart she'd resurrected warmed in his chest, sending tendrils of energy all through his body.

He jogged down the stairs, caught the scent of coffee brewing. When he reached the kitchen, he saw the coffee was only half-done, which meant she hadn't been up that long. He decided not to wait for it, bypassed the therillium glowing orange under the heat lamp in the corner of the kitchen, and pushed the screen door open.

Night and water. Those were two things he'd learned she loved. Wherever they ended up, it had to be on a beach like this. So she could have the water. So she could spend time out here at night. So they could make love under the stars with the waves rolling gently against the shore.

Cool water brushed over his bare feet as he wrapped his arms around her waist from behind and nuzzled her neck. "Good morning."

She reached for his arms at her waist, tipped her head to give him more room. "Mmm…good morning to you."

He kissed her cheek, then her mouth when she turned. He loved the way she tasted, loved the way she smelled, loved that she didn't shy away from him. She shifted in his arms, ran her hands up around his neck. Opened to him when the tip of his tongue slid along her bottom lip. Moaned just the slightest bit as he dipped inside for a taste.

When he eased back, her eyes had that sleepy, dreamy look to them. The one he loved to see.

"You're up early this morning," she said as she rested her cheek against his chest and he tightened his arms around her back. "I heard the shower running."

"I didn't mean to wake you."

"It's okay." Her lips curled against him. "As long as you let me sleep at least a little later."

His chest tightened. "Maelea, I need to talk to you about later."

She eased back and looked up with a furrow between her perfect eyebrows. "Why doesn't that sound all sweet and sexy like I want it to sound?"

Because she was smart. He let go of her when she stepped back. "I told you yesterday that I only have six months to find Atalanta."

"I remember."

"I'm running out of time. If I don't go now I could find myself in trouble."

Understanding dawned immediately in her eyes. "I'll go pack." She took a step around him. "How long should I—?"

He snagged her arm, turned her back to him, awed by the fact she didn't even hesitate. "No."

"What?"

He reached for her other hand, laced his fingers with hers. Tried like hell to find the right words and knew he never could, so he just said what he'd already decided. "I don't want you to come with me."

Confusion crossed her face. "Why not? I thought you needed me? I thought last night we decided—"

He tightened his grip on her hands. "I do need you.

More than you will ever know. Which is why you have to stay here."

"Gryphon—"

"Just listen to me. I used you. At first it was to get out of the colony. And then when I realized how you calmed me, I used you so I could think clearly. I was even willing to use you in spite of what might happen to you along the way, but not anymore. All that time at the colony, after Orpheus brought me back, when he'd lost Skyla…I didn't understand what he was going through, how he could hurt so bad after just finding her. But now I do. I can't lose you like that, Maelea. I won't put you at risk."

"But you need me if you're—"

"I need you alive. I need to know you're safe. If Atalanta has any idea what you mean to me, she'll use you against me. She'll hurt you, and I can't—won't—let that happen."

Worry filled her eyes. "But—"

"This is not about you not being strong, *sotiria*. You're the strongest woman I know. The bravest too, to face down not only me, but daemons and hellhounds and, *skata*, my brother." He tried to smile, knew from her worried expression it didn't help. "This is about knowing that when I'm finally free, I have you to come back to."

"But how will you be able to focus without me there to block the darkness?"

"Look in my eyes, Maelea. They're clear. For the first time in months. I'm not going to lose that when I'm gone. Not if I know I've got you to come back to. If I'm going to find Atalanta, I have to let the darkness pull me toward her." He brushed his thumb across her smooth cheek. "But I'm not afraid of it anymore. I know I can fight it now. Thanks to you."

She stared at his T-shirt, her expression so filled with worry and dread, he let go of her hand, threaded his fingers in her hair, stepped close, and tipped her face up to his. "I'm coming back. I promise you that. This is real. This is everything to me. Now that I know what I have to live for, I'm not about to lose it."

Her eyes slid closed. And when he brushed his lips over hers, she gripped his elbows and kissed him back, telling him with her mouth what he already knew in his heart.

She was his. For better or worse, for however long they had together. She was his alone.

He wrapped his arms around her, held her tight. Her hands slid up his back. Her fingers gripped his shoulder blades as she turned her head against his chest and he rested his cheek on her hair.

"Will you wait for me?" he asked.

"That depends," she said with a hitch to her voice. "How long do you plan to be gone?"

He smiled and hugged her closer because he recognized the teasing in her words. And the heartache. "As short as possible."

She pushed back again. "How will you get to her? She has daemons all around her. What will you—?"

He placed his fingers over her lips. "Don't think about it. I don't want you to worry."

"But—"

"I know how she thinks. I spent three months with her. I'll find a way."

Her gaze raked his face. He couldn't tell what she was thinking. Only feeling. She hated this. She was scared. She didn't want him to go.

"I'm coming back, Maelea. I promise. My heart beats because of you. It will always find its way back to you."

Her eyes filled with tears. She pulled him close again, held on tight. So tight, he felt her everywhere. And as the waves washed against their feet, he knew no matter what happened, this was the best moment of his life. He was loved. Not because of his title. Not because of what he could do. Even in spite of everything he'd done in the Underworld. He was loved simply for who he was.

"Come inside and help me gather my things?"

She eased out of his arms when he let go, swiped at her cheeks. "You go ahead. I need a minute."

She was hurting. He knew he'd sprung this on her without warning. He could give her a few minutes. He kissed her cheek, knowing he was going to remember that jasmine scent of hers wherever he went. That just the memory would give him strength. "Don't be long."

The weight of what lay ahead hung heavy on his shoulders, but for the first time in months—ever, really—his heart felt light. Alive. As if it had wings. It felt…right.

The screen slapped behind him when he stepped into the house. He wiped the sand from his feet on the rug, then crossed to the kitchen and poured himself a cup of coffee. As he headed up the stairs, he tried to remember where he'd put the sword he'd picked up in that cave. He'd have to get new weapons, knew Maelea would have money for him to buy more. Calculated—

His feet stilled halfway up the steps when he realized

the therillium hadn't been glowing orange under the heat lamp the way it had the whole time they'd been here.

He headed back into the kitchen, set his cup on the counter, wound around the island to look at the ore. The heat lamp was still on, but the ore definitely wasn't glowing. It was nothing but a hard, solid, greenish-black glob. It wasn't even glowing green, as it had been in the water of that underground river.

Tendrils of unease rushed over his spine, and his pulse picked up speed. Carefully, he touched it. The rock was cold and hard, and not an inkling of energy or power radiated from its surface.

A growl echoed from outside.

His head darted up. And his heart lurched into his throat just before Maelea screamed.

Chapter Nineteen

GRYPHON GRABBED A BUTCHER KNIFE FROM THE BLOCK on the counter and tore the screen door open.

Maelea was climbing up on an outcropping of rock to the left of the bay in an attempt to escape. Across the sand, five snarling hellhounds were advancing on her.

Gryphon screamed to get their attention. Waved his arms above his head, tore off the deck, and raced toward the water to put himself between them and Maelea.

They had to have been waiting for the therillium to lose its power. He was so stupid. Stupid to think she would be safe here alone. That Hades wouldn't continue to track her. That no one had noticed he'd taken that therillium in the first place.

He charged the closest beast, already at the rocks, ready to lurch toward Maelea with snapping jaws. Sand and water flicked up from Gryphon's feet. He hurled himself at the beast. They rolled across the sand, a tumble of arms and legs and teeth. Gryphon scrambled to his feet before the beast could pin him down and arced out with the knife in his hand. He caught the beast across the foreleg. It howled and dropped back. Then snapped its massive jaws and charged.

Maelea screamed again. Gryphon looked over just as she reached the top of the five-foot-high boulder. She twisted around, threw mussel shells and pebbles, whatever she could find, at another hound trying to reach her.

He stabbed out with his knife again. Blood dripped down the snarling hound's neck. Behind him, growls echoed as the other three advanced on Maelea. Then the ground shook beneath his feet, just as it had in the colony's caves, just as it had in that motel room. Only he didn't know where it was coming from or if it could help.

There were too many, he realized. His only hope was to use his gift and freeze them so she could get away.

He arced out, caught the hound at the jugular. Blood squirted all over him and the ground. The beast stilled, made no sound, then dropped to the sand. He looked for Maelea. Three hellhounds jumped and snarled and snapped at the base of her rock. The fourth was headed straight for him with glowing red eyes.

He centered himself. The ground shook harder. His eyes fell closed as he drew on his gift. But Maelea's scream jolted him out of focus.

His eyes shot open. Maelea's arms swung out for balance, but her footing slipped on the rocks. And then she was falling.

No!

Panic and bone-chilling fear rocketed through him. He pushed his muscles forward, sprinted through the water toward her. A hound slammed into him from the side. They rolled through the shallow surf. The knife went flying. The hound pinned him to the ground and closed his jaws over his shoulder.

Pain spiraled through his body, and he roared. A blinding red ignited behind his eyes. He jabbed at the beast's face, couldn't seem to get the thing to let go.

Maelea. He had to get to Maelea...

He shoved up hard with his knee. Clawed out with

as much force as he could. A whir sounded close. Then another. The beast let go and howled. Then dropped to his side next to Gryphon in the surf.

Chest heaving, Gryphon pushed himself up. Two arrows stuck out of the side of the dead hellhound. His gaze shifted out over the beach, to Titus and Skyla killing what was left of the hellhounds. Then to the water, where Orpheus was hauling a soaking wet and bloody Maelea to her feet in the waist-high surf.

She sputtered, coughed, held on to Orpheus as he lifted her into his arms and walked toward the beach.

She was alive. Relief poured through Gryphon like a tidal wave. He pushed to his feet. Needed to touch her. To hold her. Blood gushed from his shoulder. A wave of dizziness dropped him back on his ass. Water sprayed around him.

"Shit," Skyla said. "Orpheus! He's hurt. And, uh, boys? Look up there."

Gryphon looked toward the cliff Skyla was pointing to. The cliff was covered in seething, glowing green-eyed daemons.

Holy fuck, they'd been found by everyone.

"We need to get them both back to Argolea," Skyla said. "Like now."

Argolea? No. Gryphon tried to push up again. A wave crashed into him, jostling his body against the sand. "Maelea—"

"I'm all for that," Titus said, stalking Gryphon's way at a fast pace. "Is she okay?"

"I don't know," Orpheus said somewhere close. "Let's get the fuck out of here before those daemons figure out how to get down that cliff."

"Relax, Gryphon," Skyla said at his side, kneeling beside him. "We'll get you home."

He didn't want to go home. He just wanted Maelea. He struggled to see past Skyla, but Titus stepped in his way. Then looked down at him and shook his head with a *you're such a dumbshit* expression.

Before Gryphon could ask where they'd come from or what the hell was going on, Titus brought his fingers together and opened the portal. A burst of light blinded Gryphon's eyes. And then he was flying.

—∿∿—

"I'm fine," Maelea said for the hundredth time. "I'm not hurt. Stop fussing over me."

She tried to get up, but Callia pushed on her shoulder, keeping her prone against the bed. "You hit your head and have a concussion. You're not going anywhere just yet, missy. Relax. You're safe here."

Maelea wasn't worried about being safe. She was worried about Gryphon.

She hadn't seen him since they were brought to the castle in Argolea. The Argonauts had whisked him off somewhere as soon as they came through the portal, and every time she asked what was going on, she'd been told not to worry.

Not worry? That wasn't possible. She knew the Argonauts hadn't been happy with Gryphon before he kidnapped her. Likely were even less thrilled with him now. She needed to find them. To set things right. She'd seen the anger in Orpheus's eyes when he hauled her out of the water. Had seen the way he cut Gryphon a bitter glare, as if her falling in the water and hitting her head was his fault. He couldn't be more wrong. It was her own stupid fault. She knew now there was some sort of hidden power in her, one she'd called on out there on that rock. One that vibrated from her into the ground and caused it to shake. And it was that power that had knocked her off her own feet and tossed her into the waves.

All of them couldn't be more wrong about Gryphon. She had to get to him. She had to make them understand…

She pushed up again. "If you'll just let me—"

The door whooshed open, and Skyla stuck her blond head inside the room. "Is it okay for me to be here?"

Skyla. Relief pinged through Maelea's chest. Yes, Skyla would help her.

Callia glanced toward the door. "Actually, you have good timing. I need to go check on Gryphon. Can you stay with Maelea?"

"Sure."

Callia looked back at Maelea. "You, stay put."

Maelea's nerves bounced in her stomach as Callia left. When she and Skyla were alone, she focused on the Siren's green eyes. "Tell me how he is."

"He'll live. Getting patched up. I'm a little surprised at your concern, though."

"He didn't do anything to me."

"That's not what it looked like when we got there. It looked like you were trying to get away from him and those hellhounds showed up."

Maelea blew out a breath of frustration. "That's not what was happening at all. I was looking out at the water, trying to get my head on straight when those hellhounds appeared. Gryphon was in the house packing to leave. He wasn't anywhere near me. And even if he had been near me, I wouldn't have been trying to get away from him."

Confusion crossed Skyla's face as she eased down on the side of Maelea's bed. "Maybe you'd better tell me just what happened while you were with Gryphon these last few weeks. Because when Orpheus saw you with him in the caves beneath the colony, just before the floor broke open, getting away from him was the only thing you—or we—wanted."

Maelea swiped both hands over her still damp hair as her pulse picked up speed. How could she explain what had happened? She couldn't. All she could do was try to convince Skyla he wasn't the monster the rest of the Argonauts were undoubtedly sure he'd become.

She fought back the rush of emotions. But wasn't strong enough to stop the tears that stung her eyes. "You want to know what happened?" When Skyla nodded, she said, "I realized how special he is. And I fell in love with him. That's what happened."

The voice was back.

Which meant Maelea wasn't close.

Gryphon ground his teeth as he sat on the bed in nothing but wet jeans while the med tech wrapped his shoulder, fighting to hold back his temper.

"What the hell were you thinking, Gryphon?" Theron roared at him. "Do you have any idea what kind of fucking mess you've made for the rest of us to clean up? Hellhounds. *Skata*. Not to mention the line of dead daemons you left in your wake. You're damn lucky Titus and Orpheus came through after you. Not that it fucking matters, since the Council's already caught wind of this disaster."

Gryphon cut a look at Orpheus near the door. His brother's arms were crossed over his chest, his eyes as hard and cold as Gryphon had ever seen them.

Oh yeah, his brother was pissed at him. And with good reason.

He looked toward Titus, leaning against the wall behind Theron, a toothpick sticking out of the corner of his mouth. Luckily, the Argonaut had healed from his wounds. Which was about the only good news right now. Even so, a burst of remorse trickled through Gryphon's veins.

"Nick's ready to have you skewered," Theron went on, pinning him with a look. "He's banned you from the colony." His black eyes narrowed. "Are you listening to any fucking thing I'm saying?"

No, actually, Gryphon wasn't. All he could think about was Maelea. "Where is she?"

"Safe from you, finally," Theron said with dead calm.

Gryphon's heart cinched down tight. And panic slid through his veins. "You have to let her stay. She can't go back to the colony. She won't stay there, and Hades is hunting her."

"Why the hell would you care?" Theron asked. "You fucking kidnapped her."

His pulse pounded hard in his chest. Yeah, he had, but he'd also found something in her he'd never expected to find anywhere else. Something he now knew he couldn't live without.

"Well?" Theron asked.

Before Gryphon could answer, the door opened and

Cerek stuck his head in the room. "Um, Theron. Sorry, man. I need you for a minute. We have a...situation downstairs."

"What kind of situation?" Theron asked.

"A Council situation."

"This is all I need," Theron muttered. He looked to Gryphon. "You. Stay put. We're not done."

As he left, Gryphon couldn't help but worry that the Council had found out Maelea was in their realm. They'd never allow that. Not the daughter of Persephone and Zeus. His stomach tightened.

Titus pushed away from the wall. "O? Can I see you outside in the hall for a minute?"

Gryphon's wariness kicked in as he watched the two leave. Now what the hell was going on? As the med tech continued to bandage his shoulder, he tried to listen to what was happening beyond the door. Couldn't hear anything but that voice echoing in his head. It was there, but not strong, which meant Maelea had to be somewhere in the castle. If she were outside the castle walls, the voice would be a blaring roar in his ears.

The door pushed open again, but instead of his kin, Callia stepped into the room. "I'll finish that for you," she said to the tech.

The female nodded, then slipped out of the room without a word.

Callia glanced at the bandage job, then pressed her fingers all around the outside of the wounds on his shoulder, using her healing gift to feel for problems. "It's not as deep as it could have been. You were lucky."

"How is she?" he asked, knowing Callia had to have seen Maelea. "Is she going to be okay?"

"She's fine," Callia answered as she continued to wrap his shoulder. "She has a slight concussion from hitting her head. Nothing more. Skyla's with her now."

Skyla. Gryphon's eyes slid closed, and he drew in a breath, let it out slowly. Just hearing from someone that Maelea was okay eased the pressure on his chest.

"She seems quite worried about you," Callia said.

The space around his heart warmed. "I—I need to see her."

"I'm not sure that's a good id—"

The door pushed open, but instead of Theron and the others, Orpheus came back into the room alone. The anger was gone from his eyes. In its place was shock and…confusion.

"Orpheus?" Callia asked as she applied the last bit of tape. "Are you okay?"

"Yeah. I'm fine." He ran a hand down his face. Then nodded Gryphon's way. "Are you done with him?"

"Yeah. He's done." She set down her supplies, handed Gryphon a new shirt from the counter at her side and said, "Put this on."

"Good," Orpheus said. "I, uh, need to talk to my brother." When Callia glanced at each of them curiously he added, "Alone."

"Sure." Callia cast him a weak smile. "I'll just be outside."

Gryphon pushed off the bed and tugged the shirt over his head as the door snapped closed behind Callia. Every muscle in his body hurt, but he couldn't relax until he saw for himself that Maelea was okay.

As he pulled the shirt down, he looked toward Orpheus, who was staring at him with a freaked-out expression. He dropped back onto the side of the bed, bent down to tie his boots. "I know you're pissed at me. Just lay into me already and get it over with."

"I—" Orpheus shoved his hands into the front pockets of his jeans. "When did you figure it out? That she was your soul mate?"

Gryphon froze. Looked up. How the hell did Orpheus know that?

His brain spun. And then he realized…Titus. He must have thought it when Titus was standing in the room.

No wonder the guardian had pulled Orpheus out into the hall.

He braced his hands on his knees, pushed up. Blew out a shaky breath. "Not soon enough."

Anger raced back over Orpheus's face. "Did you—"

"I didn't hurt her," he snapped, hating the burst of jealousy he felt at Orpheus's obvious concern. He knew his brother was head over heels in love with Skyla, but there was a connection between Maelea and Orpheus. One that rubbed Gryphon the wrong way. She was *his* soul mate, dammit.

Still…he'd really done a fucking good job protecting her, hadn't he? How many times had she almost been killed because of him? His anger dissipated. Morphed to guilt.

"I didn't hurt her," he said again, gentler this time, more for his benefit than Orpheus's. "I… I…"

Shit. What could he say that would make any kind of logical sense? He'd kidnapped her, made her his prisoner, dragged her halfway across the country, then fallen for her. If he said that, he'd sound more insane than they already thought he was. And the longer he sat here trying to explain something he couldn't, the longer it would be before he could see for himself that Maelea was in one piece. That she wasn't hurt. That she truly was okay.

"Did you know before you left the colony?" Orpheus asked.

This one, he could answer. "No. I'd wanted to leave for weeks. Getting out of my room was easy, but I didn't know how to get past the tunnels. I'd been watching her for a while and I knew she'd figured it out. So I intercepted her. I only planned to use her to get away, but then the tunnel crashed in and we ended up underground, and then…"

"Then what?"

His heart cinched down. "Then I figured out she was more than I thought she was."

"*Skata*," Orpheus said in a stunned voice. "She's not just your soul mate. You're in love with her."

When Gryphon's eyes snapped to his, Orpheus added hesitantly, "Does she feel the same way about you?"

Gryphon thought back to their last night together at the beach house. And his heart warmed when he remembered Maelea's words. Words he was pretty sure he was going to remember for the rest of his life. *I love you, Gryphon. Nothing else matters to me. Nothing from before can change that. This—you and me together now—this is all that matters.*

"Yeah," he said, unable to fight the curl of his lips. "She does. Crazy, huh?"

Voices echoed from the hallway before Orpheus could answer. They both looked toward the door. "Where is he?" One voice rang out above the others. "I want to see him."

"Fuck," Orpheus muttered.

Gryphon tensed and pushed off the bed. He knew that voice. Knew it well, because it belonged to Lord Lucian, the leader of the Council of Elders. His—and Orpheus's—uncle. "How does he know what's going on?"

"Beats me," Orpheus muttered. "But that's why Titus and I didn't tell Theron when we figured out where you and Maelea were holed up."

"You think the Council's planted a spy at the half-breed colony?"

"You bet your ass I do. Otherwise they wouldn't have known about your escape, about the fact you took Maelea with you, about those daemon remains you left behind. And before I forget, let me just ask…what the hell were you thinking, not destroying them? Lucian and the rest of the Council's gonna use this as another excuse to try to get rid of the Argonauts altogether."

Gryphon knew Orpheus was right. The Council saw the Argonauts as rogue warriors who weren't needed. Even after everything Atalanta had done and was doing to try to destroy Argolea, they still didn't think she was a big enough threat to warrant the guardians. They'd been trying to disband the Argonauts for ages. But underneath, Gryphon knew the Council's hatred of the Argonauts had nothing to do with perceived threats or protection. It had to do with power. They saw the Argonauts as the monarchy's personal warriors. And they couldn't overthrow the queen until the Argonauts were gone.

It didn't matter that Orpheus and Gryphon were Lucian's nephews. Familial ties meant nothing to their uncle. They'd both learned that long ago. Power was all that mattered.

The fact that Orpheus seemed so pissed off by that thought hit Gryphon right in the chest. Because before—before Gryphon had gone to the Underworld, before Orpheus had stepped in to fill his shoes with the Argonauts, before Isadora had asked Orpheus to stay on, even though Gryphon was back—Orpheus had despised and undermined the guardians as much as Lucian.

Gryphon sighed. "I couldn't. There were hellhounds chasing Maelea. We barely got away from the first bunch of daemons alive. I didn't have time to destroy the remains before Hades's hounds were on us. And the second set—at the motel—they surprised us. There were too many. I had to use my gift to freeze them, then Maelea killed them because I was too weak to move."

He omitted the fact he'd handcuffed Maelea to the bed, which was why he hadn't been able to protect her in that fight, but from the look on Orpheus's face, it was clear he'd already figured out something else had gone down in that motel room.

"Maelea killed them," Orpheus said with a hint of pride in his voice. "Well, I'll be damned."

"The lords and I want to see him," Lucian bellowed in the hall. "He has much to answer for. The first of which is why he brought Persephone and Zeus's daughter into our realm. We will not stand for this."

Panic rushed over Gryphon as he glanced toward the closed door again. Out in the hall he could hear Theron arguing with his uncle. He had to get to Maelea before the Council did. He didn't doubt for a minute that they wouldn't just boot her right out of the realm on her ass. And if they did that, she'd be a prime target for Hades.

He looked to Orpheus. "Where is she?"

Orpheus turned from the door. Didn't even hesitate to say, "Second floor. Northwest wing. Skyla's with her." When Gryphon moved for the balcony of the suite he'd been tucked into, Orpheus added, "What about your shoulder?"

Gryphon was already thinking through how he'd climb one floor up the outside of the building onto another balcony, then find a back set of stairs down to Maelea's level. "It's fine."

He was out on the balcony before Orpheus caught his good arm, stopping him. "Gryphon, wait. Take this."

He took the small, clear electronic device from Orpheus. "What is it? A phone?"

"Some kind of fancy techno gadget Titus came up with. This one works like a human sat phone but is way cooler. Integrates your brain waves or some shit. I don't know how it works, but all you have to do is have this puppy turned on in your pocket and think about contacting me, and it sends a signal. Only problem is it only works here, not in the human realm. Titus hasn't perfected it yet. But at least you'll be able to get in touch with me."

Gryphon looked down at the device in his hand. "Titus…"

Shit. He needed to apologize to the guardian. Try to make up for what he'd done.

"Callia couldn't keep him in bed," Orpheus said. "He was as adamant about finding you as I was."

"Yeah, to kick my ass, I'm sure. I have it coming."

"No," Orpheus said, "To make sure Nick and his men didn't. He doesn't blame you, Gryph. He understands. If anyone knows what was happening in your head, it's him."

That thought didn't exactly put Gryphon at ease. But it helped. At least, leaving, he knew Titus didn't hate him.

"If you get into trouble," Orpheus added, "look to the witches. Tell them you're my brother. Delia and her crew will do whatever they can to help you."

Delia was the leader of the witch enclave that resided in the Aegis Mountains. Her witches had been instrumental in helping the Argonauts rescue Isadora from the warlock Apophis's castle. And Orpheus's mother had been part of their coven.

Gryphon didn't know what to say. His relationship with Orpheus had not been one of brotherly love and admiration. For years Gryphon had tried to break through Orpheus's outer shell, but Orpheus had always done whatever he wanted, whenever he wanted. And then, after Gryphon had come back from the Underworld, it was Orpheus trying to get through to Gryphon. So many years lost and wasted because of animosity and jealousy and lack of understanding. And now, after everything they'd both been through—lies and mistakes and secrets on both sides—they'd finally found common ground. All because of the Underworld.

But when he looked into his brother's gray eyes, he didn't see anger or even sympathy anymore as he'd seen since coming back from hell. He saw respect. A respect he hadn't realized he was missing.

"Get her out of Tiyrns," Orpheus said softly. "Take her into the mountains if you have to. The Council will be looking for her. And you."

"I know."

"You're safer here than you are in the human realm."

He knew that too. He also knew that what Orpheus

was doing now, letting them both go, he wasn't doing as an Argonaut, but as his brother. And that it would mean the end of Gryphon's days with the Argonauts. "What will you tell Theron and the others?"

One side of Orpheus's mouth tipped up. "That I finally came to my senses."

"You're gonna bring down a shitstorm of trouble. Not just from the Argonauts, but from the Council as well."

Orpheus's smirk turned into a full-fledged grin. "I've been on the straight and narrow for several months now. It's time I did something to shake things up. Besides, Lucian's still considering retiring, which means I'm still in line for his Council seat."

"You're an Argonaut now. They'll never let you sit on the Council."

Orpheus's eyes sparked with challenge. "All the more reason I'm gonna push for just that."

Gryphon didn't doubt that. When Orpheus put his mind to something, he usually found a way to make it happen. He closed his hand over his brother's forearm, locking them together. "I owe you. For…a lot more than I can ever repay."

"Just take care of her. That's all the payment I ask for. She's special, Gryph."

"I know." Emotions closed his throat. "And I will. I promise."

Chapter Twenty

"Wow," Skyla said, brushing her blond hair back from her face. "I didn't see that one coming."

Maelea twisted her hands in her lap. Part of her was relieved she'd been able to tell someone what had happened between her and Gryphon. The other part was scared to death, now that it was out there. "I know. I didn't see it coming either. Neither of us planned it."

"No one ever does," Skyla said with a curl of her lips.

"What's going to happen to him?" Maelea asked.

"I don't know," Skyla answered. "I'm new to all this Argonaut brotherhood stuff. But it's not just the Argonauts he has to answer to. The Council of Elders here—the lords that advise the queen—found out what happened at the colony. And somehow they found out about the string of daemon remains he left from Montana to British Columbia."

"That wasn't all his fault," Maelea cut in. "I was responsible for a few of those kills myself."

Admiration swam in Skyla's eyes. "You were, huh? Good for you. I always knew you had it in you. But regardless"—she frowned—"the Council's always looking for any excuse to undermine the Argonauts. I have a feeling this could turn into a political nightmare."

"I could talk to them. Tell them what really happened."

"Uh, no." Skyla's face grew wary. "They get one whiff of you and things will go from bad to worse.

Remember Nick's reaction at the colony when we showed up with you?"

Sickness brewed in Maelea's stomach as she remembered back. Yeah, Nick had not been happy to see her.

"The Council will freak if they think Gryphon did anything to draw Hades's attention to the Argolean realm," Skyla added.

Maelea hadn't thought of that. She didn't want to do anything to make things worse for Gryphon.

"I need to see him," she whispered, almost afraid to say the words out loud.

"I don't know if that's going to be possible," Skyla answered. "At least right now. He's with Theron and the others. And Orpheus. Orpheus is more than a little pissed at him."

"Because of me."

"He cares about you."

Maelea knew that. She also knew that Orpheus was wrestling with his own guilt, where she was concerned. He felt responsible for bringing her to the half-breed colony. For exposing her to Hades. For putting her in Gryphon's path. But he had nothing to feel sorry for anymore. In fact, if she could thank him right now, she would. "He has no reason to be mad at Gryphon."

Skyla's face softened. "I'll try to talk to him. See if I can smooth it over."

If anyone could, it would be Skyla. She had a way with Orpheus. She—

The French doors that led to the balcony pushed open. And Maelea's heart lurched into her throat when Gryphon stepped into the room. "Oh my gods."

She didn't remember pushing off the bed. Didn't

remember crossing the floor. But she would forever remember the way his arms closed around her with stinging force when she reached him. The way his eyes brightened. The way he whispered "*Sotiria*" and lowered his mouth to hers with a fierceness that stole her breath.

She wrapped her arms around his neck, kissed him back with everything she had in her. Didn't even care that Skyla was watching.

Worry filled his light blue eyes when he finally eased back. "You're okay? I saw you fall. I was so worried." His gaze strayed to her forehead. "*Skata*, your head."

Her fingers passed over the bandage near her hairline. "It's okay. It's not bad. I didn't even need stitches."

"Thank the Fates," he breathed, pulling her tight again and burying his face in her hair. "Scared me, *sotiria*."

She closed her eyes, wrapped her arms around him again, and just luxuriated in being close to him. She'd been so scared too. When she saw those hellhounds, she'd thought that was it. The end of everything. Just when she'd finally found a reason to live. When she'd finally been given a reason to let go of her dream of Olympus.

His body stiffened against her, and she eased back, watched his eyes narrow and focus over her shoulder.

She turned to look behind her. Skyla eased off the bed, a smug expression on her face.

Gryphon tried to push her behind him, but Maelea wasn't having any of that. "It's okay, Gryphon. Skyla knows."

His gaze dropped to her with surprise. "You told her?"

"I told her everything."

His eyes widened. "Everything?"

Maelea's lips curled, because she knew he was

thinking back to that boat. And the stairs at her beach house. And the beach. And the kitchen table. And the sofa… "Well, not *every*thing."

Heat flared in his eyes. He leaned down and kissed her. "Don't tease me. Not yet." Before she could answer, he looked back to Skyla. "I'm taking her with me."

"I figured you might," Skyla said.

"Don't try to stop me."

"I wouldn't dream of it. How did you get away from the Argonauts?"

"Orpheus."

Surprise flashed in her green eyes, followed by approval. "Well, I'll be."

"The Council's already looking for me. They'll be down here soon enough."

"The Council?" Skyla's gaze shifted to Maelea. "Shit. You two need to get out of here now, then." She moved to the door, opened it, and peeked out. "Coast is clear."

Maelea lifted the cardigan someone had brought for her from the bed, tugged it on. "Where are we going?"

"As far from Tiyrns as we can," Gryphon said, nudging her toward the door.

"Gryphon, wait." Skyla stopped him at the door. "Don't take her back to the human realm. She's safer here. Even with the Council."

"Don't worry. They won't get their hands on her."

A smile spread across Skyla's face. "It's good to see you looking…human."

A slow smile turned Gryphon's lips. "It's good not to need your singing, Siren."

Skyla chuckled as she pulled the door open, then

sobered. "Go. Before it's too late. And good luck. To both of you."

Gryphon looked right and left, pulled Maelea out into the wide hall with him. "What was that about?" Maelea whispered as they headed for a back set of stairs.

"What?"

"The 'singing' comment?"

"Skyla has a way of taming…things…with her voice. It's how she and Orpheus got me out of the Underworld when I was freaking out."

Maelea's heart bumped as they headed for a steel door. Thank the Fates for Skyla, too.

Gryphon typed numbers into a keypad and the door hissed open. A small, dimly lit set of circular stairs looked as if they led down into the bowels of the realm. They moved inside. The door closed behind them. They seemed to descend forever. When they reached the bottom step, Gryphon dragged her toward a wooden door, illuminated only by the dim yellow lights in the ceiling.

"Where are we?" she asked.

"The undercroft. It's where we store extra weapons."

He typed another code into yet another access panel. The door swung open. Inside sat racks and racks of weapons—knives, swords, throwing stars, things with serrated teeth she didn't know how to define.

He grabbed a multitude of weapons. Strapped on a scabbard, which he slung over his head so it cut across his back. Slipped others into pockets she didn't know he had. He handed her a dagger.

Her stomach rolled at the thought of having to use the weapons. Obviously, he expected someone to come after them. The Argonauts? This so-called Council?

Would they really try to kill them? For the first time she realized everything he was leaving behind by being with her. "Gryphon—"

He grasped her hand, pulled her back out of the room. "Come on, we don't have a lot of time."

The door closed and locked behind them. He led her down a long narrow tunnel through a maze of twists and turns that made her thankful he was with her. And then finally they came to a third access panel. He typed in more numbers. The door hissed open. Nothing but darkness beckoned.

Trepidation rushed over her spine as she stared into the black abyss. "Gryphon, maybe we should rethink this."

"Rethink what? This tunnel leads out into the mountains."

She turned to face him. "Rethink leaving. I don't want you to get in trouble."

"I'm not."

"You are. You're walking away from your kin, from your order. From your life. I don't want to be responsible for that. I—"

"*Sotiria.*" His hands framed her face, forced her to look up. Heat rushed over her spine when she saw the soft, needy look in his eyes. "Don't you know that I would give up anything for you?"

"Oh, Gryphon." Tears filled her eyes, and love wrapped around her heart, squeezed tight as a vise, making words nearly impossible to get out. "Ditto" was all she could manage in a rough whisper.

She melted when he eased down and kissed her. When his body brushed up against hers. When his tongue slid into her mouth and his heart beat so close to hers she could feel it inside her chest.

He nipped her bottom lip. "I will keep you safe, *sotiria*. Trust in me."

She had no idea where they were heading or what would happen when they got there, but she trusted him more than she'd ever trusted anyone before. Her fingers gripped the denim at his hips. "I do."

A ghost of a smile splayed across his face as he let go of her, as his hand closed over hers and he pulled her into the darkness of the tunnel. "Good. Because I won't let you down."

The door snapped closed behind them. At her side, Gryphon flicked on a flashlight. "In a few minutes we'll be home free."

Home free. Maelea closed her hand around his and hoped he was right. But something in the back of her head warned there was no such thing as home free for her.

—–∿∿–—

Gryphon was gone.

Word had spread through the castle quickly. The Executive Guard and the Argonauts were already searching for him. The Council was in an uproar. It was like a repeat of what had happened at the half-breed colony, except this time Max was thankful for the distraction. His parents were too busy with other things to pay any attention to what he was doing.

He stood outside the queen's chamber and breathed slowly to settle his nerves. And had a flashback of standing outside Atalanta's chamber, doing almost the same thing.

The difference now was, he knew exactly what came next. Thanks to Lachesis.

Something in the back of his head said Lachesis would never encourage him to get the Orb, but he ignored it. Because he knew its strength. And he knew that with it, he could do what needed to be done. He could finally prove to everyone he was as strong as the Argonauts.

He turned the knob, was relieved when he found the door unlocked. He stepped inside, shut the door softly at his back. The queen's personal suite consisted of several rooms with high ceilings and arching windows that looked out at a view of the Aegis Mountains. But the view wasn't what he'd come for. He closed his eyes, focused on the energy swirling in the room. Tried to locate it.

There.

Power seeped into his veins. Now that he knew how to consciously use his gift of transference, he could feel the power radiating through his skin. Could feel every ounce of strength settle in his limbs.

He opened his eyes, crossed the sitting room toward the wall of bookshelves on the far side. The energy was stronger here. He scanned the leather tomes and trinkets on the shelves. Paused when his eyes locked on a wooden box marked with nothing more than the winged omega symbol.

He lifted it from the shelf, set it on the desk to his left. Flipped the latch on the front.

But the top didn't budge. It was protected by some kind of magic.

Frustration welled inside him. He'd take the box, but he sensed whatever spell kept the lid latched likely also kept the box confined to this room. And now that he could sense the spell, he could also sense another, near

the doorway, preventing any sort of magic from enter-
ing the room. The queen's mate was part witch. He'd
obviously set up a host of spells in an attempt to keep
the thing safe.

Damn Demetrius. Max ground his teeth. Ran though
options in his head. Nothing would work. Nothing—

The door opened in the antechamber. Max's heart rate
shot up. He let go of the box and dove under the bed. If
he got caught in here, his father would skin him alive.

His pulse roared in his ears as he peered out from
under the bedskirt. Heavy boots clomped across the
floor. Then stopped near the desk. "*Skata.* What the hell
is this?"

Demetrius. Oh, shit. Demetrius.

Every muscle in Max's body froze.

He definitely didn't want to get caught by Demetrius.
Not only was he the biggest of the Argonauts, he was
Atalanta's son.

Max held his breath while Demetrius's boots turned
a full circle. He knew the Argonaut was searching the
room, looking for anything else out of the ordinary. If he
looked under the bed...

Demetrius's witch powers hit Max square in the
chest, the force so strong, it drew a gasp from Max's
lips. He slapped a hand over his mouth, held his breath.
But power was seeping into his veins. Power and spells
he'd never known before. All without consciously pulling them forward.

Demetrius's boots echoed across the floor. Stopped
in front of the bookshelf, then retreated toward the door.
Max stayed still as stone until the door closed and silence
settled back over the room. Only when he'd counted to

twenty and he was sure he was alone did he crawl out from under the bed.

He crossed quickly to the bookshelf. Took the box down again. And used the powers and witchcraft he'd pulled from Demetrius to open the latch. Inside sat nothing but a gold bracelet. Disappointment trickled through him, but he lifted it out of the box anyway. Then realized it wasn't a bracelet at all. It was only enchanted to look like a bracelet.

A wide smile spread across his face. And revenge—a revenge he'd been plotting since he'd escaped Atalanta's clutches—reformed in his mind all over again.

Chapter Twenty-one

GRYPHON'S HEART HAMMERED AGAINST HIS RIBS AS HE led Maelea through the dark tunnel. Things had gone more smoothly than he'd expected. More smoothly than they should have. In a matter of minutes they'd be in the mountains beyond the walls of Tiyrns. He tried to shake the tickle in the back of his throat, the one that warned something would inevitably go wrong—but couldn't.

He gripped Maelea's hand tighter. Tried to calm the nerves radiating from her skin. When they reached the far side of the long tunnel, he shined his light over another access panel and typed in the same code he'd used before.

The steel door opened with a hiss. Sunlight burned his eyes as they stepped from darkness into light. As seasons in Argolea mirrored those in the human realm, it was late spring in the Aegis Mountains, and the trees rising around them swayed in the light breeze, the leaves rustling with their movement.

He closed the door behind Maelea. While she blinked several times, he took his first good look at her in the daylight. Someone had brought her fresh clothes. She was dressed in slim jeans, a white fitted T-shirt, and a cardigan. But the bandage on her forehead near her temple stood out in stark relief against her dark hair, and the stress of the day's activities showed heavily in her eyes.

"Hey, come here." He wrapped his arm around her waist, drew her close. Loved the way her hands felt against his biceps and her head tipped up to his. And when he kissed her, his own worry over what lay ahead slowly dissipated into the high mountain air.

"It's all going to be okay," he said when he eased back, trying to reassure her.

"You do too much for me."

"I would do more if I could. I love you."

Her eyes darkened as she brushed soft fingertips over his cheek. "I love you, too, Gryphon. So much more than I expected. So much more than I can even explain. This…it's sudden and crazy, but…for the first time in my life, everything feels right. Being with you feels… like home."

She eased up on her toes and kissed him again. Wrapped her arms around his shoulders and held on tight. And in her kiss he tasted relief and desperation and hunger. The same things he'd been feeling the whole damn day.

"What an attractive couple you make."

Gryphon pulled back from Maelea's mouth and whipped around. Only to falter when he came face-to-face with Persephone.

"Oh, gods," Maelea muttered at his side.

Oh, gods was right. Not only was the goddess Hades's wife, she was also Maelea's mother. What the hell was she doing in Argolea?

Gryphon pushed Maelea behind him. Reached back for his blade, but as soon as he pulled it from his scabbard, some sort of power latched on and yanked. The weapon flew through the air and landed in the trees to his right.

Persephone lowered her arm and grinned. "You won't be needing that."

"What are you—?" Gryphon started.

"Doing here?" Persephone finished for him, stalking across the forest floor in a long, black gown, her jet-black hair so much like Maelea's tumbling down her back, like a river of onyx silk. She looked past Gryphon toward Maelea. "Should I tell him, darling, or do you want to?"

"Oh, gods," Maelea whispered again, growing tense against his back.

Unease made Gryphon looking over his shoulder. "Tell me what? What's going on here?"

Guilt rushed over Maelea's face.

"What's going on here," Persephone answered, drawing his attention her way again, "is that I've come for the Orb. I'll take it now, darling daughter."

"The *what*?" Gryphon's eyes shot to Maelea.

"I…I don't have it," Maelea sputtered, looking past him toward her mother.

His brow lowered. "Why would she think you would?"

"Because…" Her eyes darted around like a cornered animal, searching for an escape. And in the silence that followed, that tickle in the back of Gryphon's throat grew to a roaring vibration that echoed all through his skin.

"Because," Persephone said when Maelea wouldn't go on, "we made a deal. She gets the Argonaut to trust her, gets him to take her to Argolea, gets the Orb for me, then I get her into Olympus. You gave him the elixir, did you not, daughter? That's why he's so besotted with you, right? So where is it? I grow tired of this delay."

Maelea's gaze darted to his. And fear erupted in her

eyes. A fear that said she knew exactly what Persephone was talking about. Because she'd made that deal.

I would do anything to get to Olympus.

Her words from the beach house ricocheted through his mind. Stole his breath. Words she'd spoken with conviction. Words he thought meant nothing after their week together. But now he knew that had just been an act. The *anything* she'd needed to say and do to get her here. To Argolea. To the castle. To the Orb.

Holy *Hades*. He thought back to how groggy he'd been after using his gifts at the motel. Way groggier than he should have been. To that drugged-out feeling on the boat. To being hornier than hell. And now he knew why. Because she'd fucking drugged him with some potion her mother had given her.

Fury erupted inside him. Obviously, screwing him blind and professing undying love was no big deal to her. After all, she'd tried to kill Orpheus to get to Olympus months ago. And thievery…well, that was way easier than going after Zagreus, Hades's son, as she'd told him she'd planned to try next. All this time he'd been telling himself she was different from any other female he'd ever met. And now he knew why. Because she was the daughter of the Queen of the Underworld. The most conniving, backstabbing, and licentious goddess ever to walk the planet. And obviously, she was just like her mother.

His heart shattered at his feet. Leaving behind a black, gaping hole, as deep as the darkness that lived in his soul, all thanks to Krónos and Atalanta.

Skata. Could he be more fucking gullible? He'd left her alone in the castle. Others probably had as well.

Could she have found the Orb so quickly? Knowing her and her desperation to get to Olympus, yeah, she probably had.

"Where is it?" he asked in a low voice, fighting back the darkness bubbling up from the depths of his soul.

"Gryphon." She stepped toward him. "I didn't take it. I promise. I didn't make that deal. I wouldn't use you like that. She offered, but I didn't agree to it. I only used the potion because I needed you to cooperate so we could get away from those daemons. You weren't listening to me and I needed your help. I didn't…What are you doing?"

His hands landed on her shoulders. Harder than necessary, but he just couldn't seem to be gentle as he patted her down all the way to her feet, ignoring the curves at her waist, the softness of her breasts, fighting back—even now—the desire building inside when he touched her.

Dammit, he was such a fucking idiot!

He didn't find the Orb. Which only inflamed his anger. As he pushed to his feet, Persephone chuckled at his back. "Where did you hide it, daughter? Tell me and we'll be on our way."

"Go back to hell!" Maelea yelled at her mother. "I didn't take it!" She looked at Gryphon, heartache and panic alive in her eyes. "Now do you believe me?"

He wanted to. Needed her to be telling the truth. Prayed he wasn't the fool he suddenly felt.

A beeping sound echoed around him. Gryphon looked right and left, then realized it was coming from him. He pulled the high-tech gadget that Orpheus had given him from his pocket and pressed a button. Orpheus's voice boomed through the clearing. "Gryphon, shit, where are you?"

All kinds of chaos could be heard on Orpheus's end of the line. Voices and footsteps and the beep of several machines. "Why? What's going on?"

"What's going on? I'll tell you what's going on. The Orb is fucking missing. They think you took it, you dumbass. Please tell me you didn't touch the damn thing. Because if you did—"

Gryphon didn't hear the rest of his brother's words. Because rage and anger and darkness erupted as he stared at Maelea's guilt-ridden and now very panicked face.

He'd been so naïve to think there was any kind of happily-ever-after for him. She was his soul mate, after all. And like all the Argonauts, he'd been cursed by Hera because of her hatred for Heracles—the first guardian. Fated to be drawn forever to the one woman who would torment his existence. That right there was a great big red warning flag he should have paid attention to.

"Gryphon," she whispered. "Just listen to me. Please. I—"

"Maelea has it," he said to Orpheus. Her face blanched, but he didn't care. He suddenly didn't care about anything anymore. Anything except revenge.

"What?" Orpheus said in a shocked voice.

"She took it. Was planning to give it to Persephone in exchange for entrance to Olympus. I just found out. We're standing outside the tunnel that runs from the undercroft. Get here now."

Persephone swore at his back.

He clicked the end button before Orpheus could ask anything else. And in the silence, tears filled

Maelea's eyes as she stared at him. Tears that only enraged him more.

"I trusted you," he said with more calm than he expected, though inside, retribution cut through him like a hot, sharp knife. "I should have known better than to put my faith in a female whose soul is as black as mine."

"Gryphon—"

"Thanks to your mother, I realized what you really are before it's too late. I can't believe I nearly got killed protecting you from Hades's hellhounds."

At his back, Persephone hissed. And he felt, rather than saw, the goddess dissipate into nothing but her own fit of rage.

Beside him, Orpheus materialized. "Gryphon, what the hell—"

Tears ran down Maelea's cheeks as she stepped forward. "Just let me explain—"

Gryphon flinched out of her grip and stepped far, far away from her. "No, I've wasted way too much time on you as it is. You're good, female. I have to admit that much. But like I said before, you're not irresistible. Thank your mother for reminding me what really matters in this life."

Orpheus called out to him, but he was already flashing, flying over land and water and reappearing at the gatehouse, where the portal that led into the human realm was housed.

The two executive guards on duty lurched to their feet, but the darkness inside had all but consumed him, and Gryphon moved faster than both, disarming them and leaving them in a tangle of limbs on the floor before either could draw a weapon. "Stay fucking down," he growled as he kicked their weapons aside. "If you know what's good for you, you won't follow."

He moved for the portal, hesitated at the edge, and closed his eyes to listen for the voice.

Now that he was away from Maelea, he could hear it. Could feel the pull in the center of his chest, calling him back. All he had to do was follow it. As he let it guide him, he let go of all those silly fantasies he'd had the last few days and refocused on what was important.

Freedom.

Not from the Argonauts or the Council or the half-breed colony, but from Atalanta. From the voice and darkness. From the threat of the Underworld lingering over him like a black cloud. A threat he should have been thinking about all along.

"I didn't take it," Maelea said in a frantic voice to Orpheus. A voice she couldn't control.

"What the hell is going on?" Orpheus asked.

Beside him, three more Argonauts appeared— Theron, Demetrius, and Zander—all sporting the same pissed-off expressions. But Maelea didn't shrivel into the background the way she normally would when faced with four gigantic warriors. She stood her ground and focused on Orpheus. "Persephone appeared to me in that motel when Gryphon stepped outside, and she offered me a deal. She wanted me to get her the Orb. To convince Gryphon to bring me here so I could take it. But I didn't. I didn't agree to anything, I swear it. I didn't even plan to come here. You and Titus and Skyla brought us here. I haven't even been alone. Callia or

Skyla have been with me the whole time. Orpheus, I'm not lying to you. I wasn't lying to Gryphon, but he…"

Oh, gods. Her heart contracted so hard, the pain stole her breath. She covered her mouth with her hand to hold back the sob. He thought she'd betrayed him. That she'd used him. And why wouldn't he? Look at her parents. Lies and betrayal and thievery ruled all the gods. Genetics weren't on her side. And then there was her own admitted obsession with Olympus. And his abuse at the hands of another god, Atalanta.

Her stomach rolled. Tears burned her eyes. Dammit, she never should have used that elixir her mother had given her. She hadn't been trying to seduce him as Persephone wanted. She'd simply been trying to get him to cooperate so she could save their lives.

Orpheus gripped her upper arms. "Focus, Maelea. Where did Gryphon go? He said something about thanking Persephone for reminding him what matters most."

She blinked back the tears. Told herself to keep it together. She had to make this right. She had to find a way. "He…he's been planning to go after Atalanta all along. It's why he left the colony. He was getting ready to leave me at the beach house and do just that when you and Skyla and Titus showed up. It's her voice he hears in his head. When he was in the Underworld, Krónos bound them together. She's been calling to him. He thinks the only way he's going to be free of her is to kill her."

"*Skata*," Theron said at Orpheus's side. "Did he say where she is?"

"No." Maelea shook her head. "He never said, and I don't think he knows. But he can find her, just by listening to the voice. By giving in to the pull. Krónos gave them six months to find the Orb or he'll drag them both back to the Underworld, and he's running out of time."

"*Skata*," Theron said again, glancing toward Zander. "That fucking Orb. We'll never find him."

"I gave him Titus's fancy transmitter," Orpheus said, letting go of Maelea and pulling his out of his pocket.

"It'll only work if he's still in Argolea," Theron said.

"Does he have the Orb on him?" Zander asked as Orpheus tried to contact Gryphon.

"I don't think so," Maelea answered. "I didn't sense it. But I can only sense the Orb if it's being used, and it—oh, my gods."

She gripped Orpheus's arm, swayed on her feet.

He reached out to steady her. "Maelea? What's wrong?"

Energy whipped through her. An energy with power like no other. A power that was definitely being used.

"The Orb," she managed in a shaky voice. "Someone just used it to open a portal to the human realm."

"Gryphon?" Orpheus asked.

She swallowed hard. Shook her head. Turned toward Zander, because the face she saw now in her mind was one she'd seen at the half-breed colony. "No," she whispered. "Your son."

———※———

Max wasn't sure where to open the portal, so he picked the woods surrounding the old half-breed colony in Oregon. He knew patrols still ran in that area, looking for half-breeds who'd yet to move over to the new location. Hoped he'd run into one today.

Rustling in the trees at his back caught his attention and he whipped that way, only to freeze when the god stepped out of the darkness, heading right for him, a smirk across his menacing face.

Max moved back a step. He didn't know who the god was, but he sensed his power. And a whole lot of darkness—darkness like Atalanta's.

"You proved to be quite the Argonaut, boy. And completely predictable. Now I'll take the Orb and we can both be on our way."

Max's mind spun. Then his eyes caught sight of the mark of the Underworld peeking out from under the collar of the god's shirt.

Hades.

Max swallowed hard. And fear burst in his chest. What was Hades doing here? How did he know Max had the Orb? How did he...?

Lachesis.

Oh, shit.

He hadn't once thought to question the Fate in the woods outside Tiyrns. He'd been too upset. But thinking back now, he realized the eyes were different from the last time he'd spoken to the Fate. The eyes, he realized now, were dead black shards of coal like those in Hades's head.

The Orb burned hot against his flesh where it rested on a chain around his neck under his shirt. Infused him with power. He still wasn't any match for a god, but he'd gotten away from Atalanta with nothing but the Orb. Maybe, if he played his cards right...

"You son of a bitch," a female voice hissed. "You are not to go after my daughter."

Hades's head swiveled to the side. Toward the dark-haired female dressed in a black robe, also appearing from the darkness of the trees, hatred and retribution alive on her pale, perfect face. "My love—"

"Don't 'my love' me," she growled. "My daughter is not to be touched. You sent hellhounds after her again, you bastard."

Persephone. Double shit. Max glanced between the two, his eyes growing even wider as he took another step back.

"She was not harmed," Hades said, trying to brush off her anger with a roll of his eyes. "There's no reason for you to be in such a tizzy."

"I'll show you a tizzy." Persephone lifted her hands. Electricity arced out of her fingertips and hit Hades square in the chest. He flew back ten feet and slammed into the ground with a grunt. "That's for attacking my daughter." She lifted her hands again before he could get up, sent another current of electricity through his body that made him shake and writhe on the ground. "And that's for interfering in my quest for the Orb. It will not be yours, husband. It will never be yours."

She turned her icy glare on Max. And under her dead stare, every hair on Max's flesh stood straight. "You."

Before she could attack, Hades lurched to his feet and hurled a whip of fire out from the palm of his hand. It wrapped around Persephone, locking her hands at her sides, and yanked her backward. Her skirts flew up. She screamed as she was dragged toward Hades.

Her body slammed into his. He closed his arms around her. "It seems all your time on Olympus has made you forget who's in control, little wife. I think it's time I reminded you."

He bit into her neck. And Persephone screamed again. But as her cries of protest turned to moans of pleasure, Max knew if he didn't get out of here right now, he was going to be in even deeper shit than he already was.

He turned and ran. And hoped like hell they were too distracted to realize he was gone.

His heart pounded hard in his chest, was a roar in his ears, as he zigzagged around tree trunks and jumped over logs. He slipped on a wet patch of moss, hit the earth face-first. Pushed up again and tore off through the trees. Only when he was at least a half mile away did he slow and realize he could use the Orb to open a portal to a different location, far away from here.

With shaking hands he unzipped his jacket, was just about to pull the Orb from under his shirt when a growl echoed close.

"Well, well, well. What do we have here?"

Slowly, he turned and peered up at the five daemons moving toward him from the shadows.

"He's an Argonaut," the one on the right said, drawing in a deep whiff.

"He's Atalanta's son," the one in front said, a sinister smile twisting his gruesome lips. "We've been looking for you, boy."

Max dropped his hand from his shirt. Zipped his coat. Tried to quell his racing pulse. But it didn't work. Because this increase in tempo wasn't from fear. It was from excitement. And the promise of retribution yet to come.

This time, he had no intention of running.

"Really?" he said in a voice that was calmer than he expected. "Well, here I am, dog-breath. What are you waiting for?"

Chapter Twenty-two

GRYPHON SAT CROUCHED IN THE TREES OUTSIDE Atalanta's new stronghold, a stone fortress set deep in the Scandinavian Mountains of Sweden. Scanning the compound, he took stock of the daemons on patrol around the property, the sharp-rising ridge to the west, the river to the east, and the lake not far beyond.

Snow littered the ground, but spring was trying hard to make itself known this late in May, though nothing—not even the sun trying to peek through the trees—could cut the chill in Gryphon's soul. The darkness inside vibrated with too much intensity this close to its source. And the voice was all but screaming to draw him the rest of the way in.

He ground his teeth, blinked hard, and shook his head to fight off the urge. He'd let the voice and darkness pull him this far, but he needed to think. To regroup. To figure out how he was going to get inside without being caught. Everything hinged on that. On staying focused now more than ever. If only he had Maelea with him...

I didn't take it. I promise. I didn't make that deal.

Her words outside the castle spiraled back through his mind. And with it, the conviction in her voice when she'd added, *I wouldn't use you like that.*

The way he'd used her?

Skata, he didn't know what was real and what was a lie. He wanted to believe her, knew he'd jumped to conclusions without giving her any chance to explain, but he'd been duped before. By that warlock who'd sent his soul to Tartarus. By Atalanta, when she'd offered him freedom from his suffering. By Hera, with that damn soul-mate curse. He didn't want to be the fool again.

This...it's sudden and crazy, but...for the first time in my life, everything feels right.

Warmth slid through his veins when he remembered the way she'd looked at him, encircled his heart, squeezed until he could barely breathe. Being with her felt right to him too. In a way nothing else had ever felt right, even before the Underworld.

That was real. The way she made him feel, the connection they shared, the emotions he'd heard in her voice when she told him she loved him, the way she'd held him that night in her beach house when he told her about his time in the Underworld...that was all real. No matter what she'd arranged with her mother before their week together, he knew in the bottom of his heart what she'd said outside the castle in Tiyrns was true.

His pulse beat hard as he scanned the compound again. *Skata*, he was an idiot. So sure she had to be as dark as her mother, he'd ignored what he knew to be true in his heart. And now he'd probably lost her because he'd let that fear control him. Just as he'd let Atalanta control him for far too long.

Urgency pushed at him. He was done living in fear. Done letting others manipulate him. He still had just over three months before his deadline with Krónos. He could come back. He could bring Orpheus and some of the other Argonauts to help him. Demetrius, Zander, even Titus...they'd all relish a go at Atalanta. And thanks to the darkness inside him, he could lead them back to her. He could—maybe—be the key to finally bringing her down once and for all.

Dooouuulas…come to me.

The screaming voice, the darkness…they pulled at the center of his chest, drawing him in, but he knew now he could fight it. Thanks to Maelea and her faith in him, he knew he could fight anything.

He backed away from the compound, into the darkness of the trees, intent on getting far enough away so he could open a portal back to Argolea without drawing attention, but froze when a portal popped open not far from him, and five daemons stepped through.

"Atalanta will be most pleased with our catch," the one in front said, staring down at something in his hand.

The one on the right chuckled. "Maybe she'll make all of us archdaemons. Screw that sonofabitch Naberus."

Gryphon narrowed his eyes to see what they held. The middle daemon in the back of the pack carried something that wiggled and turned as if trying to get away.

"Put me down! I can walk, you morons!"

Gryphon's blood ran cold when he recognized Max's voice.

Shit. *Shit!* Had the kid followed him? How would he even know how to get here?

He scanned the area. The daemons were marching for the front gate of the compound. If Gryphon didn't do something right now, the kid was toast.

He grasped his blade at his back and stepped out of the trees into the daemons' line of sight. "Looks like you boys found something that doesn't belong to you."

The daemon in front, the one holding something in

his gloved hand, drew in a long whiff, then growled, "Argonaut."

"He's alone," another said, sniffing the air, moving up next to the first. "And he's the one we've been looking for."

The remaining daemons stepped into line with the first two. The fifth hovered at the back of the group with Max in his arms. Max's eyes grew wide but he didn't speak. Didn't even move.

Four—make that five, if the one in the back dropped Max and joined the fight—against one. Not great odds, but Gryphon had faced worse. However, he needed to take these fuckers down quietly and quickly or else they'd have an army of daemons on top of them within seconds.

"Max," he called, ignoring the growls from the daemons already inching toward him. "Remember how you got away before?"

"Yeah," Max called back before the daemon could stop him from answering.

"Do it again."

The daemon in front chuckled. "That boy's not going anywhere but to Atalanta."

Gryphon closed his eyes, drew on his forefather Perseus's power from deep in his core. Energy radiated up from the soles of his feet, through his body, and out his limbs. And when he opened his eyes and fixed them on the daemons in front of him, their gasps of surprise as their muscles stopped working and their bodies stilled was like music to his ears.

A thwack, followed by a grunt, echoed ahead. Gryphon stumbled back a step as his energy waned, then slowly slumped to the ground. He watched through hazy vision as Max scrambled up from the snow where the daemon had dropped him when he stopped midstep, and grasped the beast's sword. Then he knocked the monster to the ground with his boot and decapitated him.

Minutes later, all that remained were steaming bodies and the kid—looking and acting more like Zander's son with every passing second—wiping the bloody blade on his pants. He leaned over, picked something up from the ground, then stalked toward Gryphon. "Are you okay?"

Gryphon blinked several times. Tried to get up. Couldn't. "No…that…drains me. I'll be…okay. In a while."

A smile slinked across Max's face. "That was way cool. I wish I—"

A rumble sounded from inside the walls of the compound.

Max's smile faded. He shot a look over his shoulder then handed Gryphon the object he'd picked up. "We might not have a while. Here, use this. It'll help you regain your strength faster."

Max shoved a metal disk into Gryphon's hand. And only when power radiated through his chest to warm him from the outside in did Gryphon realize the kid had given him the Orb of Krónos.

Gryphon's eyes shot to the glowing disk pressed against his chest, then up to Max's face. "You took it?"

Nervousness crept over Max's face. "I wasn't going to give it to Atalanta, if that's what you're thinking. I just needed the extra power. So I could open a portal. So I could get here and win."

"Holy shit," Gryphon breathed, already feeling better from the Orb's power. "Your dad's probably busting a few thousand blood vessels right now wondering where the hell you went. And your mom—"

"My dad doesn't care. He treats me like a baby. And I'm not. A baby couldn't kill those daemons."

Max's eyes leveled on Gryphon's. Eyes, Gryphon noticed, that were the exact same shape and color and intensity as his father's when Zander was angry. And he heard his own thoughts ricochet through his head. Thinking no one cared about him. That no one missed him. He'd been so wrong. Just as Max was wrong.

He knew they needed to move, that they didn't have time for this powwow, but this was important enough to take a moment for.

"Your dad loves you, Max. It's just not always easy for us Argonauts to show it. He did everything he could to find you when you were with Atalanta. He'd die for you. He'd do anything for you. If he's protective, it's because he wants to make sure nothing happens to you again. And because he can't stand the thought of losing you again. I know because my brother's done the same thing to me. We have to cut them some slack."

Max's brow furrowed. "Maybe, but he thinks—"

A roar echoed near the main gate.

Max turned to look. Though he still wasn't back to 100 percent yet, Gryphon struggled to his feet. Looping the Orb's chain over his head and tucking the medallion under his shirt, he grasped his parazonium from the ground and tugged on Max's arm. "Come on. We'll finish this later. Right now we need to hustle."

As he hobbled into the trees after Max, he fought the shrieking voice calling to him and tried to calculate how far they needed to get before they could open a portal home. If they were too close, they'd—

His feet skidded to a stop when the voice dimmed. He whipped around, looked through the forest around him. Light replaced the darkness hovering inside his soul.

"Maelea," he whispered.

Max jogged back to him, his small chest rising and falling under his open jacket with his breaths. "What? What's wrong?"

"Maelea's here," Gryphon said louder.

Oh shit, she was here. That was the only reason the voice would be dimmed, the only reason he'd be feeling that light. He scanned the forest again, searching for her. How had she gotten here? How had she—?

There. On the far side of the compound. She was looking for him. She was…

He took off running in that direction, his only thought to get to her before Atalanta did. At his back, Max yelled, "Gryphon? Wait!"

His boots crunched on snow and downed limbs. When he reached a small brook, he ran right through the ankle-deep, freezing water, only barely registering the cold liquid seeping into his boots. Urgency pushed at every side of him. Whatever commotion was happening at the main gate couldn't be good. He had to get to Maelea. He had to find her…

Blood pounded in his ears. His heart thumped hard against his ribs. He threaded through a cluster of trees only to skid to a stop at the opening of a small meadow.

Atalanta appeared not more than ten feet in front of him, her blood-red robe brushing the ground, her jet-black hair waving in the wind at her back as he remembered from the Underworld. A wicked smile turned her lips as her onyx eyes focused on his. And being this close to her, that darkness resurged deep inside his soul. "*Doulas*. I felt you close. I knew you'd come to me, eventually."

Footsteps pounded at Gryphon's back. And too late he remembered Max had been chasing after him.

Atalanta's gaze shot past him to the trees, then narrowed and held as Max skidded to a stop too. "Maximus," she whispered.

Her gaze shot back to Gryphon, and her smile widened. This one a malevolent, victorious grin that curled his insides, even as the darkness inside twisted and urged him to give in. "I knew I could count on you, *doulas*."

"Run," Gryphon whispered to Max as he stepped in front of the boy and lifted his blade, fighting her pull with every bit of strength he had left inside. "You can't have him," he said to Atalanta. Then, "Max, run!"

Atalanta chuckled. "You can't fight me, *doulas*. I'm your master." She extended her hand, and an invisible force arced out, ripping the blade from Gryphon's hand. The metal flew through the air, over her head, to land on the frozen ground at her back. Then she moved forward with all the empty, dead hatred he remembered from his time with her in Tartarus and extended both arms toward him. The darkness inside him surged to life, forcing his feet forward, forcing him toward her, even though he tried to stop it. "Come to me. Come to your destiny."

It was taking him. The darkness overwhelmed Gryphon. Panic surged again. Atalanta was going to win. And thanks to him she was going to wind up with not only him but with the Orb and with Max, a descendent of the Horae, whom she needed to wield the Orb's powers.

No, no, no. He fought, struggled, tried to see through the darkening haze, but knew he was slipping. Even with the Orb's power, the Underworld darkness was too strong. Her lure too great. And because of his weakness, because Maelea had come here trying to save him, he'd led her to her death too.

She had to get away. She had to survive. Why the hell hadn't he taught her to fight like she'd wanted at the beach hou—

"Gryphon!"

The haze cleared, and the pull inside dimmed. He looked past Atalanta, toward a body rushing close. Toward Maelea at a dead run. And behind her, Theron, Zander, Orpheus, Titus, and Skyla.

Atalanta whipped around, and growled as she extended her hands toward Maelea.

Everything inside Gryphon lurched in fear. "No!"

Chapter Twenty-three

MAELEA'S HEART JUMPED INTO HER THROAT WHEN SHE saw Atalanta with Gryphon. She'd tried to stay still and hide in the trees, as the Argonauts had told her to, while half of them, along with Nick, had attacked the front gate. But as soon as she felt Gryphon's darkness rushing toward her, she hadn't been able to stop her feet.

"Maelea, stop!"

She didn't know which Argonaut had called out to her. All she could focus on was the goddess whipping her way, narrowing dead eyes, zeroing in right on her.

"You," Atalanta growled as Maelea skidded to a stop. "You kept him from me. You and that disgusting light. Your light will be no more."

Atalanta lifted her hands, and Maelea braced herself for the fury, but before power arced from the goddess's fingertips, Gryphon hurled his body at her back, taking her down like a linebacker. She screamed. Energy arced out of her fingers and shot toward the sky. They both landed with a grunt on the hard earth, rolled across the ground. Gryphon reared back and smacked his head into hers. She hollered in pain. In her disorientation, he looked around, spotted his blade on the ground yards away. Climbed off her and moved for it.

A roar erupted from Atalanta. And when she looked up, rage flashed in her eyes. She scrambled to her knees, pulled her hand back. "You will pay for that, *doulas*!"

No! Fear gripped Maelea's chest. He'd never reach the weapon in time. It was closer to her than it was to him. She lurched for it on the ground in front of her, and before she realized what was happening, the ground shook. Power—energy—vibrated from her into the earth. An electrical current shot across the clearing, then erupted in a bolt of lightning that speared up from the dirt and charged through Atalanta.

The demigod's entire body shook. Her eyes rolled back. Smoke erupted from her ears and singed her hair as she landed against the frozen ground.

At Maelea's side, Orpheus grasped her arm, pulled her to a stop before she could reach the weapon, and muttered, "Holy shit."

Stunned, Maelea stared across the field. Gryphon whipped around. Shouts echoed at her back. Footsteps pounded the earth. But all Maelea could focus on was what she'd done—the power that had come from her—and on the goddess whose eyes weren't black anymore, but blood red as she narrowed them on Gryphon and pushed to her feet, seven feet of seething fury.

"Now you will pay, *doulas*," she growled.

"Don't touch him." From the trees behind Gryphon, a boy stepped out of the darkness, lifted his hands, and sent a steady stream of energy from his fingertips. A stream that hit Atalanta in the chest and knocked her off her feet again.

She screamed, hit the ground, rolled, and pushed herself up. Dark, singed hair stuck out all over her head. This time she fixed her rage on the boy. On the boy and Gryphon, who'd scooted over and put himself between her and the child. "Not a mortal wound, *yios*. Now, you will both pay!"

"Max!" someone at Maelea's back screamed.

The ground rumbled again. Power surged within Maelea. She jerked out of Orpheus's hold. Ignored his cry for her to stop. Swept the blade into her hand from the ground. The weapon was heavy, but instinct guided her now. Instinct and a need to get to Gryphon before it was too late.

Atalanta climbed to her knees. Growled. Lifted her arms.

Gryphon's eyes grew wide. He pushed up from the ground, stepped fully in front of the boy.

Electricity rushed from Maelea through the ground before Atalanta could hit him with her powers, speared up right beneath Atalanta's feet. A bolt of lightning pummeled her body from the ground up. Flames ignited on her skin and a scream like a thousand harpies howling echoed through the clearing.

She dropped to her knees. A dazed look passed over her face. Her gaze skipped from Gryphon to Max, then drifted out across the field, past the Argonauts, and seemed to focus on something far off in the distance. "My love," she whispered. "I tried...for you."

Adrenaline surging, Maelea ran up behind the goddess, and just as Gryphon had told her to do in that motel room, she swung out with the blade held tight in both hands.

Metal met flesh and bone. And a thump echoed when Atalanta's severed head hit the ground, followed seconds later by her smoking, burning body.

Footsteps pounded across the ground. Chest heaving, Maelea dropped the blade and stared at what she'd done. The meadow, the snow, the Argonauts...everything seemed to fade away. She stumbled back a step, but strong arms closed around her before her legs gave out. Strong, warm, familiar arms.

"Hold on to me, *sotiria*," Gryphon whispered. "Don't let go."

She gripped his arms, but her gaze drifted past him, toward the tree line Atalanta had been staring at when she'd dropped to her knees. Toward the lone daemon wearing a trench coat, watching from the shadows. And though she couldn't be sure, Maelea thought... No, that couldn't be right. Did he just *nod* at her? Like he approved of what she'd done?

She blinked, sure she had to be imagining things, but when she opened her eyes the daemon was already turning for the forest. Disappearing into the darkness of the trees as if he'd never been there.

Sound returned slowly. The heat of Gryphon's body seeped into hers, warmed her from the outside in, drawing her back to what was most important. Gripping his arms, she looked up into dazzling, Caribbean blue eyes she only wanted to stare into forever. "I didn't take it," she whispered. "I didn't take the Orb."

"I know. Shh." He tugged her close and buried his face in her hair. "I know."

She closed her eyes and held on tight, feeling the strong steady beat of his heart against her own, letting his heat chase away the chill inside her.

"I should have trusted you. I should have..." His arms tightened around her back. "I'm sorry. I'm so sorry." He swallowed. Then whispered, "It's gone. The voice, the darkness. It's all gone because of you."

It was gone. She couldn't feel even an ounce of the

Underworld inside him anymore. But even as he held her, fear crept in.

Would he want her, now that he didn't need her light?

She opened her eyes and looked over Gryphon's shoulder toward Zander, who was crouched on his knees, hugging Max across the clearing in much the same way Gryphon was hugging her, tears in his eyes as he checked to make sure the boy was okay. Then to Theron, Titus, Orpheus, and Skyla, who were all staring down at Atalanta's smoking body with wide and surprised eyes.

Orpheus looked toward Skyla and smirked. "Now that's what I call a mortal wound." Then toward Maelea. "Way to go, Ghoul Girl."

From the front of the compound, roars erupted, then faded to nothing. The dark energy that had permeated the compound—this whole area—dissipated until only light, blessed peace remained.

Maelea pushed back and looked up. Gryphon's blue eyes sparkled, and as he stared down at her, one corner of his lips curled in a smile that shot heat straight to her belly. "Thank you," he whispered. "Thank you for everything you've done for me."

She waited for more. Waited for him to tell her he still loved her. Fought back the panic rushing through her veins. Looking down at his chest, she caught sight of the circular outline of something disk-shaped beneath the fabric of his shirt.

The Orb of Krónos. He had the Orb. He really didn't need her anymore. None from his world did. They had what they'd been seeking.

A burst of light erupted behind her before she could

figure out what to say. Gryphon shoved her behind him. She blinked at the burn in her retinas, held up a hand to block the glare. Slowly, the light dimmed until what faced them wasn't man or creature or monster. It was a god. The King of the Gods. Her father.

A collective curse rumbled from the group.

Stunned, Maelea stepped out from behind Gryphon, shrugged off his hand when he tried to stop her. Three thousand years she'd waited for this moment. To look upon her father with her own eyes. He wasn't gray and aged, as she'd envisioned over the long years of her life. He was youthful and strong with short, dark hair and a lean body covered in…very human-looking jeans, a T-shirt, and a light jacket.

His eyes softened when they landed on her. And a smile—a real smile—spread across his lips. "My child, this has been a long time coming."

Light radiating from him drew on something in the center of her chest. She took a step toward him.

"Maelea," Gryphon said warily at her back.

She stopped in front of her father, still unable to believe any of this was real.

Zeus's smile widened. "You've finally earned your place on Olympus. You found the strength to call upon your gift. And you killed what my brother Hades created with his darkness." He held out his hand. "Come, child. It's far past time. Come and secure your place with the gods."

She looked down at his hand. Everything she'd ever wanted was only inches from her. All she had to do was reach out and take it.

Slowly, she turned to look behind her. At the Argonauts standing with their feet apart, arms at their sides, bodies ready for whatever battle Zeus might throw their way. To Sklya at Orpheus's side with her hand at her lower back, reaching, Maelea already knew, for her dagger. At Atalanta's smoldering body at their feet. And finally to Gryphon, at the front of the group, staring at her with wide, light blue, mesmerizing eyes.

I would give up anything for you.

Her heart contracted. And the road home, a home that had nothing to do with Olympus, spread out in front of her like a winding trail of gleaming gold.

She turned back to face her father. And knew as soon as she made this choice, she could never take it back. Even if it turned out Gryphon didn't want her anymore. "I'm not going with you."

Zeus's smile dimmed. "What did you say?"

"I said…I'm not going." Her chest warmed. Telling her yes. It was the right choice. The only choice. "I don't want to leave."

Shock filled Zeus's eyes, and his gaze shot past her. "You stay because of *him*?"

Maelea moved fully in front of Gryphon. "I stay because I choose to. My choice has nothing to do with you."

"So like your mother." Disbelief morphed to contempt in his eyes, and a chill spread down Maelea's spine at how quickly her father could go from wanting her to hating her. "Conniving and treacherous. He'll not give you the Orb, if that's what you're after. In fact, in a minute, it will be mine. But you, child, because you turned your back to me, you will be left to dwell in this realm all alone, just as you were cursed by my brother." His dark eyes narrowed. "I gave you a chance."

Maelea's adrenaline shot up, and she felt—and heard—the Argonauts move up around Gryphon, protecting both him and the Orb. "I'm not after the Orb. But you just confirmed to me that you are. And I'm pretty sure you'll not get it. Not without a fight."

Zeus chuckled, and his gaze swept over the group, hovering on Skyla to Maelea's right before swinging back her way. "Do you think the Argonauts and one backstabbing Siren scare me?"

Maelea tensed at the venom in his eyes. Behind her the clink of weapons being drawn drifted to her ears.

Oh gods, what had she done? Even with the Orb the Argonauts were no match for Zeus. Had she just condemned them all as she'd condemned herself? Her pulse soared.

"They might not scare you, Zeus, but I do."

Zeus cursed, and, shocked by the new voice, Maelea turned toward the left. Toward the frail-looking creature hovering over the frozen ground, her diaphanous robe shimmering in a ray of golden sunlight.

"Lachesis," Gryphon whispered at Maelea's back.

A Fate. Maelea's pulse beat even faster as the female floated toward them and stopped between Maelea and the King of the Gods.

"She's made her choice," Lachesis said. "Go back to Olympus."

Fury erupted in Zeus's eyes. "This is not over."

"For now it is," Lachesis said matter of factly. "The Orb belongs not to you, not to your father, and very definitely not to your brother. It belongs to them. And what they choose to do with it is their choice. Much as Maelea's future is her own."

Zeus's enraged eyes shot over the group again. "If you think you're safe because Atalanta is dead, you're sorely mistaken. You do not want to take on the gods. You will lose, I guarantee it. Give me the Orb now and I'll let you and those who dwell within your realm live."

Silence echoed through the clearing.

"You've been given your answer," Lachesis said, a smug grin across her face as she extended her arm and closed her fingers into a fist. "Go back to the light once and for all!"

She threw her hand forward, opened her fist, and whatever power had gathered there shot toward Zeus. In a poof of smoke and flames, he disappeared into nothingness.

"Whoa," someone whispered.

"Holy shit," another said.

As Lachesis turned to face her, Maelea caught sight of the rest of the Argonauts—Demetrius, Cerek, Phineus—and Nick emerging from the trees at her back, *holy shit* looks on their faces at the scene they'd just witnessed.

"This is the reason Orpheus's soul was given a second chance, child," Lachesis said, drawing Maelea's attention her way. "So that he could find you, and so that you could fulfill your destiny." The Fate lifted both hands in front of her and pulled them back as if drawing on two invisible ropes. "I release you from both the light and darkness. Your life is your own. You will remain ageless—I can't change that—but when you choose to move to the Isles of the Blessed, so it will be."

Maelea gasped as her links to both the Underworld and Olympus were pulled right out of her body. Her legs sagged, and she would have slumped to the ground, but Gryphon was right there to catch her, his arms sliding around her waist, his body pressing up tight against her back to support her all over again.

Lachesis looked his way and smiled. "Take care of her, Guardian."

"I will," Gryphon answered, glancing at Maelea, a smile on his lips and a sparkle in his eye that banished whatever lingering fear remained.

Lachesis's smile faded, and she moved back, looked over the rest of the group. "The race to find the last remaining elements will intensify. And revenge now burns hot in the gods' veins. You've won the battle, but not the war, my friends. Every moment the remaining elements are hidden, Krónos plots his freedom. Find them, guardians, and end this war once and for all."

The Fate faded into nothing. And around her, whispered "No way that just happened" and "Holy *skata*, did you see that?" comments echoed. But she couldn't focus on any of them, because all she could see was Gryphon looking down at her with all the love and longing she'd searched for her whole life.

"You gave up Olympus."

She turned in his arms, rested her hands against his strong, familiar chest. "I knew it wouldn't be half what I'd dreamed without you."

"*Sotiria*," he whispered, framing her face with his hands. "You give up too much for me."

She gripped his forearms, and her skin warmed at the contact. "Haven't you figured out by now, Guardian, I would give up anything for you?"

His eyes softened, and as he lowered his lips to hers, kissing her so gently, so thoroughly, she knew the sacrifice she'd made wasn't a sacrifice at all.

"I will make you happy," he whispered against her lips. "I promise."

Someone chuckled. From somewhere close Titus muttered, "Way to go, Gryph." Then to the rest of the group, "Another one bites the dust."

A thwack echoed through the clearing, followed by Skyla's voice saying, "Leave them alone. I think it's sweet."

But Maelea didn't care what Gryphon's kin thought. All she cared about was spending her life with the man she'd feared and hated and loved and lost. With the man she'd never lose again.

She pulled back from his mouth. "What about your Council? They won't let me—"

"Don't worry about them," Theron said nearby. "We'll handle the Council. I think it's the least we can do, after what you did for us."

Gryphon looked to Theron, smiled his thanks, then glanced back down at her, this time with eyes she knew she would lose herself in forever. "Anything else you need?"

"Just you," she whispered. "You're all I ever need."

"Ditto, *sotiria*." His lips curled higher as he leaned down to kiss her again. And as his arms tightened around her waist, she couldn't tell where he stopped and she began.

Which, after all this time, was exactly the way it should be.

Eternal Guardians Lexicon

ándras; **pl.** *andres*. Male Argolean

Argolea. Realm established by Zeus for the blessed heroes and their descendants

Argonauts. Eternal guardian warriors who protect Argolea. In every generation, one from the original seven bloodlines (Heracles, Achilles, Jason, Odysseus, Perseus, Theseus, and Bellerophon) is chosen to continue the guardian tradition

Council of Elders. Twelve lords of Argolea who advise the king

daemons. Beasts who were once human, recruited from the Fields of Asphodel (purgatory) by Atalanta to join her army

doulas. Slave

élencho. Mind-control technique Argonauts use on humans

Fates. Three goddesses who control the thread of life for all mortals from birth until death

gynaíka; **pl.** *gynaíkes*. Female Argolean

Horae. Three goddesses of balance, controlling life and order

Isles of the Blessed. Heaven

kardia. Term of endearment; my heart

kobalos; **pl.** *kobaloi*. Gnomelike creatures who mine Hades's invisibility ore

meli. Term of endearment; beloved

Misos. Half-human/half-Argolean race that lives hidden among humans

Olympians. Current ruling gods of the Greek pantheon, led by Zeus

Orb of Krónos. Four-chambered disk that, when filled with the four classic elements—earth, wind, fire, and water—has the power to release the Titans from Tartarus

Siren Order. Zeus's elite band of personal warriors. Commanded by Athena

skata. Swear word

sotiria. Term of endearment; my salvation

Tartarus. Realm of the Underworld similar to hell

Titans. The ruling gods before the Olympians

thea. Term of endearment; goddess

yios. Son

About the Author

Elisabeth Naughton is the bestselling author of more than ten paranormal and romantic suspense novels. Her work has been nominated for numerous awards, including the prestigious RITA awards, the Australian Romance Readers Awards, the Golden Leaf, and the Golden Heart. *Enraptured*, the fourth book in her Eternal Guardians series, was listed as one of the *Publishers Weekly* top-ten romances for the spring of 2012 and garnered rave reviews. To learn more about her and her books, visit www.elisabethnaughton.com.